RECKLESS HAWKE

A SECOND GENERATION HAWKE FAMILY
NOVEL

BILLIONAIRES OF NEW ORLEANS: THE HAWKE
FAMILY SECOND GENERATION
BOOK 4

GWYN MCNAMEE

RECKLESS HAWKE
© 2024 Gwyn McNamee

Cover Model: Chain; Photographer: Wander Aguiar

Cover Design: Michelle Johnson at Bluesky Design

Editing: Stephie Walls at Wallflower Edits ; Renita Lofton McKinney at A Book A Day Author Services

To anyone who ever lost love and found it again...

HAWKE FAMILY TREE

THE HAWKE FAMILY
Antonia and Sam "The Savage" Hawke

SAVAGE COLLISION

Savage Hawke & Danika Eriksson

Kennedy Hawke

STONE SOBER

Stone Hawke & Nora Eriksson

Isaac Hawke   Coen Hawke

TAINTED SAINT

Solomon "Saint" Clarke & Caroline Brooks

Pope Clarke   Bishop Clarke

TORTURED SKYE

Skye Hawke & Gabe Anderson

Atlas Anderson   Astrid Anderson

BUILDING STORM

Storm Hawke (Matthews) & Landon McCabe

Angelina Matthews   Alessandra McCabe

STEELE RESOLVE

Luca "Steele" Abello & Byron Harris

Jude Harris-Abello (ad)

1

ALESSANDRA

The tears welling in my eyes make it almost impossible to see the ultrasound screen and the tiny human growing inside me right now.

I swipe at them to try to get a better look, but when it comes into focus—the cherub face and tiny hands and feet—the panic returns as quickly as the tears do.

No.

Breathe.

I swallow back the terrified sob threatening to launch out of my throat as I watch the movement on the screen, then take a shaky breath.

Dr. Brennan shifts the wand across my belly, happily focused on the screen and examining what she needs to. "I know we've talked about this before, and you said you didn't want to know, but do you want me to tell you the sex of the baby?"

Squeezing my eyes closed, I shake my head.

God no.

That would only make this worse.

Make the threat more real.

I open my eyes, but I look at *her*, not the screen, afraid a full-on panic attack is going to hit me if I peek at my baby again. Somehow, I force a smile even though I want to throw up. "I don't want to know." At her slight frown, I quickly add, "I want it to be a surprise."

Partially true.

She grins at me. "Your Aunt Nora has been harassing me, trying to get the inside info and to see if she can make me accidentally let the gender slip..."

Despite currently dancing along the thin line between a complete meltdown and barely holding it together, that makes my lips twitch—genuinely this time. "That doesn't surprise me at all. Nora can be persistent. Although, by now, I would've expected her to go into my medical records and figure it out herself."

Dr. Brennan laughs, returning to check whatever else she needs to on the scan. "Well, I guess she *could* do that, but it would be a HIPAA violation since she's not your treating doctor."

I laugh lightly. "You think Nora cares about that?"

Her returned chuckle fills the room, and Dr. Brennan shakes her head. "Probably not. She's very protective of you."

That's an understatement if I've ever heard one.

Since the moment she told me I was pregnant, Aunt Nora has hovered over me worse than Jude, Ang, or even Mom and Dad, like it's single-handedly her job to ensure my pregnancy goes smoothly.

I release a little sigh. "I know, and I appreciate it, but the closer I get to my due date, the more everyone seems to be doing the helicopter routine."

She sets down the ultrasound wand and takes my hand in hers, squeezing it gently. "I know this is your first baby, and it can be scary and overwhelming, but you're lucky to have your entire family there for you to support you through this."

Since the baby's father isn't...

Those words never actually leave her lips, but it's what she means.

Mom, Ang, Nora, even Skye, Dani, and Caroline have *all* come to at least one appointment, but Dr. Brennan has never questioned where the baby's father is—either because she's incredibly intuitive or because Nora warned her not to bring it up.

The tears well again, and I nod.

I am lucky.

I know that.

Their constant pestering, checking in on me, and circling me like military choppers is all done with the best of intentions. But lately, I've been feeling suffocated, like this heavy weight is sitting on my chest and making it impossible to breathe.

And it isn't just the baby taking up space my organs used to.

It's because of the reality of what having this child means— potentially for all of us. The danger it presents that I can't even warn them about because merely thinking about it gives me hives and makes me to want to curl into a ball in a dark closet and hide out forever.

Each appointment only reminds me of how quickly the day of reckoning is coming.

Four weeks...

I only have *four more weeks* before this baby comes into the world and turns it upside down for all the Hawkes.

Dr. Brennan hands me a towel to wipe off the ultrasound gel.

I swipe it across my stomach. "So...how are things looking?"

My due date looms over me, so damn close and foreboding. A dark, sinister danger I can't avoid forever. I haven't been able to shake the growing unease as I tick the dates off the calendar —one by one, moving closer and closer.

All I want is to be able to hold this baby, love him or her, and give my child the best life possible, free of any fears or worries—and knowing I won't be able to do that is already breaking me before the sweet child even enters the world.

Dr. Brennan smiles. "The baby is in a good position, and typically, by now, there isn't much room for him or her to rotate comfortably, so I think we'll be good. You're only a centimeter dilated, which is completely normal at thirty-six weeks, so you'll likely deliver right around your due date."

I release a relieved sigh. "Good..."

Because I still need time to figure out what the hell I'm going to do.

The warning Uncle Stone gave me when Kennedy and Cass dragged me to see him a few months ago rings in my head. *"You can't hide who the father of this child is forever, especially if he comes knocking, wanting to be involved in his or her life. Kennedy said you were scared of him. If there's something we need to know, that we need to be prepared for, we should start doing that now rather than later."*

He's right, of course.

I should tell them all the truth. Explain what a mess I've gotten myself into—again. But I can't bring myself to put it into words.

Not yet.

It's too raw.

Too painful.

Too unfathomable that I've fucked up this badly.

But at least I have another month to figure out how to get myself out of this and protect the baby.

Right now, none of the options are great: run and leave New Orleans—but I have nowhere to go and haven't had to survive by myself *ever*, let alone with a new baby. Or stay and wait for the fireworks sure to happen when I give birth and the shit hits the fan—not good for any of us.

Dr. Brennan waits at the bottom of the exam table. "Do you have any other questions?"

Yeah, any ideas on how to handle a dangerous-as-hell baby's father?

"Any way to stop the Braxton-Hicks contractions?"

Those fuckers have been plaguing me for months, and I could really do without them on top of everything else. They almost feel like they're some kind of punishment for bringing this danger into our lives...

She offers a kind smile. "Relax. Stress can make them worse, but other than that, unfortunately, no. However, they're completely normal. And if anything *doesn't* feel right, you're very lucky to have your Aunt Nora and Pope around. Either one of them could help you, should there be an issue."

Pope...

I cringe at the mention of his name. That alone is enough to form a tremendous pit of hurt and regret in my stomach. "Yeah..."

The poor doctor has no idea how the innocent things she's saying are affecting me, ramping up my anxiety and reminding me that Pope is likely here, somewhere in the hospital building.

Unless it's his day off...but I wouldn't be so lucky.

I slide from the table and pull my shirt down over my protruding belly.

Dr. Brennan wraps her arm around my shoulder. "I'll see you again next week, but if this storm ends up hitting us, we may need to adjust a day or two either way from our current appointment." She squeezes, giving me a motherly smile. "You're going to be a great mom, Allie. You have a lot of amazing ones in your family to help you. Don't be so worried."

Don't be so worried.

So many people have said those words to me over the

course of my pregnancy, then told me that everything's going to be okay, that *I'm* going to be all right.

But no one knows the truth.

No one knows the cataclysm I'm about to bring to their lives when we already have so much to worry about with the hotel going up, Satriano still a very real threat, and the uncertainty in New Orleans since Roselli's murder. Not to mention the potential hurricane the weathermen say may be coming our way.

It's a swirling maelstrom that threatens to swallow the Hawkes whole.

I push out of Dr. Brennan's office and into the hallway, releasing a heavy breath and sucking in air with lungs that don't seem to want to fill. The panic heightens with each appointment, with every inch my belly grows, as each day passes and I come closer to meeting this baby. This innocent who is going to cause so much trouble.

My phone buzzes in my purse, and I pull it out, that relief at being done with my appointment instantly switching to renewed terror as I stare at the message.

UNKNOWN NUMBER:

You can't ignore me forever, Allie. We need to talk.

Oh, God...

That vise that always seems to be strapped to my chest cranks even tighter.

Ever since the day he came into The Grind and told me we needed to talk about the baby, I've been dodging him, avoiding him at all costs. I only managed to end *that* conversation before getting into the nitty gritty with him because Angelina reappeared at the counter. But that's only going to work for so long —even I know that.

And right now, if I don't get out of this sterile, hospital-scented hallway and get some fresh air, I'm going to hyperventilate and drop right here on the linoleum.

I make my way over to the bank of elevators and press the down button, quickly deleting the message from him, as if that's somehow going to make him go away and fix this quagmire I've created.

The baby kicks, almost like he or she can sense the turmoil, and I press my hand over the spot and rub gently.

"I love you, kid, but we're not ready for you yet. Not even close."

Maybe I never will be...

It certainly feels like I'm teetering on the edge of a gigantic cliff, about to jump off and hope I can fly when my wings are battered and destroyed. At least for now, I can take an elevator down instead of leaping and hoping I don't crash face-first into the unforgiving ground.

The doors slide open, and I step into the empty cab, then punch the button for the first floor and lean back against the metal wall, letting my eyes drift closed and tilting my head to try to work out the kinks in my neck.

These checkups always leave me so tense. Even when I can't sneak in without Ang or Mom or someone else showing up to support me at the appointment, their presence just ends up making things worse. Having them with me, so happy, excited, completely oblivious to all the reasons this baby is going to unleash a tidal wave of problems on the Hawkes, makes my guilt eat me alive the entire time they're in the room.

The elevator stops on the next floor down, and the doors part.

Someone inhales sharply, and my eyes fly open and meet the beautiful cognac ones I had hoped I wouldn't see today.

You have to be kidding me.

Pope hesitates a second before he steps into the elevator, wearing dark-gray slacks that hang off his trim hips perfectly, a white button-down shirt with his lab coat over it, a stethoscope around his neck, and a tablet in hand. His eyes never leave mine as the doors slide closed behind him.

We stare each other down, and the elevator drops another floor along with my stomach, the air thickening around us.

After all these years, nothing has changed. The man standing in front of me still manages to render me completely speechless with a single look. And why does *he* always have to look so damn good—toned, lean muscle moving fluidly under his clothes, smooth umber skin, and those dazzling eyes I always get lost in.

A million questions lie in his gaze—ones he never voices even though we're forced to see each other constantly at family events. Probably because I've spent the last decade avoiding situations like *this*.

Being alone with Pope Clarke in any sort of confined space is a recipe for disaster...

The cab keeps descending, and his lips part like he's about to say something when the elevator stops and the doors spread behind him.

A pretty redhead wearing pink scrubs steps in, grinning at Pope as she presses the button for her floor. "Dr. Clarke, I was hoping I would see you today."

My gut twists as Pope finally drags his eyes from me and turns toward her. "Melody..."

The nurse peers up at him through thick lashes, batting them like a teenager at her crush. "What time are you off today? Maybe we can grab dinner again?"

Again.

My spine stiffens, and my gut twists violently.

Pope peers back at me, and the woman follows his gaze, her eyes dropping to my hand resting protectively over my belly.

"Oh!" Her brows rise. "I'm sorry. Were you talking to a patient?"

Red-hot anger mixes with the kind of raging green-monster jealousy I have no right to feel over him anymore.

Before he can answer, the ding fills the tight space, and Melody glances at the panel above the door. "This is my floor." Her green eyes dart back to Pope. "Call me later, okay?"

He doesn't respond before she slips out and the silver slabs close behind her, sealing us back into what suddenly feels very much like a tomb.

I grip the rail behind me, squeezing it so tightly that my fingers actually hurt. Pope slowly turns back toward me as we descend again, his eyes hard and unreadable even with as well as I know him.

"Al..."

I raise my hand off my stomach. "Don't. Please...I can't."

The cab jerks to a halt on the first floor, the signaling ding ringing in my ears like a warning bell to get the hell out of here.

Great idea.

Before he can say anything else, the two huge slabs of metal keeping us in part, revealing my escape route into the bustling main hallway of the hospital.

Averting my gaze from the man who is so damn good at breaking my heart, I hustle around him, my shoes squeaking on the linoleum as I race past the ER nurses' station without a look back.

His heavy footsteps follow me, echoing through my head the same way his heartbeat used to.

I can't do this today.

I can't.

My phone buzzes in my purse again, and bile climbs in my throat at the possibility that it's *him* again with another threatening text.

Time is running out.

And I won't be able to run forever.

POPE

ALLIE'S THICK, dark hair bobs with her strong, determined steps away from me and through the ER toward the front desk and waiting room. Her short legs might not be able to move her very fast—especially given her current condition—but she is using them to evade me like a thief running from the cops.

Ironic, considering the way she stole my heart all those years ago...

She makes it to the waiting area and peeks over her shoulder at me just long enough for me to see the telltale shimmer in her Hawke-blue eyes.

Fuck.

Her tears always did me in, and time hasn't changed that.

Go after her.

The voice in my head that has screamed those words at me so often over the last decade begins the same incessant command.

Go after her. Go after her. Go after her.

I've ignored it so many times. Talked myself out of it, knowing it was for the best that I stay away and let her live her life without me in it the way I want to be. Watched her slide into the passenger seat of someone else's car. Kiss someone else's lips. Stare into someone else's eyes with affection when it should have been me.

Go. After. Her.

This time, I almost follow the instruction, but Nora steps from one of the exam rooms to my right, blocking my path. I skid to a halt on the linoleum, and Nora turns her head to follow my gaze in time to see Allie dart out the sliding glass doors to the parking lot.

Nora sets her inquisitive aquamarine gaze on me. "Was that Allie running out of here like her ass was on fire?"

"Mmhmm."

I stare at the doors, as if she might actually come back when I know damn well that woman isn't voluntarily going to be in my vicinity under any circumstances.

Maybe rightfully so.

But even with her gone, I still feel her presence, the suffocating weight of knowing what she thought when Melody came into that elevator. What she's always thought of me. What I *let* her and everyone else think because it's easier and far less painful than admitting the truth.

"Pope?" Something waves in my peripheral vision. "Earth to Pope."

I jerk my head away from staring after Alessandra and turn toward Nora, who watches me expectantly with a blond brow raised.

The corner of her mouth twitches into a grin. "Did you hear me?"

Fuck no.

I was too busy obsessing over the woman I can never have. Shaking my head, I run a hand over my cheek. "No, sorry. What'd you say?"

She glances toward the door, then back at me. "I asked how your patient was doing, but you seem a little preoccupied with something else."

More like someone *else.*

Shit.

Nora is far too observant for me to get away with that and have her *not* notice. It's what makes her so damn good at her job and such a good teacher to me and the others who did their residency here.

Even if I hadn't worked at this hospital for several years, through my internship and now residency, she would still see right through any attempts I make at bullshitting her. Growing up with her as basically an aunt, she knows me about as well as anyone and isn't afraid to call me out when she feels it's necessary.

Some may suspect nepotism got me my placement, but I busted my ass to get here. And Nora never would have given me *any* inappropriate help since she sure as hell never had any when she went through medical school and all her training. Truly, working for Dr. Nora Hawke is ten times harder for me than anyone else here—and today proves it.

Damn the Hawkes and their ability to unravel people with a look.

I need to get my head back in the game.

My shift has barely started, and I've already let Allie distract me from what I *should* be focused on—my patients. Like the one upstairs I was checking on before I walked into that quicksand with her in the elevator.

"He's doing well. Settled in upstairs, and he's on Dr. Pierce's schedule for surgery later tonight."

She nods and sets her tablet on the nurse's station counter before she leans against it and studies me. "And what about you?"

I raise a brow at her. "What *about* me?"

"How are *you* doing?"

Her question takes me aback for a moment, and I wrack my brain, trying to figure out why the hell she's asking. "I'm fine. Why wouldn't I be?"

Her slender shoulders rise and fall, her gaze darting around the ER and toward the half-full waiting area Allie escaped through. "We've been awfully busy around here." Those too-knowing eyes of hers meet mine again. "But really, I was referring to what just happened with Allie."

I grit my teeth, making a vain attempt at keeping any reaction to her statement neutral. "Nothing happened with Allie."

Like always.

We dance around each other, each pretending the other doesn't affect them and going through the motions by rote. Neither of us saying what we want to, what we *should*. It's gone on for so long, it's become the normal routine—an elegant waltz that allows us to spend as much time together as we're often forced to without losing our sanity. Until someone steps on the other's toes...

Nora releases a little laugh, drawing a look from the nurse, Zoe, at the desk, who quickly diverts her eyes back to the paperwork in front of her, even though we both know she's still listening in. "Bullshit. She *ran* out of here and away from *you*. And, we both know that girl is hiding something."

Yeah, like who the damn father of her baby is.

"But what I want to know"—Nora takes a step closer to me and leans in conspiratorially—"is what happened between you two?"

My back stiffens. "I am not sure what you mean."

"Come on, Pope." Nora sighs. "Everyone has noticed it. The tension, the way you two can't seem to be in a room alone together anymore..." She offers a light smack of the back of her hand against my chest. "You two used to be thick as thieves, inseparable when she wasn't with Jude, or she'd just drag him along wherever you were going. But"—she shakes her head, sending her blond hair floating around her face—"something changed years ago, and it seems to have only gotten worse as you guys have grown older."

Well, fucking hell.

It's not that we really thought we were fooling anybody. It would be impossible to do in this family. The way she constantly glares at me, the hatred simmering in her eyes every time she looks my way.

Of course, they've noticed it.

But I am not about to get into ancient history with Aunt

Nora or anyone else.

I give her a half-smile, one I hope is convincing enough that she'll buy it and be off on her way. "It's nothing you need to worry about."

"But I am worried, Pope." She scans the ER again, always watchful over her domain. "That girl has been a mess for years, and you and I both know it. Bouncing from relationship to relationship, guy to guy, always getting her heart broken, never giving herself time to heal or be on her own for a while. Now she's having this baby and won't even tell anybody who the father is. She is jumpy. She's secretive. She won't even talk to Jude or Angelina..."

Which is, undoubtedly, the most concerning part about what's been happening with her for the last several months.

Jude is her rock, the one person she can always count on to be there for her and the only person she *wants* to run to when she's dodging questions from any of the rest of the Hawkes. Now her lips are sealed, even with him.

I tighten my hands into fists inside the pockets of my lab coat so Nora can't see how truly bothered I am. "I know."

"I thought maybe you could get through to her, but after seeing the way she bolted from you, I'm guessing that's a no."

My frustration comes out as a barked laugh, and I shake my head, rubbing the back of my neck and trying to work away some of the tension there. "Definitely not."

And now I need to change the subject before she asks a question I can't dodge my way out of.

I motion toward the TV hanging on the wall behind the nurse's station. "Did you watch the weather update?"

She glances at the screen where the weatherman points to a cloud formation in the Caribbean. "Yep. The storm that's forming could hit us on its current projected path."

Resting my elbows on the counter, I watch the update where he predicts the tropical storm will grow into one of the earliest hurricanes in history. It's barely spring, and we're already having to worry about landfall in likely less than a week. "Yeah, we should know in a day or two, I would think. And then we'll need to start preparations around here."

"Is it affecting any of your family in Jamaica right now?"

I shake my head. "Dad called all the cousins and his aunt and confirmed they're just getting a lot of rain. They'll be fine where they are...it's us I'm worried about."

Nora elbows me. "Your first hurricane as a full-fledged doctor."

I offer her a half-grin. "It's not like I haven't experienced it before here during my internship."

"I know, but back then, you were still learning the ropes. You have more responsibility now as a resident, and I rely on you to be the incredible doctor I know you are."

I let my jaw drop in mock offense. "Are you saying I was a bad one back then?"

Grinning, she shakes her head. "You've always been brilliant. I'm just messing with you. But we need to keep an eye on this. If it hits us directly"—she glances out across the emergency room—"this place is going to turn into a madhouse."

Maybe that's exactly what I need.

Something to take my mind off Allie and everything that's been going on with the Hawkes recently.

There was a time when being alone with her in a confined space like that elevator would've ended up with her in my arms and my lips pressed to hers.

It simultaneously feels like ages ago and only yesterday.

I can still taste her on my lips, smell her, feel the way her body molded against mine. After all this time and the emotional distance she's put between us, I still can't get Alessandra McCabe out of my head—and maybe I never will.

She isn't the kind of woman you can ever forget.

No matter how hard I tried to push her away for her own

good, to protect her from the mistake she was about to make, all it did was create anger and resentment.

It's never going to dissipate...and it is going to continue to break my heart every time I see her.

Like today.

She's about to have another man's baby, and that knowledge makes my skin crawl and my stomach turn.

But I have no right to be angry at her.

No right to be jealous.

She was never truly mine—not in the way I wanted her to be.

And now, it's too late for that.

Zoe rises from her seat at the nurse's station and approaches. "Dr. Hawke, we have three incoming. Motor vehicle accident."

Nora looks at me. "Let's go."

We start making our way toward the ambulance bay, Zoe hot on our heels.

"One has penetrating trauma to the abdomen but seems stable. The second has neck and back injuries which are stabilized. The third is in v-fib..."

Fuck.

Adrenaline courses through my system, washing away the lingering concern about Alessandra. My laser-sharp focus immediately moves to what I'll need to do the moment they arrive, mentally running through the steps and ensuring I'm prepared for anything that might come through the door.

I've spent my life working for this, to become an ER doctor, to help the people who need me most when their lives hang in the balance. The things I've missed out on, that I've given up... all of it is worth it if I can save someone who might otherwise not make it.

There will be plenty of time to worry about Allie later.

There always is.

2

ALESSANDRA

Jude's hand slides over on top of mine, where it rests on the table, and he interlaces our fingers and squeezes. "Are you okay?"

His question pulls me from the trance I've been in, staring at Nana's home-cooked meal I can't even enjoy. I glance over at him, still picking at the food I've mostly been moving around on my plate, hoping no one would notice I'm not really eating it.

As if I could ever really get away with that at Nana's Sunday dinner table...

The people seated around me—some family by blood, others by choice—all see far too much to get away with that.

Especially Jude.

Best friends are incredible when you need them or they need you, but not so much when you're trying to hide a massive secret from them and they can read you like an open book. And, unfortunately for me, books are Jude's specialty.

I force a smile he will never buy rather than have to get into it with him. *Again.* Here, of all places. He'll surely be right up my ass as soon as we're alone, but for now, the lie will have to do. "I'm good."

Angie leans forward from his other side and narrows her eyes on me. "You don't look *good*, and you're barely eating."

I scowl at her.

She points her fork at me. "Don't give me that look, Alessandra Rose McCabe. You're about to have a baby. You need to feed it and yourself."

She's right, of course.

And I've been careful to ensure I do, even when my nerves make it difficult to want to eat, but I can't seem to get anything down tonight.

Not only because these Braxton Hicks contractions keep me uncomfortable but also because every time I try to take a bite, my stomach turns thinking about the decision I need to make soon—potentially to leave New Orleans and all these people I love so much.

As the entire table chatters on, mostly about the incoming storm and preparations for it, I can't stop thinking about the text messages I've been deleting for the last several days since my run-in with Pope at the hospital. Hoping they'll simply disappear. Praying it won't become the showdown I think it will.

It would be easier to work through my predicament in my head if Pope weren't sitting directly across from me at the table, his entrancing gaze locked on me far more than it should be at any typical family gathering.

Jude pulls his hand from mine and slides it along the back of my chair so he can lean in closer, brushing his lips against my ear. "What's going on, Allie Cat? You look spooked."

I turn my head toward him, and those crystal-blue eyes stare back at me, far too knowingly for me to be able to bullshit my way out of this. "I'm just nervous about the storm."

Good lie, Al.

That seemed completely legit.

His blond brows rise slowly, his disbelief obvious—not only because I'm a shitty liar but also because he knows me better than *anyone* at this table. "Why? It isn't like we haven't been through them before."

Called the fuck out.

We've had at least half a dozen serious storms that I can remember, and the Hawkes always operate like clockwork when these things hit. We all know our duties and our places, and gathering here at Nana's in Metairie to ride it out is the family tradition no one would ever dare break.

Together, we're safe.

An unshatterable unit.

At least...that's the theory.

The last year has tested that belief in so many ways. Between Jack and Vivi showing up with Satriano hot on their heels, the explosion at The Grind, Roselli's threat, and then the shooting and Damiano showing up...the only good thing that's come of any of it has been Isaac's new son.

I glance over at him where he sits with his family, baby Giovanni sleeping against his chest, head resting on Isaac's shoulder, his tiny little fingers clutching his father's shirt.

Gio looks so happy.

Peaceful.

Despite entering this world in the midst of all the turmoil the Hawkes have been through.

And I'm only about to make things worse.

Swallowing through the panic threatening to choke me, I turn back to Jude. "I know. But I wasn't a month away from having a baby then."

The corners of his lips curl. "We'll all be safe and sound here at Nana's."

I offer him a tight smile and nod, and he reaches up and

tousles my hair playfully. Groaning with annoyance, I elbow him to push him back toward his seat, and Ang gives us a look that tells me he's going to be filling her in on our little private conversation as soon as they get home tonight.

Savage clinks his knife against the side of his wineglass, suddenly taking on his very serious head-of-the-family role. "Everyone. Everyone."

Oh, Lord, here we go.

He's been in one of his moods ever since we all got here. Whenever a storm builds and threatens New Orleans, Savage gets all up in his feelings after he almost lost Uncle Gabe all those years ago during one.

The man himself couldn't seem to care less. Gabe reclines casually in his chair with his arm behind Aunt Skye, and she leans over and whispers something to him that makes him smirk.

Savage glowers at his best friend and sister. "Will you two knock it off for a second? I'm hoping we can avoid anyone getting kidnapped or shot during this hurricane."

Gabe rolls his eyes and his hand along with them to encourage Savage to continue.

The patriarch of the Hawkes releases an annoyed huff while half the table tries to cover their smirks. "I just want to make sure everyone knows what they're doing over the next two days before the predicted landfall. We have a lot of locations to get locked down and ready."

Nana pushes back from her seat on the other end of the table, her plate empty, and starts walking around behind everyone, clearing the others from anyone who has finished. "They all know to come here, Savage. We don't have to go over this like everyone at this table is a child." She looks at Jude and me, the two youngest, and gives us a bright smile. "I think, at this point, Jude and Alessandra are perfectly capable of taking care of themselves."

If she only knew...

A muscle in Savage's jaw tics. "Thanks. Mom. Yes, we all know the plan is to come here. But there's a lot to take care of before that point."

There always is.

With dozens of businesses under the Hawke Enterprises umbrella and the major external construction on the hotel almost completed, splitting them up and ensuring each and every one is locked up and protected from damage takes top priority before we all hunker down in Nana's house on high ground.

Saint grins at Savage from his seat between Aunt Caroline and Bishop. "I have the security teams boarding up windows already at all of our locations, and we'll be officially shut down as of tomorrow night."

Isaac's brow furrows, and he looks to Savage while he rubs Gio's back gently, trying to keep the baby calm and asleep with all the loud voices around the table. "Do we need to be shutting down for a full twenty-four hours before the storm?"

Savage waves a hand dismissively. "Stop worrying about the money. A one-day shutdown isn't going to break the bank."

Stone snorts and shakes his head. "I am just glad he's the one worrying about it, so I don't have to."

It's meant as a joke. But my chest tightens at the statement and the way his hand shakes as he brings his wineglass to his mouth.

His injuries from the shooting were far worse than anything Isaac or Kennedy suffered, and the potentially permanent damage remains visible to anyone who knew him before.

The slight tremor in his hands.

The cane he now uses to move around because he's so unstable and can't trust his body anymore.

He hasn't lost any of his mental faculties or attitude, though.

Nora leans in and says something to him before looking to Pope. "Pope and I will likely both be at the hospital starting around then and stay throughout the whole storm."

Pope nods. "We know what a shitshow it's going to become as soon as it makes landfall."

Savage snorts. "That's an understatement. I want *everyone* here by Tuesday morning, at the latest, since the worst is supposed to come that night."

Everyone nods their agreement, and the buzz of various conversations resumes, leaving me staring at my plate again, unable to make myself worry about the incoming storm.

My phone vibrates in my purse, hanging on the back of the chair, and I cringe.

Shit.

Anyone who would be texting me is already here, seated around this table we've had to expand over the last year to make room for Jack, Vivi, Cass, and Charlotte. Which means it's *him* again.

He's getting more persistent.

More forceful.

More angry.

I'm surprised he hasn't come looking for me at The Grind again. But given the current situation in New Orleans, he's likely too busy—or he's afraid of the same thing I am...the family finding out he fathered this baby.

I push back my chair, and Jude and Ang both look up at me.

Ang's dark brow furrows, her mothering instinct kicking in immediately. "You all right?"

Another fake smile. "Just going to go use the bathroom."

I snatch my purse off the back of the chair and try to hurry down the hallway, pulling my phone out to review the message.

UNKNOWN NUMBER:

I'm serious, Allie! You and I are going to talk. If that means I need to hunt you down, I know where to find you.

"Shit, shit, shit."

My stomach roils, the few bites of Nana's lasagna I managed to eat churning and threatening to come back up, and the baby kicks, almost like it's reacting to my blood pressure spikes.

I walk straight past the hallway bathroom and into Mom's old room, closing the door behind me and beelining to the bed. If I don't get away from everyone soon, I'm going to lose it. Keeping this secret, knowing what's coming, it's all too much.

Slowly lowering myself to the mattress, I release a heavy breath, but another damn contraction hits me, making me grit my teeth.

How did I get myself in this goddamn situation?

I squeeze my eyes closed against the answer screaming at me in my head.

Because you're reckless...

Everyone at that table always accused me of being just that. Reckless with my life and my heart. Jumping before I look. Going all-in without knowing the stakes or consequences. And they're right.

My own actions brought me to this moment, and this sweet baby is going to pay for it.

The pain passes, and I rest my hands protectively over my stomach. "I'm so sorry your life is starting out this way."

I'm already a shitty mother and I haven't even started yet.

Tears sting my eyes, and I blink them away as footsteps move down the hall toward my hiding spot.

Please don't let it be Uncle Stone, or Isaac, or Kennedy, or Cass, or anyone else who's going to be on me about the very subject I can't talk about right now without completely losing my shit.

The doorknob turns, and the solid slab of wood pushes

inward, revealing the one person who could actually be worse than any of them.

"Pope, what are you—"

He steps in and closes the door behind him with a deafening click of the latch securing. I hold my breath as he turns to face me, his jaw hard, determination in the set of his strong, lean shoulders. Frustration vibrates off him as he places himself directly between me and the only way out of the room.

Crossing his arms over his chest, all six-four of him towers over the bed—a gentle giant like his father. But right now, he's using his size to ensure I can't run from him again.

Pope locks his heated gaze on me. "You are not running from me this time, Teeny. You may shut everyone else out. But we're going to talk, whether you like it or not."

POPE

As soon as I call her "Teeny," she knows she's in trouble. I don't even know why I said it when I don't think I've used the nickname for her since we were in high school.

Likely not since *that* night.

It didn't feel right afterward. After what I did, what I said. But in this moment, I need her to remember who I was to her before all the bullshit so she'll talk to me.

A friend.

A confidant.

Someone she could always trust and run *to* instead of away from.

Because this can't go on any longer.

I can't bear it, and everyone else around that table is feeling the same way. When one of us is suffering, the entire Hawke clan seems to suffer with them, and her utter silence on this matter while we can see it destroying her isn't healthy for her or that baby.

Watching her not eat at dinner, pushing her food around on her plate, had both the friend—or at least, former one—and doctor in me tensing up with concern. Even more so than I already was after her flight from the hospital the other day.

By this point in her pregnancy, she should be over any bouts with morning sickness and her appetite should be back, if not even greater, than it was before—yet she's barely gained any weight and was hardly showing until almost the end of her second trimester.

Whatever she's hiding and holding back is literally eating her alive.

And I can't watch it anymore.

She shifts nervously on the bed, her hands over her belly, clearly uneasy with my arrival and pronouncement. The blue eyes she inherited from her mother plead with me, and she shakes her head, sending dark strands floating around her face. "Please, Pope, I don't want to do this. I can't talk about—"

A slight sob cuts off her words, and her pain permeates the air so heavily I can feel it with each breath I take, like acid burning through my lungs.

I take a step toward her, then kneel, putting me at eye level with the tiny woman who holds so much power over me even after all this time. Seeing her like this—lost, hurt, terrified— claws at something deep in my chest that I've pushed down for so long. Trying to pretend that it doesn't exist anymore. Trying to pretend it *never* did. To protect myself because if I acknowledged it, it would drive me utterly mad.

Time hasn't changed anything, though.

She's still the only woman who ever held my heart and the one who is still breaking it. With her vulnerability. With her desperate plea for the wrong fucking thing. This isn't when she should be shutting down and pulling away. She should be reaching out to the lifeline I'm throwing her, grasping it, and clinging to it so she isn't lost, floating out in the abyss she's been living in by trying to keep this secret.

"Then you're going to listen, Al. Something is wrong. Everyone can see it. Kennedy told me you had a conversation with Uncle Stone, and he told you we need to know what's going on so we can help and be prepared for whatever's coming. The same way we always do with these hurricanes. But you keep pushing everyone away. Even Jude…"

A tear falls from the corner of her eye, and I force myself not to reach out and brush it away. My fingers itch to do just that. To touch her again. To comfort her. To be that person for her.

Allie swipes at her cheeks, leaving wet streaks across her pale skin. Her body trembles, but she doesn't respond. She merely keeps staring at me like she's searching for something in my gaze but isn't finding it.

"You have to let us help you, Al."

She stiffens, her pretty pink lips falling open slightly. "*Help* me? Don't pretend you all of a sudden *care*, Pope. This savior complex might serve you well at the hospital, but don't turn it toward me to ease your guilt over what you did to me."

Each word she throws at me hits like the tip of a poisoned arrow designed to tear straight through my chest and directly to my heart.

That's what she thinks.

I see the truth as she believes it to be darkening her eyes. And I can't let her go on with such a tremendously huge misconception about me or why I'm in here with her.

It has nothing to do with being a doctor with a "savior complex," nor the fact that we were raised together and are basically family.

Shifting closer, I reach out and grasp her chin, tilting it to force her to hold my gaze. Heat radiates from where I touch her, into my hand, up my arm, and through me, warming me in a way no one else can. "I always cared, Allie. Too much."

Before I can talk myself out of it, I do what comes so naturally, what I used to do without even thinking about it. I lean in and brush my lips over hers.

A fleeting whisper of a touch.

Barely a kiss.

But the instant our mouths connect, that same crackle of energy that did me in where Alessandra McCabe is concerned so long ago hits me like a freight train, sizzling through my body and going directly to the places it shouldn't.

Where it *can't*.

After initially leaning into the kiss, Allie jerks back like she felt it, too, her eyes wide, tears brimming and threatening to spill over again. Her gaze dips to my lips, like she's debating whether she wants to do that again or smack me there. Then her small hand comes to my chest, and she pushes, urging me to back away.

I've always given Allie what she needed—even when she didn't realize it—so I rise to my feet and retreat a step, letting her have her personal space.

With one hand pressed to the mattress to give her leverage, she pushes herself to her feet. Leveling her icy gaze at me, she straightens her shoulders that don't even come up to the middle of my chest, gathering her courage for whatever she's about to do.

Staring down at her now, she looks so small, so fragile.

But looks can be deceiving.

Alessandra McCabe isn't a porcelain doll. She's one of those Russian nesting things—beautiful for sure, but with multiple strong layers you have to fight through to get to the core of who she is.

I was there once...and I hurt her more than anyone else

probably has in her entire life. Now, I'm paying the price for that.

The eyes that once looked at me with such affection now glare at me with a fiery hatred. "You say you care, Pope, but you didn't act like it then. Don't try to start now."

She brushes past me, leaving me standing in Storm's old bedroom, dazed and pissed in a way I haven't been in a long time.

Not because of her reaction to the kiss.

I shouldn't have done that.

But because she didn't tell me anything.

I came in here for answers. To *help* her. And all I managed to do was send her running away from me again.

Footsteps make me turn toward the hallway, hope that it could be Alessandra returning blooming in my chest, but instead, Bishop appears in the open doorway, dark whiskey eyes wide when they find me.

"Oh, there you are. I've been looking for you." She motions over her shoulder as she leans against the jamb, her long braids falling past her shoulders, down for once instead of twisted up into the bun she usually keeps them in. "Nana is putting out the tiramisu, and Dad and I made gizzada this morning."

Normally, the mere mention of my favorite Jamaican dessert would send me running for the table, but I can't think about eating right now, not after what went down with Allie.

I scrub my hands across my face. "I'll...be there in a minute."

Bishop narrows her eyes on me. "What's wrong with you?"

"Nothing."

My answer comes a little too quickly to be believable, and leave it to big sis to pick up on it immediately.

She takes a step into the room, determination written all over her face. It's the same look she wears before she gets into the ring to destroy an opponent, so I never want it directed at me. "Spill, or I'll take you down and put you in an arm bar until you break."

Fucking hell.

I turn away from her, pacing over to the window to stare out at the darkening sky and light rain already being brought in by the coming storm. "I just tried to get Allie to come clean with me about whatever is going on with her."

"*Aaaaah.*" She snorts. "Well, that's a lost cause. You shouldn't have wasted your time. She sat with me for a bit last week while I was getting my braids done, brought me coffee a couple times and some snacks from The Grind, and yet, somehow, she managed to dodge every question I asked about that baby's father and why she's been so cagey about him." She *tsks.* "That girl plays a mean defense. It's too bad Atlas and I can't convince her to step into the ring. She'd be a natural."

Turning back to her, I grin. "She certainly knows how to throw a jab, too."

Bishop smirks. "And I'm sure you did absolutely *nothing* to justify her ire, right, baby bro?"

One of her dark brows rises, and I stare her down, trying to decipher if she really knows anything about the past Al and I don't talk about or if she's fishing.

Thankfully, I don't have to answer.

Mom appears in the doorway and props her hands on her hips. "There you two are! You're missing dessert. Alessandra already left because she was tired, but everyone else is still here. We're thinking maybe a Scrabble tournament."

I point at Bishop. "Watch me take *you* down." I amble toward the door, intentionally bumping my shoulder against hers. "You may have gotten all the brawn, but I got the brains."

She scowls at me and punches my bicep hard enough to make it sting. "Shut up."

Grinning, I wrap my arm around her shoulder and maneuver us toward the door, where Mom watches with a careful eye to ensure we're joking around and not actually fighting.

But Bishop knows I'm just messing with her.

We both understand how easily our roles could have been reversed.

Everyone always expected me to go into the "family busi-ness" and work for Dad, organizing all the security for the various Hawke Enterprises businesses, and for Brainiac Bishop, with her perfect SAT score, to go the lawyer or doctor route. But she always leaned toward more physical pursuits, wanting to spend time with Dad and the rest of the guys at the gym or setting up new surveillance equipment. Strapping a gun on my hip and using my size and strength as a weapon was never my calling.

I knew it from a young age, watching Aunt Nora at the free clinic Hawke Enterprises hosts once a month. Treating ill patients. Patching up wounds. Giving them the care they couldn't get anywhere else.

That was what I was meant to do.

Helping people.

Saving them.

But they have to want it.

And right now, it seems Allie doesn't.

Bishop is right...I was wasting my breath to even try.

3

ALESSANDRA

The fierce wind rattles the apartment windows, the gnarly, haunting howl filling my ears and sending a shiver down my spine.

I need to leave for Nana's now.

If anyone had known what Hurricane Analise was going to do overnight, I would already be there, but she strengthened and altered course, throwing off the best-laid plans. What we expected late this afternoon or early evening has already hit us, dropping buckets of rain and violent, dangerous gusts. And it's only the front edge of the storm.

Things are only going to get worse.

Another of the annoying Braxton Hicks contractions that have plagued my entire third trimester hits me, and I curse and try to breathe through it, wishing like hell Dr. Brennan had given me a way to stop these suckers other than the one thing I *cannot* do—relax.

When it finally passes, I glance down at the group text message with the rest of the family.

JUDE:

> Ang and I just got done double-checking the
> alarm at The Grind and resecuring the sensors.
> We're heading to Nana's. Allie, are you on your
> way? Do you need us to come get you?

For a brief moment, I consider saying *yes*, but they'd have to go in the opposite direction to get me from the apartment, and there's no reason to make them spend any more time on the streets in this if they don't have to. Not when I'm perfectly capable of driving myself, even in this mess.

ALLIE:

> No. I'm good. Leaving now.

Scanning the apartment, I mentally go through everything I'll need for the next few days and ensure it's all in my bag. Even if I forgot something, I shouldn't waste any time looking for it.

I slide the strap over my shoulder, tucking my phone into the side pocket, and trudge toward the front door, already formulating a plan for how I'm going to handle the next few days locked down with the entire family when I can barely handle a few hours here and there as it is now.

Once I'm at Nana's, I can lock myself in one of the bedrooms and pretend I'm exhausted and sleeping or that these damn contractions won't stop until I rest and take it easy —alone.

Hopefully to avoid a repeat of Sunday.

That conversation with Pope nearly broke me, but knowing he's at the hospital with Aunt Nora for the duration of the storm means I can get a temporary reprieve—at least from him. No doubt someone else will step into his place with the questions I don't have good answers to right now.

I rub the top of my belly, where the kiddo has been pressing a tiny foot for the last few days. "Time to go, peanut."

Releasing a heavy breath, I flip off the lights and slip out into the hallway, closing and locking the door behind me. It feels strange not to be leaving with Angelina—our first hurricane since she moved in with Jude. But I'm happy for her, for them, and soon, I won't be alone in this place.

This baby will be my new roommate if I stay.

Despite everything weighing me down, I smile at that thought and turn toward the elevator and stairwell and freeze, all the momentarily pleasant thoughts evaporating in a split second.

Oh, God...

He stands at the top of the stairs, somehow looking just as handsome as ever, even soaked to the bone by the torrential rain. But he isn't wearing the slow, easy grin he used to always give me—and any other girl interested him. The one that got me into his bed and him into my pants far too easily.

His lips press into a hard line.

His normally bright, playful amber eyes flash dark as the storm clouds outside.

His hands fist at his sides.

Now I can see exactly who and what he is, even though I was blind to it for so long.

"I'm glad I caught you, Allie." His smooth voice dips low, his anger barely restrained—and so much worse than I thought it would be when we finally faced each other. "It's been so difficult getting ahold of you recently."

His gaze dips to my belly, and I rest my hand over it, as if it's going to do anything to protect me or this baby from what's coming.

I swallow through the fear clogging my throat. "I am on my way out..."

Please let me go.

Please...

I take a couple of tentative steps toward the elevator and the stairwell, my only ways to get out of here, but it means moving closer to *him,* too.

He holds out a hand, blocking the width of the hallway easily, stopping my advance toward freedom. "You really think I'm about to let you and my baby walk out without us having a fucking conversation?"

My heart pounds wildly against my rib cage. "This isn't the time. I promise, once the storm is over, I'll meet with you. We'll talk. I swear. But I have to go now before it gets too dangerous out there."

He releases a hollow laugh that echoes down the empty hallway. "You shouldn't be worried about the storm, Al."

Ice replaces the blood in my veins, instantly chilling any hope I was hanging on to that things might not be as bad as I was anticipating with him. That there might be *any* way this all works out.

I shift my keys between my fingers to leave them poking up between each knuckle, exactly as Saint and Bishop taught me, giving me the only weapon I'll ever have standing out here.

"Please..." Blood rushes in my ears as I try to think of a way —*any* way—to get myself out of this. "I give you my word. I promise."

Another sharp pain bands my abdomen, and I grit my teeth, trying to hide it from the man so intent on keeping me here.

A muscle in his jaw tics as he searches my face. "No, you're coming with me. We'll ride out the storm together. It'll give us *plenty* of time to talk."

This was his plan all along—to catch me and bring me somewhere I couldn't escape from.

I shake my head as tears well in my eyes, despite not wanting to give him the satisfaction. "If I don't show up at my grandmother's house, the family is going to come looking for me." Holding his gaze with more bravado than I'm actually feeling, I lay down a warning. "You don't want that."

Of anyone, he should know what the Hawkes are capable of, how protective the entire family is of anyone under our wings. If they knew what he was doing right now, it would be the end of him, regardless of who he is and what other predicament it would drag us into.

He sneers, something menacing in the tilt of the lips I used to kiss. "You think they're going to find you?" He shakes his head. "I don't believe for one minute that you've told anybody I'm the father of this baby, which means they'd have no reason to come looking for you with *me*."

Shit.

He's right.

My brilliant plan has backfired.

By keeping his identity from everyone, all I've done is make it impossible for them to find me should he manage to get me the fuck out of here against my will.

He grabs my upper arm, and though I'm tempted to take a swing at him with my weapon in hand, with the door locked, he's far too big and too fast and would catch me before I could get back into the apartment. And certainly before I could get down the stairs into my car when I'm waddling around like this.

I have to bide my time.

Wait for the right moment and opportunity.

Which definitely isn't now since another pang wraps around my belly.

I inhale sharply, trying not to show any outward signs of my pain. These damn Braxton-Hicks contractions are only getting worse with the stress of the storm and this man deciding *now* is the appropriate time to have this conversation.

While I try to figure out how to get away from this asshole and the contraction ebbs, he leads me to the stairs and marches me down them slowly, keeping his eye on me almost protectively despite his rough grip.

Ironic, considering he's the only threat right now.

We reach the bottom, and a clap of thunder close enough to rattle the whole building makes me jump. He tightens his hold on my arm, pushing open the exterior door, and leads me out into the driving rain and blowing wind that almost topples me over. Only his firm grasp keeps me upright as he marches me toward the parking lot at the side of the building.

You can do this, Al.

It would be much easier without this torrent, though. I can barely see the few cars left in the lot through the deluge, but a big, black SUV sits three spots down from my red Porsche Cayenne.

Close enough for me to make this attempt.

I glance at him out of the corner of my eye, but he's focused on his vehicle and keeping his hand around my arm, forcing me to keep walking through the puddles already forming and starting to flood the parking lot.

He reaches into his pocket for his keys.

That's my opening.

I swing up with my right hand and jab the keys sharply into his side closest to me.

With a howl of pain, he buckles inward, his grip on me loosening. "Fuck!"

Jerking free of him, I drop my bag and run, racing as fast as my legs will carry me across the slick pavement toward my car. I hit the remote start and unlock buttons and jump in, throwing it into drive as he regains his feet.

Fury burns in his gaze as it meets mine through the violent tempest outside. This single pane of glass in my window isn't going to stop him. And if he gets his hands on me again, I won't fare well.

But I have no intention of letting him ever touch me again.

I pull forward out of the spot, and he lunges toward the car. The tires slip on the wet asphalt, and I hydroplane, almost doing a three-sixty before I finally regain control of the car and direct it toward the street.

He runs after me for a few steps, then seems to think better of it and moves toward his SUV.

Shit, shit, shit, shit, shit.

I definitely didn't think this through.

All he has to do is try to follow me straight to Nana's and attempt to intercept me along the way to continue the "conversation" he seems so desperate for.

Between the storm raging around me and the tears pooling in my eyes, I can barely make him out anymore in the rearview. My only hope now is to put some distance between him and me—fast.

I pull out onto the street and hammer the gas pedal.

The wind buffets my car, making the whole thing rock slightly as my back end spins out, unable to find purchase on the slippery road. But all those defensive driving lessons Bishop insisted I take with her kick in, and I regain control before I completely lose it.

You can do this, Al.

There isn't any other option.

I turn at the first intersection before he can even get out of the parking lot, then make four more quick turns through slowly flooding streets, trying to prevent him from following my route.

Another sharp pain bands around my stomach.

"Shit..."

Gritting my teeth, I breathe through it, one hand white-knuckling the wheel, the other pressed to my side.

I need to slow my heart rate, calm myself down, if I want these to stop.

Deep breaths.

Over and over.

My body relaxes slightly, and I release the death grip on the wheel, taking the final turn to bring me back to the main road I need to take to get to Nana's—that happens to go right past The Hawkeye Club.

It stands only a few hundred yards ahead of me on the left side of the road—sign dark, windows boarded up in preparation for this bitch of a storm.

Lightning shoots down from the sky and slams into a tree along the side of the street. Half of it falls onto the power lines, dragging them down onto the grass, and the other massive portion topples onto the road right in front of the building where I've spent so much time.

I stomp on the brakes, hydroplaning as the massive half of the tree falls toward the road, colliding with the wet asphalt.

And I just keep sliding toward it.

POPE

CHAOS HAS ALREADY INFECTED the ER before the worst of the storm has even hit us.

It's a madhouse.

Beds at capacity.

Waiting room full.

People angry about wait times, demanding to be seen by a doctor immediately.

Though most of the people only have minor injuries sustained trying to ready their homes or attempting to evacuate.

Some broken bones. Contusions. Lacerations that will require stitches. The easy stuff—an appetizer to the entrée of major injuries sure to come.

It's the same every time one of these things strikes New Orleans, and as the largest hospital and only level-one trauma center in the city, we end up accepting the most cases—and the most-dire ones.

Thankfully, no life-threatening injuries have come through the sliding doors—the only glass not boarded up in preparation for the storm per our emergency plan—but the way the storm is ramping up, we all know what's coming.

Utter bedlam.

Almost as if on cue, Nora rushes over, out of breath and looking a little frazzled instead of her normal cool, calm, and collected. Strands of blond hair fall around her face, having escaped from the ponytail she wears it in while on duty when it gets like this. "How are you doing, Dr. Clarke?" Her gaze darts to my patient. "All good?"

I finish the last stitch and glance at her. "All good. We should be able to discharge a few people soon and open up some beds."

She nods, already backing away to touch base with the rest of the staff in the ER. Of all the departments, the ER gets hit the worst in times like this, and Nora oversees her domain with absolute precision. "All right, let me know if you need anything."

"Will do."

An incredible doctor *and* a great boss.

It isn't a combination many people in her position possess. So many great doctors have no idea how to manage others or play nice, but Nora takes it all in stride, making it look easy. Always checking in on everyone, making sure we're okay and that we have everything we need because, on a day like this, anything is possible.

"You're all done, Mr. Knight." I place the bandage over the wound on his arm. "Try not to fall off any more ladders, okay?"

He chuckles low, examining his injury, and nods, his gray hair falling over his forehead. "I will do my best."

"We'll get you discharged soon." I glance toward the main ER doors near the waiting area, out at the thick black clouds and flashing lightning. "It's pretty rough out there already. You may be stuck here for a bit even after we discharge you."

He follows my line of sight, his old eyes crinkling around the corners. "I have lived through worse, kid."

I smirk at him and squeeze his shoulder. "I'm sure you have, but still, be careful."

There's nothing I can do to keep him here once he's discharged, even if it would be in his best interest. That's the problem with living here—so many people think they're invincible because they're survived other storms in the past, but this city learned the hard way with Katrina that the unthinkable can happen.

Everything is fine.

Until it isn't.

That thought immediately brings the fear in Allie's eyes on Sunday flashing through my head, and a familiar unease creeps along my spine. Some would argue it's merely the charge in the air, the power and electricity of the storm I'm feeling, but deep down, I know it's something else.

That sixth sense I've always had when she needed something.

When she was upset or frightened.

When she needed me.

It's been years since I've let myself acknowledge it. A decade of forcing it down and pretending I don't feel it so I can justify what I did that pushed her so far out of my reach.

But I can't fight it today.

Not after that conversation.

Not with this storm raging.

I head to the nurses' station to get Mr. Knight discharged

and pull out my cell, scrolling back through the messages in the Hawke family group chat I typically avoid like the plague, to the ones that started this morning.

Mostly everyone confirming they were on their way to Nana's or had arrived.

ALLIE:

No. I'm good. Leaving now.

Sent almost two hours ago.

A little of the tension in my shoulders releases, and I keep moving through the newer messages. That momentary relief disappears in a millisecond as a new one comes through.

DAD:

Pope, have you heard from Allie?

She should have arrived at Nana's by now.

Even with the storm already causing issues, the worst of it hasn't hit, and the news reports said flooding is minimal. The roads should have been fine...wet but passable when she left.

Nora approaches with her phone in hand. "Are you seeing this?"

I nod. "You haven't heard anything from her, have you?"

She shakes her head, "No. You?"

"Of course not. I'm the last person she'd call if there were a problem. I'm calling my dad." I connect the call and put it on speakerphone so Nora can hear it, too. "I need to figure out what's going on."

He answers on the second ring, his deep voice wavering slightly through the line. "We can't find Allie."

Squeezing my eyes closed, I rub at my temple, willing myself to keep my cool and assess the situation the way I would any medical crisis that comes through those ER doors. "I saw the message."

"Everyone is here except her—"

But it isn't possible to be rational when it comes to Allie.

I slam my fist on the counter, making Nora flinch slightly. "Why the hell didn't one of you go pick her up?"

"Pope..." The reproach in the way he says my name makes me stiffen, bringing me back to being a small child when all he had to do was utter that one syllable to stop me in my tracks. "This isn't the time, son."

"I'm sorry. I just don't understand why she was by herself."

Dad releases a sigh filled with his shared worry and regret. "She was with Angelina and Jude last night helping them, but she wanted to sleep in her own bed. I can't say I blame her for that. Probably most comfortable for her right now. Ang was going to pick her up this morning, but an alarm went off at The Grind, so they had to go check it. Allie said she would drive herself while they dealt with it, and no one expected it to get this bad this fast. In hindsight..."

Yeah, no shit.

So many things look *so* different when they're in the rearview.

If I had known what would happen to Alessandra, the path she would take in her life and the resentment she would harbor toward me for the entirety of it, I might have made a different choice that night. I might have listened to my heart instead of my head and never hurt her.

I release a heavy breath, trying to tamp down the panic I haven't ever felt in these hospital walls—even dealing with the worst of traumas—but that is somehow a crushing weight on me now over one small woman. "She was at her place?"

"Yes."

Opening my eyes, I glance at Nora. "Then, I'm the closest. You guys are all out at Nana's, and with the storm picking up, the roads are going to deteriorate. It could take you hours to get to her apartment."

Dad issues a low growl. "Yeah, we all fucking know that,

kid. But you and Nora need to stay at the hospital, which means I'm going to take Bishop, Gabe, Atlas, and Coen and go find her."

Nora presses her lips together, staring at my phone on the counter. "No." Her eyes dart to meet mine. "Go, Pope. We're closer. She could be in trouble..."

I scan the ER, which hasn't calmed any since I first discovered the worrying text. "Are you going to be okay here without me?"

Technically, I'm required to be here, and leaving during a natural disaster like this could be grounds for dismissal from my residency.

Nora huffs. "I don't care if you're supposed to be here. We'll cover for you, and if the administration has a problem with that, they'll have to answer to me. You go find Allie."

I grab my phone and take it off speaker, already on the move toward the staff locker rooms. "Dad, do you know what route she normally takes to get to Nana's?"

"Yeah, I've ridden with her a few times. I'll text it to you. We're still going to try to get there."

"I'll be in touch."

I end the call and slide my phone back into my pocket, ducking into the locker room to grab my keys. Given the thousands of possible horrific scenarios racing through my head, I don't bother to change out of my scrubs and into the extra clothes I keep here. I toss my lab coat into a pile and slam it closed.

Thunder shakes the building again, and I rush through the hallways toward the staff parking lot at the back of the hospital, checking the message from Dad for the route Allie typically takes to Nana's.

I push the door open, and the gale-force winds catch it, wrenching it from my hand and slamming it back against the brick wall. Rain pummels me, coming in almost horizontally, and I raise my arm to block it as I grab the door and fight against the gusts to get it closed.

As soon as it clicks back into place, I refocus on getting through this squall to my car.

Each step feels like fighting Mother Nature herself. Shielding my eyes from the pelting drops, I navigate through an inch of accumulating water on the pavement to my car, beeping it unlocked so I can slide in and start it up immediately.

It roars to life, the seat under me rumbling and giving me a surge of confidence that I can find her.

She can't have gone far.

Not three weeks short of delivering that baby.

Not in this storm.

Dad and the others will check the stretch from the hospital to Nana's, which leaves me to cover the portion to her place. If she's still there, I'll get to her. And if she had car trouble or got stuck in flooding, she knows to stay where it's safe and to call for help. She'll be along the route Dad texted me.

Theoretically...

I peel out of the parking lot on wet asphalt and head that way, my heart in my throat, regret sitting heavily on my shoulders.

This shouldn't have happened.

Someone should have been with her.

I should have been.

"Fuck! Fuck! Fuck!" I slam my hand against my steering wheel. "Where are you, Al?"

The roads are mostly deserted, as most of this zone has evacuated already, but the few out creep by the flooding inter-sections. Rain comes down so hard that I can barely see a few feet in front of me. I brake and pull out my phone to check for any text updates from anyone.

No service.

Shit.

Lightning splits the sky, and thunder booms so close that it shakes my car, a warning of how imminent the worst of the storm is. Wind powers through the trees, threatening to topple them right onto the road in front of me. I weave around debris blocking the lane, squinting through the windshield, straining to see what's in front of me.

I need to find her—quickly.

If I didn't know this road so well, I wouldn't even know The Hawkeye Club stands a handful of yards ahead. I move slowly through the partially flooded street, scanning for any sign of her or her vehicle.

She had to come this way—no way she would have risked going any other route in this weather.

Come on, Al. Where are you?

Something comes into view ahead.

An obstruction on the road blocking my path.

I inch closer, unable to make it out through the deluge, until I'm almost on it—a massive tree blocking all lanes of traffic.

Shit.

I slam on the brakes, the car sliding and coming to a stop before colliding with what appears to be a shattered oak. Leaning forward, struggling to see past the windshield wipers that are doing their best to deal with the water—and failing miserably—I can just barely make out something red on the other side of it...

Fucking hell.

Allie's car.

4

ALESSANDRA

The absolute dead silence coming from the phone pressed against my ear instead of a dial tone adds to my rising panic, and I shiver in my soaked clothes, willing myself not to fall apart completely.

My cell was in the bag I threw in the parking lot of my building to get away...and that tree falling on the power line outside must have taken out *all* power to the area.

Hence, the stupid, useless phone in my hand.

Shit, shit, shit, shit, shit.

This storm has really fucked things up—almost as badly as I have.

Well, maybe not that much.

But close.

I slam the phone back into the cradle on the wall, scanning the main bar area of The Hawkeye Club, looking for any other options, any possible way to reach someone and let them know where I am—but short of Byron having an old-school CB radio stashed somewhere I don't know about, it appears I'm fucked.

The place looks so strange like this, with the power out, only the emergency floodlights and exit signs lit by their battery backups. Normally filled with thumping bass, bright lights, and women shaking their asses for the clientele, it's more like a ghost town now.

The tables all empty.

The stage and pole dark.

And I'm stuck here until power gets restored or until someone finds me.

But who the hell would be coming?

Everybody's already out at Nana's house. And the way the storm is building, no one's getting here anytime soon, even if they *thought* to look for me here.

Another contraction hits me, the pain radiating across my lower back and around my stomach. Harder than the ones earlier today, this pain almost blinds me. I double over, pressing my hand against my belly and gritting my teeth.

Fuck!

The baby kicks, and I rub over the spot. "If you could just chill out for a while"—I gasp through the pain—"that would be great."

Thunder booms, shaking the entire building, making the glasses in the bar rattle and the bottles of alcohol lining the back wall threaten to topple.

I look up at the ceiling. "If you could chill, too, I would appreciate it."

The front door I entered through only a few minutes ago bangs open, slamming against the wall, and the blustery wind swirls into the club, bringing rain, leaves, and other small debris across the normally immaculate, shiny black tile.

Shit.

It's getting even worse.

I waddle out from behind the bar and toward it to lock it back into place. Which I should have done when I first got in here. But I was so happy to be inside, out of the storm, where I might find a damn phone, that I didn't even think to fully secure the door behind me.

All I could see was that phone on the wall—which is utterly useless now.

Damn storm.

Wrapping my hand around the solid wood, I start to push it closed against the battling wind that doesn't seem to want me to do it. Lightning flashes and thunder rolls again, even louder through the open jamb, reverberating through the empty club and making me jump slightly at its intensity.

Something moves out in the whirlwind—a figure struggling through the driving rain and gusts strong enough to knock someone over.

My heart catches in my throat.

Did he follow me?

Panic surges through me, and I shove at the door harder, trying to get it closed before he reaches it.

But the person gets closer.

No. No. No.

Lightning flashes again, illuminating Pope for a millisecond before he nudges the door open wide enough to push me back slightly and slip inside the club.

He urges me to retreat all the way, then slams the door closed and throws the lock.

Water drips off him, like it has been me since I got in, leaving little puddles all over the tile, and he turns to face me. "Jesus, Al." His gaze sweeps over me, checking me closely as he tries to catch his breath after fighting the storm. "Are you okay?"

It takes a moment to process that he's really here, standing in front of me, waiting for me to answer.

Finally, I nod, even though I am *far* from okay with this entire situation and the confrontation earlier this morning.

"Um, yeah. I guess." I wave absently toward the road. "The tree fell in the road, and my car skidded into it. I couldn't back up. My tires must have been stuck on a branch."

His eyes widen. "Did your airbags deploy?"

I shake my head. "No, I think I slowed down enough...what are *you* doing here?"

He runs a hand over his face, wiping away some of the water. "My dad told me you didn't make it to Nana's. I was trying to get to your place and saw your car on the road."

"How did you get past the tree?"

It was lying across the entire road, blocking his route to the club from that direction.

"The alley that runs along the building next to this...I parked in their lot and hopped the fence to get over here. I was on my way to your car to see if you were inside when I saw the door to the club bang open in the wind and figured you must have come inside."

I release a heavy sigh of relief.

No matter how hard I've been avoiding Pope—and don't want a repeat of the other night—at least I'm not riding out this stupid storm alone until help comes.

He gives me another concerned look. "You're sure you're okay?"

I open my mouth to assure him I'm fine when another contraction hits and doubles me over. "Fuck!"

Pope steps forward, and strong arms wrap around me. "Shit, what's wrong, Al?"

Fucking EVERYTHING!

And I can't even scream that at him because the pain is stealing my ability to speak. "I've...been...having...contractions..."

"What?" His brow furrows, the instant shift into doctor mode visible in his intense examination of my face. "When did they start?"

"They've been happening for months, Braxton-Hicks. Dr. Brennan said I was only a centimeter dilated at my appointment last week, so it's probably nothing to worry about, just a little intense."

Keep telling yourself that.

Pope doesn't seem convinced, either. His penetrating gaze travels over my soaked clothes and hands clutched across my stomach. "Everything in your records suggested you weren't going to deliver early, but stress can induce early labor—"

I narrow my eyes on him, righting myself now that the pain has passed. "You looked at my records?"

He tenses, darting his eyes around the club instead of keeping them on me.

"I'm pretty sure that's a fucking crime, Pope. A HIPAA violation..."

His head snaps back toward me, eyes blazing. "How the hell else was I supposed to know you were doing okay when you wouldn't talk to me?"

"I talk to you." My reply comes out a little too fast and a little too defensive.

He snorts incredulously and shakes his head, water dripping down the sides of his face. "Glaring at me from across the room and grunting 'hi' when we're around other people doesn't count as talking to me, Allie. Now"—he scans the club again —"let's get you somewhere I can examine you."

I tense and try to pull out of his hold. "What? No."

He narrows his eyes on me. "Allie, I have to examine you to see if you're in active labor or not."

Shaking my head, I take a step back, freeing myself from his arms. "No, I'm fine. It's just Braxton-Hicks. I'm sure."

For a split second, I almost believe it.

Want to believe it.

Because the other option is unfathomable at this point.

Pope holds out his hand, palm up. A request to trust him, to let him do what he's trained to do, no matter how fucking awkward it will be for both of us. "Then let *me* be sure. *Please.*"

Years of fighting him, of keeping up this wall between us that I need in order to be able to spend time around him, have created the natural instinct to move *away* from rather than *toward* Pope Clarke.

But I also know he's right—that we need to know what's happening with the baby, especially given our current predicament.

I reach a shaky hand out to his, sliding our palms together. He tightens his grip and turns us to face the club.

He scans everything visible in the dim emergency lighting. "I assume there's no power?"

"None. I don't have my cell. That's why I came in here, but the landline isn't working..."

"Shit. My phone doesn't have service, either. That power line must have fed the local cell tower." His eyes dart to the elevator and door that leads to the stairs to the second floor. "And no power means the elevator is out of the question."

He releases my hand and drops his shoulder, sliding his arms around me and lifting me up before I can protest.

"Hey"—I flail slightly in his hold—"what are you doing?"

His cognac eyes dip down to me as he stalks across the club floor, avoiding the debris the wind brought in. "I'm taking you upstairs to Savage's office. It'll be the most comfortable place for us to ride this out for however long we have to."

"I can *walk.*"

He shoulders his way through the emergency exit door into the stairwell. "If you're in labor, I don't want you climbing two flights of stairs."

The baby seems to agree with him.

Another contraction hits me, and I wince and cling to Pope, tightening my fingers into his soaked scrub top. Twisting in his arms, I suck in a sharp breath and release a sound that is wholly inhuman, fighting the agony.

His ascent falters, and he pauses, staring down at me with concern darkening his gaze. "Fuck, another one that quick?"

I nod, gritting my teeth, and he mutters something under his breath I can't quite catch. Then he resumes his climb, picking up the pace.

We reach the top of the second flight of steps, and he pushes that door open and stalks down the hallway with determination toward Uncle Savage's office.

The storm continues to rage on, windows rattling despite being boarded up from the outside, wind howling and blowing things against the building.

Pope makes it to the door of Savage's office as the pain finally releases me from its grip. He shifts his hold on me so he can grab the knob and turn it, pushing into the familiar space that always smells like bourbon and my favorite uncle.

He walks over to the leather couch and slowly lowers me onto it, dropping to his knees next to me. "How are you feeling?"

"I'm okay right now..."

Big. Fucking. Lie.

I am so *not* okay.

"I can't be in labor, Pope." Tears well in my eyes, and I swallow the sob threatening to slip out. "It's too early..."

He eyes me sympathetically. "You've been under tremendous stress for most of your pregnancy. Between the fire at The Grind, the shooting, and the threats from Satriano...not to mention whatever's happening with the baby's father. All that stress releases adrenalin and cortisol into your system, and it can induce early labor, Al." He rests his hand over mine. "But you're thirty-seven weeks. That's not technically full term, but a lot of babies are born at this gestation, and going into labor now isn't all that unusual."

That sob I've been fighting falls from my lips, and I suck in a shuddering breath. "But I'm not *ready*."

He squeezes my hand tightly. "You might have to be."

POPE

I HUSTLE down the stairs I climbed a moment ago, checking my phone again to find that damn SOS symbol signaling no service.

"Fuck, fuck, fuck..."

My curses echo through the stairwell, only heightening my awareness of how of how truly precarious this situation we are in really is.

If that power line fed the local cell tower and the club, we're not making *any* calls out of here.

Which is not fucking ideal.

Even without examining Allie, I can already tell I'm not going to like what I find. She seems to understand it, too, no matter how much she wishes it weren't true. The fear in her eyes has nothing to do with the storm outside and everything to do with that baby coming early.

I hit the door at the bottom of the stairwell and step out into the club, only lit by the single floodlight in the corner near the exit sign, and beeline for the bar to get what I'm going to need.

Compared to the fully stocked ER I just left, scrounging for anything I can find here at the club feels more like dumpster diving, despite how nicely Savage and Gabe keep the place.

I snag four bottles of water, the pump of hand soap next to the sink, a bottle of moonshine, and a stack of clean towels from under the counter before I make my return to Savage's office.

Each step I take closer to Allie ratchets up the anxiety I typically *never* feel in these circumstances. I'm trained to handle emergencies—the more *dire*, life-threatening injuries imaginable, and I've done it without even breaking a sweat. I've delivered dozens of babies, many with complications that required quick thinking and some serious medical intervention, but the vast majority of births go smoothly.

Then why does it feel like that tree outside is crushing my chest?

As much as I don't want to admit it, I know the answer to that.

Because it's Alessandra McCabe.

Because I haven't stopped worrying about her from the day I found out she was pregnant.

Hell, I haven't stopped worrying since the day I broke her heart and let her walk away from me.

But I can't let her see my nerves. Not when she's barely keeping it together. I need to be Dr. Clarke right now, *not* Pope.

This is merely a routine exam that might lead to a completely routine delivery...that just happens to be in a strip club.

I step back into the office to find Allie still lying on the couch in her wet clothes, tears streaming down her temples, jaw locked through another contraction. "Don't hold your breath. Breathe *through* it."

Her head whips toward me, and she glares but does as I say, sucking in a long, deep breath and letting it out slowly. Over and over again, while I count how long this one goes on.

Sixty seconds...

Ninety...

Allie finally relaxes, slumping back against the pillow on the couch. "That one was...intense."

And long.

Even without knowing when it actually started, it's enough to confirm my fears.

I drop to my knees next to her and set down my supplies,

contemplating how to approach what I'm going to have to do. She tenses at my closeness, eyeing me the same way she did when I cornered her in the bedroom at Nana's house on Sunday.

Trepidation.

Distrust.

The heat of lingering hatred over our shared past.

God knows Allie doesn't want me to examine her, and I'd be the last person she would pick to deliver her baby—but she doesn't have any choice. It's not like I'm in any position to give her another option.

Still, I can't force her to accept my help.

I need her to *want* it.

To trust me again—even if it's just to get through what's likely coming in the next few hours if someone doesn't rescue us—fast.

Which means laying the truth out for her as calmly and directly as I can.

I twist the cap off a bottle of water, setting it down next to me. "I know you're pissed at me, Al, but you have to think about that baby and what's best for him or her, not about how much you hate me right now, okay?"

She opens her mouth to say something, but if I let her start an argument, it's going to eat into the time I have before her next contraction.

I hold up a hand to stop her from interrupting me. "I'm a doctor, Al. I've done an OB rotation. I've delivered dozens of babies both there and in the ER when they came in too late to get them moved. You have to let me check you out because, by the looks of the storm and the way it sounds out there, we might be stuck here for a while. And given my experience, I don't think you have *a while* before we're going to meet your baby."

"Oh, God..." The panic rises in her voice as she shifts restlessly on the couch. "I can't—"

"Please, Teeny, trust me."

It's hard for her to do after everything we've been through, all the resentment she's held the past decade, and I fully expect her to tell me to fuck off and that she'll do it herself.

That would be a very "Allie" thing to do.

The woman loves to push people away when they try to help her, but she finally inhales sharply, turns her head toward me, and opens her eyes, offering a tight nod of approval.

A tear slides down her cheek, and I have to look away, not only because seeing her distress shreds me from the inside out but because I have to get ready.

I spread out one of the towels, pour water on my hands, then pump some soap onto them, scrubbing them until my skin feels raw.

"What are you doing?"

"Sterilizing the best I can. This isn't exactly the ideal environment to be doing this."

She releases a laugh, the sound stilted and filled with her unease. "Uncle Savage keeps this place about as clean as a hospital."

That draws a smirk to my lips. "You are right about that, but still..." I glance up at her, my humor draining with what I'm going to have to ask of her. "I'm going to need you to take off your pants and underwear."

Her jaw hardens again, and I turn away, giving her my back, as I pour the moonshine over my hands, too.

God knows I'd rather be downing it than sanitizing with it right now...

I hear her struggle behind me and almost turn around to help, but I force myself to keep facing Savage's desk, staring at all the family pictures on it and on the shelf behind.

Him and Gabe the day they opened this place.

Him with Dani and Kennedy when she was a baby, sitting on his lap, staring up at him while her mother kisses him.

Him with Star—which makes my chest ache for the woman I never got to meet.

"Okay, I'm ready."

She sure as hell doesn't sound ready.

I'm not so sure I am, either, but I turn back around to face her and lower myself to my knees, keeping my hands up. "I'll do this as quickly as I can, all right?"

She squeezes her eyes closed and nods, and I spread her knees to begin my examination.

Fuck.

What I find makes me clench my jaw. "You are definitely in active labor."

"What?" She jerks up and looks at me, still between her legs. "No..." She shakes her head. "No, no, no. No, I can't be."

"You're seven, maybe eight centimeters dilated already." I reach up and palpate her belly. "And the baby has dropped."

"No. No, no, no, no, no, no, no."

The more she chants, the harder and faster her chest heaves, and I can see the panic starting to well up inside her. How hard it's becoming for her to contain her fear.

I climb to my feet and rinse my hands again, then settle on the edge of the couch next to her the best I can while I dry them on one of the towels.

Her sobs fill the room, and another contraction makes her wince, gripping her stomach and twisting, the leather creaking under her.

Fuck, I hate this for her.

No way to help her manage the pain she must be in— emotionally or physically.

But I still have to try.

I take her face between my palms and hold her steady,

forcing her to look at me. "You need to breathe, Al. Calm down. I'm right here."

If she hyperventilates and passes out, that will make an already complicated situation downright dangerous.

She attempts to breathe through the contraction, then sags slightly when it releases her from its grip. "I'm not ready." Her bottom lip quivers, and she shakes her head in my hold. "I thought I had a few more weeks. I thought..."

"It's going to be okay, Al. You and the baby are going to be *fine*. And we'll get you out of here, okay? But unless help gets here in the next hour or so, maybe two, I don't think you're going to make it to the hospital before this baby makes an appearance."

She swallows thickly. "I fucked up everything."

Her words stab directly into the part of me that feels the same way every time I look at her.

I wipe the tears from the corners of her eyes. "It'll be all right. I'll take care of you."

"You said that once before..."

Wincing, I squeeze my eyes closed at the memory that's haunted me endlessly.

What started out so good became so painful in only a matter of minutes. When I realized what I had to do. The decision I was going to have to make. The words I was going to have to say to her. How I was going to have to destroy her...

It all comes rushing back, hitting me so hard I almost say something to her that would only further complicate the situation and our lives.

Don't, Pope.

This isn't the time or the place.

Opening my eyes, I meet her blue ones filled with so much fear and uncertainty. "I'm going to go gather some more things that I need for the delivery and try to find us some dry clothes to change into, all right? You need to breathe through the contractions. Don't hold your breath again."

She sucks in an unsteady one and nods. "Okay. All right."

I climb to my feet and head toward the door but pause to look back at her.

What would she have done if I didn't show up? If I didn't find her?

The thought makes acid fill my throat, and I swallow it and hustle downstairs and straight for the dancers' changing rooms behind the stage.

These girls are prepared for any scenario, and Savage, Gabe, and Byron make sure they are fully stocked with anything they might need while here at work.

They take care of their girls...and I need to do the same for Allie.

I dig through the cabinets and the bags in their lockers, grabbing larger towels, blankets, clothes—anything I can find that might be useful.

Scanning the dressing tables, a white and gray chevron bag tucked under it catches my eye. I snag it and throw it over my shoulder, hoping it's what I think it is, before I head back to the bar to grab a knife they normally use to cut citrus for the drinks.

God, I hope I only have to use this to cut the umbilical cord.

If there's a complication, if the baby gets stuck or Allie starts crashing and I need to do a C-section, she will bleed out before anyone ever gets here.

Even though I know the Hawke posse left Nana's house the moment they realized Allie should have been there, the storm is going to prevent them from getting here quickly.

Which means Al and I are on our own.

5

POPE

Even with the windows in Savage's office boarded up, the storm makes its presence known, growing stronger and angrier in conjunction with Allie's contractions and mood.

Though, I can't say I blame her.

With all the stress she's clearly under, having to deliver her baby here, like this, instead of at the hospital where she planned, must be another blow to a woman already fighting something that's had her twisted up for months.

The catastrophic winds batter the building and rattle the glass against the wood set up to protect it, a reminder that we are at Mother Nature's mercy right now, no matter how badly we both would prefer to be anywhere else.

I'd do anything to help her through this, but deep down, I worry when all is said and done, whatever happens tonight is going to make things between us even worse.

Allie's head snaps toward the violent sound, and she sucks in a sharp breath, her body tensing. I want to tell her to stop worrying about it, to concentrate on what we're about to do, but maybe agonizing about the storm offers the distraction she needs so that she's not focusing on the pain that I can do absolutely nothing about.

Or the fact that I'm the one here helping bring her first child into the world.

No matter the tiny glimpses of our old rapport peeking up since I arrived, the trust she's placed in me to do this, she still has an impenetrable wall up around her. The same one she put there firmly that night everything between us came crumbling apart, and she refuses to bring it down for me even in this moment when she needs a lifeline to cling to.

Despite knowing the reason she put it in place, I want her to at least consider the possibility that I did what I did for *her.*

Not for *me.*

The fact that she can't see that has been a festering wound in my soul for a decade. And today is only making it worse.

So many times over the last few hours, I've almost brought it up, tried to explain my actions that drove this wedge between us. Each time, I gulped the truth back down—afraid it would drive her further away and possibly make her fight me when it comes time to do the really hard work required to bring her baby into this world.

Her eyes move back to me, wide, full of fear, but I don't know if it's due to the hurricane or the fact that we're about to do *this.*

I tug her hand into mine, relief flooding me when she doesn't immediately jerk it away. "We'll be okay."

This building has weathered worse storms and come out unscathed, remained the heart and soul of Hawke Enterprises for almost fifty years. It isn't going anywhere, despite what Mother Nature may attempt outside.

"*You'll* be okay."

Women deliver babies all the time, often without any

medical support at all. We're warm, dry, and safe here to do this.

"The *baby* will be okay."

It's coming early, but there's no reason to think anything will go wrong as long as I can keep Allie's head in the game and prevent her from panicking.

"You need to take some deep breaths and try to slow your heart rate a little for me, all right?"

Without the benefit of any of the typical equipment we use to monitor mothers in active labor, I've had to resort to the most basic of measurements and assessments—the things I can see and feel with my own eyes and hands.

And I don't like what I see.

Her breathing is too raggedy.

Her heart racing.

Her body too tense.

She gives me a sharp nod, fighting the tears, but before she can make any attempt to relax, another contraction makes her stiffen, squeezing my hand so tightly she crushes my fingers enough to make *me* wince.

"Breathe, Al. You're fully dilated. We're going to start pushing soon, okay?"

She grits her teeth and shakes her head. "I. Can. Wait."

God fucking love her...

Even in this much pain, lying on her uncle's office couch, minutes away from delivering this baby, she still clings to hope that Dad, Gabe, Coen, and Atlas might actually find us in time to get her to the hospital. But from the sounds of what's going on outside, I wouldn't be surprised if they had to turn back completely. You don't mess with this type of weather unless you want to end up where I should be right now, back at the ER.

Guilt claws at my chest at abandoning Nora and my station, my job, my duty, to come looking for Allie. But seeing how close she is to delivering, it almost feels like it was fate that I would be the one to find her.

Her clenched hand relaxes slightly, and I pull mine free of it and shake it, trying to get the tingling to stop.

"I'm sorry, Teeny, but this baby isn't waiting. But we can do this—you and me."

Maybe they weren't the right words to say because her tears immediately start flowing down her cheeks again.

Fuck.

I never could stand watching her cry, but this feels like some new form of torture designed to bring me to my knees for the woman who doesn't want me here, doesn't want my help or offered comfort.

Do your job, Pope.

Pretend she's just another patient.

It's impossible.

But it's the only way I'll get through this.

I scan the supplies I managed to scrounge together, including a pile of Hawkeye Club T-shirts that match the ones we both currently wear—replacements for the soaked clothes we had on when we came up to Savage's office. The too-short jeans I found in Gabe's office at least stay up on my hips, but I would much rather be in a fresh set of scrubs for this.

Allie tenses again, and I check her progress as a crack of thunder shakes the whole building, making even me flinch.

"All right, Al. We're going to push on the next one, okay?"

"Shit." She takes a sharp breath. "Shit." Another gasp. "Shit."

She relaxes slightly, as this contraction ebbs, and I grab the towels and knife and set them next to me on the coffee table.

"I need you to turn and face me."

Her eyes widen slightly, like she's about to argue, but I shake my head. There isn't any way she'll be able to push without her feet propped on this, and I need her open to me to ensure the birth canal is wide and clear.

"Al, we don't have time." I lock eyes with her, ensuring she sees how serious I am. "Turn."

I slide my hand under her, helping her move on the couch until she's propped against the back and can put her feet up on the coffee table on either side of me.

"As soon as the next one comes, I need you to bear down and push, okay?"

She nods, the tears trickling down the established red lines on her cheeks. The combined physical and mental anguish she's going through almost make words I should never say fall from my lips—ones that wouldn't be fair.

I swallow them back and get ready, but it doesn't take long before she tenses again and starts to strain. "Good. Keep pushing as long and as hard as you can..."

Five seconds...

Ten...

Twenty...

Thirty...

Forty...

The baby moves closer to this world with each passing second and effort on her part, and the contraction finally stops.

Allie slumps back, a sob slipping from her throat. "I can't-I can't do this—"

So many women have said the same words to me during their labors, and every single one of them was wrong. The pain gets into their heads, and Allie is doing this under the most unpleasant of circumstances.

"You can. You will."

I give her a moment to just cry while I keep my eyes on my watch, preparing for the next contraction. She needs the moment. She needs to let it out so that when it comes time to push again, she can breathe and use all the energy she has left to advance her labor instead of panicking.

"We're almost there, Al. A few more hard pushes. That's all it will take. Another one will be coming soo—"

I don't even get the word out before the next one hits, and despite her insistence that she can't, Allie pushes hard, gritting her teeth and clutching the edges of the couch. The leather creaks in protest the longer the contraction goes on, but the baby makes great progress.

"Good, keep pushing. As much as you can..."

She does as I count my way through it, and when she relaxes again and opens her eyes, I offer her a reassuring smile.

"You did good, Al. Keep it up." I slide my hand over hers and squeeze it. "We're almost there."

She huffs, shifting on the couch. "*We?* I'm doing all the work..."

I fight a grin and pull my hand back, ready for the next contraction because the baby will likely crown with another good push.

It doesn't take long before she bears down again, her anguished cry filling the room, combining with the fierce sounds of the storm battering the club.

The baby starts crowning, and I position myself to grab it. "Keep pushing, keep pushing."

Allie sags back as the contractions stop, her breathing heavy, chest heaving.

"That was good, Al. One more, two tops."

Her head shifts from side to side against the leather, her damp hair twisting behind her. "God, why does this hurt so much?"

"Do you want me to give you the clinical explanation?"

She rolls her eyes. "It was a rhetorical question, Pope."

That draws a grin across my face.

I've missed this with her—the back and forth, the banter.

Despite the hostility still permeating her words, it feels good to actually be talking to her. Incredible to be the one who's able to help her through this, even if she doesn't want me here.

"Next one, big push."

"Easier said than done, Pope—"

The contraction steals whatever her words were, and she bears down again, forcing the baby's head farther out before her body relaxes.

Sweat drips down her temples, mixing with the tears that have been flowing non-stop since we started pushing. "Women voluntarily do this without medication?"

Fighting a laugh, I nod. "Actually, a lot do."

"They're fucking *insane.*"

"I'll mention that next time someone tells me they want a natural birth."

She scowls at me. "No, you won't."

I shake my head and grin at her. "No, I won't."

But keeping her talking and maybe even getting a laugh or a smile out of her will help her relax slightly going into the final effort.

Her fingers tighten around the edges of the couch cushions, and without me even having to tell her, she pushes hard, using every last ounce of strength she has left to get the baby's shoulders through.

She collapses back as I scoop him up in one of the towels I had waiting.

"Good job, Al..."

Her eyes flutter open. "Why isn't the baby crying?"

Terror fills her voice, and I immediately move to do what's necessary.

"It's okay, Al. Sometimes they need a second and some encouragement." Adjusting my hold on the baby, I rub the chest and back, and a few seconds later, the first startled cry fills the air. "It's a boy."

Allie freezes and squeezes her eyes closed, releasing one of the most anguished sobs I've ever heard.

Relief.

Fear.

Maybe both.

I clean him up a little as he kicks and squeals, then hold him up so she can fully see him. "Pull your shirt up."

She only hesitates a moment before doing it, exposing her breasts and smooth peachy skin the baby needs to feel against him right now.

I settle him to her chest, letting my gaze drift to her face. The sheer awe and love there makes my heart stall for a second, and I have to look away, or I might end up crying like she is.

Pushing to my feet, I retreat a half-step, trying to get myself back into *doctor* mode. "You should see if he'll latch to feed. The colostrum you're producing right now has a lot of important antibodies and other things he needs, and we don't know how long we'll be stuck here. He's going to be hungry..."

Her eyes dart up to meet mine, the tears still flowing freely as she stares up at me. She uses her free hand to swipe them away and nods. "Okay. I'll try."

She adjusts the baby, giving him access to her breast, and he latches on and clings to her like the lifeline she is for him.

That's always the way I felt about her.

Like she was the thing that kept me rooted in the real world when I spent so much time pushing myself to achieve stratospheric heights academically and could so easily get lost in those endeavors.

But that was a long time ago.

Emotion clogs my throat, and I have to turn back to ready her for the afterbirth and cleaning her up. Because God knows

I can't sit and watch her nurse another man's baby right now without losing my soul completely.

ALESSANDRA

A LOUD CRASH jerks me awake, the heavy fog of sleep still trying to drag me back under, but Pope rests his hand on my shoulder, urging my head back down onto his lap.

"It was outside."

It takes a few seconds for his words to sink in and for me to get my bearings.

Uncle Savage's office.

The couch.

The storm screams outside, the wind rattling the windows again, fighting them for a way in.

Did I fall asleep like this?

I blink up at him, trying to remember, but everything is enveloped in a thick haze of bone-deep exhaustion I've never experienced before. Every part of my body aches, especially my chest, with each breath, but compared to the vivid memory of the pain that wracked me only a short time ago, this is more than bearable.

Especially snuggled up on Pope's lap, his familiar scent enveloping me and bringing me back to the moment, even though my brain seems to want me to go back to sleep.

My gaze drifts up over Pope's bare chest to my son, snuggled closely against his shoulder, wrapped up in what looks like one of the Hawkeye Club T-shirts, sleeping contently. "Did I fall asleep?"

He nods, his bourbon eyes examining me in the dark room. "Yes..."

The last thing I remember was Pope moving around the

office, cleaning up after he had examined me for any complications post-delivery, averting his gaze while I fed the baby. Which means he settled onto the couch and moved me onto his lap at some point once I had passed out.

Just like any other time we've had to be in each other's vicinity over the last decade, my first instinct is to pull away, no matter how comfortable I might be. To put much-needed space between us. But I'm too exhausted. My body and mind are both wrung out more than I knew possible.

The baby shifts slightly against him, and my chest tightens even more, worry immediately taking hold. "Is he all right?"

Pope glances at the little guy, rubbing his back gently to soothe him back to sleep. "He's fine. They sleep a lot at this age."

I try to swallow back the sob, but I can't.

Not staring at the baby.

My baby.

The last few months, I've been terrified of this day, of what bringing this life into the world would mean for him, me, and the rest of the Hawkes. But now that he's here, I can't see any of the complications, just a perfect little angel with thick, dark hair and a tiny hand pressed against Pope's chest.

Another sob slips free with the tears. "He's so beautiful."

Pope grins, glancing down at him. "He is. You did really well." His eyes dart to meet mine. "I know this wasn't easy for you..."

That's the understatement of the century.

Nobody wants the ex-love of their life delivering their child, especially in the middle of this storm that seems intent on keeping us cooped up in here for any foreseeable future.

Whatever crashed outside was big—maybe the Hawkeye Club sign coming down. We're going to have a lot of repair work to do when all this is said and done, and not only to the various Hawke Enterprises buildings. Getting stuck here with

Pope ripped open old wounds I've tried so hard to let scar over and brought up memories I long attempted to forget.

I reach up and touch my son's tiny fingers, inadvertently brushing against Pope's bare chest with the movement. "Where's your shirt?"

He smirks. "It was a little dirty, and skin-to-skin contact is good for babies."

"So I've heard."

All the books I read, trying to prepare myself for the delivery and having a newborn, threw so many things at me. It was too much to absorb, especially when I was caught in the abyss of trying to figure out how to protect my baby from his father.

One of Pope's dark brows rises. "You want to take him?"

That vise cranks around my ribs, the same fear that I'm going to fail at this the way I did at keeping him safe gripping me. "He looks comfortable with you at the moment."

Happy.

Safe.

All the things I can't give him.

I let my eyes drift closed again, unable to look at the picture-perfect moment, knowing that everything is going to go to shit even worse than it already has as soon as we get out of here and the storm settles.

"Hey, Al?"

Pope drags his fingers through my hair gently, the familiar feeling relaxing me even more into him.

"What?"

"You seemed..."—he considers his words for a moment—"distressed by the fact that it was a boy."

My entire body stiffens with his observation.

Of course, he would notice that.

Of course, he would ask.

Pope knows me too well not to.

He shifts slightly under me, never stopping the calming movement through my hair. "Were you hoping it was a girl?"

Shit.

I hadn't intended to get into this with anyone—especially not Pope—today, or anytime, until I had some sort of plan, an idea of what I might be able to do to keep that dangerous man away from my child.

But he's here now.

I don't have any more time.

And if I don't share the truth soon, no one will be able to stop his father from coming for him.

"No." I shake my head. "It isn't that. I just..." I suck in a deep breath and release it slowly before the words come tumbling out in a rush, racing to fill the room after I've held them back for so long. "I thought maybe if I had a girl that he wouldn't care so much, that he might not be as likely to want to be involved in her life as if he had a son."

Pope mutters something under his breath and shifts again. "Al, everyone's been really patient with you and tried to respect your privacy during your pregnancy, but at this point, I think you need to tell me what the fuck is going on with the father of this baby."

He's right.

I open my eyes to meet his.

Gone is the professional doctor version of Pope Clarke, replaced by the one I used to run to when I needed comfort or advice growing up. The one who became so much more, only to snatch it away from me.

His eyes plead with me for the answers I haven't given anyone. "Please, Al."

Another sob rips from my throat, the tears welling and sliding down my temples. "I swear...I didn't know who he was..."

Pope's brow furrows as his shoulders tense, bracing himself

for whatever truth I'm about to unload on him. "What do you mean?"

It's going to sound so stupid.

Proof of how reckless and naïve I really am.

How could I not see it?

How could I not know?

Swallowing my fear and regret to try to get through this explanation, I turn my head back to fully face Pope. "When we got together, I just thought he was, you know, a handsome, talented, flirty musician."

"Musician?"

He repeats the word, and I can almost see him running it over in his mind, trying to think of anyone he might know who would fall under that category.

"You remember Dan, right? Dan Roe, who used to play at The Grind?"

Pope's eyes widen, his jaw dropping slightly. "*He's* the father of this baby?"

I give a sharp nod, then press my hand over my mouth to fight another hysterical sound from slipping out, shaking my head. "But you don't understand..."

"Don't understand what?"

"Who he *really* is."

"Jesus, Al." He tilts my chin, forcing me to look up at him. "Stop with the cryptic shit and just *tell* me."

After keeping the truth locked away in a vault inside for so long, actually telling someone feels all kinds of wrong, like I'm revealing something meant to stay buried. But everything Pope said the other night at Nana's was right—the Hawkes can't help me if they don't know what they're up against.

"When I first got pregnant, I held off on telling him because we had so much going on with the fire at The Grind, and I knew he was not a serious relationship type of guy, that he was unlikely to want to be involved. I wanted to approach him carefully about it, but I *was* going to *tell* him because he had a right to know. I had planned to have that talk with him when he played at the reopening, but…"

Pope's jaw hardens. "But then, the place got shot up."

Vivid images flash through my head.

The joy of getting The Grind open again after the catastrophic fire.

All our regulars back for their favorite drinks after months of being shut down.

Even seeing Dan up on the small stage, singing and grinning at me, completely unaware that I was hiding my pregnancy from him.

Then everything changed.

"It wasn't just the shooting that stopped me from telling him."

The cracks of gunfire.

Breaking glass.

Screams.

People scrambling.

"That was the day I figured it out…"

The day everything came crashing down around me. All the plans I had for this baby, for a potential future for him—or her—changed the instant I realized I was completely wrong about the man I had let into my heart and my bed for that brief time.

"Figured what out, Al?"

I inhale deeply before unleashing the truth. "That Dan Roe is actually Daniele Roselli."

Pope's entire body stiffens, and his hand freezes in my hair. "Roselli?"

Another sob tumbles out of my mouth and fills the room, and I can't fight the full tidal wave of tears anymore. "I swear, I didn't know. No one did. Angelina sure as hell didn't, or she never would've allowed him to play there."

"What the fuck?" The sheer astonishment in Pope's voice matches what I felt that day.

"We always assumed he asked for his payments in cash because he wanted to avoid taxes on them. Ang didn't care. He brought in so much business when he played, and he was so nice and—"

Pope squeezes his eyes closed, his jaw locking. "I don't want to hear about you and him together. Just tell me what I need to know."

Shit.

His pain at thinking about me with someone else echoes precisely what I've felt over the last ten years, seeing him with other women, hearing him joke with everyone about all his romantic entanglements.

Why does he care?

He was the one who ended things back then.

It was his call.

So callous.

So abrupt.

So shockingly thoughtless that I never could have imagined anything I do in my life could affect him now.

But I can't bear to see that pain flashing in his eyes, so I focus on the baby, so comfortable lying against Pope's strong, hard chest.

"I was going to tell him that day, after everyone cleared out from the party. But then the shooting happened. Everybody inside ducked for cover or ran for the kitchen and the back door, and you and Nora and Skye and the rest of the family ran to the front to help Stone and Isaac and Kennedy. I was behind the register, kind of frozen for a minute, and then I peeked over it and saw Dan head straight for where the front windows had been. He stared at Roselli's body while you all helped Stone, Isaac, and Kennedy..."

The memory of the look in his eyes when he turned back in my direction sends a shiver down my spine.

"He called someone as he grabbed his guitar and moved toward the back of the café to leave. He told whoever it was that his father was dead."

Pope shakes his head. "How did we all miss this? I don't...in all the time we've been dealing with Roselli, how did we not know he had a son?"

It's the same question I've asked myself for months now as I struggled with what to do about the revelation and berated myself for not knowing who I was involved with.

Even though it was a casual thing.

I should have known.

Should have but *didn't*—until it was too late.

"I don't know, either. Maybe he was raised by his mom? I remember Dan telling me he spent a lot of time in Baton Rouge when he was younger, not here."

A muscle in Pope's jaw tics, and the baby fusses restlessly against him, perhaps sensing the shift in the mood. Pope lifts his hand from my hair and rubs the baby's back gently, soothing him, quieting him back down, and he presses his tiny little hand flat against Pope's chest again.

My breath catches in my throat. "With his dad dead, I didn't know what was going to happen, but then he came in a few weeks later when we reopened, and he told me that we needed to talk about the baby. He *knew*, Pope. He fucking *knew* it was his..."

"Have you talked to him about it?"

I shake my head. "I've been avoiding him, making sure I'm never alone at The Grind so he can't pop in and corner me. I know he won't talk about it in front of anyone. He knows how much the Hawkes hate the Rosellis. He knows how complicated the situation is, but then he showed up at my place this morning, and I realized he's never going to let this baby go."

"What the hell do you mean he showed up at your place?"

Oh, shit.

My body starts trembling thinking about it, and I want nothing more than to pretend it never happened so I never have to relive it again. But Pope needs to know how dangerous Dan really is.

"He was at my apartment when I was leaving...tried to stop me." Each breath I take makes my lungs burn. "I-I thought he was going to take me. Hurt me or the baby...but I got away from him. Tried to get to Nana's."

"Jesus Christ, Al." He tips my chin up. "I'm so sorry that fucker ever touched you." Anger darkens his eyes. "You need to talk to everyone. The whole family needs to know what's happening. Isaac and Stone can figure out what we need to do legally, and Gabe and my dad will come up with a way to protect both of you..."

Each inhalation becomes more of a struggle, my sobs coming so hard and heavy now that it feels like it's impossible to stop. "I'm so sorry, Pope."

"Are you really apologizing to me for falling for the wrong guy, Al?"

There have been so many "wrong guys" since Pope and I split.

Far too many.

None of them were even a fraction of the man Pope was at seventeen.

I shake my head, locking gazes with him before lowering mine to my son. "No, for the shitstorm that's about to hit us."

My head starts spinning, making the already dim room somehow darken even more around the edges of my vision. "Pope, I don't...feel...so good."

His gaze quickly narrows on me. "Shit. What's wrong, Al? Tell me what you're feeling."

He gently lifts my head off his lap and slides out from under me, settling me flat on the couch. I try to follow him to see where he is going with the baby, but my eyes won't seem to focus.

Pope's face suddenly fills my vision, and he takes my cheeks in his warm palms. "Al, can you hear me? Tell me what's going on."

"I can't..."

Breathe.

Seem to form words.

See beyond the pinpoint in front of me occupied by Pope's concerned eyes.

Stay awake...

"No." He shakes my face slightly, and then his hands roam over me. His fingers press against my throat. "Al, no. Stay awake. Stay with me. Al? Jesus Christ. Al?" The rising panic in his voice and his touch can't keep me connected. "Stay awake until help gets here. Stay with me!"

I want to do that.

I want to stay with him and the baby.

But the darkness is too inviting.

6

ALESSANDRA

Aunt Nora leans against the wall next to the door, waiting for Dr.—

Crap, what's his name?

Boggs?

I've seen so many in the last several hours I don't even remember their names, let alone what each one's specialty is or why they are seeing me. Forcing a smile, I nod, pretending I have the faintest fucking clue what he's trying to relay.

Nora raises a blond brow at me from over his shoulder.

Dr. Boggs stops talking, his gaze following mine to her and then cutting back to me. "Do you have any questions?"

About a zillion, but I will not be asking you when you talk like an encyclopedia.

I shake my head, and the corners of Nora's lips twitch because she knows damn well I'm going to ask her to dumb it down to non-medical terms as soon as he leaves and give me the bare-bones, bottom-line info.

The older man offers me a kind smile and pats my hand.

"You'll be okay, sweetheart. You have Dr. Hawke and Dr. Clarke watching over you."

My spine stiffens at the mention of Pope, who has remained absent since I first woke in the hospital, confused as hell about how I got here.

He's avoiding me.

And after what happened, what I told him, I can't say I blame him for not wanting to see me. If the roles were reversed, I don't know that I could look him in the eye after a confession like that.

Dr. Boggs leaves my room, and Nora closes the door behind him, then settles into the chair beside my bed, ready to delve into her non-doctor explanation of what happened to me that I've been waiting for since I woke up.

But I stop her before she even starts. "How's the baby doing?"

Her eyes light up, and she grins. "Just like the last time you asked, he's completely fine. He's in the nursery, and I can tell you, the staff there is taking incredibly good care of him."

The tiniest bit of tension coiled inside me releases, but no matter how many times she tells me everything is fine with him —reiterating what Pope told me when he first examined him after the birth—there's still a part of me that worries because he came so early.

And for what his arrival means for us all.

I suck in a sharp breath and let it out slowly, my chest tight each time I try to get some oxygen. "What did that doctor say? Something about an echo something or other."

Nora nods. "Pope was worried when you passed out that you might have internal bleeding, something that he wouldn't have any way to stop there at the club. I think you sucked a little bit of life out of him during that hour he was there with you while you were unconscious and he could do nothing but wait before those firefighters who finally found you."

I rub at the spot over my heart. "And the echo whatever?"

She instantly slips from aunt mode into doctor mode, her humor fading. "You have postpartum cardiomyopathy. Basically, your heart is struggling and not working properly. It can cause shortness of breath, irregular heartbeat, water retention, and in extreme cases, it can get very severe and life threatening."

Life threatening?

My baby just came into this fucked up world and impossible situation, and now, I might not even be here to raise him.

God, could this get any worse?

Nora squeezes my hand tightly. "Don't panic, Al. You're going to take some medication, ones chosen because they're still safe if you want to keep breastfeeding. And you're going to have to be monitored very closely."

"Will it go away?"

Her smile this time doesn't come as quickly, reservation in her gaze. "About fifty percent of people fully recover, fewer partially, and there's a percentage who never do."

"And what does that mean if my heart doesn't recover?"

The couple of seconds pause she takes before answering tells me all I need to know before she even says the words. "Then you would need a heart transplant."

She moves from the chair to the edge of my bed, wrapping her arms around me to intervene before I go into full meltdown mode. "But the chances of that happening are slim. All right? You're healthy otherwise. Your drop in blood pressure from this condition is what caused you to pass out. There's every reason to believe that with the proper medication and a little bit of time, your heart has a chance to recover. You shouldn't be thinking worst-case scenario."

A tear trickles out of my eye, and I bury my face against her shoulder. "Not think worst-case scenario? I had my baby at the club during a hurricane, for Christ's sake. Now you're telling me my heart might be failing?"

"I know it's a lot, Al." She pulls back slightly and offers a half-grin. "But just like you'll improve, so does the weather. The hurricane has moved inland and is already dissipating, which means in a few hours, cleanup is going to start."

"How long do I have to stay here?"

She releases me and stands. "A few more days, to make sure you're stable on the prescribed medications and your heart hasn't suffered any further damage, then you can go home."

Home.

Panic claws at my chest, remembering the last time I was there, when Dan blocked me and tried to force me to go with him.

That place has been home for so long.

All the years I shared it with Angelina, where it was our safe space.

Our place to sit on the couch and binge shitty television and rant about the long days spent on our feet at The Grind.

Even after she moved in with Jude, it still felt like home —*my* place. Where I had prepared for the baby's arrival. Where I planned to raise him and create a warm, loving place for him to grow up despite the complications I was bringing him into— if I didn't have to flee New Orleans altogether to escape Daniele.

Nora makes her way to the door and grabs the handle. "Can I get you anything? I know your parents, Angelina, and Jude are going to leave Nana's as soon as the roads are clear enough to get here. Then one of them will sit with you, but I need to head back to the ER."

No mention of Pope...

"I'm okay." I put on my practiced fake smile. "I promise."

"You're a tough girl, Al. I'm proud of you. You did good. He's beautiful." She pauses. "Have you thought of a name yet?"

Everything happened so fast that I didn't even have the chance to tell anyone what I've been considering for his name.

I look down at my hands and twist them in the thin hospital blanket covering me for a moment before I meet her gaze again. "I was thinking about Benjamin."

Nora freezes, her body stiffening.

"Yeah"—I nod at her reaction, the same one I expect from everyone—"I wanted to talk to my mom and dad and Ang first. Make sure they were okay with it..."

Unshed tears shimmer in her eyes, and she clears her throat like there's something stuck in it. "They'll be fine with it. I think it's a wonderful tribute to him."

"I never knew him, but Mom and Ang talk about him so much...all their happy memories. I've heard the same stories from them and everyone else for so long that I feel like I lived them and *did* know him."

She swipes away a tear from the corner of her eye. "It's a great name, but I won't say anything to anybody until you talk to them, okay?"

I nod, unable to speak through the emotion. Nora slips out of my room, the door clicking shut behind her, and I relax back, staring up at the tiled ceiling.

After so many hours stuck in the dark with Pope, even the low lighting in the room seems bright, harsh to my eyes, and I let them drift closed, running through the cyclone of events that have left me here.

One mistake after another.

All mine.

Tears leak from my eyes and move down to the pillow under my head while my guilt threatens to drown me.

I brought all this onto myself, onto all the people who love me and will risk themselves, trying to correct my mistakes. Each and every one of them will bend over backward to protect me and the baby from the demon I invited into their lives.

That realization and the bone-deep exhaustion I've been battling since I woke finally get to be too much to fight. I roll slightly onto my side, wincing at the twinge of pain that reminds me I just gave birth, and snuggle until I get as comfortable as you can be in a hospital bed.

The first fingers of sleep start to creep into the edges of my mind, but one truth keeps screaming at me through the encroaching darkness.

Once the storm ends, the real tempest is going to begin.

I may not be safe from what's coming after this hurricane blows over, but at least for now, in this brief moment, I can pretend like I am—before the hard stuff starts.

A soft knock sounds at the door, and I lift my head, blinking away those first vestiges of sleep. "Come in."

The door opens inward, and a nurse in pink scrubs comes in, carrying Benjamin snuggled in her arms. I push myself up and shift slightly until I'm sitting better.

She approaches and speaks softly. "He just woke up. I thought you might want to try feeding him. I checked with Dr. Boggs, and he cleared it. But if you're not up for it, we have formula in the nursery. He took that well while you weren't available—"

I shake my head. "No, I want to."

Even though I've only spent a few hours away from him, the thought of her taking him now that he's here makes me want to leap out of this bed and snatch him from her arms so I can keep him with me—never let him out of my sight again.

That protective, mama bear instinct has certainly kicked in.

I hold out my arms, and she slips the tiny bundle into them. Cradling him against my chest, I get my first real look at him in the light after only seeing him in Savage's dark office during the storm. He stares back up at me with familiar Caribbean blue eyes. "Will his eyes stay blue?"

The nurse smiles. "I don't know. A lot of babies have them

and they darken or change as they get older. But considering how many members of your family I've met with that very color blue, I'd say it's a strong possibility he keeps them." She brushes her fingers over his thick mop of dark hair. "I'll come back in a little while for him, okay? Unless you want me to bring a bassinet in here for you so you can keep him with you?"

"I can do that?"

She nods. "Of course. They needed to get you stabilized and wanted to give you some time to rest, but we can absolutely move him here. There's no reason he needs to be in the nursery."

"I'd feel a lot better if I had him here with me..."

A knowing smile curls her lips. "No problem. I'll let your doctor and the other nurses know, and we'll get one in here."

She leaves my room, and he releases a little wail, clearly annoyed he wasn't immediately fed upon waking.

"Sorry, buddy. I'm new at this..."

Failing from the beginning.

I tug down the side of my gown, giving him access to feed, and he latches on, snuggling in close. His eyes flutter closed as I hold him tightly to me, never wanting to let go again. Examining every detail of my son in the light.

He's so tiny.

So perfect.

Absolutely angelic.

And he sure drew the short straw to end up with me as a mother.

I've managed to fuck up everything, and I've only just started.

Dragging my finger across his nose and over his soft cheeks, I search for the resolution to our current predicament—the same one I've been looking for since I first realized who Dan was.

"What do you think, Benjamin? Are we going to be okay?"

I wish he could give me an answer because I sure don't know it.

POPE

MY KNEE BOUNCES RAPIDLY, the only movement in the room besides the rise and fall of Allie's chest and the occasional shifting of the baby resting in the bassinet set up next to her bed.

I watch her eyelids flutter in her fitful sleep, her soft, pink lips parted slightly, breath alternating between short, hard spurts and level, normal rhythm.

Whatever she's dreaming about, it isn't completely pleasant.

My fingers itch to reach out and touch her. To brush the thick, dark strands back from her face. To place a comforting hand on her and tell her she's safe. But I force myself to stay seated beside her bed in the god-awful, hard-plastic chair, terrified I might wake her inadvertently when her body so badly needs the rest.

Peripartum cardiomyopathy...

Jesus...

I scrub my palms over the rough stubble on my face and relive that horrific hour again and again in my head. When she wasn't responding. When her breathing was so shallow. Her heartbeat erratic and slow.

It could have killed her.

It still *could.*

It doesn't matter that I know—medically speaking—she has a very mild case or that it's treatable with the medications she's on. That doesn't guarantee recovery.

This disease doesn't work like that.

It's an unpredictable monster that often shows up out of

nowhere—like with Allie—and can seriously harm a new mother.

She could be fine in two months, or if things take a turn for the worse and her heart muscle doesn't heal, she could end up on a damn transplant list.

Benjamin could lose his mother.

I could lose *her*.

Not that I've ever really *had* her. Even when I did, it was sneaking around and constantly worrying about anyone finding out what we were doing. It was secrets and dark corners and praying we wouldn't get caught. And then, it was ten years of throwing myself into school and this job while she led the life she was never meant to have, all because of what I did to her.

Boy, did that backfire.

The thought that I might never get a chance to explain to her why I did what I did has been rolling around in my head since that moment she passed out on me, and something tells me it's not going to go away, no matter how clearly I know I can never say the words I want to.

Too much time has passed.

Too much pain has been endured.

She's a different person now, not that sweet, innocent, inquisitive, bright-eyed girl who wanted to explore the world that she was at sixteen. No matter how peaceful she may look sleeping in between her fits of nightmares, internally, she's a woman torn apart and in agony.

And having me around only makes things worse.

Which is why I should go before she wakes up.

I start to push to my feet as the door clicks open behind me. Dad and Gabe enter quietly, and Dad's eyes dart over to her. He starts to back out when he sees that she's sleeping, but Allie shifts up onto her elbow, blinking lazily.

Her gaze lands on me first, and she jerks a little, like she's surprised to see me. "Were you sitting there, watching me sleep?"

Despite the distress currently filling my heart, I can't fight the quirk of my lips. "Maybe."

She rolls her eyes. "Yeah, because that's not creepy." Her attention darts to her other visitors. "Saint, Uncle Gabe, is anyone else here?"

Gabe shakes his head as he advances into the room, toward her and the bassinet, Dad hot on his heels. They stand over Benjamin's bed and lean down to stare at him, their large hands gently ghosting over his hair and tiny fingers and anything they can get away with touching without waking him.

Finally, Gabe looks up at her and grins. "Wow. And I thought I had the whole calamity-during-a-hurricane belt formally won. But you just had to outdo me, didn't you, kid?"

Allie grins at him and shifts in the bed, wincing slightly.

I immediately climb from the chair, scanning her face for signs of further distress and the heart monitor beside her bed. "Are you in pain? I can order—"

She holds up a hand. "I'm okay, Dr. Clarke."

Ouch.

Dr. Clarke...

I shouldn't be so quick to jump down her throat and into action. I'm not even her treating physician now that she's here in the hospital. But seeing any discomfort makes me want to fix it for her. Even if it isn't my place.

Dad's dark gaze cuts to me, then to the baby and Allie, silently asking the question they came here to discuss.

"So..." I release a heavy sigh, bracing myself for the coming onslaught of anger from Allie when she finds out what I've done. "I know it wasn't my place to say anything, Al, but you were unconscious. I didn't know what was wrong, and I—"

Her shoulders tense, and her eyes dart up to Gabe and Dad. "You told them."

Lowering my face into my palms, I wince at the note of hurt in her voice. "I had to." I pull my hands away to meet her accusatory glare. "We already know Roselli and Satriano have both hacked the hospital system in the past, and even with our attempts to make upgrades on the tech since then, we don't know that they didn't see you get registered as an inpatient..." My focus drifts to the baby. "Or that *he* was."

She presses her lips together firmly.

"I had to make sure we got both of you safe, extra security on your room and the nursery—"

"Did you tell Nora, too? She didn't say a word while she was in here."

I nod. "I'm sorry."

She may never forgive me for telling everyone her secret, but there are so many things on that list now that one more doesn't matter. The number of mistakes I've made when it comes to Allie could fill the damn gulf and then some. And I just seem to keep doing it.

Her bottom lip quivering, Allie lies back against the pillow, staring at the ceiling. "So, everyone knows what a fuck-up I am."

Dad steps forward and leans over her, pressing a kiss against her forehead. "You're not a fuck-up, Al. No one knew. Roselli did a damn fine job keeping his son protected. Either Daniele was never part of the business and was simply the musician he appeared to be, or it was one really good deep-fake, a way to infiltrate us and have nobody question it."

As the man in charge of security for the entire Hawke Enterprises empire, those words should mean something coming from him, but given the tears falling to her pillow, I don't think they're much comfort to Allie.

Gabe nods his agreement and crosses his arms over his chest, leaning back against the wall beside the bed. "And if it's that, then we all fell for it, hook, line, and sinker. Every single one of us sat there and listened to him perform when he played at The Grind and none of us saw it. None of us suspected a fucking thing—not even when Roselli showed up *twice* while Dan was performing."

Again...hindsight.

Dad watches her carefully, considering his words, not wanting to scare her. But he and Gabe have worked far too hard for far too long protecting this family to mince words in a situation like this. "But you were right to be worried, Al."

Now it's time to really get down to brass tacks. This is going to be a very uncomfortable conversation for her, and she knows it, shifting nervously on the bed.

She stares up at Dad, her brow furrowed. "What do you mean?"

He glances from me to Gabe. "I mean, you were right to think he would be a problem if he knew he was the father. If he came to your apartment in the middle of a fucking hurricane to grab you and take you against your will, then there's nothing that's going to stop him now that the baby's born."

Gabe nods. "If it were my son, I'd burn down the world to get to him."

Fucking hell.

I cast a glare toward him. "Did you really have to put it like that? You're going to scare the shit out of her."

Allie starts trembling, her eyes immediately darting to the baby, soundly asleep despite us talking around him. "What can I do? How do I protect him?"

Gabe issues a long sigh, as frustrated as I am with a lack of good options. "I have already talked to Stone and Isaac, and they're going to work on some protective orders. But"—his broad shoulders rise and fall—"do you really think a piece of paper is going to stop a Roselli?"

It's the painful, ugly truth she knew deep down the minute she saw Dan for who he really was. That's why she's been terrified. It's the reason for all her secrecy and desire to hide away from all of us.

A sob slips from her throat, and she shakes her head. "No."

I reach forward and pull her hand in mine, squeezing it. "We're not going to let anything happen to you or the baby."

Her gaze cuts to me. "But how can you say that? How can you promise it? You can't know that. You can't—"

"Yes, I can."

She tugs her hand from mine and pushes herself up until she's sitting, her bottom lip still quivering, the tears streaking her face. "Once I leave the hospital, he's going to find me."

Her statement is so definitive.

But that will never fucking happen.

A surge of rage rushes through me, igniting a fire deep in my belly I only felt before one other time—when she told me what that fucker did, trying to take her from her apartment. "He'll never get to you, not if you're with me."

Her eyebrows fly up. "What?"

Gabe pushes off the wall, stepping closer, narrowing his eyes on me. "What do you mean '*with you?*'"

Running my hands over my head, I pace alongside the bed. "Look, I've been thinking about this. She obviously can't go back home, right? Like, ever. He knows that apartment. He knows she lives there. He was waiting to fucking ambush her. She can't go back there."

Allie releases another small sob. "All my stuff, all the stuff for the baby..."

Gabe glances at her. "We'll pick it up. We'll get everything you need. But he's right. What are you thinking, Pope?"

I chew on my lip as I consider any other option that isn't going to piss her off as much as this one. But I don't come up with any. The only way this works is the plan I came up with while she was undergoing all the testing—the one sure to upset more than just her. "She's going to need constant medical attention, monitoring to make sure that her heart is functioning properly and isn't deteriorating any further."

Dad nods. "So, she goes to stay with Gabe and Skye. She can—"

"No." My objection comes a little too forcefully, enough that Dad's dark eyebrows fly up.

Gabe fights a smirk.

I hold up a hand to him. "Look, Skye is a very talented nurse practitioner, but we'll need to do echocardiograms and ECGs, and I would feel a lot safer if I could personally monitor her and make sure she was doing okay."

Allie releases a shocked little sound. "Don't you have a *job*"—she waves her hands around—"here, at this very hospital, that you need to do? You can't just—"

I approach the bed, standing over her the same way I did at Nana's what feels like an eternity ago, looking down at a broken woman I can't walk away from when I can help her. "I already took a leave of absence."

Dad whirls to face me. "You did *what*?"

Shit. Maybe I shouldn't have sprung this on him like that.

After all the years of special summer school programs that I made him and Mom put me in because I always knew what I wanted to do and was determined to do whatever it took to get here, then college and medical school—I'm walking away from it.

But it will only be temporary.

And I don't see any other way we can do this and protect Allie and the baby.

Dad worries his jaw, then motions toward the door. "But your residency..."

"Will be here when I get back." My gaze drifts over Allie and the sleeping baby. "This is more important."

A flush spreads over Allie's pale cheeks, and she averts her eyes, reaching into the bassinet beside her bed to fuss over Benjamin even though he's still sleeping soundly.

Gabe returns to his position against the wall, drumming his fingers against it. "What do you plan on doing? You can't bring her to your place. Anywhere connected to the Hawkes isn't safe."

I nod slowly. "I know, which is why I was thinking we have to take her somewhere no one would ever look, and it has to be *just* me. Of everyone in the family, I'm the one who's almost never seen with her. I'm the person they would least expect her to be with. They're not going to search for me."

Dad and Gabe exchange a look while Allie cuts her gaze to me.

"And I don't have any say in this?" She looks to the other two men for help. "Why can't I go to Mom and Dad's or Gabe and Skye's? Gabe is perfectly capable of protecting me there, and Nora can show Skye how to do any tests I need."

Gabe gives her a half-smirk. "While I appreciate your confidence in Skye and me, Pope's right. It would be the safest thing for you and the baby to get out of town, away from here, somewhere they'll never look for you until we can handle the Roselli situation. Besides"—he motions toward the lone window in the room—"the city's a fucking mess, flooding in some areas, lots of wind damage. The Hawke Enterprises Foundation is going to be busy helping clean up, which means a lot of us will be pulled in different directions. Plus, there was some damage to the hotel..."

Her brow furrows. "Was it bad?"

Gabe runs a hand through his hair and shakes his head. "Nothing too serious from what we can tell so far. Kennedy, Cass, and your mom and dad will be heading over there once the last of the storm clears to do a better visual inspection. They've been going off what they can see from the cameras at the site."

"Shit." She glances up at me, telling me in no uncertain words that she doesn't like this idea at all. "Is this *really* our only option?"

I should be used to seeing this trepidation in her blue eyes when she looks at me, but it still stings, knowing I'm her last choice. "This is about protecting you, Al, you and the baby, making sure you're healthy and safe."

If that doesn't guilt her into agreeing to it, nothing will.

No matter how messed up this situation is, one thing I know absolutely, without a shadow of a doubt, is that she will do *anything* to protect her son.

She looks over at the baby again, then releases a heavy sigh. "You know, I thought about leaving New Orleans..." Her eyes meet mine, then drift to Dad and Gabe. "I thought I could hide out somewhere he would never find me and have the baby, and maybe I could just"—she shrugs—"find a way to be safe."

A little hiccupped sob slips from her lips.

"But that never would have worked." She shakes her head. "I don't know the first thing about surviving on my own or taking care of a baby. I need everyone to help me. I can't do this by myself. I can't protect him—"

I sit on the edge of her bed, taking her hand in mine again. "I can. Until this gets sorted. Okay?"

She hesitates for only a second this time before she nods. "Okay, but where are we going?"

7

ALESSANDRA

The narrow two-lane highway cuts through the dense green forest, carving a path across parts of Louisiana that man appears to have never touched. After spending my entire life in and around New Orleans—with little to zero interest in exploring Mother Nature—the sheer vastness of what surrounds us the deeper we make our way into the wilderness only cranks up the anxiety already consuming me.

My knee bouncing, hand gripping the door handle, I try to take deep breaths and control my racing heart, like I'd been attempting to do for the last two days before I was discharged.

Sitting in that hospital, *waiting* for something to happen, the saying, "felt like a sitting duck" finally made sense. Because that's exactly what Ben and I were. Even with the extra security at the main doors of the hospital and outside my room, despite the entire family taking turns staying with me to try to keep me calm, none of it did any good.

I still couldn't catch my breath...

Couldn't stop my heart from thundering against my ribcage...

The blood from rushing in my ears...

My hands shaking each time I held Ben or watched him sleep...

Nora kept telling me a lot of that was just this heart condition, but it was aggravated by the fact that I couldn't *stop* myself from imagining Dan charging into the hospital, guns blazing, to get to us.

Even now, hours away from home and the man causing all this, I keep glancing into the backseat to check on Benjamin.

Needing to see him.

Needing to know he's all right.

Because I sure as hell am not.

Babies have it so easy. Never having to worry about anything except sleeping, eating, and pooping. Completely oblivious to what goes on around them. Content to be held and rocked. All their troubles melting away as soon as they have a full belly and warm arms around them.

If only it were like that for adults...

Pope's large hand settles on my knee. "He's fine."

I glance over at him in the driver's seat, free hand on the wheel and eyes on the narrow road that seems to stretch on forever through the thick trees. "For now. Where are you taking us? Murdersville?"

It certainly reminds me of the start of some slasher flick—the lone car traveling down a desolate road until it reaches some remote, ramshackle cabin occupied by a violent serial killer.

The corner of Pope's lips curves into a smirk, and he peeks over at me, shaking his head. "We're almost there. You'll see."

There.

Seems ominous, even with his assurances that our destination is safe.

All I know is we're somewhere near Shreveport, and I only have *that* information from the last sign I saw before we turned off the highway.

"*If I need to get you or Ben to the hospital for any reason, I can do it quickly. That's all you need to know.*"

Pope's words echo through my head. They were supposed to be reassuring, but instead, they only remind me how tenuous my situation really is. Though the medications have stabilized me for the time being, there's no telling how my heart will act over the next few months.

And stress is the one thing Dr. Boggs said to avoid.

As if that's possible.

Fleeing from the father of my child with the first man to break my heart was *not* on my bingo card for this year—or ever.

Sending me out into the wilderness with my new baby and Pope probably isn't the best way to keep my cardiac health stable, but no one else would know that.

Not really.

Not when we've kept everyone in the dark about what happened between us for a very good reason.

Pope peeks over at me again, his hand tightening around the wheel. "Are you doing okay?"

I'm so sick of everyone asking me how I'm doing when I am so *obviously* not okay, but when Pope asks, he usually means medically speaking. And I can't get annoyed with it. Part of this deal is that I have to be honest with him. I need to tell him if I'm feeling dizzy or light-headed or if I have tightness in my chest or difficulty breathing.

All signs that my heart is struggling—so he can bring out the high-tech, expensive equipment we lugged along with us that he most certainly should *not* have taken out of the hospital. But paying for an entire wing has its benefits. Along with Nora's role as the chief of the emergency department, he was able to get what he needed without too much finagling.

"I'm okay." I take several deep breaths. "Just nervous."

"Don't be. You know they'll take care of everything." He checks the rearview mirror like he has been incessantly since we left New Orleans to ensure no one is following us. "They'll figure out a way to protect you and Ben."

"I know."

Or, at least, I should know that and believe it.

Everyone's been telling me the same thing for days, trying to reassure me that it isn't as bad as I think it is. But I can see it in their eyes, especially with Stone and Savage, that this is bad.

We would be idiots to believe a Roselli is going to walk away from a son voluntarily. That leaves either murdering someone who could possibly be in line to take over control of the city's largest criminal empire or coming to an agreement with him that I could live with. And I can't imagine that *ever* happening when it comes to the little boy back there.

My little boy.

I couldn't ever agree to give him to Dan for *any* amount of time, not with his resources to take him out of the country, the threats he's made, and his lack of qualms about resorting to physical violence with me.

He's not touching Benjamin.

Ever.

That pain returns to my chest again, and I try to focus on the trees so I won't drag myself into another panic spiral.

How do people do this?

I didn't know I could love something and want to protect it so much, be so willing to do *anything* to ensure he never experiences the kind of fear I did when I saw Dan in my hallway. It makes what Isaac went through with Giacomina and Vivi even more terrifying now that I understand what he must have been feeling when he discovered he had a daughter and she was in danger.

The constant worry and pain are almost unbearable, and something tells me this is only the beginning.

Pope slows, drawing my focus back to the road, and he turns down a narrow drive, barely visible in the dense forest.

I glance around the SUV, branches and leaves obscuring my view of anything but endless trees. "This is where we're going?"

He nods.

More murdery vibes.

"Not instilling much confidence in the situation, Pope."

He huffs slightly. "Can't you ever trust me?"

The frustration tightening his voice makes a pang of guilt hit my gut.

He has done nothing but help me since he found me at the club, but constantly having him around has put me even more on edge, making me snippy and angry about things that happened such a long time ago.

I thought I had moved past our shared history.

I've spent the last ten years looking for ways to do just that, but clearly, I haven't been able to as easily as he has.

This doesn't seem to affect him at all.

Always so strong and stoic.

He does what he has to do.

What he feels is his *duty* as a doctor.

And somehow, manages to pretend nothing about *this* makes the past seem so fresh like it does for me.

Before I can even attempt to figure out a way to answer his question, we pull through the last of the thicket into a small clearing.

"Whoa." I lean forward, staring up through the windshield. "I wasn't expecting this back here..."

Instead of the run-down, old, murdery-vibes cabin I expected this deep into the wilderness, a huge, modern two-story house rises above us—looking decidedly out of place in this setting.

Pope pulls the SUV to a stop in front of the steps leading up to the front porch, throws it into park, and looks at me with an I-told-you-so grin. "Trust me next time."

"What is this place?" I unbuckle my belt and open my door, stepping out and gawking at the beautiful home. "Seriously..."

Pope pops his door and climbs out, watching me over the roof. "It belongs to one of Dad's old Saints teammates. A guy he still talks to but hasn't really been seen with in years, so it isn't someone Roselli or anyone else would think to contact. And no one will ever look for us here. We'll be safe."

He says it so casually, but I have a harder time believing it.

Somehow, it doesn't seem like I'll ever feel safe again.

I release a heavy sigh and push my door closed, wincing at the loud slam it makes. Almost instantly, Benjamin flails and starts screaming in the backseat.

Pope raises a brow at me.

I hold up my hands. "I know, I know. It's going to take some getting used to, the constantly being quiet part."

He shakes his head. "Don't constantly be quiet."

"What?"

His door slams closed with no attempt to quiet it. "A lot of babies will learn to sleep through different noises, even loud ones, if you expose them enough."

I tug open the rear door. "Yeah, somehow I don't think I'll be that lucky..."

Not when I never have been, and Benjamin sure hasn't hit the lottery, either.

Born to a hot mess of a mother and a likely dangerous, mob-connected father at a strip club during a hurricane and already on the run at only three days old...

Not exactly a jackpot.

I unclip his car seat, lifting it and pulling him from the backseat to continued wails of displeasure. "It's okay, buddy. We'll get you inside and fed."

Pope jogs up onto the porch and punches in a code on a keypad on the door. The sound of the door unlocking fills the quiet air. "We're all set. Why don't you take him in and get him fed, and I'll bring in all the bags?"

God knows there are enough of them for that to take hours.

I glance at the back of the massive SUV we drove, full of all the baby requirements I had ready at my apartment for him. The bassinet, stroller, clothes, diapers, and everything else we might need, plus our clothes, the medical equipment Pope "procured" from the hospital, and enough food to last two weeks, so we won't have to go into town or see anyone while we're up here.

Hopefully, not for long.

The thought of being cooped up in this house with Pope sends goosebumps breaking out across my skin, and I shiver and climb the steps to the porch.

Pope raises a brow at me. "You good?"

Shit.

Apparently, he saw that.

But there are a thousand other explanations I can give him for my full-body shake a moment ago besides his proximity. Top of the list is the son of a ruthless mobster who may, for all I know, be just as bad, coming after me to take my baby.

I'm far from good, but I force a smile and nod. "Right as rain."

Almost as if on cue, a rumble escapes the darkening clouds overhead, and Pope looks to the sky at the weather moving in.

"The storm didn't do much damage this far north. Just a lot of rain and some minor flooding." He scans the small clearing. "But on the drive up, this area looked unscathed. Likely one of the reasons Saint suggested sending us here."

Since New Orleans took the direct hit from the storm, the majority of the damage seemed to be centered there, leaving plenty of work for the rest of the family who aren't actively hunting Dan while we're hiding out.

The Hawke Enterprises Foundation and most of the Hawke clan will be busy assisting with repairs and relief efforts for those affected by the flooding and wind damage, and Cass and Kennedy will have to focus on the repairs needed to the Hawke Hotel if they still want to make the grand opening date. Savage won't tolerate any more delays—even ones out of our control.

Which leaves me alone with the tall, dark, and insanely handsome man with deep, haunting eyes who gave up his job to take us up here, currently waiting for me to enter the house before he returns to get our things.

This should be interesting.

I step through the front door to a massive foyer that rises two floors, a chandelier of antlers hanging in the middle of it, matching the rustic, woodsy décor in the rest of the visible space.

This guy wanted a hunting cabin, but instead, he built a hunting *mansion*—complete with heads of various game animals visible on the walls in a living room to the left.

I carry a very fussy Benjamin down the hall that leads straight past a formal dining room and into a large kitchen with a massive center island. A long table runs in front of sliding glass doors that open out to a large patio surrounded by a beautiful but foreboding forest.

It would almost be peaceful if my mind didn't keep seeing shadows and danger lurking behind every tree trunk and bush.

Benjamin's wails echo off all the dark marble and cabinets, and I set him on the floor, unbuckle him, and pull him from his carrier, snuggling his tiny body up against me.

"All right, you hungry, buddy? Let's go find somewhere to eat."

With the huge glass doors, I can't shake the feeling of being exposed, and if I have to keep staring out of them, I'll never be able to relax.

I wander into a less formal living area with a large black leather couch facing a big-screen TV. Football memorabilia decorates this room—helmets and framed jerseys on walls and built-in shelves.

If—*no...when*—we get out of here, I'll have to call Saint's friend to thank him for letting us use this place. After a day at the club riding out the storm, and two more in the hospital, this feels downright luxurious.

Almost *too* nice for what we're doing.

And for what the rest of the Hawkes are doing back at home —trying to clean up my mess as well as the one the hurricane left.

I blink away the prick of tears in my eyes and lower myself onto the couch, settling Benjamin in position to start feeding. He stops fussing immediately, relaxing against me as Pope appears in the connected kitchen with grocery bags hanging off both arms.

His dark whiskey eyes cut to me, the look he gives me bringing those damn goosebumps again. I quickly whip my head away to stare down at Benjamin nursing, unable to hold Pope's gaze any longer.

He doesn't say anything, just drops the bags in the kitchen before disappearing again out to the SUV.

But I saw it there in that split second that our eyes connected—this is going to be as difficult for him as it is for me, but for a completely different reason.

POPE

My bare feet don't make a sound as I pace the halls of the massive house. Again and again. I make the rounds—circling the whole downstairs, then back up to the second floor, where Allie and Benjamin sleep.

It's what I should be doing, but I'm too amped up, my body too jittery, unable to sit still, let alone try to actually get some rest.

Not when my brain won't stop churning.

Not with so much up in the air.

Not when there's the possibility of so many things going so wrong.

Even with all the equipment I brought up here to monitor her, Allie could have a setback. If she gets sick enough, if her stats tank or her heart shows evidence of any further damage, I'll have to take her into Shreveport to the hospital, which would undoubtedly ping on Roselli's radar.

A shudder rolls through me at the thought of him rolling up with his father's old crew—the men who threatened, maimed, and killed in the Roselli name.

And would undoubtedly do it again for Cristiano's son.

I peek in the cracked door of Allie's room for the hundredth time tonight, but only the soft sound of her even breaths floats to me.

At least someone is getting some rest.

God knows she needs it.

That woman has been through the wringer, and it's far from over, a fact that keeps me pacing the halls. Checking the doors. Running through the plan in my head for the hundredth time to assure myself it's solid. Peeking in on her and Benjamin in his bassinet next to her bed.

I slip in and head for him, gazing down at his sleeping form in the darkness. So small, yet already so strong and feisty. He isn't afraid to voice his displeasure or tell us what he wants.

Benjamin has his mother's spirit, which means he's going to

always be a handful—full of "piss and vinegar," as Mom would say.

It's the thing that drew me to Alessandra our whole lives, but it's also the reason she has wandered down so many wrong paths.

Ones I gave her an inadvertent nudge toward.

Almost as if he can sense me watching him, Benjamin's face scrunches up and he lets out a wail that shatters the still night. I quickly scoop him up, settling him against my bare chest. "Shhhh. Let's not wake up your mom. She needs to sleep."

The fact that his cry didn't wake her is evidence enough that I need to let her be. I check his diaper while he continues to protest, but he's just hungry.

I slip out of the room and down the hall to the staircase, then descend and head for the kitchen to grab one of the pre-made bottles and throw it in the warmer.

He continues to fuss about the delay, and I rock with him, trying to soothe his protests when all he wants is Allie.

I know the feeling...

For years, I held onto it, let it eat me alive from the inside out. But I forced it back, for my own good as well as hers. Because she will never forgive me for what I did to her, and I can never get back that inherent trust or bond we once had.

Things can never be the same, a reality I'm beginning to understand the longer we're thrust together during this impossible situation.

I just need her to trust me—for now.

Long enough for the rest of the family back home to come up with some way to *fix* this. Hopefully, before I wear a groove in the floors with my pacing.

Knowing there are half a dozen loaded weapons placed strategically around the house doesn't help ease any of my nerves. It doesn't feel like enough firepower for what we might face.

Benjamin seems to sense my stress, his wails growing stronger until the warmer beeps and I'm able to get him the bottle he so desperately wants. He takes it between his lips right away, finally relaxing against me and allowing me to crack my neck and release some of the tension his distress was building in me, too.

I walk over to stand in front of the sliding glass doors that look out into the dark forest behind the house. With the cloud cover overhead, I can barely make out the distinct shapes of the trees. It's merely a thick, dense blackness that feels like an endless void I could get lost in if I stare out at it for too long.

Ignoring the desire to throw on the exterior lights and illuminate the whole yard for my own sanity, I look down at Benjamin, all soft cheeks, little black eyelashes spread out across them. Tiny fingers press against my chest, warm and comforting in a way I didn't know they could be.

A knife hits me in that exact spot and twists the longer I look at him. "I am sorry you're caught up in this, buddy, but don't blame your mom. It isn't her fault. None of this is. It's all mine."

I lower my head and press a kiss to his—the wispy, dark hair soft against my lips.

This sweet, innocent baby is stuck in the middle of something he has no control over, and it's up to *me* to keep him and Allie safe. But despite what I told her, I'll never *truly* feel safe here, or anywhere, for that matter. Not until the situation with Roselli is resolved.

I can't see how that's going to happen without bloodshed.

Even if he wasn't involved in his dad's business over the years, which I have a hard time believing, he still demonstrated his intention by trying to grab Allie the morning the hurricane hit.

Anger burns through my blood again, like it did while

Allie's head rested in my lap on Savage's couch and she recounted what happened.

It was all I needed to know to confirm he's not going to let this baby go.

But he also greatly underestimates the Hawkes and what we're willing to do to protect our own if he thought he would get away with that. "I will make sure you're safe, kid. You and your mom."

My words hang in the silent air for a moment, then soft footsteps sound behind me. I freeze and glance over my shoulder as Allie approaches, her hair disheveled, eyes still sleepy.

Wrapping her arms around herself, she rubs at her bare skin, the tank top and tiny shorts she's wearing barely covering her. "I thought I heard something down here."

I force myself to ignore my body's instant reaction to her, instead focusing on the fact that she's here at all. "And you came down to investigate a noise without me? Don't do that unless you're going to grab one of the guns."

She flinches slightly at my reproach.

I hate having to say it to her, despise having to even suggest she would need to use one of the weapons we have, but it's the reality of where we are right now.

We both need to be alert at all times, ready for any potential threats to arise, and prepared to act like we've both been trained to do our entire lives.

Allie nods slowly. "You're right. I'm sorry. I'm just...still kind of asleep..." She approaches cautiously and peeks into my arms. "When did he wake up?"

I stare back out at the forest as the clouds move away from the moon, letting it illuminate the treetops swaying in the wind. "A few minutes ago."

Stepping forward, Allie places her hands flat against the glass, watching the same elegant movement, almost as if they're dancing. She's silent for a few moments before she peeks at me out of the corner of her eye. "How long do you think we'll have to stay here?"

I shake my head. "I don't know."

And that's the God's honest truth.

No one knows.

Finding out Roselli had a son was shocking enough, and now everyone is scrambling to figure out what Daniele has been doing since his father's death and after his confrontation with Allie.

A distressed noise slips from her trembling lips. "They're going to kill him, aren't they?"

Her softly spoken question is so innocent yet filled with the understanding that it's true. Something a Hawke like Alessandra knows all too well.

"I don't know for sure, but..." I look down at Benjamin again, still content in my arms, and I can't help but imagine what must be going through Daniele's head—knowing he has a son out there. "I don't know how we get out of this without that happening."

Allie presses her forehead against the glass and closes her eyes. "I never should have gotten involved with him. I don't know what I was thinking..."

I don't want to have this conversation with her again, but she seems to need the reassurance. And I'm not going to let her blame herself when it was my fault.

All of it.

This was all set in motion by what I did that night.

"You didn't know."

She lifts her head and looks over at me, her eyes dipping to the baby. A sad smile crosses her lips. "Things could have been so different, you know?"

Fucking hell.

My heart lodges my throat, and I hold her gaze, unable to

look away. The weight of her words crushes both of us, yet we refuse to let that string that's always held us together break.

It's been there forever—changing texture and length, at times thinning until it's close to snapping and letting us both walk away, trailing the jagged edges with us.

Only it never did.

Benjamin releases a tiny cry, finally shattering that connection—at least momentarily—and I glance down at the empty bottle and turn toward her. "I'm going to clean up."

She reaches out and takes him from me, cradling him softly against her chest and murmuring something to him I can't make out. My hand holding the bottle shakes violently as I take it to the sink and throw on the water, letting the noise of it running into the basin fill the kitchen.

I rinse the bottle, then drop it into the washer, my eyes following her as she moves around the kitchen and living room, rocking him gently. Without the water running, her soft hum reaches me, the familiar tune making my throat dry.

She starts singing the Jamaican lullaby Dad used on all of us when we were little, and my entire body starts to tremble.

Allie may have been terrified of becoming a mother, given the circumstances, but she loves that kid more than anything, and she'll do anything to protect him. Even if it means staying here with me. Which must be as painful for her as it is for me.

It's only the first night, and already, both of us are starting to crack.

This is precisely why we've avoided each other for so long.

It wasn't just the anger she had for me; it was the knowledge that whatever we had together never really died.

We've both felt it every time our eyes met across a room for the last ten years, and neither one of us wants to admit it because we both know we can't change the past.

That pain and betrayal will always live in her heart.

And what I did will always come back to bite me.

8

POPE

Allie fidgets, shifting around on her left side where she lies on the bed, facing me, unable to keep herself still. I freeze the ultrasound wand on her exposed chest and give her the third glare in the last five minutes.

"Stop. Moving."

She narrows her eyes on me, the blue almost icy with her annoyance. "It's been a week. Do we really have to do this every day?"

I scowl at her, pressing on her shoulder to adjust her position so I can get the wand back where I need it. "You have postpartum cardiomyopathy, Allie. So, *yes*. I'm going to check you *every* fucking day." I watch the image on the screen, trying to get the right angle. "I'm going to do an echocardiogram. I'm going to do an ECG. I'm going to check your blood pressure constantly. I'm going to do everything in my damn power to make sure you're monitored as well as possible outside Dr. Boggs' office." I lock my gaze with hers, using my best "Dr.

Clarke" look so she understands how serious I'm being. "This can cause full-blown heart failure, Al."

She presses her lips into a hard line and averts her eyes, the reproach hitting its mark. "You think I don't know that?"

The sadness in her voice almost makes me regret being so hard on her.

Almost.

She has to take this seriously and stop giving me a hard time about it, but I know she's only being difficult and trying to make light of it because she's terrified.

I lean in until I am probably a little too close to her. "Stop moving and stop talking so I can get this done."

Little Miss I-Always-Have-Something-To-Say looks like she wants to, but she scowls and remains still, and I adjust the wand again to get a good view of her heart.

Finally.

If I hadn't been able to get the portable ultrasound and ECG from the hospital and bring them with me, we would have to be doing this in Shreveport, and God knows that would draw way too much attention.

I can't take the chance that Roselli might be looking for me to get to Allie and Benjamin. If he is, using my hospital credentials anywhere else would send up a giant red flag saying, "Here we are. Come and get us."

So, while I may not be a cardiologist or have the level of equipment Dr. Boggs would back at UMC, I sure as hell will do my best to monitor her and keep her as healthy as possible while we're trapped up here together.

Even if she hates me for it.

Silence falls over us while I continue to scan, searching for any signs that her condition has progressed. I hold my breath, sending up another silent prayer, and like every other day since we got here, while things don't look "normal," they haven't advanced, either.

A minor win in what could potentially be a very long battle.

I release a heavy breath and pull away the wand, handing her a towel so she can clean off the ultrasound gel. "Everything looks good."

She pushes herself up with one hand, wiping her chest while I quickly avert my gaze and work on cleaning up the machine. "You'd be able to see it, though, if things were getting worse?"

"Between these two machines"—keeping my back to her, I motion between the ultrasound and ECG we already ran —"something would show up to give me an indication that things have gone downhill since you left UMC."

"What would happen then?"

Besides me completely losing my fucking mind?

I bite back the words and return to my work, putting everything back on top of the dresser in the spare bedroom we've been using to conduct these daily exams.

"Pope...what would happen?"

Slowly, I turn back to face her, planting my hands on my hips, trying to conceal how truly terrified I am of that happening. "Well, you could go into full-blown heart failure, and if that happened out here..." I trail off, not ready to discuss that potential. "We're relatively close to a hospital, but still..."

She nods. "Aunt Nora said if that happens, I would eventually need a heart transplant."

I give her a sharp nod. "But, hopefully, it won't come to that. The fact that nothing's progressed in the last week is a good sign that your mild case isn't going to get any worse—"

"But it might not get better, either."

Hearing the worry in her voice, my hands itch to tug her into my arms and make her promises I know I can't as a doctor, but I don't, leaning back against the dresser instead, watching her with her back to me as she re-buttons her shirt then pushes up from the bed. "How are you feeling otherwise?"

Allie clears her throat, running her hand over her shirt and pants, smoothing them out. "Okay, actually. Still a little sore, but"—she shrugs as if she didn't give birth less than two weeks ago on a couch at a strip club—"good, I guess."

"Good."

I want to delve deeper, ask her to *talk* to me, not just about how she's feeling physically, but what's going on in that beautiful head of hers. Because I see how bad she needs to. But I also know pushing Alessandra McCabe into *anything* will only make her retreat further.

And there isn't anywhere else for her to go out here.

She'll talk when she's ready.

I rub a hand along the back of my neck. "You'll go back and see Dr. Brennan in a few weeks, but if you feel any pain, anything unusual, tell me and I can—"

Allie holds up a hand. "Nope, we're not doing that again."

She walks out of the room without another word, and I squeeze my eyes closed, pinching the bridge of my nose.

Fucking hell, did I really offer to give her a pelvic exam?

As if delivering the baby wasn't awkward enough.

Please, God, don't make me have to do that...

I'm not sure I could live through it, and neither could she.

We've gone back to dancing around each other—that same elegant waltz we've always performed.

She spends all her time alone with the baby. Playing with the few toys we brought when he's awake. Wandering around the house with him in the carrier, strapped to her chest, while he sleeps or sitting with him on the bed, reading a book on her tablet. Anything to avoid being in the same room as me.

While I spend my time digging through the internet or on calls with Dad, Bishop, Gabe, and Savage, trying to get any sort of update that might suggest this is close to being over. But in the seven days we've been here, the Hawkes have come up with exactly diddly squat.

Daniele Roselli is doing a damn good job of hiding.

After what went down with Allie at her apartment building, he had to know we'd be coming for him and what we were capable of—both through his father and by hanging around Allie and The Grind so much.

Daniele isn't an innocent caught up in his father's world.

In fact, the more digging we've done, the scarier the prospect of actually finding him gets.

In the last several months since his father's death, New Orleans has been stuck in a tense standoff. Everyone waiting to see what's going to happen and who is going to step up to fill the seat at the head of the Italian family left vacant when Cristiano Roselli bled out on the sidewalk in front of The Grind.

Of course, we were all waiting for Satriano to do just that after he showed up, throwing down his threats and leaving us all speechless at the hotel's groundbreaking ceremony.

But the man has remained suspiciously quiet and absent from the public eye.

Nothing but a rumor popping up here or there of him being seen around NOLA and a few other Gulf Coast cities, but he certainly isn't making any big moves, not like we expected.

And now that we know Roselli has a son, the hints of infighting amongst the remaining Roselli men makes a lot more sense. Daniele may be going after his father's empire, biding his time until he's reconsolidated the power of the Roselli name before he makes any major moves.

Which means if he gets his hands on that baby, Benjamin will potentially be caught in the crossfire of another mob war in New Orleans.

I shake my head to clear that thought before I drive myself mad and push off from the dresser, heading out of the room and down the hallway past Allie's closed door to the staircase. Ignoring the pull to twist that knob and check on her, I hustle down the steps and make my way to the kitchen, where my laptop is set up on the long table overlooking the woods.

My makeshift office has started to almost feel like home now, even though this house still makes me uneasy. I slide into my usual chair and flip open my computer, scanning my emails for any updates that might have come through while I was examining Al.

Absolutely nothing.

Again.

I stare at my phone sitting next to my computer and drum my fingers on the tabletop to stop myself from calling Dad to demand some answers that he certainly doesn't have or I would have heard from him.

It isn't fair to keep harping on him because he can't find the douchebag.

Not when it isn't really his fault.

Daniele has the Roselli resources, and that means he could literally be *anywhere* in the world, under any number of assumed names. Finding him could take time—far more than we anticipated.

And it's making both Allie and me antsy.

Instead of tearing into Dad, I grab my phone and call the other person who might understand my level of anxiety at this point.

Bishop answers on the first ring. "Is everything okay?"

"Yeah." I lean back in the chair and stare at the light fixture hanging above the kitchen table that I've memorized over the last week. "Fine. Just going a little stir-crazy here."

She snorts. "I bet so. How is the patient?"

"Pissed off."

Her laughter floats through the line. "And Benjamin?"

"He's great." His bright-blue eyes flash through my head— so observant even at such a young age. Always watching me and his mom. "Perfect."

"Good. But if you're calling for an update, I don't have one."

I sigh and lean forward, resting my elbow on the table and my face in my palm. "I figured as much. I talked to Dad this morning already."

And I've been nothing but a pent-up ball of tension since then.

Each day gets harder.

Waiting.

Watching her.

Being this close.

"What are we supposed to do, Bishop? Hide up here forever?"

She releases a sigh filled with understanding only an older sister can offer. "You know that won't happen."

"But how long do we wait? We're going to have to go into town in the next week or so anyway to restock food and supplies if nothing changes. We never intended to have to stay this long."

We all thought finding Roselli would be easy, that our contacts all across New Orleans and the rest of the Gulf Coast would find him quickly so we could take care of it and get Allie back to her life.

That looks more and more unlikely as the hours tick by.

Bishop jostles the phone slightly and says something to someone before she comes back. "We could have someone drive stuff up?"

"Nah." I shake my head, my frustration tightening my hand around the phone. "Too dangerous. If he's watching any of the family, he could follow you guys straight to us."

"You think it's safer for you to go into town and leave her alone at the house?"

Leave it to one of the resident security experts in the family to bring up the exact fear that's set up permanent residence in my chest.

"Fuck no." I scrub my free palm over my face. "I'm taking them with me."

"What if you're spotted?"

I release a heavy sigh. "As far as we know, Roselli never had any major connections in the Shreveport area. We'll be quick, and I'll make sure to watch for any tails. But we need to find this fucker, Bishop. I can't keep doing this."

"Doing what?"

"This. Up here with her—"

The sharp inhalation of breath from my right makes me drag my head up and toward the sound.

Allie stands in the archway near the bottom of the staircase, mouth open slightly, Benjamin nestled in the carrier against her chest. She places her hands protectively over him, then turns and rushes back toward the stairs, the mist of tears already clouding her eyes.

"Shit."

ALESSANDRA

I LIE BACK on the bed, staring at the ceiling I've become well-acquainted with the last week, listening to the gentle sound of the lullaby playing from the small speaker shaped like a stuffed lamb in the corner of the room near where I moved Benjamin's bassinet earlier.

The light, familiar notes should be soothing—it's the entire purpose of the damn thing—but I can't relax. I can't stop my damn heart from racing or my chest from tightening uncomfortably.

Pope would be pissed at me for not telling him.

But apparently, he's pissed about having to be here with me in the first place.

So, fuck it...

It isn't the first time that man has said words that hurt my heart, but this time, I won't give him the satisfaction of knowing what he's done to me.

Nope.

Not this time.

I peek over at Benjamin, still sound asleep, content with the music that doesn't seem to be doing anything to help me. If I get out of bed to do anything, like continuously pacing and staring out the window, which seems to be my constant activity beyond reading, I might wake him.

And if he starts fussing, that will send Pope running up to check on him.

After what I heard Pope say, I don't want to be a burden anymore.

To him or to anyone else.

We don't need him.

I'm getting stronger, feeling better every day, at least physically, but his words keep hitting me like Atlas' blows in a title match—over and over again. To the chest. To the gut. To the head. All threatening to undo any semblance of calm I might manage to find if I could get them out of my head.

My phone rings on the nightstand, and I lunge for it, trying to stop the shrill sound before it wakes the baby. I grab it and silence the ringer, checking the name on the screen.

Oh, thank God.

If anyone can get me out of this shitty headspace, it's Jude.

I answer his call and return to reclining against the pillows. "Hey."

"Hey, yourself. You doing all right?"

Even though we've talked twice a day, every day since I got up here, Jude still asks each time—as if anything will drastically change between our morning and evening chats.

If it were anyone else, it would annoy me. Make me feel like

I'm the baby—though, technically, I guess I still am, along with Jude. But coming from him, the best friend I've been keeping so many secrets from, it makes tears burn in my eyes.

Not being able to see him, to hug him, to come clean about everything that's been weighing on me for so long has been killing me. But I can't tell him I'm not all right because he doesn't know the truth about Pope. If he did, it would change everything. So, I keep that old secret, holding it tightly in that place that haunts my dreams.

And lying to my best friend well and truly sucks.

"Yeah, I'm okay."

He snorts incredulously. "You don't *sound* okay. What's wrong, Allie Cat?"

I swipe at my eyes, trying to suck in a deep breath that will keep me from releasing a sob. "It's just been a long time since we came up here. I miss you and Ang and everyone else."

"Well, I'm glad I'm at the top of the list."

His lopsided smirk flashes in my head. "Of course you are. What are you doing?"

Paper rustles in the background. "I'm actually at Novel Idea but have mostly been editing the book. It's been slow today. Not a lot of people out buying new reading material when they're busy repairing hurricane damage."

"I bet not." I pick at the comforter, playing with the decorative fringe along the top seam. Guilt at abandoning Angelina to handle the entire café alone eats away at my stomach. "What about The Grind?"

"Well, I can see your sister bustling around through the window. She looks plenty busy..."

Which is good for business, not so good for feeling bad about not being there to help.

"I hope Astrid has been able to step in."

"You know she always will."

Of course she will.

All the Hawkes are constantly offering to help at the café, the bookstore, or any of the other businesses that might need temporary help, but Astrid has her own life and people who rely on her, too. And by being at The Grind, filling in for me, she's not where she would elsewhere be, assisting those who need her expertise.

"I don't want her tutoring students to suffer because she has to take over my role at The Grind..."

"Al, stop it." Jude's chastisement silences me. "Stop apologizing. We knew we were going to lose you for a while after you had the baby, anyway. Right? We've been planning for this. Just because you went into hiding with Pope doesn't change anything in that regard. It just came a few weeks earlier than we had thought it would. And it won't be forever."

I release a mirthless laugh that fills the room, then slap my hand over my mouth and quickly sit up to ensure I didn't wake up Benjamin. But he's still asleep, head turned toward me, perfect lips parted slightly in his slumber.

"Shit." I try to return to speaking quietly, barely above a whisper. "I almost woke the baby."

He chuckles lightly. "What was so funny?"

I sigh, running my free hand through my hair. "You saying it won't last forever. I'm sure Pope would tell you it feels like it already has been a lifetime since we came up here..."

Jude snort-laughs. "How is he doing with all this?"

This would be the ideal opportunity to tell him all the things I've longed to for the last ten years. To discuss what happened with Pope and why things have been so weird between us for so long, but I bite back that truth, too embarrassed and hurt by what went down to admit it even to him.

"I don't think he's doing very well, to be honest."

I push myself up and scoot back until I'm seated against the headboard, staring at the room that has become mine.

It feels absolutely nothing like my room in my apartment.

It isn't warm.

It isn't inviting.

It isn't *mine*.

But I guess my apartment isn't mine anymore.

Christ, I don't even know where I'm going to go when I do go back to New Orleans.

Concern tightens Jude's voice. "Al...what did he say?"

Fighting back tears, I close my eyes and envision him sitting there at the table, head lowered, his entire body language screaming exhaustion and frustration. "I heard him on the phone with someone. I think it was Bishop. He said...he said he can't keep doing this up here with me."

Fuck.

This time, the sob slips out before I can stop it, and I slap my hand over my mouth again—both to stop me from waking Benjamin and to make sure Pope doesn't hear me and come running in like a superhero with a red cape.

The last thing I need is for him to see me like this right now, after what I heard.

"Al, stop crying. I'm sure he didn't mean it the way you are reading it, okay? He's just used to being at the hospital, you know, being in that fast-paced ER, working with Nora, saving lives. You guys have been stuck in a house together for a week. You're probably *both* going stir-crazy, right?"

His words make sense—if you don't know the history.

"Yeah, I guess."

"Don't take it personally, Allie Cat."

"I'm trying not to. But..."

I let my thought trail off, the ugly, painful trauma of what happened between Pope and me all those years ago sitting on the tip of my tongue. I've wanted to tell Jude so many times, especially back then. But we all knew what everyone would think, how much drama it would cause. And opening that old wound now wouldn't solve anything.

"Hey, Al..." Jude's voice drops low, his seriousness coming through the line. "I don't know exactly what happened between you and Pope—"

"Jude, I'm sorry. I—"

"No, let me finish. I don't know what happened between you two. Of course, I have had my suspicions. I knew you were up to something those nights we weren't together when I had that advanced English class at the college. Plus, I saw the way you looked at each other."

Shit.

"You don't have to go into details, Al. You don't have to tell me anything you don't want to. But regardless of what happened back then, I can tell you what's happening now. Pope is there because he *wants* to be, because he cares about you and Benjamin and wants to make sure you're both safe, like any of us would." He pauses for a moment, collecting himself, emotion heavy in his voice. "If I could, I would have gone with you. But I—"

"You don't have to apologize, Jude. Never for that. *Ever.*"

My heart breaks to see him continue to struggle with going to new places, with leaving his condo to go anywhere besides the bookstore, The Grind, or Nana's house. It seems to be a few steps forward and then one back with him, but at least he's not alone anymore, cooped up inside his place and lost in his own head.

I smile to myself and picture him in this big house with me and the baby. "You'd be sick of me, too, if you were up here."

He barks out a laugh. "No, impossible. In fact, I wanted to talk to you about that."

"About what?"

"About when this is all over with *Dan* and you come home."

The anger in the way he says his name makes me grin. Jude is a lover and a poet, not a fighter. But something tells me he'd rip that man's head off if he could get his hands on him.

"Ang and I want you to bring Benjamin and come live here."

"At the condo?" I chuckle. "How the hell would that work?"

The one-bedroom loft space is Jude's entire world and has been for a long time, and it certainly isn't set up for a third adult and a baby.

"Ang and I will get a Murphy bed for out in the living room. You and the baby can take the bedroom."

My heart aches and feels like it might burst, and my lip trembles as I try to fight back the tears again. "Wow. Thank you, Jude. You have no idea how much I appreciate that. But I'm not going to do that to you and Angelina. You guys need your privacy, your space."

"We want you here, both of you."

"I believe you. I just...I'm not going to do that. If I can't go back to my place, then I'll go stay with Mom and Dad. You know they'd be thrilled to have Benjamin under their roof."

He laughs lightly. "I'm sure they would. But will *you* be able to handle living under the same roof?"

That's the harder question.

Much harder.

They're incredibly overprotective, maybe rightfully so, given the current circumstances, but they mean well.

When they offered to let me stay with them when I found out I was pregnant, and again after Ang moved in with Jude and left me alone at our apartment, I said no both times. Mostly because I didn't think I could handle living with them again under the weight of their judgments and hovering. With the baby there, it would be even worse.

"It'll be okay, Jude. It'll work out."

"Wasn't I supposed to be the one reassuring *you*?"

I smile and sigh, rubbing at my tired eyes. "Yeah, you were. But I'm okay now. I promise. I'll talk to you tomorrow..."

"You say that like it's a bad thing."

"Of course, it isn't. I love you."

"I love you, too, Allie Cat. Give that baby a kiss for me."

"I will."

I end the call and toss my phone back onto the nightstand, cringing as it slides off and careens onto the floor, the noise filling the room and startling Benjamin awake.

Shit.

He cries out, his tiny face scrunching up in anger, and I climb from the bed and pull him into my arms, immediately rocking him gently to try to stave off a full-on meltdown.

And before Pope comes rushing in...

Everyone's bending over backward to help me, to make my problem go away—permanently—and all I can do is sit here, trying not to have a goddam heart attack while the man determined to keep me alive can't even stand to be near me but feels obligated to do just that.

I thought things were bad before when I was keeping all this a secret and trying to come up with a plan to handle it all, but it's so much worse than I ever could have imagined.

Maybe I should have left New Orleans...

Everyone would be better off if I had.

9

POPE

The cool, damp evening breeze coasts over my exposed skin, and I take a sip from the beer in my hand and lean against the porch rail, staring out at the dirt road that brought us here. Or, at least, what I can see of it in the almost pitch-black of night.

It disappears into the thick trees—the only way in or out. Something about that makes goosebumps rise all over my body, and I shake myself, trying to lose the unnerving feeling creeping over me.

By now, I would have thought I'd be used to this place, to its remoteness, the intricacies of the land, and the quiet stillness of the evenings during which I barely sleep—but I'm not.

In fact, tonight is the worst so far, though that may have something to do with the look on Allie's face when she overheard me on the phone with Bishop earlier.

You're such a fucking idiot.

I should know better than to say shit like that when she might be around to hear me. And I've started up those steps a dozen times since then, stopping myself each time before ever reaching the second floor. Not because I don't want to correct her *very* wrong interpretation of what I said, but because it's probably best that she continues to misunderstand.

It makes it easier for both of us.

At least, that's what I tell myself.

There are so many lies I've forced myself to believe in order to make it through the days and nights here with Alessandra and Benjamin. Lies about what I want and what's possible.

I take another long swig of my beer, hoping the hoppy, cold liquid will erase the feelings I can't seem to escape while I'm trapped here, but before I can even swallow it, a scream rips through the still night air.

The bottle falls from my hand, shattering on the porch, and I turn toward the cracked front door and race inside. Scrambling through the foyer, I jerk open the drawer on the table at the base of the stairs to grab one of the guns I hid there when we arrived, racking a round as I ascend the steps.

Three at a time.

But it isn't fast enough.

Blood whooshes in my ears, my vision narrowing on the closed door at the end of the hall as I rush toward it. Allie's low sob slips under the crack, and I turn the knob and push it open, holding my breath, unsure what I'll find but prepared to do whatever I have to if there's a reason to pull this trigger.

She stands over the bassinet, her hand over her mouth, trembling so violently that she has to grip the side of it to even keep herself upright.

I scan the room for signs of an intruder or threat, but all appears normal.

"Jesus, Allie, what's wrong?"

Lowering my weapon, I approach her, searching for an injury. She shakes her head, pulls her shaking hand from her mouth, and another anguished sound rips from her chest.

I reach out and pull her to me while I check on Benjamin. He shifts restlessly in the bassinet, but he appears okay, probably just woken by the unexpected noise. Allie sobs against my chest, and I slip the gun into my waistband and wrap her fully in my arms, holding her close.

"What happened, Al?"

"He-he was here. He-he took Benjamin..."

Relief floods my veins.

A nightmare.

She was having a nightmare.

I take her face in my palms, forcing her to focus on me. "Allie, it was a dream. Benjamin is fine. He's right here, asleep." I tilt her head that way so she can see him in the bassinet before bringing her eyes back to mine. "He's *safe*. You are *safe.*"

Another sob tumbles from her lips, her hysteria growing rather than going in the right direction.

I tug her against me fully, and she clutches my T-shirt tightly in her hands, her tears falling to my skin. Each warm drop only seems to add to her distress, so I scoop her up and carry her to the bed.

She keeps weeping, the sound of her anguish enough to make my eyes mist over as I carefully switch her weight so I can pull the gun from my pants and set it on the nightstand. I climb onto the mattress and settle myself against the headboard, draping her on my lap so I can hold her tightly and try to stop her rising panic.

"Shh." I run my hand over her hair gently, my other hand keeping her close. "Al, it's all right. It was just a dream."

But I, of all people, know how vivid and real a dream can be.

I've had them about Allie for so long, sometimes I can't figure out if they're a memory of that night or a wish for more of what I never should have had in the first place.

She clings to me like a lifeline, the same way she did so

freely back then, the way I've wished she would again without reservation. With *trust* that hasn't been there for a very long time.

I rub her back and let her cry, rocking her while she tries to find reason again.

"Take some deep breaths, Al."

She tries, sucking in a shaky one that sounds more like a hiccup. "I-I'm s-sorry...I—"

"You don't have anything to apologize for, Teeny."

Frankly, I'm surprised this didn't happen sooner.

With the threat from Roselli looming over us, time moving at a snail's pace without resolution, it's only natural for her to have nightmares about the man who poses such a danger to her and her son.

Nodding, she pulls her head back, her tear-soaked eyes meeting mine in the dark room. "You shouldn't be here. You shouldn't have left the hospital, your job, your life—"

Hell.

That has absolutely nothing to do with her dream.

Her apology is about what she heard me say to Bishop, the words I wish I could take back because they hurt her, even if I never meant them the way she interpreted them.

Cradling her face again, I tilt it up, forcing her to meet my gaze. "I'm *exactly* where I want to be, Al. Where I *need* to be. Protecting you and Benjamin and making sure you're both healthy and safe."

Her eyes soften, like whatever anger she held over what I said is starting to evaporate with her tears. "What about earlier...you said..."

Stupid woman.

She has no idea what she still does to me, how fucking impossible it is to concentrate on keeping her safe when all I want to do is kiss her senseless every time we're in the same room.

I was *this close* to coming clean with Bishop, seconds away from telling her everything that happened between Allie and me back then, everything we kept hidden for what we thought was a very good reason. If Allie hadn't let me know she was standing there, listening, I probably would have, so I could get some help from another woman, one I trust implicitly, with how to handle this impossible situation.

Allie swallows thickly, searching my face for something. "I don't want you to stay here because you feel obligated to treat me as a doctor and protect me from something you have nothing to do with—"

After what she heard, of course Allie would think that's why I'm here.

Obligation.

When we were in her hospital room, discussing a way to keep her safe, I made it seem like this was the most logical solution because I'm a doctor and wouldn't be tied so readily to her as anyone else in the family.

She has every reason to believe those words were true—and the *only* reason I came with her.

I drop my head back against the headboard, releasing a sigh. "Al, that isn't why I'm here."

"Then...*why?*"

Her question sounds so innocent.

So simple.

Something that should be *easy* to answer.

But it's tangled up with ten years of things we never said to each other. A decade of unspoken truths and lies I let her continue to believe.

Maybe it's time to let the skeletons out of the closet...

Lifting my head again, I meet her questioning gaze. "Being here with you is hard because I want to wring that fucker's neck personally. I took an oath to do no harm, to use these hands to heal and not hurt." I hold them up, flexing my long fingers. "But

I want to use them to hurt him, to make him feel the terror he has made *you* feel."

A tiny gasp falls from her lips, and she grasps my hand, placing it back against her cheek and leaning into it, her soft skin against mine sending a low sizzle through me, making me feel things I shouldn't be right now. "I'm sorry, Pope, for what I said that night at Nana's..."

Her words have always stung, but I always took the pain as a proper punishment for the way I treated her, for the agony I caused her. But I don't want to read too much into anything she says right now. I don't want to misinterpret something that she only regrets because she's upset about the nightmare.

I brush my thumb over her cheek. "You said a lot of things that night, Al."

She nods slowly, a stray tear slipping from her right eye and making its way down to my palm. "About you never caring..."

ALESSANDRA

As soon as I said those words that night in Mom's old bedroom, I knew they weren't true. I *knew* they were a lie said to hurt him as much as I was hurting so he would feel everything he made *me* feel.

I knew they were a lie because every memory I have of Pope from my childhood through to that very day he broke my heart were of the man I've seen the last few weeks. The one who tried to help me even when I didn't want it. The one who abandoned his duty to come find me in a storm. The one who left his dream job without a second thought to take care of me and keep me alive and safe. The one who has handled my son with love and not in a cold, clinical way he could be.

Pope is a lot of things, but uncaring could *never* be one of them.

Compassionate.

Protective.

Gentle.

A calming presence I needed in my life then.

He always cared.

Always.

And he still does.

His dark eyes lock with mine, unwavering. "You know I did, Allie."

The pain in his voice as he says that while holding me so closely, the same way he has my son since he helped bring him into the world, brings a new wave of tears.

"Then why did you..." I swallow through another sob, stuck between not wanting to relive that painful moment again and finally getting the answer I've sought for so long. "Why did you say it was a mistake?"

Those four words have haunted me for a decade. They're the reason for all of this distance between us, for all the ire I held for him for so long.

"Fuck..." Pope scrubs a hand over his face, staring at the wall behind me instead of meeting my gaze. "That was...a shitty choice of words."

"But—"

There is a *but* there. I can see it all over his face. How much he doesn't want to be having this conversation with me right now—or maybe ever.

He's going to leave.

For a moment, I firmly believe he will without giving me the answer I need, but he finally lets his eyes meet mine, and the corner of his lip quirks up. "You know...I still remember the exact moment."

I raise a brow. "The exact moment what?"

His fingers feather across my cheek. "The exact moment I stopped seeing you as little Allie and started seeing you as the woman you were becoming, the woman who could stop my heart with one look."

My breath catches at his words, how genuine and heartfelt they are. "What was it?"

He grins. "My sixteenth birthday..."

Without even having to think about it, I know exactly the moment he's talking about. "I came straight to your party from the salon."

Pope bobs his head, lifting his fingers to thread them through my hair. "I saw you from the back, with that dark bob after you had chopped off like eight inches of your hair..."

I can't fight the smile pulling at my lips. "I turned around and saw you."

He matches my grin. "You turned around, and it was like I was seeing a totally different person. You weren't that little girl anymore. You were all grown up, running toward me with your arms open, screaming, '*Happy birthday,*' before you launched yourself at me."

"So that was *the* moment, huh?"

Twirling a strand of my hair around his finger, he nods again. "Yep."

"I remember mine, too."

His brows rise.

"It was when I saw that look in your eyes that day...after I turned around."

He probably thinks I'm fucking with him, but that moment in time has been seared into my brain since then. That day, Pope looked at me so differently. Not like I was his little "cousin" who he had to watch over and ensure I wasn't getting into trouble; he looked at me like I was an equal, like the year that separated us in age no longer mattered at all and I was my own person—not just a Hawke.

That was it.

The beginning of the end.

We just didn't know it would lead to so much heartache.

My humor fades, and the question he so deftly avoided answering only a few moments ago throbs in my head.

Why did you say it was a mistake?

I don't repeat it.

I don't have to.

His smile falters, as if he can read my mind, and he drops my hair and rubs his hands over his face, sighing.

Our entire relationship, if you can even call it that, plays on repeat, like I'm watching a movie rather than scenes from my own love story. Starting from our first kiss out in the rain that summer between his senior year and my junior one. Through the stolen moments we somehow found at family events and intimate ones when we managed to end up somewhere truly alone. And then that night...when we finally became each other's firsts and it all came crashing down.

Pope stares at the ceiling. "After we...you know...that night, I was on cloud nine. I honestly couldn't remember ever being happier in my entire life as I was being with you in that moment. But then"—he finally lets his gaze drop to meet mine—"you immediately started talking about how this changed everything. About how you didn't want to submit all those college applications you had stacked up in your bedroom. How you didn't want to travel the world and study abroad anymore—something you had been talking about for years. You said you were going to stay in New Orleans because it was where I would be for at least the next four years for undergrad..."

His gaze moves to the bassinet, an affectionate smile pulling at his lips. He reaches out to brush his hand over Benjamin's head.

"I didn't want that for you, Al." His eyes meet mine again. "I didn't want you to be stuck, stagnant, always waiting for me to find free time to spend with you when I knew how hard I was going to have to study in undergrad, not to mention medical school. Then work in my internship and residency. I knew what that would be like. And that wouldn't have been fair to you to make you give up all your dreams for life so you could sit by watching mine."

What?

The explanation isn't what I thought I knew and understood for all these years.

Far from it.

"But"—I open and close my mouth, unable to voice the question threatening to choke me—"how could you just *end* it? How could you walk away so easily?" I never could have. "Didn't you...love me?"

He releases a heavy breath, wincing and squeezing his eyes closed. "You think I ended things with you because I didn't *love* you?" The sheer agony in his whispered question slashes at my heart like a fresh scalpel. "I ended things because I've always loved you...more than anything in this world. And I wanted you to grow up and make your own decisions about your life, not controlled by the ones I'd made for myself."

Oh, God.

"Why didn't you *tell* me any of this that night?"

Pope lifts his hand and cups my cheek again, brushing away the tears now streaming down it. "Because as soon as I said it was a mistake, you shut down and shut me out. You didn't want to hear anything I had to say, and I realized it would be easier for me to let you go and easier for you to let me go if I let you hate me for ending things for whatever reason you had already created in your head."

"I thought..." I shake my head. "I thought you wanted to be single when you went to college, so you could—"

He raises a brow. "So I could play the field?"

"Well...yeah."

A mirthless laugh slips from his lips, and he shakes his head. "You couldn't be more wrong, Al. I didn't date in college. I was too busy studying and pushing myself to finish in three years instead of four so I could start medical school earlier. And for the record, it was even *worse* when I got there. All my time and energy were on that singular focus, not looking for someone to take to bed."

"What about all the girls we all saw you with..."

"Friends." He shrugs slightly. "Some who maybe wanted to be more. But most of them never were. In fact, the *vast* majority were nothing but pleasant company I shared a laugh and maybe dinner and a movie with."

The redhead from the elevator in the hospital pops into my head, bringing with her the green monster. "Melody?"

He smirks. "We went to dinner *once*. One time, Al. Dinner. Nothing else."

God, I was so fucking wrong.

About everything.

"But..." Another sob slips from my throat. "Why did you let me and everyone else think that you were sleeping with all those women?"

His sad smile almost undoes me completely. "Because I needed you to keep hating me so I wouldn't be tempted to try to get you back. Nothing has changed, Al. I am still all about the job. I work insane hours. I miss more family events than anyone else—which I only get away with because Nana knows I'm 'saving lives.' But I don't have one, Al. None. I work, I go home exhausted and crash hard, and then I get up and do it all over again in an endless loop. There isn't room for anything else. For anyone else. It wouldn't be fair..."

Oh, God.

I can physically see him pulling away again, shutting down exactly like he did that night. He shifts me off his lap, setting me beside him on the bed and climbing from it.

Without looking at me, he grabs the gun, tucking it into his waistband as he wanders over to check on Benjamin. His eyes linger on my son, the true affection there making everything he said hurt even more.

Slowly, he cuts his gaze to where I sit dumbstruck on the mattress. For a split second, I hold out hope that he's not going to turn and walk away.

Please stay.

God doesn't hear my plea, just like He didn't that night when I begged Him to make Pope change his mind.

Pope walks to the door and pauses inside the jamb. He looks over his shoulder. "Remember, you're safe here, Al. No matter *what*, I won't let anything happen to you or your baby."

The door clicks back into place behind him, sealing me in with the realization that I fucked up things even more than I ever knew.

10

ALESSANDRA

For so long, I avoided Pope, tried to run from him each time there was even a flicker of a chance of us being within ten feet of each other because every time I saw him, I was dragged back to that day.

To those four words: *It was a mistake.*

The instant he said them, I shut down completely. Didn't want to hear anything else he had to say. Not his stupid explanation. Not his excuses for what he was doing to me.

Pope was right—I did block him out.

I never gave him a chance to explain back then or any time since. And now that he has, now that we've cleared the air and I know the truth, things are far from fixed between us. If anything, it's only made it worse.

The past several days since our conversation, he's grown more nervous, appears increasingly exhausted, like he hasn't slept at all in the almost two weeks we've been here.

For all I know, he hasn't.

I've been so drained since the moment we set foot in this

house—physically and emotionally—that other than that nightmare and a few others, I've slept like a rock. Dead to anything outside my room. Only Benjamin's cries have woken me, and even then, it felt like I was only half awake, going through the motions necessary to get him fed and changed and back to sleep without fully coming back to the world myself.

Maybe Pope hasn't slept.

Knowing him, he's been pacing and worrying, trying to work out some logical way out of this situation and letting it control his thoughts day and night.

He was always an overthinker, one who would study all the angles and try to solve a riddle or problem the way no one else could. Even now, as he watches me load Benjamin into his car seat, his knee bounces incessantly, where he leans against the kitchen counter, arms crossed over his chest. That dark, penetrating gaze of his never leaves me and the baby as he tries to work out our current predicament.

I click the final buckle on the car seat, securing Benjamin, and climb to my feet. "All right. Ready to go."

Pope presses his lips together, his forehead creasing. "Maybe we shouldn't…"

Here we go again.

"Look, you've been debating this for days." I motion toward the kitchen behind him. "But we're almost out of food. No one thought we would be here this long. If you don't think it's safe for anyone to drive it up to us like Bishop suggested last week, then we have to go to a store. Unless you want to reconsider and let me stay here with the baby and you just go."

He shakes his head, biting the inside of his cheek as he contemplates our options, none of which seem particularly great. "I don't want to leave you two alone here."

I scowl at him, starting to feel like this man sees me as some breakable thing made of glass. "I can handle a gun, Pope. You know that. If anybody comes within five feet of this place—I shoot first and ask questions later."

The corner of his mouth twitches like he's fighting a grin at my words. Still, he shakes his head. "Not leaving you. We'll go. I just need to make a decision on where. If we head into Shreveport, there'll be a lot more people. It might be easier to blend in without anyone really noticing us. But if we go to one of the smaller towns, it means less exposure overall and less of a chance someone might recognize us."

"I'm good with whatever you want to do, Pope." Again, neither seems like one we want to leap at. "It's your call."

He rubs at the back of his neck, staring down at Benjamin, who has resettled and fallen back to sleep already. "Shreveport. I feel like the three of us would stick out like a sore thumb in some tiny town where they're not used to strangers and everyone knows everyone."

I reach down to grab the car seat, but Pope pushes off the counter and almost beats me to it with his long arms, his hand wrapping around the handle next to mine. Skin brushes skin, and heat travels up my arm and through my body in an instant.

We both lift our heads, and our eyes meet. So close I can smell his crisp soap and a faint whiff of his morning coffee— which we used the last of, so we *definitely* need to make this grocery run.

A clock in the living room ticks off a few seconds, and we stand frozen, examining each other like we haven't spent our entire lives together before he gently urges my hand off.

I pull it back slowly, my eyes never leaving his as he stands to his full height, lifting Benjamin easily.

He clears his throat. "You have the list?"

What?

Oh, the list. For food. Because that's what we were doing...

I reach into my pocket to pull out the scrap of paper. "Yep."

Everything we need—at least in the food department—is

neatly listed in Pope's meticulously perfect handwriting. Although, it would be nice to know how much we need to get and how much longer we'll be here.

The uncertainty of it all makes planning for anything nearly impossible, and with Dan in the wind, it's starting to feel like we may be stuck here forever.

Don't even think that, Al.

If I can't get home and see everyone soon, I might have a full-blown breakdown.

How did I ever think I could leave New Orleans and the rest of the family? I can barely make it two weeks without them...

If Pope weren't here, I wouldn't have even gotten this far.

He takes a hesitant step toward me and uses his free hand against my lower back to walk me toward the front of the house. His large palm radiates his familiar heat into me, and I almost whimper at the loss of his touch when he removes it to unlock and open the door to the porch.

Knock it off, Al.

This isn't the time or place, and Pope made it very clear the other night that this isn't happening. Even if I *could* get past the years of pain and the animosity I've harbored toward him, my current anger at myself for letting it be that way for so long seems unsurmountable.

All that time lost.

So many years have gone by with him letting me believe a lie.

It's all so twisted up inside me now—like my own little hurricane of uncertainty and complications named Pope that has already hit and is wreaking havoc on me.

I step out into the warm morning air and inhale a long, deep breath of the heavily woodsy scent, hoping it will replace Pope's still lingering in my lungs.

It doesn't.

Aside from occasionally coming out here or on the back

patio with Pope right at my side to break up the monotony of being in this house the last few weeks, it feels like it's been *years* since I've experienced the outside world.

My chest starts to tighten—a combination of excitement to be getting out of here, even if only for a short while, and the constant fear that we might be recognized and word would somehow get to the very person we're trying to hide from swirl inside me. Caught up in the blustering winds of uncertainty Hurricane Pope has already brought.

Pope moves past me and down the steps toward the SUV with long, fluid strides, seemingly unaffected by what happened in the kitchen. He pulls open the rear door, secures Benjamin's car seat, and turns back to me. His brows rise when he finds me still standing motionless on the porch. "Al?"

Shit.

I shake my head to clear away the lingering thoughts that will only drive me mad if I let them and descend the steps toward him. He opens my door, watching me carefully, his always observant eyes taking in every nuance of my movement and expression.

His lips part like he's about to say something, but before he can, the sound of tires on gravel echoes down the road.

Pope freezes, immediately switching his intense focus on the path leading through the trees that we were just about to take out of here. "Get in the car."

"What?"

"Get in the car and get *down*."

Oh, God...

I quickly scramble into the passenger seat and duck down as low as I can into the floorboard. Pope closes my door and the rear one, securing Benjamin inside, and I watch through the window as he reaches for his gun in the holster he attached to his jeans earlier.

He remains on my side of the vehicle, partially obscured by

my door, peeking over the hood, using the SUV as a shield against whoever is coming our way.

Oh, God. Oh, God. Oh, God.

Pope raises the gun, aiming it toward the end of the road that will soon be filled by *someone.*

Please don't let it be Dan. Please. Please. Please.

My heart hammers against my ribs, blood rushing in my ears, making it impossible to hear anything else. The edges of my vision blur, my breaths coming shorter and harder.

No.

Not now.

I press my hand over my chest, trying to stop my stupid heart from exploding or making me pass out again, and I blink through the fog, straining to see Pope.

With his eyes locked on the approaching intruder, he keeps the gun far steadier than I could right now. Despite not being able to hear anything over my own body's attempt to have a damn heart attack, I know the moment the other vehicle reaches the clearing because Pope's shoulders sag, and he relaxes completely.

What the hell?

He smacks his free hand against my door. "It's safe. Come out."

I scramble up and look out the driver's side window to see who's here.

Saint's familiar Land Rover pulls up alongside our SUV, Pope's father at the wheel and Uncle Gabe in the passenger seat.

Oh, thank God.

All the air whooshes from my lungs on a relieved cry. I reach for the handle with a trembling hand, but Pope pops my door and holds it open for me, the rush of fresh air helping to clear my spinning head.

Saint turns off his vehicle, and Gabe climbs from it first.

Pope approaches him, some of the tension returning to his shoulders given the unexpected visit. "What are you doing here?"

Gabe exchanges a look with Saint as he rounds the hood, but before they can say anything, I make it to them and throw my arms around Gabe.

"I'm so happy to see you, but I thought it was too dangerous for anyone to come up here."

He squeezes me tightly. "It is."

Gabe lifts his head and scans the surrounding woods. Always vigilant. That sixth sense of his undoubtedly picks up everything around us, taking in all the variables and calculating plans.

Pulling back slightly, he motions to the house. "Let's go inside and talk."

My stomach drops as he fully releases me. Pope appears to share my unease, his back stiff as he gives them a sharp nod, then pops the back door and grabs Benjamin.

Saint smiles and takes the carrier from him. "Hey, little guy. Wow, you've grown a lot since I saw you last." He looks up at me with a grin. "What are you feeding this kid?"

I know he's trying to make me feel better, to calm some of the anxiety their sudden arrival has brought up, so I force a smile through the panic still coursing through my veins as we all climb the steps.

Pope leads everyone back to the kitchen, and Gabe continues examining the place like he's searching for faults or hidden dangers. Not being able to check it out *before* they sent us here has likely been driving the former Army Ranger mad.

Saint sets Benjamin on the floor, unbuckles him, and pulls him out gently—his massive hands so huge he could hold him in one if he wants to. He cradles him against his chest. One of the biggest and sweetest men I've ever met with the tiniest baby...

Pope watches his father and leans back against the counter in the exact place he just vacated. "So, what's going on? Why did you two come up?"

Gabe wanders around the table and stops at the head of it, gripping the top of the wooden chair. "Savage and I got a call this morning."

I suck in a sharp breath, grabbing the counter next to me to keep from passing out as my world keeps going fuzzy at the edges. "From Dan?"

Offering a sympathetic look, Gabe shakes his head. "No, from someone we never expected to hear from. At least, not this way." He looks from Saint to Pope, then finally back to me, his green eyes hard. "Satriano."

"What?" Pope's body stiffens as mine does. "Why the hell did he call?"

Benjamin releases a little noise, finally starting to wake up at the most inopportune time, and Saint begins pacing around the kitchen, rocking the baby.

"This is where it gets...interesting."

Gabe sighs and runs a hand back through blond hair starting to gray at the temples. "That's an *interesting* way to put it." His hands tighten on the chair back, his knuckles whitening. "Satriano said that he was aware that you had your baby." He clears his throat. "And that he knows the father is Daniele Roselli."

It takes a second for his words to process through the fog that's trying to envelop my brain. "What? How could he *possibly* know that?"

We all know the only people I told sit around Nana's dinner table with us on Sunday and would never utter it to another soul—certainly *not* the mobster who has not only caused so much destruction and turmoil for us but also threatened to do a lot more.

So how could he know?

Gabe grimaces. "That's the most concerning part of all this. We don't know where he is getting his information."

"Shit." I wince and waver slightly on my feet, fumbling to get my hand around the lip of the counter again.

Pope's hand wraps around my arm, keeping me upright, and he lowers his face to my level, his eyes meeting mine. "Al, you feeling okay?"

I nod and take several deep breaths—or as deep as my chest will allow at the moment.

"You need to sit." He ushers me to one of the chairs around the table, pulls it out, and helps me lower myself onto it. Squatting in front of me, he takes my wrist between his hands and presses his fingers to it. "Are you dizzy? Lightheaded? Pain anywhere?"

I wave my free hand at him absently. "I'm fine, just...a little lightheaded with all the excitement." And until I get some answers, I am not letting him shift the focus to me instead of what they drove up here to tell us. "So, he was just calling to let us know he knew?"

Saint gives me a tight, almost smile. "Not exactly. He wants to have a sit-down."

Pope scowls, releasing my wrist, apparently—at least temporarily—appeased with the stability of my medical situation. "What, with you and Savage?"

Gabe shakes his head. "No, with Allie, and he told her to come alone."

An arctic chill washes over me, initiating a full-body shiver, and Pope pushes up to his full height.

"No fucking way that's happening." Jaw locked, Pope storms over to the fridge, grabs a bottle of water, slams the door, and twists off the cap as he returns to the table. He hands it to me, giving me a concerned look. "Drink."

This isn't the time to argue with him, so I accept the bottle and force myself to take several sips. The cold doesn't help with the icy chill raising goosebumps on my kin, but the water does help clear my head and even out my breathing a bit.

Gabe sighs, holding up his hands that look so innocuous but that have killed too many people to count—both during his time as a Ranger sniper and since. "Look, I understand your reluctance, believe me. But what if he has information on where to find Dan? It's been almost two weeks, and we've come up with nothing despite using our best resources. Hell, I even called Cutter and had our buddy Preacher try to find him."

And if one of the best hackers in the world can't find the guy... what hope do we have?

Saint offers a shrug of his enormous shoulders, still cradling Benjamin against his chest. "If Allie goes and meets with Satriano, at least we'll find out what he wants and what he knows."

Pope shakes his head, glancing over at me as my entire body starts trembling again. "Absolutely *not*. Look at her! She has a form of heart failure and we're going to send her into probably the single most stressful situation I can think of with the man who threatened all the Hawkes?"

Gabe steps away from the chair he's been leaning on and squats in front of me. He rubs my shaking arms and presses a kiss to my forehead. "I promise you will be safe during the meeting, Al. We'll pick somewhere public. Somewhere he wouldn't dare try anything, and you know we'll always be prepared for any scenario."

Which likely means he, Bishop, and Saint—the three people with the best shots and most time on the range—with rifles trained on Satriano from multiple points.

Saint approaches Pope and squeezes his shoulder. "Son, think about this rationally. You know we'd never put Alessandra in danger, and if Satriano can help us keep her and Benjamin safe, then we have to consider if we have any better options. And none have presented themselves."

"Fuck!" Pope throws up his hands and paces away, scrubbing them over his face and muttering something under his breath he probably doesn't want to say out loud in front of his father. "Fuck! Fuck! Fuck!"

Gabe squeezes my arms. "If you don't want to do this, we'll find another way to—"

"No." I shake my head, clearing the last remaining cobwebs and doubts about whether I really have the strength to face that man. "We can't go on like this. We have to try something. I'll do it."

POPE

STARING out the window with the binoculars, I watch Allie pace along Fulton Alley, watching for any signs that she may be in any sort of medical distress. Her heart may be slowly recovering, but this is precisely the type of situation that could send her spiraling again.

And it isn't good for mine, either.

The popular tourist area bustles with visitors to New Orleans as well as the heavy lunch crowd, who are here to grab food at the various restaurants with patio seating.

Theoretically, it's the perfect spot to meet Satriano.

Very public.

Somewhere he wouldn't dare try anything.

Not with so many witnesses.

At least, that was the thought when we had the family meeting last night and discussed picking a location to meet.

But now that we're here, I can't shake the feeling that this could also be the perfect ambush spot. With so many people milling about, someone could grab her and get lost in the crowd before any of us could get to her. And even with three rifles at the ready to take out any threats, there are so many innocents that avoiding collateral damage could be impossible.

Something Satriano would know, too.

Allie scans the buildings rising on either side of the alley, searching for us, even though we specifically told her not to, her anxiety making her twist her hands in front of her and chew on her bottom lip.

"I don't like this..."

Bishop glances up from the scope on her rifle, her braids pulled back in her usual bun to keep them out of her face. "Duly noted, and none of us do, but a little late to do anything about that, isn't it?"

She's right.

If anyone left their posts now to try to get her out of here before Satriano arrives, it will likely only make him even more of a threat to all of us. That man despises the Hawkes and everything we stand for and has big plans for his revenge against us for his brother's death. The last thing we need to do is give him any more reason to act.

My in-ear radio crackles to life, and Gabe's voice fills my head. "He's here. Everyone be alert and ready."

How can I ever be ready for this?

To have to stand in this building and watch Allie meet with such a dangerous man...

Even knowing Bishop, Dad, and Gabe already have him in their crosshairs can't relieve the barely restrained panic engulfing my body right now.

Each step Satriano takes closer to Allie only makes it worse.

Dressed in a perfectly tailored suit, Damiano Satriano approaches her with a grin and offers her his hand in greeting. "Alessandra, *mia carissima*, it is so lovely to see you again."

His lightly accented words play in my ear, picked up through the hidden mic Gabe insisted she wear for the entire meeting so we can all hear what's going on.

And hearing *that* man call her "my dear" makes me want to grab the gun from Bishop's hands and empty the whole fucking magazine into him.

The fact that she served him coffee and exchanged pleasantries with him for so long before any of us knew his true identity was bad enough, but for this man to attempt to touch her and throw around terms of endearment is seriously making me consider crossing the line to use my hands for something *other* than saving lives.

Allie doesn't accept his proffered hand. She just stares at it, then lifts her gaze to meet his. "Mr. Satriano...why did you want to meet?"

Good girl, Al.

Don't give him any opening to get your guard down.

"Mr. Satriano?" He presses his hands to his chest in mock offense, shaking his head, making his perfectly coiffed silver hair shimmer in the sun. "Have we really come to that? You always used to call me Damon."

She scowls at him, crossing her arms over her chest defensively. "That was before I knew *who* and *what* you really are."

His lips quirk slightly, and he crosses his arms behind his back, wrapping one hand around the other wrist—a casual move for a conversation that is far from it. "Fair enough." He turns and scans the surrounding buildings on all sides. "Hello to the other Hawkes watching and listening from above..."

Shit.

We should have expected him to know we wouldn't ever send her *truly* alone but hearing him call us out directly sends a shiver through me.

The silver-haired mobster is one smooth operator.

Don't let him intimidate or charm you, Al.

She searches the hundreds of windows that line Fulton Alley, trying to locate us, but we didn't tell her exactly where we would be for this very reason—so she couldn't inadvertently give away our positions.

Finally, she returns her focus to Satriano. "Why did you want to meet?"

He motions toward one of the benches near them, and Allie gives one more uncertain look at the windows in search of us before she reluctantly walks over and takes a seat.

Satriano settles next to her, stretching one arm along the back, like they're just two friends enjoying a chat on a pleasant morning. "First, I wanted to offer my congratulations on the birth of your son. And so soon after Giacomina gave Isaac a son. Such *blessings* for the Hawke family."

Smug fucking bastard.

Letting us know he has been following *exactly* what's happening with us, even if we haven't heard from him in a while. A veiled threat wrapped in congratulations.

"Second, I wished to offer my assistance in dealing with your difficult situation with the father..."

He doesn't say Roselli's name, but he doesn't have to for me to see how much Allie is affected by his words. Her body stiffens, and she twists her hands on her lap, averting her gaze from Satriano.

Come on, Al.

Savage, Gabe, Stone, Isaac, and Dad prepped her for this the best they could, going over every possible scenario for what Satriano could say. And she seemed ready. But now that she's alone with him, I can see her nerves getting the better of her, even from here.

Some of the Hawkes are built for these types of situations— Isaac and Stone taking down opposition in court, Gabe and Dad assessing and neutralizing physical threats, Savage and Kennedy addressing business ones—but Allie has always stayed sheltered from those uncomfortable parts of running their empire.

Under normal circumstances, she might be able to handle it. That attitude that always seems to get her into trouble could be her best defense. But this is about her son, and that changes everything.

If she doesn't get herself under control, this could go south very fast.

Her shoulders rise with her deep inhalation, and she clears her throat, like she's trying to dispel the threat he just made. "Well, what is it you think you can assist with?"

Satriano grins—a slow, cold pull of his lips that doesn't hold any actual humor or warmth. "I'm aware your family has been looking for him for several weeks without much luck. While I don't typically like to make assumptions in my line of work, in this case, I can only presume this isn't a manhunt to invite him into the Hawke fold with open arms."

No, it sure as hell isn't.

Allie shakes her head, confirming Satriano's suspicions.

He nods slowly. "I know where Daniele Roselli is staying and how to arrange a *meeting* with him. I would be happy to provide that information to your family or even send some of my people to have a *conversation* with the father of your son."

My hands tighten around the binoculars.

Satriano is offering to "take care" of our problem *for* us... which can only mean he expects something *major* in return. He isn't the type of man you want to owe anything, but Allie is vulnerable right now. Perhaps in the most exposed position she's ever been in her entire life. Which means she may be willing to do something stupid to protect Benjamin.

Allie seems to understand the situation as well as I do, narrowing her blue eyes on him. "And what would you expect us to do for this *favor*?"

That slow grin that seems to signal Satriano is contemplating something sinister makes an appearance. "Right now, all I would ask in return is that the Hawkes don't get in my way."

Her brow furrows. "In your way, how?"

He scans the buildings again. "I assume, at the very least, that your uncles, Savage and Gabe, are somewhere up there." His gaze cuts back to hers. "And the former Ranger likely has a rifle aimed right at me. I'd be surprised if there weren't at least one more, too."

Allie smiles, the first genuine one I've seen from her today. "Two more, actually."

Atta girl! Let him know we have him.

Satriano bobs his head. "Well prepared. I'm impressed. And despite our differences, I've also been impressed with the way the Hawkes have built this empire in New Orleans, only rivaled by that of the late Cristiano Roselli."

"We aren't criminals."

His silver brows rise. "Aren't you? From what I've observed since my arrival, it sure seems as though spilling blood, threatening or paying to get what you want, and any number of other questionable moves are all on the table for your family."

He isn't wrong about any of that. The Hawkes do whatever is necessary to protect our business and each other, but comparing us to the Rosellis is a far stretch.

We don't blindly use violence without considering the consequences or collateral damage—something both the late Roselli and Satriano himself did frequently.

We look for ways to resolve difficult situations in a positive manner for all parties without the sort of bloodshed they so easily leap to.

Satriano is merely trying to get a rise out of Allie, but she doesn't take the bait, remaining silent in the face of his hard stare.

The longer they hold the stalemate, the more I want to run to her rescue.

Before I can, Satriano grins again, almost like he appreciates Allie's gusto.

"Daniele Roselli is young, inexperienced, nowhere even remotely on the level of his father. When Cristiano died, he left a power vacuum in New Orleans. His men still fight to this day over who should lead and take control—one camp supports his only son taking over, another rallied for his former right-hand man, Francis Gilardi. Neither has emerged victor yet, but I intend to ensure neither of them is sitting on his throne."

And there it is.

Confirmation of exactly what we've all suspected since the moment Satriano revealed himself to us—he wants to control New Orleans, take over Roselli's territory. Perhaps even expand beyond those current borders.

He certainly has the resources to do it.

Satriano waves out a hand. "If the Hawkes agree to stay out of my way as I make the necessary moves to achieve that end, removing Roselli will benefit us both."

Self-serving piece of shit.

He gets an adversary removed *and* something he clearly wants from us.

Allie looks to the windows again, searching for guidance from Savage and Gabe, who are also listening in and hearing every word from their vantage point in the building across from us.

A moment of tomb-like silence settles over everyone before Savage's voice comes through the comm. "Ask him if this would be a formal truce."

We've spent months living in fear of that man, of the unknown, after he issued his vague threat and let us know he would be coming for us. He left us intentionally off-balance and paranoid so we are always looking over our shoulders, afraid of what he might do next.

A truce would mean relief from that—if we can trust a word he says.

Allie turns toward him again to relay the message from the man, who ultimately speaks for the family. "A truce?"

He grins again, his pleasure obvious. "For now...and I may also need to call in a favor from you from time to time. The Hawkes have a great deal of power in this city and connections I cannot ever hope to create. That could be beneficial to me in my new role."

Fucking hell.

Satriano wants us to sell our souls to him to get Roselli out of the picture.

Watching from this distance, my hands itch to throttle the man for even suggesting it, but seeing Allie's increased distress the longer this drags out, knowing her bone-deep fear for her son and herself, I already know what she wants to say.

She would agree—*if* it were up to her.

But it isn't.

So, she waits until Savage's voice comes through the comm again. "Tell him if it removes Roselli and he promises that you and Benjamin will be safe, he has a deal..."

We just signed our souls over to the devil himself.

11

POPE

The click of the key twisting in the lock reverberates through the empty hallway, and I push in the door to my condo, hoping things might have improved since I left an hour ago.

Aunt Skye and Bishop's chatter carries through from the kitchen in the open loft space, and I let the door close behind me. They both pop their heads out to see who arrived, then duck back to whatever they were doing as soon as they know they don't have to be concerned.

I sure do, though.

My attention immediately goes to Allie, who stands at the bank of windows at the far side of the living room, staring out at the dark river and pitch-black night—completely unmoved since I left.

She doesn't turn to acknowledge me entering, and I can't even be sure she heard me, despite how everything seems to echo in here.

I lock the door—extra protection we probably don't need

here, given the fact that we own the building and I live in the penthouse that occupies the entire top floor. Gabe and Dad have so much extra security downstairs that I think it would be hard for even the police to get in here, but it makes everyone more comfortable, including me.

Well, maybe not everyone.

No amount of reassurances or security measures seem to have helped Allie over the last two weeks since we returned to New Orleans and she met with Satriano. Even being back with the rest of the family, seeing Jude, Angelina, and her parents, hasn't helped.

Storm has been here every day for hours, trying to get through to her, doing anything she can as her mother to attempt to make this better—but it seems to have failed.

I beeline for the kitchen and set the grocery bags on the counter, raising a brow. "How is she?"

Bishop leans against the counter near the sink, tossing a towel she apparently used to dry our dinner dishes behind her.

Skye bumps me with her hip, urging me out of the way, and starts unpacking the bags. "The same." She offers a slight shrug. "She's barely talking to anyone. She just stares out that window when she isn't with Benjamin..."

Dammit.

I wasn't gone *that* long—only an hour, tops, to pick up the few items we needed and the special treat for Allie that I pray will lift her spirits. But I had held on to a sliver of hope that Bishop and Skye could get her to open up and talk once I was out of the condo.

About *anything.*

Just as long as she's not locked inside her own head anymore.

Two fucking weeks like this since she sat down with that mobster...

Fourteen fucking days of Allie being practically catatonic.

It isn't like her to be so quiet, barely interacting with anyone who comes to my place to see her and the baby. Even Jude, who somehow fought his own demons to make it over here and stay with her one day, said she barely spoke to him, either, unless it was to answer a question about Benjamin.

I don't have to be a doctor to know how unhealthy it is. And she appears to be losing the battle despite every single one of the Hawkes doing their best to spend as much time with her as possible and get her to open up about what's been happening since she met with Satriano.

Which is basically fucking *nothing*.

Skye reaches into one of the bags and pulls out the massive tub of ice cream. She raises a brow and holds it up to me.

Given how healthy I normally eat, I can already anticipate her question. I hold up a finger. "Not for me." I motion toward the living room. "For Al. Her favorite—Brownie Batter."

Bishop smirks, and I glare at her.

"Hey, you have any better ideas?" I throw up my hands. "Because I sure as hell don't."

I've tried everything I can think of—short of calling one of the psychiatrists at the hospital to come meet with her. But if I even attempted that, she would only see it as an act of betrayal and push me away more.

I didn't know it *was* possible to put a bigger rift between us, but each day, I feel like she's slipping further away, the tide of uncertainty pulling her out into deeper water without a lifeboat or any signs of rescue.

And no matter *what* I do or say, she doesn't want to talk to me.

What happened at that house, the conversation we long ago should have had, hasn't changed anything. Not really. Maybe she better understands what I did that night and why, but that hurt is still there. The wound I made with my words and actions still stings her every day. She still harbors that anger toward me and what I did, and I still can't give her what she needs and deserves, even if she wants me to.

Which puts us back exactly where we were ten years ago.

Only now, she and Benjamin are living at my place until Satriano can fulfill his end of this deal, which is taking way too fucking long.

Bishop ignores my outburst and doesn't offer any suggestions—because we've literally tried *everything*. She moves out of the way so Skye can start putting things away in the refrigerator. "No more updates from Satriano then, huh?"

I sigh and rub my neck, trying to release some of the tension there. My stop at Savage and Dani's place on the way home ended up being a fruitless effort to get something positive and substantive to tell Allie before I came back. "Not according to Savage. Just like we already knew, they last spoke with him a few days ago, and he said Roselli was on the move again—that he was either tipped off or far smarter than he gave him credit for. He told Savage that he intends to uphold his end of the bargain and take care of it for us, no matter how long it takes."

Bishop rolls her eyes. "Yeah, what a *bargain*. All we had to do was make a deal with Satan himself."

Skye scowls and finishes with the groceries, folding the reusable grocery bags and stuffing them into their spot under my sink. "We didn't have much choice, did we?"

After living through what she did with Dom Abello when she was our age, all the pain and loss that befell the Hawkes due to that man and their connection to him, I can only imagine how hard this must be for her. Almost like history repeating itself, with the family being pulled into another mob war.

She offers me a tight smile and pats my arm. "Well, since you're home, that's where I'm going to head."

"Thank you so much for staying with her."

Knowing Skye was here should anything go wrong medically has made leaving the condo when I need to so much easier. Between her, Nora, and me, it makes it possible to keep one of us always here who can treat her if her symptoms worsen or the unthinkable happens.

Just in case.

Thankfully, Allie's condition has remained stable and even improved slightly over the last month since she gave birth, but she isn't completely out of the woods yet. There's still a chance her heart won't completely heal, and she may be at risk of issues for the rest of her life.

The continued uncertainty and fear don't help anything.

Which means we continue watching her and monitoring her, praying nothing sets off a progression of the disease.

"Of course." Skye hesitates for a moment, glancing toward the living room even though Allie seems completely oblivious to our conversation or that I'm even back. "Do you have any plans to go back to work at the hospital, given how long this is taking?"

One more thing weighing on my mind on top of Allie's medical condition and keeping her and Benjamin safe.

My six weeks of personal leave is almost up. Only two more weeks, and if I don't make a decision fast, there may not be a job for me to go back to, regardless of how close I am to my direct boss.

Nora can't operate the ER short-staffed for much longer. I probably wouldn't have even been *granted* the leave in the first place if she hadn't gone to bat for me with the head of the residency program. But she can only do so much. Ultimately, it will be what's best for UMC and not what's best for Allie, even though I continue to think that's me here monitoring her while she's forced to stay cooped up with the baby.

"I don't know yet." And it seems like an utterly impossible decision to make. "I have a couple weeks to decide..."

Bishop scowls at me. "Have you told Mom and Dad that?"

I shake my head. "They'll kill me if I don't go back."

"*I* might kill you if you don't go back."

She always was one of my biggest supporters, the one quizzing me before exams and helping me through so much of the complicated medical school shit that I might have stumbled on without her. It all comes so easily to her, as simple as a jiu jitsu flip of an opponent, firing off the perfect rifle shot, or decking Atlas in the ring.

At times, it still surprises me she isn't the one with the M.D. after her name, but I sure as hell know I wouldn't have gotten mine without her. So, she has every right to be angry at the thought that I might risk my career to stay here and monitor Allie when Skye is perfectly capable of doing it and we all know it.

"I have no intention of *never* going back. I'll figure it out..."

Eventually.

Hopefully.

Skye and Bishop both give me unconvinced looks.

Time to change the subject.

I raise a brow at Bishop. "Are you staying tonight?"

She shakes her head. "No. Dad is going to take the overnight shift down in the lobby and should be here soon. Gabe will be here in the morning, and I'll be back tomorrow afternoon." Her gaze darts to the living room, where Allie still stands near the windows. "Unless you need me to stay..."

After her meeting with Satriano, Allie needed a friend here—either Angelina, Astrid, or Bishop—spending the night in her room. It wasn't enough that I was right down the hall. With the vast chasm between us, she was never going to come to me for what she needed. And when I checked on whoever stayed over, I always found them curled around each other like the way they used to when they had slumber parties as kids, crashed out in the massive bed in my guest room with Benjamin sleeping peacefully nearby in his bassinet.

It would have been a cute throwback had I not known how deeply Allie hurt and craved that comfort I can't provide her— that she won't let me give her.

Bishop drums her nails on the counter. "What do you think? Should I ask her?"

I shake my head. "Leave her be. If she needs you, I'll call and you can come back."

She releases a long, slow breath, her worry furrowing her brow. "Okay." Stepping up, she gives me a look that tells me I *better* make that call if Allie even hints at wanting her here. Then she throws her arms around me and squeezes. "See you later, baby bro."

"Goodnight."

Skye does the same, patting me on the chest as she pulls away. "You'll get through to her eventually. You and Jude were always the only ones who could."

That might be reassuring if he hadn't tried—and failed—a hundred times over the last few weeks, too.

They move out of the kitchen toward the door.

Bishop waves at Allie's back. "Bye, Al, we're taking off."

"Bye, sweetheart." Skye pauses to examine her niece, tears misting in her eyes. "I'll see you soon."

The front door opens and closes, and one of them clicks the lock back into place, leaving me with Allie again—minus the buffer of having another Hawke around provides.

I give myself a minute before I go talk to her.

Maybe this isn't the best place for her.

It seemed logical to bring her here when we returned from Shreveport since Nora's at the hospital so much and wouldn't be at her place enough to really monitor her, and I already had my leave set. Add how easily defensible this condo is and it made sense.

But the longer we're here, the more I begin to question whether I should have let her go to her parents' house or Gabe and Skye's. If it would've been easier on her not to be around me so much. Maybe easier on everyone.

I run my hands over my head and push off the counter, slowly making my way toward where she stands in the living room, still staring out at the river.

City lights reflect off the water, sparkling and glinting in the rippling flow. Constantly moving and advancing, unlike our lives over the last month. The juxtaposition against the stagnation we've all experienced isn't lost on me.

Is that why she's been staring out at it for so long? Wishing she could move forward in life the way the water does?

Stopping next to her, I mirror her stance, trying to see what she does. "What are you looking at?"

Dumb fucking question.

But I need something to break the ice because, otherwise, Al will stand next to me for hours without uttering a word. Silence has become the fourth person living here, occupying all the empty space not taken up by Al, Benjamin, or me. Pervading the voids that should be filled with us actually discussing all the trauma she's endured and the demons chasing her.

Her slender shoulders rise and fall, but she doesn't look at me. "The water."

"Is it that interesting?"

Not to me, though I guess I'm spoiled seeing it every day since I've lived here. I've seen the water violent and rushing; I've seen it meandering, slow and lazy. But I've never stood staring at it for literally hours.

Allie tilts her head to the side. "I was wondering how cold it is this time of year."

"Probably not too bad. Why?"

She offers another half shrug. "I don't know, just something to think about, I guess."

Other than where she is and why.

That's what she means but doesn't or can't say.

She's spent the last month locked away from her life, hidden and in fear of a man she once trusted and gave herself to. It gets worse for her with each day that passes without a resolution. Cooped up here when she's always been one to spread her wings and fly.

Allie isn't the type of girl who can be caged, yet that's exactly what we've done to her.

It doesn't matter that she knows and understands *why*—it's breaking her spirit all the same.

"I got you brownie batter ice cream."

She finally turns her head to look at me, her blue eyes rimmed with red from the tears she tries to hide from us. "Thank you, but I'm not hungry."

I bite back the desire to tell her she needs to eat more, especially because she's breastfeeding and burning through calories like crazy. But every time I slip into doctor mode, she gets angrier with me. So, I redirect to the one topic she actually *will* talk about. "How's Benjamin?"

"Asleep for a while now."

"Good."

The uncomfortable silence lingers between us, like it has the last few weeks while we've waited to know her fate.

Finally, she issues a long sigh. "I'm going to take a shower and go to bed."

And pretend you haven't just stood here for hours, lost in your head.

"Okay. Goodnight." I almost leave it at that and let her walk away, but that damn invisible thread that keeps us tied together won't let me do that without reminding her why she's *here*. "You know where I'll be if you need anything."

Right down the hall from her.

So close, yet so far away from each other.

It feels like miles separate us—ones we will never be able to close.

She turns and slowly retreats down the hallway toward the bedrooms, and I step up to the glass and stare down at the water, trying to see whatever she did that was so fascinating.

It actually *is* quite beautiful if you stop and look at it, but my guess is, she wasn't really seeing it.

Her meeting with Satriano spooked her badly. Knowing what the family gave up to protect her. Knowing we made that deal because of what she sees as *her* huge mistake. It's been tearing her up inside, bit by bit. And the longer it takes for Satriano and us to find Roselli, the more it feels like it will never happen.

I understand her frustration because I feel it, too.

Battering my rib cage.

Clawing at the inside of my brain.

I want that fucker gone so Allie can return to a normal life again, so she can be the mother she wants to be outside of the prison we've had to keep her in.

"Shit."

No wonder she wants nothing to do with me.

I slam my palm against the glass, and it rattles violently, mirroring the way I've felt since she told me about Benjamin's father—so close to shattering.

Things could have been so different...

Those words keep playing in my head, a taunt from another life, one I might have had if I'd made different decisions.

Fuck hindsight.

Letting my head drop, I stretch my neck and close my eyes, willing my anger to recede before I make my way back to the bedroom. It won't do me any good to lie down if I'm amped up. I won't sleep—not that I do much anymore.

After a few minutes of slow, deliberate, deep breaths, I

finally push away from the window and head around the condo, flicking off all the lights, triple-checking the front lock, and throwing the two newly installed extra deadbolts into place.

My feet barely make a sound down the eerily quiet hallway, and I pause outside the guest room, listening for any sound from Allie or Benjamin, ready to take him if she needs some time to shower. But the soft sob that slips under the door isn't from the baby.

I've heard her cry so much over the last month that you'd think I'd be used to the sound, used to what it does to me, but it's worse than Benjamin crying.

He usually just needs a clean diaper or to be fed or snuggled. All very easy to accomplish successfully. For Allie, there's absolutely nothing I can do to ease her distress.

But it doesn't mean I won't keep trying.

I rap my knuckles on the door lightly and crack it. "Al?"

The darkness of the room—only broken by the light streaming out of the cracked bathroom door—envelops me. I listen for a moment, and another sob comes, along with the sound of rushing water.

Shit.

Leave her alone, Pope.

Let her be.

That would be the smart thing to do—to walk away and give her space—rather than further insert myself into a situation I might only make worse. But the anguished cry that comes next is so bone-deep that my heart physically aches for her and drags my feet forward toward the bathroom door instead of away from it.

I peek into the bassinet on the way, relieved to see Benjamin sleeping through his mother's meltdown.

Don't do it, Pope.

Don't go in there.

I know what will happen if I do. I know seeing Allie like that will break me and make me question everything, but I can't stand to hear her suffering anymore.

Pushing aside all the reasons not to, I nudge the door the rest of the way open and step into the jamb.

She stands under the spray, face lowered into her hands, her form obscured by the frosted glass and steam filling the bathroom. Tortured sobs slip from her throat and echo off the tile.

"Allie?"

ALESSANDRA

POPE'S VOICE comes to me through the dark cloud of anguish surrounding me. A beacon of light in the inky blackness of my total despair. A lifeline thrown into this moment of absolute weakness.

"Are you..." He takes a few steps into the bathroom, nudging the door closed behind him so we don't wake Benjamin—assuming I haven't already with the violent bawling that seems to have overtaken my ability to breathe.

"Pope...I...I can't...I can't..."

Any words I hope to say get swallowed by my next sob.

I try to fight it, to rally against the pain that never wants to let me go, that I manage to keep contained when the others are here, but it always engulfs me the moment I'm alone.

But it's a hopeless effort when I'm already drowning in it.

Pope pulls off his shirt.

Kicks off his shoes.

Tugs off his jeans.

The frosted glass door slides open, and he steps into the shower in his boxer briefs, all long, lean muscle and the promise of strong arms to hold me while I'm caught in the twisted metal of the mental train wreck I've been trying to avoid all day.

It takes him less than a second to close the door and pull me against him, cocooning me in his embrace, enveloping me in the safety he's always provided me.

My hands pinned against his stomach, I bury my face in his hard chest, releasing the full-blown blubbering, devolving into the hysterical mess I've been trying so hard not to let anyone see me become.

He rubs his palms over my bare back, the rushing water pouring over us, a waterfall washing my tears down the drain, but that does nothing to actually relieve any of my pain.

"Shh, Teeny, it's okay. Everything is going to be all right."

His whispered words against my ear somehow pull a little of the fear that's threatening to cripple me and lift it from my chest, even though I know they're placations, not anything he can promise.

No one can.

Not when I've created this clusterfuck that seems never-ending.

Sliding his fingers under my chin, he lifts it until my eyes meet his. "I know it feels like things are hopeless right now, but they *will* get better."

I shake my head. "You don't know that."

He nods, the corner of his lips curling slightly. "I do. Don't you remember what I told you about the future?"

It was such a long time ago. I couldn't have been older than eight, making Pope nine at the time. But the memory appears as vividly as if it happened only yesterday.

"You said you were going to invent a time machine so you could go to the future and get the cure for every incurable disease in the world..."

He grins at me. "I didn't get that...but I did see that things will work out exactly as they're supposed to. You are going to be happy, and you'll raise your beautiful son to be an incredible person like his mother."

A laugh bubbles up my throat. "You're so full of shit that your eyes are brown..."

Pope issues a low chuckle that vibrates through my chest and fingertips, flowing through my body to all the places I probably shouldn't let it. "You haven't said that to me in years."

"I know." It used to be one of my favorite jibes, but somewhere along the way, my anger at him overtook the easy rapport we always had. "There are a lot of things I haven't said, Pope, ones I should have. I'm sorry for—"

"You don't owe me an apology, Allie. I gave you every reason to hate me and think the worst."

Reaching up, I trail my fingers along his strong jaw and up across his lips. "Yes, you did. But I know you, Pope Clarke. I have always known who you were at your core, and I should have known none of that was really you. Believing you could be that person I imagined you to be was a massive error on my part. One I know I'll never be able to remedy."

Pope shudders, his toned body moving along mine, igniting that same fire deep within me that he always used to every time we touched. He lowers his head, his temple pressed to mine, and pulls me tightly to him, clinging to me like he needs me as much as I do him.

The longer he holds me close, the heavier his breathing gets, his hard chest rising and falling against my palms, brushing against my skin. My nipples harden, and I press my thighs together against the sudden throbbing between them.

Of all the men I've been with over the years, the ones I thought would be my protectors, my confidants, who would right all my wrongs and bring me that type of pure joy people always talk about when it comes to love, Pope Clarke is the only one who has ever actually tried.

And my body remembers it as much as my heart does.

"Pope..."

He shakes his head, his temple still pressed to mine, keeping me close but not budging an inch—almost like he's afraid of what might happen if he moves. "Don't, Allie. Please don't..."

The desperation in his voice matches that currently building inside me.

For release.

From this seemingly endless waiting game.

From the pressure coiling inside me that might snap me in half.

From the battle I'm always fighting between doing what's right and doing what everyone expects of me.

From this *need* to feel alive again when it seems like I've been walking around half dead since even before Benjamin was born, letting the harsh reality of my situation affect my ability to truly live.

From the attraction and feelings I've tried to pretend were long dead for this man when they've always been there, building under the surface of the hostility I wore as a shield against him.

I score my nails down his wet chest and over his rock-hard abs, his smooth, taut skin like butter under my fingertips. Pope issues a low groan, his hands slipping between us and wrapping around my wrists to stop me from going any lower.

His body trembles against mine, his grip tightening around me as his hard cock strains against his briefs and presses into my belly. He tilts his face toward mine until his lips are a mere hairsbreadth away. "We can't, Al. Even if it wasn't a terrible idea —which it absolutely, positively, undoubtedly is—you won't be medically cleared for another two to four weeks—"

He isn't wrong about it being a bad idea, knowing how much more it will complicate things, but in this moment, standing under the hot shower spray with him, I just don't give a damn about any of it.

"But I feel fine. I want—"

Pope feathers his lips over mine, silencing my plea. A fleeting glance. A tease. A little taste of what only Pope can give me. "I know what you want, Allie, and I can't give it to you…"

He isn't only talking about right now, and we both know it.

But with both of us straining to find control, it's a losing battle.

He kisses me again. Harder this time. Still slow. Almost sweetly. Reverently. Like he's trying to make up for the painful words he just said. And when he pulls his head back from mine, a fire blazes in his eyes, igniting them with flecks of gold and a heat I don't know if I've ever seen there before—except maybe the night our lives changed forever. "But that doesn't mean I can't give you what you need right now."

A shiver of anticipation rolls through me, and goosebumps break out over my skin despite still standing under the hot spray. Those same damn butterflies I felt in my stomach the first time Pope kissed me in high school flutter back full force, making me tremble against him like I'm that inexperienced virgin with a crush on the boy I shouldn't be with.

He kisses his way across my cheek. Down my neck. Over my shoulder to my collarbone. Then dips to my breast until he flicks his tongue across my nipple, sending a jolt straight to my already throbbing clit.

"Oh, fuck!"

My nails bite into his pecs, earning me a low rumble of pleasure from him before he repeats the move. I've never been particularly sensitive there, but it appears pregnancy and breastfeeding have changed my body in a lot of unexpected ways. He gives my other nipple the same treatment, his large hand cupping it as another wave of need rolls through me.

I cling to him, my hands slipping up over his broad shoulders to the back of his neck. Pope's sinful mouth works across my body, slowly traveling south, driving me insane with each hot breath, soft press, and delicious lick.

He stops on my lower stomach, giving it worshipful attention, and I dig my nails into his shoulder blades. Another low, rumbling groan of pleasure pulses against my belly, making my hips buck toward him. He catches them in his large hands, squeezing them and urging me to step backward until my shoulders and ass hit the cool tile wall.

Warm cognac eyes gaze up at me, the shower spraying against his back, water droplets clinging to his long eyelashes, looking like a man with one clear goal in mind—to absolutely destroy me in the best way possible.

It's what I need.

This.

Him.

A goddamn release from all this pain I can't seem to find anywhere else.

Pope slips his hands between my thighs, urging them open, exposing me completely to him. But I don't feel embarrassed like I thought I would after having Benjamin.

Not with him.

Not seeing the way he looks at me with carnal hunger and unadulterated desire.

He doesn't waste any time, dipping his head to run his tongue through my arousal. My hips buck against his face, and I grip his shoulders, trying to keep myself upright, when my legs start to shake immediately. He spreads me open, focusing on my clit, flicking and lapping and languidly dragging his tongue over it with pinpoint precision.

Jesus...

This isn't the boy I was with ten years ago.

This is a *man.*

One who is bound and determined to get me off and watch me come apart in his arms.

The pleasure shooting through me makes it impossible to think, to reason. All I can do is *feel*. His hands between my legs. His mouth on me. The scrape of his facial hair against my inner thighs. His expert tongue and lips devouring me...

He skillfully works me up, alternating between intense, hard sucks and light, almost teasing licks. Each time I come close, start to feel that heat building low in my belly, he backs off slightly, leaving me hanging.

My pussy clenches, wanting more, craving what I can't have right now, and I scratch my nails over his shoulders, releasing a frustrated groan. I grind myself against him, trying to force him into the right spot, desperate to get him to take me all the way.

"Shhh..." He grips my hips tightly, holding me in place and still. "I'll get you there, Teeny. It will be worth the wait. I promise."

There he goes again—making promises.

But this one is different.

I believe him now, trust in his words, have faith that he would never leave me dangling on the precipice like this.

Pope doesn't have it in him to torture me like that, even though every day for the past ten years has *felt* like torture, believing what I did about why he broke things off.

Believing the *lie*.

Tears burn my eyes and trickle from them, mixing with the spray from the showerhead as he greedily works me over, finally going full force and pushing me closer and closer to the edge.

That delicious low burn starts again, and so does something else—that warmth somewhere deep inside me only Pope has ever reached—and I finally come.

The orgasm doesn't slam into me the way others have.

It isn't fast and hard.

It doesn't knock me over.

It does so much more than that.

It's more like being *consumed*.

Like something is physically absorbing me and wrapping me in pleasure, holding me there, in the bright prism of light. Safe. Where nothing and no one can touch me except the man with the blissfully talented mouth dragging my orgasm on and on...

He releases a satisfied groan against my wet flesh, and a gasp falls from my mouth, echoing off the tile with the sounds of the rushing water. The ecstasy coursing through me seems to never end, rolling on and on, flooding my veins and filling my head with the perfect haze I haven't felt in far too long.

My orgasm starts to ebb, and I suck in a ragged breath, trying to fill my lungs as Pope starts driving me toward another.

"Pope...oh, God...I can't..."

"You can."

I close my eyes and drop my head back against the tile, grinding against him, thrashing in his hold—simultaneously wanting more and needing him to relent his hyperfocus on my over-sensitized flesh.

But he's right.

Another orgasm hits me fast, still trailing on the echo of the first. This one blindsides me with its quick and relentless buzzing energy that lights up each nerve of my body and makes me buck against the wall and Pope's mouth.

And he just keeps going.

Sucking my clit and flicking it relentlessly.

Kissing every inch of me and lapping up my release.

Ensuring I'll be wrung out and a boneless mess by the time I come back down again.

The moment it starts to release me from its clutches, I sag, my muscles no longer responding, my brain enveloped in a foggy, messy, post-orgasmic cloud.

Pope's strong arms wrap around me as he pushes to his full height, and I manage to get my eyes to open. He's watching me carefully, licking his lips like he doesn't want to miss a single drop of my release, and leans into me, pinning me against the wall, his semi-hard cock wedged between us.

I glance down, the evidence of his own orgasm spread across the waistband and top of his briefs. "Did you—"

Jerking my gaze to meet his, he raises one dark eyebrow and gives me a satisfied grin.

"I haven't come in my pants like that since the last time you let me do this to you."

Jesus.

"But...I didn't even touch you."

He presses his lips to the corner of mine softly. "You don't need to, Al. Having my face buried in your pussy and tasting you come was more than enough to make *me* come a thousand times over."

Dammit.

Why does he have to say things like that?

Tears pool in my eyes again, and the look in his instantly shifts to concern. He takes my face in one palm, brushing his thumb across my cheek. "What's wrong?"

I shake my head. "Nothing."

At least, nothing that can be changed.

His lips twitch. "Liar. Are you feeling better?"

Better?

Better than the complete sniveling, hysterical mass of panic I was when he found me—absolutely.

I needed this—the release, the embrace, the care and affection.

But now something worse has replaced all that turmoil I felt before Pope came into the shower—the realization that I'm still fully and madly in love with Pope Clarke and I can never really have him.

12

ALESSANDRA

Angelina cradles Benjamin in her arms, rocking him as she moves around Pope's living room. "And aren't you just the happiest and most handsome baby ever?"

He stares up at her with wide blue eyes, and she tilts him so I can see better.

"Did you see that?" She grins. "He smiled at me!"

I scoff and take a sip of my sparkling water before returning the glass to the end table next to the couch. "He did *not*. He's barely six weeks old."

Her brow furrows, and she props her free hand on her hip defiantly. "So? I'm telling you, he *smiled* at me. I'm *definitely* his favorite aunt."

Rolling my eyes, I turn on the couch to face the kitchen where Mom and Aunt Skye are working on dinner with Dad "supervising" since neither of them would ever let him try to help, given how badly it's gone in the past. "Mom, how old are babies when they start smiling? Like three months old, at least, right?"

Mom narrows her eyes on us, scoping out the situation. "Actually, you smiled right around Benjamin's age, maybe a little younger even."

"Ha!" Ang grins, pointing at Mom. "Did you hear that? You're just jealous he loves me so much that *I* got his first smile."

I wave a hand at her. "Yeah, whatever. Still don't believe you."

If anyone is going to get that first smile, it will either be me or Pope.

Choosing to ignore our little tiff, Mom sighs and returns to the kitchen while Ang wanders over to the couch and plops down next to me, still cooing and fawning over her nephew.

For the first time in what feels like years, a genuine smile pulls at my lips, watching her with him. After she helped with all of us growing up, it's no surprise how amazing she is with babies.

A real natural.

Nothing like me.

Even after reading all the "what to expect" type books during my pregnancy and to eat up some of my endless free time while being locked away for a month and a half, I still feel like I know exactly zip about actually being a mother. Most of the time, I'm just trying to get through the day, keeping him fed, changed, and entertained without melting down in front of him.

"You look good with him."

Ang lifts her head and smiles. "So do you. You're doing a really great job under what are clearly *not* ideal circumstances."

Benjamin grabs a strand of Ang's dark hair that dangles within his reach, his tiny fingers wrapping around it quickly and tugging.

"Ouch..." Ang carefully uncurls his fingers and slips one of hers in place of the hair to give him something to hold on to. "We don't want to pull on anyone's hair. That hurts. Ouch."

She would be such an incredible mother, and Jude would be an amazing dad. Each time he comes to see Benjamin, watching him hold him, the awe and love in his eyes always makes my heart clench, wanting that for my best friend so much.

"Have you and Jude talked about it?"

Ang glances at me, still shaking her hand, while Benjamin pulls her finger toward his mouth. "About what?"

"Having kids of your own?"

Her shoulders stiffen slightly, and she shifts on the couch like she's uncomfortable with the question. Having your best friend and older sister fall in love makes for some seriously awkward moments and conversations. If she were with anyone else, she probably wouldn't have any issue with discussing this with me. When we still lived together, before she and Jude finally admitted their feelings for each other, she used to talk about wanting to get married and have a family, but she hasn't said a word about it since I got pregnant.

She keeps looking down at Benjamin, laid out on her legs, and she grabs one of his toys off the cushion beside her and frees her hand so she can entertain him with that.

Maybe she won't answer.

Pretend I never asked...

Finally, she lifts her head and gives me a sad smile. "I don't think kids are really in the cards for Jude and me."

I sit up straighter, shifting closer to her. "What? Why not?"

My mind goes to the abuse Jude suffered during his childhood and all the potential physical issues that could cause when it comes to having children. But Jude has never kept anything from me, and if there were some medical issue preventing him from getting Ang pregnant, it's definitely something I don't think he would hold back. Especially not when Nora has bent over backward to get him a great therapist and anything else he needs.

Ang releases a little sigh and waves her free hand over herself. "I'm pushing forty, and Jude's agoraphobia is still a major issue for him. Even if I managed to get pregnant, I'd be at high risk for any number of things due to my age, and he likely wouldn't be able to leave to come to appointments with me. Once we had the baby, I don't know how he would deal with leaving the house to take him places. It just seems...undoable right now."

Undoable right now.

I know that feeling all too well.

Ever since that night Pope joined me in the shower weeks ago, I haven't been able to stop thinking about his words. *"I know what you want, Allie, and I can't give it to you..."*

He didn't just mean sex.

That much was abundantly clear.

And given the way he's avoided me since—putting as much space and as many people between us as possible when we're here together, I can tell he meant every word. Regardless of the two earth-shattering orgasms he gave me that I needed to help break me from that vicious cycle of panic and pain that night, there can't be anything else for us.

Not now.

Not ever.

Pope lives and breathes for his job, for the career he pushed himself so hard to achieve, and if it weren't for my stupid heart, he never would have left it temporarily to care for Benjamin and me. I would have gone somewhere with Saint or Gabe or Bishop, someone who could undoubtedly keep us safe if there weren't any medical concerns.

He'll go right back to it soon. The long hours and lack of free time. The exhaustion and rush of the ER he loves so much.

He's married to that job.

Which doesn't leave any room for him to open his life to a baby and me.

I may have to accept that Pope and I can't happen, but it doesn't have to be that way for Jude and Angelina. I don't believe that for a moment.

"You're only thirty-eight, Ang. Women have babies *well* into their forties these days. And Jude is doing better. God, so much better than where he was a year ago. Yes, it's going to take time —'baby steps' with him—but having a reason to leave that's as important as *you* pregnant with his child or taking his kid to the park will only give him more incentive to work harder at making his way through his issues."

I know Jude better than anyone, and he will *fight* to have that with her.

She gives me a sad smile, her eyes filling with tears. "I hope you're right, but please, don't say anything to him about this, okay? I don't want him to feel like I'm pressuring him to—"

"He would never think that."

Jude worships the ground Angelina walks on, and he knows her to her core and that she would never push him to do anything he isn't ready for. Just like I won't push Pope for something he clearly doesn't want.

He may still be attracted to me—the other night proved that —but I am not what he wants anymore.

Not what *he* needs.

I have to focus on Benjamin and our lives after we leave here, not on what I wish would happen. That will only be setting myself up for further disappointment and heartache.

"Hey, girls..." Dad appears from the kitchen and approaches the couch, resting his hands on the back. "Dinner is almost ready. Would either of you like anything else besides water to drink?"

Ang shakes her head, and Benjamin scrunches up his face

and lets out a little whimper. She lifts him to her chest and rocks him, rubbing his back gently.

"Not for me." I climb from the couch and hold out my hands to her, scooping up Benjamin. "But I think I need to feed him before we eat, or we'll never get through the meal."

Dad grins at me, his eyes growing misty.

Here come the waterworks.

I swear I've seen him cry more since his grandson was born than I did in the full twenty-five years of my life before that. Landon McCabe doesn't cry easily, but this situation seems to have everyone's emotions heightened.

The pure joy Benjamin has brought everyone.

The danger.

The unknown.

Dad rounds the couch and pulls me into a hug, dropping a kiss to the top of my head the way he always used to when I was a child. "I'm so proud of you, kiddo. You're handling all this far better than I ever could..." He pulls back and gives me a smile, his eyes filled with tears. "It won't be like this forever—"

"Landon?" Mom's voice carries through the high ceilings from the kitchen.

He winces slightly. "That's my cue to get back to the kitchen. I was just supposed to round up your drink orders and return promptly. Go do your mom thing and dinner will be waiting when you're done."

Ang pops off the couch and walks with him toward the kitchen, and I turn down the hallway leading back to the bedrooms.

Seventeen days...

I've been here, captive in Pope's condo, for over two damn weeks. So long that it almost, sort of, has started to feel less like a prison and more like home. It would almost feel like we were a family—if Pope wasn't avoiding me, there weren't armed guards at the desk in the front lobby, and I wasn't terrified to leave because Benjamin and I might get snatched off the street.

The longer this goes on, the harder it gets to see the light at the end of the dark tunnel.

The more impossible it becomes to believe there ever *will* be an end.

I reach the open door to the room I share with Benjamin, but my gaze stays farther down the hall to the cracked door to Pope's room. In all the time he's lived here, I never visited before he brought me here after we returned from the "cabin" in the woods.

It was part of my self-preservation tactic.

I stayed as far away from Pope and anything having to do with him as possible—always making excuses not to come when he first moved and had his housewarming or for one of his football viewing parties on a free Sunday when he didn't need to be at the hospital.

But now I'm drawn toward the door the same way I always was to him. With him gone at his meeting at the hospital with Nora and the head of the residency program, the opportunity to see his space, where he lays his head at night, is too strong a temptation to pass up.

Shifting Benjamin in my arms, I hum lightly, attempting to keep him from fussing for a few moments longer while I go to the one place I probably shouldn't.

I nudge the door the rest of the way open and step inside. His scent permeates the air—a combination of the soap he uses and something deeply masculine that always clings to him.

Memories of being pressed against him in the shower invade my mind, and I inhale deeply as I move toward his king-sized bed centered in the room—made, of course, unlike mine with the sheets strewn all over haphazardly since I left it this morning.

The black duvet spread out smoothly.

Tucked in under the pillows.

Like at some luxurious resort.

So neat and meticulous.

Just like the man who did it.

Pope has always been so in control—of his life, his future, his dreams. He knew his goals and made them happen. He had everything perfectly lined up and planned down to the most minute detail.

And his room proves he still lives his life that way.

Which is why I can't be a part of it once this is over.

The chaotic, hot mess I've become and the danger and turmoil I've brought into all the Hawke lives but especially his, are the polar opposite of what a man like Pope needs.

He deserves so much better.

Someone who matches his drive, shares the dreams he has for his future, and fits into the life he's already created.

My knees wobble slightly at that thought, and I lower myself onto his bed, scooting back until my shoulders hit the black leather headboard. I look down at Benjamin, now completely pissed it's taken this long to get to his dinner.

"Here we go, buddy."

I adjust my shirt and bra to give him access, and he latches on, snuggling tightly against me, the feel of him in my arms reminding me that I have always planned a future without Pope in it.

Ever since that day he broke me, I tried to imagine and find one that did not feature Dr. Clarke. And when I found out I was pregnant, it became a life with the baby and me, the two of us against the world.

But after the time we've spent together, what he told me about what happened all those years ago, and what went down —literally—in the shower the other night, I don't know how I can live without him.

I've let down my guard.

No, he broke it down.

With his gentle hands. Reassuring words. Soft touches.

The way he cares for me and for Benjamin...

Leaving this place, leaving him, to walk out into a completely uncertain future might just kill me if Dan doesn't to get to his son.

POPE

DR. NORTHRUP LEANS BACK in his chair, steepling his fingers in front of his mouth. As the head of the entire residency program at UMC, he has the ability to make or break people's careers—and cause young doctors to wither under his wise gaze. Which has been locked on me for the last ten minutes that I've sat across from him in his office.

If I hadn't grown up around the Hawkes, I might be more susceptible to it, but with the number of strong, intimidating men in the family, his attempt to unnerve me doesn't do anything.

I stand my ground—or sit, as it may be—waiting for him to ask the ultimate question. The reason I'm here today. Deciding my fate—at least where my job is concerned.

One I hope I still have.

Dr. Northrup finally lets his gaze drift next to me, where Aunt Nora sits in the other chair, facing his desk, here as the director of my specific specialty, emergency medicine, and my direct boss. But he's well aware of our personal connection, too.

Everyone in the hospital is.

And that makes her being a part of the decision-making when it comes to my future at UMC all the more complicated.

Which is why we've danced around the real topic with

pleasantries and chatted about the hurricane recovery instead of diving right in directly.

The longer we sit here, the more my mind drifts back to where I want to be—my place.

I used to long to come here, to work another shift, to feel that adrenaline rush that only saving lives can bring, but now I can't stop the anxiety that being away from Benjamin and Allie is bringing.

Let's get down to it already…

Northrup finally releases a sigh and leans forward, resting his forearms on his desk. "Dr. Clarke, you know how much we value you here. You've done amazing work in your time as a resident, and I'm not just saying that because Dr. Hawke's sitting here and she's the one who's essentially trained you."

She fights a grin, attempting to maintain her professional demeanor when the man she's worked with for almost thirty years knows her far too well.

"When you first came to me about taking this leave"—he offers a slight shrug—"I understood it. I've known the Hawkes for decades, and they have become an integral part of the hospital family. Hell, the family charity has donated several wings as we've expanded. And given your close connection to them and what happened to Miss McCabe during the hurricane, I empathized with why you felt you needed to take leave."

There's a "but" coming.

We all know it, and silence hangs between the three of us for a moment before he presses his lips together firmly, the friendly demeanor shifting slightly, like it's time to get down to business and what he really wants to say.

"But it's been six weeks, Dr. Clarke, and I can't hold your spot indefinitely. There's *no* question about your work ethic or the quality of it. If there were, I'm sure Dr. Hawke would have informed me, no matter how difficult it might make things at family dinners."

This time, I can't fight a grin.

He has a sense of humor, which is good. but it doesn't mean he's going to go easy on me about this or anything else.

"That leaves me in a difficult position because we do need you here. And while we've been able to rearrange the schedules and cover for you during your absence, if we go on any longer, I'm going to have to find a permanent replacement."

Permanent replacement.

Those words echo in my head and make me wince. Not just because it means potentially losing my dream job and the opportunity I've worked my entire life for and given up everything in order to achieve. But because that's exactly what Allie's been doing for all these years.

She's been searching for a permanent replacement, looking for someone to become what I once was for her. I didn't see it clearly for a long time, but the last few weeks have proven to me the explanation for her spiral after our breakup.

We may have been young and dumb, without any real idea of what the world was like outside of our small, secure bubble, but we experienced something *real*. If she's anything like me, she's compared every man she's ever met to me the same way I've constantly compared other women to her and found them lacking.

And her most recent choice has brought down this rain-storm of problems.

Nora turns to me. "Pope..." She reaches over and places her hand on top of mine, patting it gently. "I know how difficult this is for you because things are so up in the air still with Alessandra."

Of course, Dr. Northrup doesn't know about Roselli or the fact that he might be willing to hurt her to get to their baby, so Nora has to choose her words carefully.

"But"—she releases a heavy sigh—"I agree with Dr. Northrup that it's time for you to return to work. Allie's cardiomyopathy seems to have stabilized. She hasn't been having shortness of breath, water retention, or any of the other outward physical symptoms recently, and all her scans have remained unchanged, showing, if anything, slight improvement. The medications seem to be working. There's no reason to believe that she's going to have any additional episodes, and things are looking great for, hopefully, a full recovery. As much as it might hurt you to hear this, she doesn't need you there every day watching over her like, well, a hawk."

I groan at her play on words, and she chuckles.

"Come on, that was a good one."

It was, but I'll never admit it.

She slaps my hand playfully. "Skye is retired now. She doesn't have any obligations that will keep her from going over there when you're on shift. I can go on my days off because you know I would love to spend as much time as possible with that adorable baby."

Benjamin's face flashes in my head, drawing my lips up into a grin. The sweetest, most perfect, innocent baby who's so goddamn lucky to have so many people who love him and are willing to do anything to protect him and his mother.

Dr. Northrup nods. "Dr. Hawke is correct. I've spoken with Dr. Boggs about Alessandra's scans, and things do seem stable. And as you know, I worked with Skye many years ago in the ER when she was still a practicing nurse. She's quite skilled, should your friend need anything."

My "friend"...

Fuck.

Why does that word tighten my chest so much?

It feels like I'm the one with the heart problem the way it seems to stutter every time I see her, the way my breathing seems to get shallow, and my ribs feel like they're caving in anytime I think about something bad happening to her.

Dr. Northrup looks to Nora, clearing his throat. "I hate to do this to you, Pope, but I need a decision today."

A decision that's going to determine my entire future.

That could make or break my career.

It's what I *should* be concerned about, yet the idea of not being there with her after six weeks, of having to get up and come into the hospital to concentrate on patients while also ensuring that Allie is safe, makes my mouth go dry.

I swallow through it and try to gather my thoughts. "I appreciate the position I've put you in, Dr. Northrup." I look at the woman who has always been my mentor and staunchest supporter. "And Nora, it's your ER and you've been short-staffed because of me."

Her gaze softens, the affection that's always been there bleeding through even heavier now. "Don't ever apologize to me for that, Pope. If I could've taken off and done the same thing for her, I would have. But you were the far better choice."

She's right—the hospital would've fallen apart without her here, especially after the storm. Of anyone, Nora is the person in the best position to understand my situation. My love of this job. How hard I've worked. And my concern over Allie. Plus, she's brilliant...and she's telling me it's time to come back.

Yet acid churns in my stomach, climbing my throat and burning me in a way that screams it's wrong.

"I don't know if I'm comfortable leaving her just yet." I somehow manage to get the words out without my voice wavering. "I know you said you need a decision tonight, but can I have until Monday?"

Dr. Northrup shares a look with Nora, and she gives him a sharp nod.

"Dr. Hawke has agreed, but no later than Monday morning, Dr. Clarke."

"I understand."

He climbs to his feet, and Nora and I do the same. As he

rounds his desk to shake my hand, I think about the day I stood on the stage and accepted my diploma, graduating from medical school after busting my ass and putting all my focus into achieving that success.

This was everything I dreamed of.

It still is.

The job that keeps me on my toes and my heart racing, that gives me a reason to get up every morning and allows me to go to sleep every night exhausted but happy, knowing I've saved so many lives and helped so many people. And now, I'm seriously considering giving it all up to help one...and a half.

Dr. Northrup ushers Nora and me out of his office, and as the door clicks shut behind us, Nora swoops up beside me, looping her arm through mine, her head barely coming to my bicep.

She looks up at me. "Are you all right? Really?"

"Of course."

"I don't know, Pope." She shakes her head. "You're not acting like the kid I helped prep for his medical school exams. The one who always wanted to come with me on Take-Your-Son-to-Work Day instead of with your dad or your mom."

I chuckle. "That's because I was at their offices almost every day anyway."

She smirks and elbows me. "Don't downplay your love for this job, Pope."

A wise warning I should take to heart, but it's too hard to hold it there tightly when it's already filled with so many confusing things.

We make our way down the hallway and pause at the top of the steps that will lead down to the back door and out to the employee parking lot.

Nora motions in the opposite direction. "I'm going to stop in my office and take care of a few things before I head home. You're going back to your place?"

I nod and push open the stairwell door.

Her small hand tightens around my arm, stopping me. "Hey, Pope?" She glances up and down the hallway before she focuses back on me. "Anyone can see how much you care about Allie and Benjamin. And believe me, we all appreciate everything you've done for them. But there are plenty of people in this family who can protect them, who can watch over them, who can do exactly what you are doing for them...and they won't lose their jobs. Unless there's some other reason that's keeping you from leaving her?"

The question hangs in the air like a 15,000-pound elephant waiting to crush me under it.

And she already knows the answer as well as I do.

But I'll never say it, not when it can't actually mean anything.

"I'll take it under advisement, Nora. See you later."

I pull out of her loose hold and jog down the steps, desperate for the clean, fresh air outside after sitting in Northrup's stuffy office for so long.

Or maybe it's the weight of the decision sitting on my chest that makes it hard to breathe.

I push out the back exit and suck in a long, deep breath, the smell of oncoming rain filling my nose.

It doesn't help as much as I had hoped, and I cut across the parking lot toward my car. Just as I reach it, tires squeal behind me, and I turn to find two dark SUVs pulling up and blocking my car in my spot.

Shit.

They aren't ours.

The hair on the back of my neck stands on end, and the early evening seems to get unnaturally still and silent.

What I wouldn't give to have a gun on me right now, but we aren't allowed to carry them into the hospital, and it doesn't do me much good in my fucking glove compartment.

I retreat a step, moving toward the passenger side, where I might stand a chance of getting to my only weapon, but the back door of one of the SUVs flies open and someone steps out.

Fucking hell.

Daniele Satriano approaches—not the amiable, friendly, almost goofy musician who used to play at The Grind. This one —dressed in a tailored suit similar to the one his father used to wear, his hair slicked back, eyes ice cold—means business.

He stops a few feet from me, a sinister smile tilting his lips. "Dr. Clarke, I think it's time you and I had a little private chat."

13

POPE

Roselli's SUV pulls to a stop in front of a towering construction project in Mid-City. Though only partially completed, several floors appear illuminated, as if already in use or under active construction. Which is unlikely this time of day.

So, this is where he's been hiding out...

I gaze up at it as one of his goons steps from the passenger seat and opens my door. An invitation to get out of the vehicle I never wanted to enter in the first place. I look over at Daniele, who has sat silently in the back seat with me the entire drive.

His hard eyes remain locked on me, assessing and examining, but the fucker hasn't said a single word. Almost as if he thinks his silence will build up the tension enough to make me actually *fear* him.

Too bad he underestimates me and what it would take to get under my skin.

The big man urges me from the car with a firm hand on my forearm, and when I stand to my full height, he gives me a once-over, probably realizing that any benefit he typically has over most people is a bit lost when it comes to me.

Though he probably has fifty pounds of muscle on me, that just means he moves slower. This guy hasn't trained at the gym with a world-class boxer like Atlas—an advantage I mentally note in case it comes into play later.

I'm not above fighting my way out of this with my fists if I have to.

Dad and Bishop are going to kill me for allowing myself to get taken like this by someone like Roselli, but Dad also always trained us to pick our battles. And there was no way I was getting out of that one without bloodshed—likely mine.

At least by going voluntarily, I might have a chance of getting out of this alive and with some information that might help us all protect Alessandra and Benjamin.

I step away from the vehicle so he can push the door closed, and another door opens and closes behind me before Daniele joins me on the cracked pavement, adjusting his suit coat.

He spreads his arm wide in invitation, like we're about to go on a tour of the building rather than have a confrontation that will surely end with some sort of ultimatum. "Shall we?"

Do I have a fucking choice?

Roselli leads me in through massive glass doors and an unfinished lobby to a bank of elevators, then punches a button and leans against the wall between the two sets of doors.

His eyes roam over me, sizing me up.

I have six inches on him and a father who's lethal and trained me to be, too. Then again, so does he.

Cristiano Roselli didn't exactly have a reputation for the warm and fuzzies, and though things are still a bit unclear about how involved Daniele was in his father's business, he certainly plays the part now.

He screams *dangerous* and determined.

If he's willing to snatch one of the Hawkes like that, then

he's capable of anything. Using me as a hostage, perhaps, to negotiate the return of his son.

The elevator dings, and his musclemen nudge me in. Daniele follows, never taking his eyes off me, and we ride up in awkward silence for six floors until it dings and allows us out into another unfinished section.

A huge wooden desk sits in the middle of the vast open space, a leather chair behind it, and a single folding chair facing the monstrosity—ostensibly for me.

He motions toward the flimsy piece of metal, then walks around and takes his seat, like the man firmly expects me to take mine.

Instead, I stand and cross my arms defiantly.

He raises a brow at me, then smirks. "Well, Dr. Pope Clarke. I guess we've never formally met, even though I believe you were at The Grind at least half a dozen times I've played there."

I don't bother acknowledging his observation.

We aren't here to discuss our shared past or to exchange pleasantries.

His jaw hardens, his hands fisting on the armrests. "And you're the man who's shacking up with my girl and my baby."

I barely fight back the low growl starting in my chest.

My girl...

My baby...

He may have been the sperm donor, but this piece of shit will never be Benjamin's father. Not in any way that matters. And Alessandra was definitely never his girl.

His eyebrows pop up. "Nothing to say? Well, then, let me do the talking." He releases an exaggerated sigh. "As you can imagine, things have been a bit *tense* since my father's death. Add onto it me finding out that Alessandra was pregnant and had been keeping it from me." He raises his hands almost innocently. "I may have gotten a little overzealous in trying to discuss the situation with her."

This time, the growl slips out. "Overzealous? Is that what you call dragging a pregnant woman with you out into a fucking hurricane and trying to hold her hostage when all she was trying to do was get to her family and safety?"

He slams his fist against the desk, the sound reverberating off all the exposed metal beams in the vast space. "Her *family*? My son is *my* fucking family, the only family I have left, and I've never even *met* him because of you and that bitch."

I physically fight the desire to lunge across the desk and wring his fucking neck until he takes his last breath, staring into my eyes. Given the fact that I'm unarmed and the two men standing on either side of me certainly are, I wouldn't get very far. "What is it you want, Dan?"

He chuckles. "Isn't that obvious? I want my son!"

"That won't happen."

His dark brows rise. "You think I don't know the Hawkes have been looking for me? You think I don't know you sent Satriano after me like a fucking bloodhound?" He grins. "He may have caught my scent a time or two over the last few weeks, but my father taught me well." Leaning back, Roselli rests his head on his hands. "I wasn't always interested in this business. I reaped the benefits of it—the money, the easy living—and I enjoyed my life as it was. Playing guitar, picking up girls, having a good time with pretty little things like Allie."

I grit my teeth.

He continues on, kicking his feet up onto the desk, showing off his Italian loafers. "The violence never appealed to me, though." His eyes harden. "Until I saw my father shot full of holes outside one of the *Hawke* businesses." He sneers. "I knew the minute it happened that the Hawkes were behind it."

I snort, shaking my head. "You know that isn't true. Stone, Isaac, and Kennedy were all shot, too."

"Collateral damage."

"You're a fucking idiot if you believe that we had anything to do with it. That was one hundred percent Satriano's doing."

Roselli shrugs. "Supposedly. But whether it was him or your family, I learned a lot that day. Mainly, that I actually *did* have an interest in my father's business...and that Allie was carrying my child." He shakes his head slowly. "She did a good job of dodging me. I'll give her that. Though, I never understood why, since we ended things on mutually agreeable terms and always had such a great time together. But she figured it out, didn't she, who I was? She heard me on the phone that day..."

I nod. "She did."

And she did the right thing trying to keep her baby from your clutches.

He drums his fingers on the table. "Smart girl. Smarter than I gave her credit for, frankly. I guess I shouldn't have underestimated her. She's a Hawke, after all. Which leads me to the current predicament..." He climbs to his feet. "You have stolen my son, and I want him back."

"I haven't stolen anything. He isn't yours to take from Allie."

"Like hell, he isn't." He smashes his fists into the desk again. "My blood flows through his veins—Roselli blood—and I have no intention of letting him go."

I square my shoulders, puffing out my chest. "Neither do we."

He smirks. "So, an impasse, then."

The bastard walks around the desk, then leans against it, only two feet in front of me. Without even moving, I could extend my arm and suffocate the bastard. It would be worth it if I thought I could do it before the bullets killed me.

I glance to either side, but the two men are watching me carefully.

Daniele chuckles. "I'd reconsider whatever you're thinking, Pope."

Shit.

I scan all around me for any weapon that might actually get me out of here alive. Because from the sounds of it, Dan intends to use me as bait to lure Allie out with Benjamin. But there are any number of people he could have grabbed, members of the family who might be considered higher-value targets. "Why'd you bring me here, Roselli?"

"Because I know Allie's at your place. After weeks of following everyone in your family, it was pretty fucking obvious why everyone kept going there." He nods. "Smart. A good, defensible location. We would never get in."

"Exactly."

His already dark eyes go almost black. "But not everywhere else your family members go is so defensible."

An icy chill floods my veins.

"Like the gym where Atlas trains and that your sister is so fond of frequenting to spar with him. In fact, I saw her there just this morning with that pretty little blonde...Astrid, isn't it? Atlas's twin sister?"

I swallow thickly.

"One day"—he raises a finger and taps it against his cheek —"I even saw Isaac with his fiancée and their two little ones." He shakes his head, tsking. "What a shame it would be if any of them suffered injury while at a location where the Hawkes love to spend time."

Fisting my hands at my sides, I snarl at him. "Fuck you, Dan."

"No, Pope, fuck you." He points at me. "You and the Hawkes are so high and mighty, thinking you're better than everyone else, thinking that you're the ones in control of this city, but not anymore."

"You don't control anything. From what I hear, half of your father's men want you dead."

He snorts. "That's a situation that's being remedied. And soon, this situation with my son will be, too."

"You're sorely mistaken if you think we would ever hand him over."

"You will." He grins. "When the Hawkes start dropping one by one, hell, maybe even two by two, there are so many of you to choose from, so many places of weakness in your security."

It isn't even a veiled threat; it's a direct one.

Either we give him Benjamin or all of us will have a target on our backs.

"The only reason I'm not killing you now or using you as bait is that I need the Hawkes to call off Satriano. He may be coming for me anyway, but I need time to consolidate my father's crew before I take him on. He doesn't need to be involved in our personal family matters. You'll relay the message to Allie and the rest of the Hawkes—I want my son back and for Satriano to stay out of our business. And the longer you take to accomplish that task, the more bodies are going to fall."

ALESSANDRA

I PACE the length of Pope's living room for the millionth time, glancing down at Benjamin to ensure he's still sound asleep against my chest. His tiny mouth parted slightly, hands curled between us, he's content and completely oblivious to what a bundle of nerves I am or all the tension in the room. "Where are they?"

It doesn't matter how many times I ask tonight; the answer never changes.

Gabe casually takes a sip of his beer, then sets the bottle on the end table next to where he sits on the couch. "They should be here soon."

I scowl at him, annoyed at another brushoff. "That's what

you said an hour ago. Wasn't Pope just going to the hospital for his meeting today? Why did he stop to talk to Savage about anything?"

His green eyes unwavering, Gabe drums his fingers on the side of the beer bottle. He isn't looking away, yet somehow not giving me anything, either.

But I can tell he's hiding something and holding back.

After he got the call from Savage earlier and told me Pope was going to be home "later," I instantly knew something was very wrong.

Gabe may be a master of many things, but I've learned to read him over the years, and when he gets like this—stoic and short with words—it usually means something has gone FUBAR.

Which typically pisses him the fuck off.

I can see the anger coiled inside his strong body. He's doing his best to conceal it, to appear unaffected, but that only shoots my anxiety straight through to orbit.

It takes a *lot* to unnerve Gabe, and I am about to lose my mind if he doesn't give me a *real* answer.

Pope, where are you?

This is the longest we've been apart since we left for that house in the woods near Shreveport. The minutes drag on to feel like hours, the hours like days.

Maybe the hospital told him he has to come back, or he's fired.

Maybe he's pissed at me for being the reason he had to take the leave in the first place.

Maybe he's—

The lock on the condo door clicks, stopping me from driving myself mad, thinking of all the potential reasons he hasn't come home.

I freeze and wait, holding my breath as the door swings open. Pope walks in and holds it for Savage, who follows closely behind, his salt-and-pepper hair in unusual disarray, like he's been running his hands through it.

Oh, shit...

When Gabe said Pope stopped to talk to Savage, I had assumed it had something to do with his leave and going back to work, perhaps to discuss a change in the plans about who will stay here with me. But Gabe and Savage exchange a hard look immediately, and my stomach drops.

It's something worse...

Pope closes the door and turns to face the room, looking completely exhausted, bags under his eyes, his forehead creased, and an unease wafting off him that he usually doesn't carry.

I hurry over to him. "What's wrong? What happened? Where have you been?"

He doesn't say anything. He just reaches out a long arm and wraps it around me, tugging me up against him. With his strong body pressed to mine and Benjamin cradled between us, he leans down and presses a kiss to the top of my head and then to the baby's. "I'm sorry I wasn't back sooner. I..."

"Jesus, what the hell happened?"

Pope hasn't touched me in weeks, not since the shower "incident," yet the moment he walked through the door, his first move was to embrace me. Whatever happened has him seriously rattled.

Savage and Gabe, too, given the way they look at each other.

"Come on, let's talk." Pope ushers me toward the living room and sits me on the couch, scooping Benjamin from my arms and holding him close like he needs to feel the baby against him to relay whatever he's about to tell me.

Dread slithers down my spine as Savage joins us, settling himself next to Gabe. Each wears a mask of worry and distrust, the kind of thing you never want to see on the faces of men like them.

Savage inclines his head toward Pope. "You need to fill her in."

Whatever it is, he went to Savage about it first.

Fuck.

I didn't think things could possibly get worse, but judging by Pope's clenched jaw and the way he clings to Benjamin, they're about to.

His dark eyes that usually hold so much concern and affection turn to me, filled with a hatred I don't know if I've ever seen there—one I didn't think such a kind, thoughtful man like Pope could ever have. "I had the meeting at the hospital."

I nod slowly. "Yeah, did it go that badly?"

He shakes his head, continuing to pace and rock Benjamin. "No. I need to make a decision by Monday..." His Adam's apple bobs with a thick swallow. "But when I was leaving the hospital, an unexpected visitor intercepted me."

Oh, God.

Bile immediately climbs my throat. "Who?"

The apology in his gaze tells me the answer before he even says it. "Dan."

"No! Oh, my God." I climb from the couch and rush over to him, scanning him from head to toe, looking for any signs of injury I might have missed when he first walked in. As aggressive as he got with me when I was heavily pregnant, I can only imagine what he would be willing to do to Pope now. "Are you okay? Did he hurt you?"

He rests his hand free hand against my back, tugging me to him again, offering me the same comfort he does Benjamin. "No, I'm fine, physically. He took me somewhere that appeared to be a temporary base of operations. My guess is they're long gone from there, though."

Savage nods, his jaw locked with his frustration. "I sent Saint and Bishop over there the moment you called after he returned you to your car, and it was already cleared out. Even the desk you mentioned was gone."

"Motherfucker..." Pope squeezes his eyes closed, trying to control his anger while he's holding us. "They must be moving a lot, keeping to locations where nobody will look for them."

Gabe leans forward, resting his elbows on his knees. "If they're constantly on the move, it would explain why we haven't been able to find him and why Satriano has failed, too."

An icy chill rolls through me, making me shudder, and I bury my face against Pope's chest next to Benjamin, not bothering to fight the tears as they come. "What did he say?"

Pope's body stiffens, and I already know what his answer's going to be. His hand rubs up and down my back, trying to soothe me before he's even told me what that asshole said. "He said he wants Benjamin, and if we don't turn him over, he's going to start taking out the Hawkes, one by one."

My breath catches. "Oh, my God..." I drag my head off Pope, shaking it as I peer back at Gabe and Savage. "What do we do? We can't-I can't—"

"No." Pope grabs my chin, forcing me to look at him. "We're *not* giving Benjamin to him, Teeny."

Tears blur his face, and I swipe them away, looking at Benjamin snuggled close between us. "Then what the hell are we going to do? He's going to come after us to get to him—"

Gabe cuts me off with a low growl. "He's not going to do anything. He's not going to hurt any of us. I don't care if we have to put the whole family into fucking lockdown until we find him. We'll do it."

Savage nods. "Please, Al, I don't want you to panic. You know we'll always protect you and Benjamin. It's *never* going to be an option to turn him over. We are going to meet with Saint and Bishop in the morning and put together a plan of action. Everyone else is going to stay on alert at all times with extra security. No one goes anywhere or does anything, period, until this is resolved."

Now the whole family has to go through what I have the last six weeks...

Because of me.

They're all going to be stuck, not living their lives, because of something I did, because of *my* mistake.

Because I *trusted* Dan and let him get close to me.

That isn't fair.

It isn't right.

This is *my* mess.

I should be the one who cleans it up.

"Maybe I should go and meet with him..."

Pope jerks slightly, his eyes hard. "No, absolutely not—"

"But maybe if I talk to him, maybe if I, I don't know, make him see reason, maybe we can—"

His large hand comes to my chin again, stopping my babbling and forcing me to look at him. "No. That type of man can't see reason. And you know what he would do to Benjamin if he got his hands on him because his own father did it to him. Look at how easily he's been two people, how quickly he flipped from the guy you spent time with to someone willing to threaten *that*." He says the words like they burn coming out of his mouth, pain lacing each one. "You're not going *anywhere* near him."

Tears stream down my face, and I fight the sob crawling up my throat. "But I have to protect everybody..."

"Leave that to us, Al."

I turn toward Gabe and see the determination in his eyes.

He pushes up from the couch and comes over, then pulls me from Pope's hold and wraps his strong arms around me.

I sag against him and let the sobs come. "Is this ever going to be over? Are we ever going to be safe?"

The man who has always protected the Hawkes, who has

always been one of us even before he and Skye got together, kisses the top of my head. "We will, kiddo. I promise. This isn't our first showdown with an asshole like Roselli, but it will hopefully be the last." He pulls back and looks down at me. "Until then, you just sit tight here with Pope." His gaze darts to Pope and the way he holds Benjamin, and he gives him a little knowing smirk. "He'll keep you and Benjamin safe. I'll be downstairs all night, and then we'll meet in the morning. Just try not to worry too much, kid."

I scoff, wiping at my tears that won't stop falling. "Yeah, right. Easy for you to say."

He shakes his head. "It isn't easy for me to say, Al. Believe me. No matter how many times I've been in life-and-death situations over the years, it never gets easier. But you have to trust that we know what we're doing, that we're going to get him, and we're going to keep everyone safe."

Savage nods his agreement. "We've all lasted this long, and Roselli isn't the first one to threaten us. He might not be the last, either, but Hawkes will always rise, right?"

I nod as the family "motto" echoes in my head. "Always rise."

Those words have been repeated so many times over the years, when things got rough, when things went wrong, when any of us were struggling, and I want so badly to believe them.

When Savage says them, I almost do.

I walk over and throw my arms around him.

He kisses my cheek and squeezes me. "It'll be all right, Al."

Believe him.

I want to.

So badly.

I want to believe all them when they say that, but after six weeks and no progress, it feels like I'm stuck in some sort of purgatory—suffering for my sins.

And now the rest of the family will pay for them, too.

Gabe approaches as Savage releases me, and he gives me another quick hug before they make their way to the door. Pope follows them, and the three of them have a very quick, very quiet conversation before they leave. Then Pope closes the door and throws the locks into place.

One.

Two.

Three.

Tonight, it doesn't seem like enough protection.

He turns back to face me. His body is so tense that it looks like he might snap in half, trying to contain the turmoil raging inside him. "Why would you even suggest going to meet with him, trying to reason with that sorry excuse for a human being?"

"Oh, God..." I sink to my knees on the living room floor and bury my face in my hands. "I don't know. I just...can't stand the thought of anyone else getting hurt because of my mistake—"

Another violent sob wracks my body, and I double over, trying to breathe but only able to cry harder as the world crumbles around me.

Pope squats next to me, still cradling Benjamin easily in his big hands. "I know, Teeny. But do you really think Gabe, my dad, and Bishop are going to let *anything* happen to anyone we care about?"

Of course not.

That's the first thought that pops into my head.

Those three have secured the family and all our holdings, protected everything and everyone from all types of threats, so logically, I know they'll use their entire arsenal to ensure the Hawkes aren't touched.

But the last year has proven that even the best-laid plans can sometimes fail.

The explosion at The Grind...

The shooting...

No one can possibly plan for every scenario. There are too many variables. Too many places we're vulnerable. Too many of us to hurt just to make a point, but Daniele seems determined to.

My gaze drifts to Benjamin, and I rest my hand on his back over Pope's. "What are we going to do?"

"Anything necessary to protect him, Al. *Anything*."

14

ALESSANDRA

Somehow, despite how awkward and intense things have been between us, it isn't even a question, isn't anything that needs any discussion...

Pope helps me from the floor and walks me past the door to my room, straight back to his. He urges me onto his bed and hands off Benjamin before he disappears and returns, rolling Benjamin's bassinet.

He *knows* what I need tonight.

That I would never survive sleeping in that bed alone.

He tugs off his shirt and stands at the edge of his bed, watching me feed Benjamin, his eyes shimmering with unshed tears I don't think I'm supposed to see, that he believes are hidden by the darkness of the room.

But even if I couldn't see them, I would still *feel* them.

Feel *this*.

The shift.

Something changed.

Maybe it did back at that house we hid in. Maybe it did

weeks ago in that shower and he just didn't want to admit it. But he hasn't looked at me like this, with his guard down and his full heart showing so openly, not in ten damn years.

Whatever reasons he built up in his head for shutting me out no longer taint his gaze.

All I see there is the same pure affection I always did when we were younger—before things got so complicated and fucked the hell up. Before he walled off his heart so he could walk away and I opened mine to anyone else who showed me even the tiniest amount of attention and warmth he always did.

Tears fill my eyes.

And my heart shatters for the millionth time because of this man.

For how I've misjudged him for so long and all the horrible things I've said to him because of it.

For how I acted, the situations I've put myself in, the heartache I allowed others to bring on me, all because I thought he didn't want me.

For the hurt I let eat away at me, thinking I wasn't enough for him.

All the years I've spent moving through life listless, without a purpose, without anything to anchor me, without the kind of security I need, seem so wasted now that I know the truth.

You really fucked things up, Al.

I have to look away from him, break the intensity of his gaze. If I keep staring at Pope, he's going to see right through me and realize I am not who he thinks I am.

It's been so long since I've been that girl he fell in love with that I don't even remember who she is or what she looked like anymore.

That girl had hope for the future. Dreams. A wild spirit that longed for adventure and the all-consuming love I thought I had with Pope. I haven't felt any of those things since, and I don't know if I'll ever be able to again.

The bed dips, and he settles next to me, peeking down at Benjamin, who has finally fallen asleep against my exposed breast. Pope reaches out and brushes his fingertips over Benjamin's soft hair, looking at him with so much affection that it only makes my tears fall faster. "Want me to put him down?"

I nod and use the moment Pope needs to take Benjamin and settle him into the bassinet in the corner of the room to attempt to swipe away the evidence of my blubbering before he returns and sees it.

But I fail miserably.

Which only makes me cry more.

It seems to be my constant state these days—unhinged.

My mind refuses to shut down—the thousand horrific possible ways Dan could hurt any of us run through it, mixing with the complex Pope situation that just seems to get more complicated the longer this goes on.

We've already suffered so much, almost lost Uncle Stone and could have easily lost Isaac and Kennedy if those bullets had been a few inches in a different direction. And now, we have my ex making these kinds of threats when he has the resources to actually carry them out. Not to mention, Satriano trying to step in so we'll owe him favors that will surely come back to bite us.

All of it blends into a volatile concoction that threatens to combust.

And it's all my fault.

I slide down on the bed, turning away from Pope and resting my head on the pillow that smells like him. I've given up on trying to control my tears. At this point, it's a fruitless effort.

They soak the silk pillowcase, and I cling to it, needing *something* to hold on to when I can't turn to the man I want to. I can't let him see me like this—again.

Pope settles in behind me, reaching out to tug me back against his chest, tucking me into his hard, warm body until I'm completely surrounded by him and his strength. "You know how much I hate to see you cry."

I sniffle. "And I hate you seeing what a fucking mess I am..."

"Oh, Al..." He squeezes me tightly, nuzzling the back of my neck. "You're not a mess. None of this is your fault, and you have every reason to be upset about what's happening." His fingers thread through mine over my stomach. "I don't know *anyone* who could go through what you have the last few months and not feel like your entire world has been thrown upside down."

His reassurance should cut through the heavy, dark cloud of regret choking me right now, but his continued patience and support only make it worse.

"I understand if you hate me for what—"

He flips me onto my back so fast that I barely have time to register it's happening. Hands braced on either side of my head, he stares down at me, his eyes flashing in the dim light from the moon streaming in the window. "I could *never* hate you, Allie. *Ever.*" He leans closer, locking his gaze with mine, holding it even when I turn my head and try to look away. "It's physically impossible."

"But"—I fight against my body trembling, trying to find a way to explain this cyclone of emotions overwhelming me right now—"I ruined your life. Two months ago, you were happy and working at your dream job. Now you might lose it, and we've invaded your home and completely fucked up your *life*..."

"Jesus, Al..." He shakes his head, sucking in a long, slow breath. "You don't get it, do you?"

"Get what?"

He lifts his hand to my cheek, feathering his fingers across it, wiping away my tears. "You *are* my life..."

Four words from him broke me once, and now four simple ones have brought me back to life again after feeling like I've been a zombie, barely moving through each day, breathing, my heart beating, but not really living for anything until Benjamin was born. But so much has happened. So many harsh things said and lines drawn in the sand.

"But I was so awful to you..."

I pushed him away, time and time again, when he tried to smooth things over, attempted to get back to some semblance of friendship, or even just be civil with me. I fought against him every time and refused to give him an opening to explain anything to me that might have ended our animosity.

Less than two months ago, I wanted *nothing* to do with Pope Clarke, and I made sure he knew it. I twisted that knife into his back, left the wounds, and poured salt into them each chance I got.

The corner of his lips twitches, though I don't know how any of this is even remotely amusing. "You were, but you had every right to be, given what I made you think. I was more upset by what you did to yourself than what you did to me."

"What I did to myself?"

He presses his lips to my forehead, letting them linger there, like he's considering how to answer and can't do it while looking at me. When he pulls his head back, he offers me a sad smile. "I had to watch you abandon all those things you said you wanted to do with your life, the reason I ended things between us in the first place. You just kind of...gave up. You always said you didn't want to work for Hawke Enterprises, yet you went to work with Angelina right after you graduated and kind of drifted through life and shitty relationships with guys I wanted to deck every time I saw you with them."

This hint of jealousy makes me smile despite still feeling like utter shit for what went down between us. Because I was in the same boat. Every girl I saw him with, anyone he ever mentioned, even in passing, to me or anyone else in the family, was automatically the enemy. "But I should have known that whole time, Pope. I should have known you would never be *that* guy I thought you were..."

He shakes his head, gliding his thumb over my bottom lip. "You did. Deep down, you knew what we had was real. That's why you were always so terrified to be near me. For the same reason I kept my distance—because I knew this would happen as soon as I allowed you in again."

"You knew what would happen?"

Pope lowers his forehead to mine again, closing his eyes and releasing a sigh. "That I wouldn't be able to let you go a second time. You hold my fucking heart, Alessandra McCabe. You've had it since you were sixteen, and no matter how hard you tried to shut me out and pretend what we shared wasn't real, I never took it back. It's always been yours. Now it's yours and Benjamin's."

His confession hits me like one of Atlas' blows in the ring, knocking the wind right from my lungs and sending me reeling.

All the reasons we kept our relationship a secret back then.

Our age difference.

The backlash we expected from the family.

Thinking no one would understand us being together considering how we had grown up.

It all seems so stupid now—especially because of how easily everyone accepted Jude and Angelina's relationship.

But it isn't just the two of us anymore.

Everything has grown harder to navigate.

Pope's career has always been so important to him—that dream he gave up everything to achieve. It *is* his life. And I've put him in the worst position possible.

He might lose all he's worked for because of me.

"But your job..."

The reason he ended things back then and continued to

push me away the last few weeks is still there. Nothing has changed in that regard.

It's *more* than a job to him; it's a calling.

And he's really damn good at it.

That hospital needs him.

The patients do.

He drags his head back, locking his gaze with mine again. "Is immensely important to me. I love being a doctor, and I have no intention of quitting. I've just realized that I'm selfish and need it *and* you, too." His lips feather over mine. "I work shitty, long hours. I come home cranky and exhausted. I am a real bear to deal with when I wake up in the morning, especially before I've had two or three cups of coffee...but I still need you here when I stumble in after a shift and climb into bed. I need you beside me when I open my eyes at four am to get ready to leave and want to stay under the covers. I don't know how I would go back to the way things were after what we've been through since the hurricane..."

Tears that have fallen from pain for so long suddenly shift into something I barely recognize—hope.

I reach up and press my palm to his cheek. "Me, either."

So much has happened.

Things I set in motion without knowing the consequences.

Leaping before I look.

No wonder everyone calls me reckless.

Pope broke my heart, and I threw the pieces at anyone who made the mangled remains beat faster for even a split second. I was supposed to go to college, travel the world, find my own purpose in life outside of those in the confines of Hawke Enterprises. Only instead of releasing me to go do that like he thought he was doing, I let my anger and despair at losing Pope destroy my dreams.

And I refuse to let him risk *his* dream, *his* career, because I've made horrible decisions.

"You have to go back to work Monday."

He freezes, his gaze hardening. "What?"

Even without being at that meeting he had at work, I already know he has seriously been considering extending his leave, and that would put his job in jeopardy. "I won't be able to forgive myself if you lose your job because of me. I'm okay. There are a lot of people who will stay here with me and keep me safe while you're working."

His jaw hardens, and he shakes his head. "I don't like being away from you and Benjamin, even for a few hours..."

"Me, either." I *really, really* don't, but this isn't about what I need. It's what I need to do for him. "You have to go. Promise you will." I can see his hesitation, the internal debate still raging in his mind. "For me." I press my lips to his, resting my hands against his bare chest. "Please, Pope."

Pope is too selfless ever to do anything for himself, so making it for me might be the only way to get him back in the white jacket where he belongs.

A resigned sigh falls from his lips, and he buries his face against my neck. "You don't play fair."

"Is that a yes?"

He kisses the sensitive skin behind my ear, then rolls beside me, bringing me with him so we lie facing each other. "It's a yes, as long as you promise to listen to whoever stays with you at all times and keep yourself and Benjamin safe."

It's an easy ask, and I nod and kiss him softly, the weight of everything that happened today and all the tears finally starting to droop my lids. Pope pulls me against him, resting my cheek over his heart—that familiar, steady rhythm, the lullaby that finally lets me drift off to sleep.

POPE

I close the door behind Landon and Storm, the last ones to leave, because they wanted to spend every second possible with Benjamin and Alessandra. Can't blame them, considering the threat to them both. If Allie hadn't finally taken the baby to the bedroom to feed him and put him down—hopefully for the night—I might not have even been able to get them to leave after the "family meeting" at all.

Thank God.

As much as I love the Hawke clan, having them *all* in my place, pretty much *all* day, trying to come up with a way to ensure *everyone* stays protected during this tumultuous time, turned out to be a lot more difficult than I imagined it would be.

Mostly because I woke this morning to Allie's ass pressed against my hard cock and her scent invading every breath I took. As she moved around the condo all day, interacting with the other Hawkes, playing with Benjamin, and snuggling against Jude on the couch with him when I should have been worrying about the *plan*, all I could think was how badly I wanted everyone to leave so I could have her all to myself again. So I could touch her, kiss her, and experience all the things I haven't *let* myself feel in so long.

But I couldn't do that in front of them.

Not yet.

Not when things are so...difficult to navigate.

I throw all the locks into place, then wander down the hallway, looking for Allie. She slips out of the guestroom, easing the door closed as I reach it and bringing her finger to her lips.

"Shh...I just got him down."

Tugging her close, I press my lips to hers for a much-needed kiss.

Slow and sweet.

At least, that was my original plan.

It goes on far longer than I had intended, and when she finally pulls back, her cheeks are flushed.

I drag my thumb over her pretty mouth. "I've wanted to do that all day."

She grins, resting her palms flat against my chest. "Me, too."

"Well, your parents left, so we're finally alone." My eyes drift to the door she just closed. "Or as alone as we're going to get."

Her soft laughter lights me up from the inside out—the sound so foreign after weeks of her walking around in a melancholy haze. "He should be down for a while..." She pulls her bottom lip between her teeth and slowly releases it. "And I set up the baby monitor in your room so we'll hear him if he wakes up."

I raise a brow. "You're okay with him in the other room tonight?"

"He's been sleeping four or five-hour stretches at night the last week or so without waking up to feed, and his pediatrician said to let him...so..."

She pulls that bottom lip between her teeth again, staring up at me with so much hope and longing in her gaze.

Fucking hell.

This woman was always my biggest weakness, and tonight is no exception.

I press my lips to hers again, gliding my tongue along the seam. Wanting to taste her. *Needing* it. She clings to me, her fingers tightening in my T-shirt, tugging me even closer as she opens to me fully.

My cock hardens against her belly, and she rocks her hips along it, urging me on, guiding the kiss even deeper, more frantically.

I jerk my head back from hers, my labored breaths matching hers. "Did Dr. Brennan clear you when she came to see you?"

It wasn't something I was going to ask when things were

still so tense and awkward between us, but if she wants what I do, I need to ensure she's prepared for it and that I won't hurt her.

Allie pulls me back to her, kissing me firmly, her hand sliding down between us to grope my erection. "Yes..."

Shit.

That single word is like the starting bell, and her touch, the first right hook in a fight I know I'll lose.

My fingertips play along the bottom hem of her dress, barely touching her soft skin until she's squirming against me. "There's nothing I wouldn't do for you and Benjamin, Al. All you have to do is ask..."

Fear briefly flashes in her gaze, but I don't think it has anything to do with me—more that she's worried it won't be the same or that she'll disappoint me somehow after all this time.

I understand it because the feeling is mutual.

Her soft blue eyes plead with me before she ever opens her mouth. "Make love to me, Pope."

It isn't the first time she's said those words to me, and she knows exactly what she is doing by repeating them now.

Taking us both back to that fateful night.

The moment we gave ourselves to each other fully.

That we connected in a way I never have with anyone else since her.

And like ten years ago, I'll be sealing my fate by giving her what she wants—what we both want tonight.

I knew back then what being with her would mean; I was just too young and stupid to see the potential fallout of our decision. I didn't anticipate the way she would try to throw away all her plans for me or that I would have the strength to let her go to try to save her dreams.

Now, we share one.

A second chance at what we both lost that day.

I drop my shoulder and lift her into my arms easily, crushing my mouth to hers as I carry her to my bedroom, only releasing her to lay her out across my mattress.

She watches me with hooded eyes, her pink lips parted, and her chest rising and falling rapidly. I strip off my shirt and jeans, then slowly lower my briefs, letting my hard cock spring free. Her eyes follow it, and the dress she's wearing lets me witness her press her thighs together.

Alessandra McCabe...in my bed and aching for me already.

I never thought this would happen, that we could *ever* get back to this, but it feels more right than anything else has in my life for a long fucking time.

And I do not want to fuck it up.

She holds out a hand to me, and I slide my palm against hers, letting her pull me down onto the bed across her body. Everywhere our skin touches, little electric sparks seem to sizzle across it, and she rolls her hips, grinding herself against my cock in a way that makes me clench my jaw to withstand the bolts of sheer pleasure.

I reach between us and grasp her dress, shifting back so she can lift her ass off the bed. With deliberate care, I allow my fingertips to graze along her skin as I tug the fabric up. Over her thighs, across her belly and breasts, until I finally pull it over her head.

By the time I toss it onto the floor, she's quivering before me, only her panties and bra separating us now.

Christ...she is beautiful.

My mouth waters to taste every inch of her, to explore her body and worship it until she's so wrung out that she collapses in a satisfied heap next to me. I slide my fingers under the waistband of her underwear, then drag them down her legs and off, watching her for any signs of trepidation. "You're sure you're ready for this, Al?"

It's only been six weeks since she gave birth. Her body may

have healed, but it's been one emotional trauma after another since then. If she's not ready, I would never push her, no matter how badly I may want this.

She raises herself up onto her elbows and slides one hand around the back of my neck to drag me down on top of her again. Her mouth finds mine, and the kiss she gives me makes my head spin—deep and dizzying—like she's trying to consume my soul as well as steal my breath.

When she finally pulls away, the intensity of the heat burning across her Caribbean-blue gaze sears straight into my heart. "Yes, Pope. Please…"

I kiss her again, tugging on her bra to free her breasts, the fabric pushing them up high, her nipples taut and pink. The way she responded in the shower told me how sensitive they are now, and I waste no time flicking my tongue across each peak.

She twitches under me, her hips rolling up.

Seeking.

Wanting.

But I am going to ensure she's good and ready before we go there, have her primed and dripping, begging for me before I slide into her wet heat.

I roll onto my back, pulling her with me, and urge her up to straddle my hips. Her dark hair falls around her as she looks down at me, and she shifts her position so her pussy aligns perfectly over my cock.

It twitches against her, eager for something that has to wait.

I squeeze her thighs. "Come up here and sit on my face."

Her eyes widen slightly, her pink lips parting. "Um…I don't think I can—"

A blush spreads across her chest and cheeks. I've known Alessandra McCabe her entire life, and I don't think I've seen her embarrassed before, but fuck if it isn't the most adorable thing ever.

I wrap my arm around her back and tug her closer, until I'm a mere hairsbreadth from kissing her—so she can *feel* my words and know I mean them. "I want your pussy on my face. I want you to come down my throat and taste every drop. Will you do that for me, Teeny?"

She stares at me for a moment, the tears beginning to form in her eyes. "Yes."

"Good girl." I lightly slap the outside of her thigh, then lie down, settling myself in the perfect position to let her straddle my face. "Grab the headboard."

Allie slides forward, reaching for the tufted leather before she drapes her knees over my shoulders, putting her exactly where I want her.

Her pussy glistens with her arousal already, only inches from my eager mouth, and I don't waste any time burying my face between her legs.

"Oh, God..." Allie's head falls back, her eyes closed, mouth open, and she bucks forward. "Fuck..."

I grasp her ass, holding her in place, the ideal angle to plunge my tongue into her. She groans, rocking her hips forward, grinding down, and making me grin against her wet flesh. "Fuck, you taste so good..."

Each glide and flick of my tongue, every squeeze of her thighs around my head, the way she releases all her inhibitions and rides my face, taking all her pleasure, makes my cock ache to be inside her. But not until she comes for me, until she's begging me to fill her the way she needs.

It doesn't take long for her whole body to tremble.

Her hands tighten on the headboard, the leather creaking.

I slip two fingers inside her, curling them into that spot I know will drive her wild and dragging them slowly along her inner wall.

"Oh, fuck, Pope! Right there!"

I probe, pump, and glide my fingers inside her while I suck

her clit hard, pulling her orgasm from her, demanding it, needing it as much as she does.

She comes on an almost silent gasp, her body spasming, hips bucking. I hold her steady, keep her where I need her to prolong her release, to taste every single drop as her pleasure rolls on. Her pussy clenches around my fingers, rippling along them, her body wanting something else there. Something *more*.

And I'll give it to her.

Let her take control.

Take what she needs from me.

She finally sags forward against the headboard, and I pull my fingers from inside her to help her slide down my body, her soaked pussy rubbing over my length, getting it wet and ready. A little satisfied moan slips from her lips, and she cants her hips so the head of my cock barely slips inside her.

I grit my teeth at the searing heat and teasing contact, and she lifts her head from my shoulder to kiss me. Her tongue probes the way mine just did inside her, almost like she wants to taste herself on me. It glides along mine, a playful battle, almost a game to her.

A dangerous one.

Each moment she drags this on, my cock aches more, desperate to be buried inside her—and she knows it.

She grins against my lips, then presses against my chest, pushing herself up across my hips. Her hooded gaze locked with mine, Allie grips my cock and lifts herself up, aligning it perfectly before she sinks down on me, taking me agonizingly slow.

Good God...

My breath rushes from my lungs. Each inch she engulfs in her slick heat draws me further away from the worries of this world and to one where the only thing that exists is this perfect moment.

Her nails bite into my chest, and she takes me even deeper,

giving herself time to adjust until I'm all the way to the hilt. Her moan fills the room, and my eyes drift closed. A groan rips from my chest, the only sound I'm capable of, and she squeezes around me in answer.

I open my eyes to meet hers. "Jesus, Allie, you feel like fucking Heaven."

We waited so long for this moment—ten *years* of dancing around each other and repressing our feelings until they were ready to destroy us both. And it took all *this* to finally bring us back together.

She lifts her hips, gliding along my cock before she sinks down again, faster this time. Harder. More determined. Grinding her clit against my pelvis when she reaches the base.

Fuck yeah.

Pleasure surges through my blood, and I grip her hips, helping her move and find her rhythm, still letting her control and take. A mewl tumbles from her lips, and she rocks against me, engulfing me on each downward thrust and riding me like a woman without any worries or fears.

And that's all I ever wanted for her.

To be content.

To be *happy.*

I am finally in this moment, seeing her like this, feeling her body move so fluidly with mine, bringing me back to the most perfect moment of my life. One I never thought I'd repeat. One we both needed.

If I could, I would let this go on forever, but her rhythm becomes erratic. Her heavy breathing and the pink flush spreading across her chest signal she's close again.

"Allie, look at me."

Her eyes flutter open as she sinks down on me again, rolling her hips to seek the friction she needs. I slip a hand between us, my thumb finding her engorged clit, and she bucks on me, her cunt tightening enough to draw my balls up tight and threaten to make me explode.

I roll my thumb as she continues to move.

Frantic.

Desperate.

Until I pinch and twist between my fingers and she detonates.

Head back, dark hair flowing behind her, her mouth falls open, a gasp fills the room, and her movements falter. I grasp her hips, digging my heels into the mattress to thrust up into her, to draw out her orgasm and find my own.

Her pussy ripples along my length as she comes, dragging it from deep inside me on a satisfied groan before she collapses on top of me.

Both of us spent and sated.

And happy.

For as long as it lasts.

15

ALESSANDRA

The rhythmic clicking of the knife against the cutting board as I chop the vegetables for the salad fills the kitchen, mixing with the soft swooshing sound of the baby swing set up at the edge of the living room that's keeping Benjamin fast asleep while Bishop and I work on preparing dinner.

It's almost peaceful.

Something I haven't felt in almost two months. And I probably *shouldn't*, given the fact that Roselli laid down his threat only a few days ago. But if that hadn't happened, I might not have spent the last two nights in Pope's bed and in his arms. I likely never would have known what it feels like to be loved again, to feel one hundred percent whole.

With him and Benjamin, I do.

And, at least momentarily, I can forget the fact that all of us have to look over our shoulders and stay locked away while the family sets the plan to end all this into action.

If it works, it will be over soon.

For most of my pregnancy, and certainly since Benjamin was born, I couldn't see a future that didn't involve some horrible form of despair. I was either going to have to leave New Orleans and everyone I love behind to protect Benjamin, or I was going to fail and lose him to a madman.

Now, I can actually start looking to the future.

A beautiful one.

With Pope in it.

"Why do you have that look on your face?"

I still the knife and jerk my head up to meet Bishop's inquisitive gaze.

Leaning against the counter, her knife in hand, Bishop narrows her eyes on me, momentarily distracted from slicing the plantains she intends to fry for dessert to question me.

"What *look*?"

She waves the knife around a little and points it at me. "You look glow-y and kind of smug."

Shit.

"I do *not*."

Those smoky-whiskey eyes of hers evaluate me, scanning from the top of my head all the way down to my bare feet. I squirm under her assessment, knowing she will use all the skills at her disposal that serve her so well in the ring— weighing up opponents—and working with Saint to analyze threats to seek out whatever it is she *thinks* she sees.

A slow grin spreads across her lips, and she nods. "Yeah, you *do*. Does this have anything to do with my brother?"

Shit, shit, shit, shit, shit.

I refocus on the carrots, celery, peppers, and other veggies laid out in front of me and keep slicing them, perhaps a little *too* aggressively. "I'm not sure what you mean..."

Bishop doesn't respond, and the seconds slowly tick by with me hacking at the vegetables like they're the ones prying instead of her.

I finally cast a quick peek at her.

As soon as my eyes meet hers, she smirks and sets her knife on her cutting board, crossing her arms over her chest, which only emphasizes the muscles she uses to take down men twice her size. "Yes, you *do*. Do you think we're all blind? Did you really believe no one would notice the looks you're giving each other or the little touches you steal when you think no one's looking?" She points a finger at me. "I know you about as well as I know my brother, so you can't hide it from *me*. Why don't you admit there's something going on between you two?"

There go my relaxed vibes...

We knew we wouldn't be able to keep it from anyone for long, but Pope and I are nowhere near ready to go public with *this* when we've only just gotten together. But Bishop isn't the type I can brush off with some half-answer.

She will needle me until I spill.

Stilling my hand, I turn to face her. "Bishop, I appreciate you coming to babysit me today..."

She scowls at my choice of words, but really, it's what it is.

We're safer here than we could be anywhere else in this city, and I can't leave again. I wouldn't survive being away from the family, and Pope is back at work, so he couldn't take off with me even if we wanted to. That means someone has to be here with us, someone who is far better with a weapon and quick thinking in life-or-death situations—like the woman trying to use her badass superpowers on me right now to get me to spill my guts.

"I love you more than you could know, especially for agreeing to make your dad's jerk chicken for dinner because you know it's my favorite, but it doesn't give you the right to give me the third degree."

Her eyes widen. "You're right, it doesn't. You boning my brother does."

"Whoa." I hold up my hands. "Who said anything about *boning*?"

Bishop laughs, shaking her head. "I knew it." She walks over and pulls me into a hug, squeezing me tightly and lifting me easily off the floor before she sets me back on my feet. "About fucking time that you two sorted out your shit."

She doesn't seem at all surprised by any of this, which means she either knows about our past or we've been *really* bad at keeping the current situation private over the last few days.

"Did you know? I mean, about before?"

We never thought anyone did, and since no one has directly ever questioned me about it, I assumed we were right in that belief. But maybe we were wrong. Jude mentioned that he suspected something happened with Pope that I had kept from him, and if *he* noticed, others probably did, too.

Bishop waves a dismissive hand, pulls open the oven, takes out the cast iron pan, and lifts the lid to check on the chicken and rice. The spicy scent fills the kitchen and makes my mouth water and stomach grumble.

I peek at the baby swing and ensure Benjamin is still sound asleep, like he would somehow know what we're talking about.

She pushes the pan back in and turns to face me. "I mean, no, I didn't *know*. But you two were always together. And I remember one time I came home early from something, and you and Pope were 'studying' at the kitchen table, but you jerked away from each other like I had walked in and caught you doing something you shouldn't have." Grinning, she taps her temple. "I had my suspicions. But then you two started acting like you hated each other, and he went off to college and wasn't around us or the house that much when he was living in the dorm." She shrugs. "I figured you guys had an argument about something, maybe. But I was right, wasn't I? Something *happened* between you guys."

I turn my back on her and busy myself throwing the

peppers, lettuce, tomato, cucumber, carrots, and everything else into the big bowl. "It was complicated back then, for obvious reasons."

"What obvious reasons?"

I peek at her out of the corner of my eye. "Seriously?"

She snorts. "God, you and your sister, both. Jesus Christ. She and Jude waited so fucking long to act on their feelings for each other because they felt like we'd all be judgy about it. And you and Pope are the same fucking way."

"It's more than that." I sigh and lean back against the counter, wondering how much to tell her. The basics. Nothing more. "Pope broke up with me. He kind of broke my heart."

She raises her brows. "Do I need to kick his ass? Because you know I will, gladly."

I shake my head. "No. He thought he was doing what was right. I've forgiven him for it, but it took a lot of really, really bad things to happen for us to get to where we are. And I don't want to ruin it by having the whole family find out and have them breathing down our necks or pressuring us to—"

She holds up her hands. "Say no more. Consider me a vault. I will not reveal your secret, but I'm telling you, girl, I'm not the only one who noticed. And if you go around looking like my brother did something to you that I absolutely do *not* want to think about my brother doing, everyone else is going to know exactly what's going on."

I scowl at her. "I do not look like Pope has been doing anything to me..."

Her laughter fills the kitchen. "Believe me, I don't want to say that about my baby bro, but you have *the look*."

"Jesus..." I drop my face into my hands, once again annoyed with how damn close we all are in this family sometimes. Groaning, I pull my head back up. "Don't ever say anything like that again."

She grins and returns to cutting the plantains. "The chicken is almost done. Twenty minutes, tops."

"Good, I'm starving, and Pope should be back in about an hour. I'm sure he'll be hungry after such a long day."

His first shift at the hospital since his leave.

Eight whole hours without him.

An entire day here with Benjamin and my mom this morning, with Gabe in the lobby, and now Bishop here and Saint downstairs.

No one is alone, ever.

No one goes anywhere without an armed driver. Savage, Saint, and Gabe's trusted people who have been on their team for years.

We're being as safe as we can be, watching for anything suspicious, always vigilant while we move the chess pieces necessary to trap Dan in a checkmate situation. But still, having Pope away all day has made me antsy.

The smell of smoke hits my nose, and I scrunch it up. "Hey, Bishop, I think you're burning something. Maybe the bottom of your rice?"

She sniffs the air, and her eyes widen as she lunges for the oven, yanks it open, and pulls off the pot cover. Her brow furrows. "No, everything looks fine." She takes a whiff of it. "It's *not* this."

What the hell?

We both turn toward the living room and step into it, sniffing, trying to determine the source of the smell. I pull Benjamin from the swing, tucking him into my arms while we search the apartment.

The scent grows strong—sharp and ominous.

"Where's that coming from?"

Bishop shakes her head, eyes scanning the living room, and then moves down the hallway to check the bedrooms with me hot on her heels.

Each one seems fine.

But the acrid smell permeates the air, growing stronger and thicker.

I cough, my lungs starting to burn with each inhalation. "What the hell, Bishop?"

We rush back out to the living room, and Bishop freezes and points to the corner of the room, where dark smoke billows from the metal vent. "There, the air duct. It must be coming from somewhere else in the building."

"Shit."

The fire alarm starts whooping, immediately waking Benjamin, who screams and starts flailing in my arms.

I hold him steady, pressing my hand over one ear and his other to my chest to try to dampen the sound. "What do we do?"

We aren't supposed to leave this condo—for any reason. We've had doctors making house calls for weeks, checking up on Benjamin and me here, where it's safe.

But our safe haven has become a damn death trap.

Bishop's hard gaze meets mine, and she pulls the gun from her hip holster. "We have to get the hell out of here."

POPE

As much as I thought I'd be distracted my first day back at work by constantly thinking and worrying about Allie and Benjamin, a slew of multi-car accidents, a shooting in the Seventh Ward, and several idiots who decided to show off for their friends on their motorcycles near Bourbon Street have kept me busy for most of my shift.

I stop at the nurses' station and glance up at the clock,

doing a double take at where the hands are on the face. "Hey, Luna?"

She looks up from her computer screen. "Yes, Dr. Clarke?"

Pointing at the clock, I raise a brow. "Is that right?"

Her eyes follow, and she smiles. "I know, right? Crazy days make the time fly, don't they?"

I lean against the counter, rubbing my lower back. After being away from the ER for six weeks, my body is reminding me why I usually work out so much—so being on my feet for these long shifts doesn't destroy it. "Yeah. I can't believe I'm almost out of here."

She twirls her pen and offers me a sympathetic look. "How was your first day back? A little chaotic, huh?"

I run my hand over my head and shake it. "No. Good, actually. It feels great to be back."

"I know Dr. Hawke is happy to have you here."

And I'm sure if Nora were on shift right now, she'd be telling me the same thing. But even though it's her day off, she's clearly been talking with the nurses about my return.

I smirk at her. "Let me guess. She's been telling all of you to kiss my ass so I won't ever take leave again?"

Luna laughs and pushes out of her chair to grab something off the printer behind her. "Not in so many words, but I *will* tell you that I do think she hopes you never miss another day."

"I don't plan on it."

Because Allie was right—I needed to come back.

That constant worry is still there in the back of my head, pushing its way forward any free moment I get, but once a new patient comes in and I'm in my element, doing what I've been trained to, it feels...right.

As right as it did having Allie in my bed and my arms all weekend.

Maybe I really can have both.

While I cannot *wait* to get back, with Dad and Bishop there, keeping them safe, I can focus on what I need to here and on them once I get home. Which won't be too long now.

The radio squawks to life, indicating incoming patients, and Zoe grabs it and starts jotting down information as I examine new lab reports that just came through on my tablet.

My eyes scan the results, and the pleasant thoughts I had vanish, as they always do when I have to deliver bad news. "Shit. Hey, Luna?"

She looks up. "What do you need, Doc?"

"Mr. Mendelson in bed six. His blood work came back." I hate this part of the job—when it stops being something simple that I can fix and I have to hand them off to someone else to do some very hard work that might not save their lives. "We're going to have to refer him to oncology."

Her face scrunches into a wince, and she nods. "I'll call up to them."

Zoe replaces the radio and turns to me, handing me the sheet. "We have twenty incoming."

"*Twenty?*"

She nods. "I know. They're sending a bunch to Tulane and Ochsner, as well. There was a fire in a condo building. A lot of smoke inhalation, a few burns."

"What are they sending us?"

"The bad ones."

Of course.

As the only level-one trauma center in New Orleans, we are always sent the people who need our help the most, which means I am not going home anytime soon—regardless of when my shift is *supposed* to end.

Which means I should text Bishop, Dad, and Allie to let them know I'll be late.

I pull out my cell as I hustle toward the ambulance bay, but the sharp whine of the incoming siren sounds outside the sliding glass doors in front of me—the first patient already arriving.

The text will have to wait.

Luna joins me, and we step into the ambulance bay as the first bus pulls in. The other doctors on shift and their nurses assemble with us, prepared to immediately assess the incoming injured.

This is the part of the job I love, why I'm here instead of the only other place I'd want to be, and I ready myself for anything that might come tonight.

The back doors of the first ambulance to arrive open, and the paramedics wheel out a victim of the fire. One of them starts rattling off his stats from a tablet as we move into the ER.

"A 56-year-old male. Suffering smoke inhalation and burns on hands and one arm. Heart rate of 92 beats per min, blood pressure of 140/98, respiratory rate of 26 breaths/min, pulse ox was 93 before giving 100% oxygen..."

My brain automatically starts cataloging the information, and I begin rattling off orders to the nurses. "Get an IV going and order a chest X-ray. We'll debride his burns once he's stabilized."

Wheeling his bed into place, the nurses set to work on my orders, and I do my visual inspection of the patient—Douglas Landry, according to the information gathered by EMS.

"Mr. Landry?" I lean over so he can see me above him. "Can you hear me?"

The man with the graying hair nods slightly.

"Good. I'm Dr. Clarke. We're going to take good care of you. Can you tell me if you're having any chest pain or trouble breathing?"

His hazy green eyes seem to focus on me better, and his brow furrows. "Pope?"

My back stiffens.

How the hell does he know my name?

I peel the oxygen mask from his face for a moment to get a better look at the patient, and my breath catches.

Holy shit.

"Doug?"

The older gentleman who always says "hello" to me in the mornings when I'm coming in from my runs and he's on his way out to walk his dog nods and coughs.

I immediately replace the mask as a wave of panic engulfs me. "Luna! What was the address of the fire?"

She quickly grabs the tablet and glances at the screen, scrolling to find the information provided by EMS. "Somewhere near the river...I want to say, oh, here it is...600 Port of New Orleans Place."

A hand circles my wrist, and I turn back to Doug, my heart in my throat.

He pulls his mask down with a shaking hand that bears evidence of the fire—second-degree burns across the back and moving up his arm. "I hope the girls got...out...okay."

I lean over him again. "Doug, what happened? Did you see my sister and Allie?"

It's been weeks since I've seen him—since I've mostly stayed cooped up in the condo with Allie and Benjamin and haven't been taking my morning runs.

How would he even know who was there unless he saw them?

Another rough coughing fit shakes his body, and he winces. I help him replace the mask so he can get the oxygen he so desperately needs, but we need to get some pain meds into him quickly.

"Doug, are you allergic to any pain medications?"

He shakes his head and tries to remove the mask again, but I place my hand on his good wrist, stopping him. "Leave it." As badly as I need information, I need to get him treated first. "Luna, get him ten milligrams of morphine to start. See if that helps."

She nods and enters the order on the tablet, then hands it to me before she dashes off to take care of the rest of my requests.

His coughing seems to have subsided for the moment, and his oxygen levels are slowly rising, which is a good sign, but it doesn't mean he's out of the woods yet. "Doug, can you tell me what happened? Where was the fire?"

"Ground floor initially...moved up...a lot of smoke."

The ground floor.

Well below the penthouse, but with a fire like that, smoke is often the biggest danger to those on higher floors.

"Did you see my sister or the brunette, Allie? She would have had a baby with her."

He closes his eyes for a moment, wheezing and struggling to take a breath after the effort of speaking. I place a hand on his uninjured arm as Luna returns with the meds and gets them into his IV.

"This will help with the pain, Mr. Landry."

And it will likely also make it impossible for him to talk or tell me anything coherent.

Dr. Fontenot passes by, her focus on her tablet, scrolling through a file on her way toward the nurses' station.

I catch up with her, pulling out my phone as we walk. "Can you monitor my patient, Mr. Landry, in bed eight for a minute?"

She narrows her eyes on me, immediately sensing something is off. "What's wrong?"

"This fire...it was my building. My sister and...some other people were at my place."

"Oh, my God." She scans the ER, the patients flooding in and already starting to fill the beds. "Are they here?"

I shake my head. "I haven't seen them. I need to make a call."

"Of course. Go ahead. I'll check your patient."

Before she even finishes speaking, I step away from the fray and call Bishop, pacing along the wall near the elevators as it rings.

"Come on. Come on. Pick up."

Instead, her voicemail greeting hits my ears, and I end the call.

"Fuck."

I dial Dad.

"*Pick up!*"

A passing nurse I don't know gives me a strange look at my outburst, but I ignore her as I continue to pace.

His phone rings and rings but eventually goes to voicemail, and my gut twists.

I scan the ER and every single incoming patient, looking for the girls. Other familiar faces occupy beds—my neighbors, the people I've seen around the building over the years—but there isn't any sign of Bishop, Allie, or Dad.

"Shit."

Where the hell are you?

My body trembling, I dial Gabe, the only other person who might actually know what the fuck is going on.

He answers on the second ring. "They're okay."

A wave of relief floods my chest, and I lean back against the wall and drop my head to it. "Thank fuck. What the hell happened? Where are they?"

"They smelled smoke, and it started coming in through the vents. Bishop got them down through the emergency stairwell and met your dad, who was on his way *up* to them. They got out, but neither Bishop nor your father felt it was safe to wait for the firefighters or paramedics. They were too exposed standing outside like that, and your dad wanted them all to get medically assessed, so they brought them to the clinic."

Oh, thank fuck.

The free clinic Hawke Enterprises runs doesn't have

anywhere near the capabilities we do here, but it has top-of-the-line equipment and the best doctor I know operating it.

Gabe says something to someone on his end, then returns to the call. "Nora is examining them right now. She said they have some minor smoke inhalation."

"Benjamin?"

"He's fine, Pope. They're all *fine*."

His assurances should release the vise from around my chest, but I can't stop thinking about how many ways this could have gone so badly.

"Did they see anything? Does anyone know what started the fire?"

Gabe clears his throat. "No, but..." It sounds like he's moving before he returns to the phone. "Sorry, I wanted to get away from Allie because we discussed this. Do you remember what Roselli said to you?"

Like I could ever forget.

"Yeah. That he could never get to them at my place because it was too defensible."

"Exactly." Gabe's voice takes on an icy chill. "And someone just made sure they're not going to be able to stay at your place."

16

POPE

"Do you two really have to do that in here?"

I land another blow on the heavy bag, and Atlas and I both glance at Isaac, where he reclines in the huge leather chair in front of his fireplace, his feet kicked up on the footstool, a file spread out across his thighs.

Scowling at him, I wipe my arm across my forehead, trying to keep the sweat out of my eyes. "You know the answer to that."

He's just giving us shit for the sake of giving us shit.

Plus, having the extra people in his place for the past few days has to be starting to wear on him, too.

It sure as hell hasn't been comfortable for us, and we're the ones invading *their* space. Still, he could lose the attitude, especially when he can see how worked up I am.

I turn back toward the heavy bag and unleash another volley of strikes. Each time my glove connects with the red leather, Atlas rocks back slightly, trying to hold it steady for me, which typically isn't a problem for him. But today, I have the kind of fury I'm not sure I've ever felt before pouring out of me, along with the sweat.

With each swing I take, I picture Roselli's face in the center of the bag, my punches and jabs pummeling him and beating him senseless, destroying him the way he keeps trying to us.

Over and over again.

Strike after strike.

Every hit containing all the pent-up rage I have for that "man" and the lengths he's gone to trying to get to Allie and Benjamin.

Finally, my muscles burn and ache too much for me to keep going. I drop my arms, panting heavily, the sweat trickling down my head and across my chest into the waistband of my gym shorts and dripping onto Isaac's living room tile.

He glances down at the forming puddle. "I suggest you clean it up before the girls get done with whatever it is they're doing back there, or you two are going to have to explain that to Jack."

His blue gaze darts toward the hallway that leads back to his kids' bedrooms and the guest one where Allie, Benjamin, and I have crashed the last two nights.

Atlas releases his hold on the bag and crosses his arms over his massive chest, his tattooed arms flexing as he scans me from head to toe. "Not half-bad, considering you haven't been to the gym in what, two months?"

I snort and shake my head. "You say that like I had a choice."

He holds up his hands with a grin. "Just saying, your cardio could use some work."

No shit.

My normal routine went out the window the day that hurricane hit New Orleans and Allie came tearing back into my life. There hasn't been time for morning runs and an hour of lifting, and even if there were, I wouldn't be able to justify leaving them alone for my vain attempts to maintain my physique.

Still, Atlas doesn't need to comment on it.

Or maybe he does.

He has always been a real smartass, loving to jab at people as much outside the ring as he does inside—and family is no exception. The words probably tumbled out of his mouth before his brain even knew he was saying them.

I scowl at him and hold up my gloves so he can unwrap them. He steps forward and does it, tossing them onto the floor beside the bag stand he dragged over from his place.

One of his blond brows rises. "Are you sure you don't want to go down to the gym? Do a couple of rounds in the ring with me?"

I mop my head with a towel and shake it. "I'm not that stupid."

Isaac laughs. "Apparently not, since it seems you finally worked things out with Allie."

And there it is...

I've been waiting for them to say something about the fact that we're sharing a bedroom since the moment I brought them back here after Nora examined them post-fire.

Everyone was so shaken, worried, even though the girls and Benjamin are completely fine, that no one said a word when Allie said she'd share my room instead of bunking with Viviana.

Frankly, I'm surprised it took this long for them to bring it up.

They've likely been waiting for the perfect opportunity to do it without prying ears from little ones like Vivi or people who tell them to mind their own business—like Allie and Jack —milling around.

But there's no avoiding the inquisition.

Especially when Isaac is leading it.

I never thought anyone would out-lawyer Uncle Stone, but Isaac has managed to step into his father's shoes and relish his new role as the primary attorney for Hawke Enterprises since Stone almost died.

He's damn good at it, which is why trying to wriggle my way out of this line of questioning is pointless. There is no pleading the fifth with Isaac Hawke.

"I'm glad you guys approve..."

I sigh and lower myself down onto the coffee table, knowing full well that if I sit on any other piece of Jack's furniture while I'm a sweaty, disgusting mess, she'll lose her mind. Resting my elbows on my knees, I let my head hang down as I try to catch my breath.

Maybe Atlas was right about the cardio thing.

When all this is over, I need to get back to the gym regularly.

Isaac snorts, flipping the page in the file he's reading. He's had his nose in it for the last hour since the girls disappeared and Atlas suggested we do a little boxing to release some of the tension I'm feeling.

I narrow my eyes on him. "What's *that* supposed to mean?"

No one makes that noise unless they have something else to say, and it isn't like him to hold anything back.

Isaac sighs and looks up from the file. "Nothing. We're all happy for you guys. Really. Now we won't have to worry about the frostbite from those icy looks you two kept throwing each other at Sunday dinners."

I smirk at him. "Yeah. Hopefully, it'll warm up a little bit. Is Nana still pissed we all missed this week?"

He nods. "Oh, yeah. I talked to her earlier, and her exact words were, and I quote"—he holds up a finger—"'whoever this asshole is who's messing up my family dinners needs to be taken care of.'"

Atlas rests his arm on the top of the bag, eyes wide. "Whoa. Are you telling me Nana authorized murder?"

Isaac's eyebrows rise. "Does that really surprise you? I mean, Grandpa wasn't exactly on the up-and-up. He was deeply connected with Abello and worked for him doing some shady stuff, and we all know what my dad did for the man..."

That sends an icy chill through the room, cooling any further humor.

Atlas runs a hand over his blond, spiky hair. "Well, I think I'm going to get this thing out of here and back to my place before your fiancée comes out here and kicks my ass."

"Oh, great." I throw up a hand. "So, you're just going to leave me here to take the punishment?"

He laughs. "I bet if you hurry, you can clean it up before she notices."

Isaac snorts again. "It's still going to smell like a gym in here..."

Shit.

We definitely didn't think this through, but options are severely limited when we're stuck living at Isaac and Jack's place—the second most defensible position we could think of since the smoke damage prevents us from returning to my condo anytime soon.

Something that, the more we look into it, seems very deliberate.

While the search continues for Roselli and any evidence to link him *directly* to the fire, pretty much everyone agrees he must be behind it.

We know the residents of the building too well for any of them to have been reckless enough to throw a lit cigarette into a garbage can. And Gabe, Dad, and Bishop have *personally* interviewed each and every one of them about what they saw or heard that night, seeking out any suspicious behavior from anyone.

But nothing has come of them putting the screws to my neighbors.

Which likely means someone else somehow got in past Dad and the rest of the security team and started that fire.

It would be easy enough to review the surveillance cameras to attempt to identify whoever did it—if the security office weren't right next to the room where the fire started, ensuring any evidence was destroyed almost immediately.

This was no accident.

It's too calculated.

Of all the potential attacks Roselli could have initiated, no one ever thought to worry about something as simple as burning us out—and now we're stuck here, invading Isaac and Jack's home—and turning their living room into a gym since we're banned from going out to Atlas' real one to burn off some energy there.

Atlas unhooks the bag from the stand and inclines his head toward his place. "Hey, asshole. Get the door for me."

I scowl at him and groan as I climb to my feet and trudge over to pull it open. Just as it has every time I've done this since we got here, the hair on the back of my neck rises, and my gaze drifts to the elevator and the stairwell.

Assessing.

Watching.

Anticipating.

Logically, I know this building is just as safe as my own, if not more so, with the amount of security Gabe and Dad have added, but if one lit cigarette could undo our best defenses there, I can't help feeling like anything is possible. The electronic keypad and code needed to operate the elevator up here or to access the stairwell seem somehow insufficient—but it's likely only my paranoia talking.

Even walking across the hall to have a little training session with our resident light heavyweight belt contender at his place

—where we wouldn't risk Giacomina's ire—was out of the question. Because just being across the hall from Allie and Benjamin is enough to give me hives.

How the hell am I going to get through my shift tonight?

Atlas easily lifts the 100-pound bag onto his shoulder like it's nothing and carries it across the hall to his place. His blue gaze cuts to me over his shoulder. "This one, too?"

I roll my eyes and cross the hall, opening his door for him.

He steps through and drops the heavy bag onto his floor, then follows me back for the stand. After he unloads it at his place, he turns back to me. "I know we will definitely give you a lot of shit about the you and Allie thing, but I haven't seen you *or* her this happy in a long time. And you both have every reason not to be with what's going on. So, that makes me think this is probably a very good thing for both of you."

"Thanks."

I didn't *need* his support or blessing, but knowing someone else recognizes how good we are together does make it easier to take their constant badgering.

"I'd do anything for you both." He shrugs and leans against the jamb. "You know I'll be the first one out here, guns blazing, if we get a trail on Roselli."

I nod and smack him on the shoulder. "I know, and I appreciate it. Really, I do. I'm going to get back in there and clean up before Jack catches me."

He smirks. "Good luck."

His door swings closed, and I push my way back into Isaac and Jack's condo as footsteps sound down the hallway.

Shit.

I might be too late.

Vivi comes barreling out into the living room, her long, dark hair in two French braids with pink ribbons wound into them. "Daddy, Daddy, look at my hair."

She jumps onto Isaac's lap, sending papers flying, and he

catches her, laughing when the old Isaac would've lost his fucking mind that his files got disturbed and out of order.

He examines her hair. "I love it. Is this what you guys were up to back there?"

She nods. "Mom and Aunt Allie washed my hair and used the blow dryer!" Her excitement draws a matching grin across her father's face. "What were you doing out here, Daddy?"

Isaac's gaze immediately darts to the wet floor and me, still sweating, standing by the door.

Motioning toward it, I hustle to the kitchen. "I am going to clean that up quick."

He tosses his thumb toward the hallway. "I would hurry if you value your life."

I grab a spray bottle of cleaner and a roll of paper towels and race back to the living room. While he whispers conspiratorially with Vivi, I do my best to wipe up our little makeshift workout area, removing any incriminating evidence before Giacomina returns and chews my head off.

Allie and Jack's voices grow louder, echoing down toward us as they move closer to the living room. I push to my feet just as they reappear, both of them narrowing their eyes on me.

Jack props her hands on her hips, her amber eyes flashing. "What are you doing?"

"Oh, I..."—I clear my throat—"spilled something, but it's all good."

Allie fights a smirk, evidently not buying my bullshit answer. "Well, Giovanni and Benjamin are both sound asleep in the nursery. I think the afternoon at the 'salon' was too much for them."

Chuckling, I wander back to the kitchen, return the cleaner to the cabinet under the sink, and shove the dirty paper towels into the garbage can.

Soft footsteps follow me. Allie's arms wrap around me from

behind, but she immediately backs away. "Eww. Why are you so sweaty?"

I turn and smile at her, tugging her against me. "Atlas and I were doing a little workout."

"Oh, I see...or should I say, I *smell* it." She motions back toward their living room. "Is that what you just lied to Jack about?"

"Was it that obvious?"

"To me, it was."

I press a kiss to her neck. "You read me too well. Hopefully, Jack didn't pick up on that."

She grins. "You afraid of her?"

I raise a brow. "Wouldn't you be?"

Daughter of a mafia queen and a ruthless killer—she is *not* the kind of woman I want to tangle with, under any circumstances. I don't care if she's basically family or not.

Allie leans in and presses a quick kiss to my lips. "Just steer clear of her the best you can for a while. When do you have to leave for work?"

I check my watch and groan. "About an hour, and I need to shower and get ready..."

Though I would *much* rather stay here with them, especially after what happened the last time I went in for a shift. But I can't take any more time off without risking my job, and there is *no way* Allie will let me do that.

She winks at me. "I'll distract her so you can sneak back to the room."

God, I fucking love this woman.

We've so easily fallen right back into this comfort zone with each other. All that animosity and uncertainty left behind in favor of us enjoying being together as much as we can and pretending—for brief moments like this—that the world isn't out to get us.

I wish it could go on forever.

But the fact of the matter is that Roselli won't stay on ice much longer, and the plan we formulated to draw him out makes me far more nervous than I ever let on.

Nervous enough to want to defy Allie's order to go back to work and instead stay here with her and Benjamin to ensure they're safe, but I don't need *two* Hawke women pissed at me today.

One is more than enough.

ALESSANDRA

I CLOSE the bedroom door behind me and throw the lock, then stride straight toward the bathroom, stripping off my dress on the way, letting it fall to the floor. The sound of rushing water filters out to me through the cracked door, immediately bringing me a mental image of Pope naked under the spray.

It shuts off just as I step into the steamy bathroom, and Pope runs his hands over his head and face, then slides back the frosted glass door and steps out, reaching for his towel.

His eyes land on me and he freezes, his brow furrowing. "What are you doing in here? Is everything okay?"

I take a step in, then another, nudging the door closed behind me, then lean back against it and take a minute to appreciate Pope Clarke in all his God-given glory.

It should be a sin to look like that and be a brilliant doctor.

And so insanely attentive and caring.

And incredible in bed.

Truly.

Not fair to my libido.

My pussy clenches as I grin at him and the way his gaze travels over me in the black bra and thong. "What does it look like I'm doing?"

He narrows his eyes and grabs the towel, wrapping it around his waist, but not fast enough to conceal his growing cock. "Something you shouldn't be. You were just in a fire a few days ago."

Like I need the reminder.

Racing down that dark, smoky stairwell behind Bishop, clutching Benjamin to my chest and trying to cover him so he didn't inhale any of the acrid smoke...

Not knowing who or what might be waiting for us at the bottom...

It was terrifying, but we're safe now.

And things are *really* good between us.

Going to sleep and waking in his arms the last few days, even here instead of at his place, helped ease those painful memories—or at least allowed me to lock them away in a vault I won't open until much later.

It isn't anything I want to dwell on right now.

Not when I feel so alive.

But I know how guilty and helpless Pope felt, not being there with us.

If I'm going to make him forget, even for a few moments, I have to downplay what happened and pray he buys it.

I offer a shrug. "I feel totally fine. My throat doesn't hurt. I'm not coughing..."

Pope gives me that *look* again, the one he always uses when he wants to go all "doctor" on me about something.

But I hold up a hand before he can. "Don't give me that 'doctor' look. Tell me, if I were *anyone* else, is there any medical reason I wouldn't be able to suck my boyfriend's cock and have a quickie with him before he goes to work?"

He runs a hand over his eyes, his whole body tensing. "Jesus, Allie..."

"What?"

His hand falls away, and an inferno blazes in his gaze. "I

have to leave for work in twenty minutes, and you come in here *looking* like *that, saying* things like *that,* and calling me your *boyfriend.*"

It just slipped out.

I hadn't intended to use that important word and potentially mess up what was supposed to be a nice release for both of us before he leaves for his shift. But now that he's brought it up, the tiniest hint of uncertainty and regret start to seep in.

Calling me your boyfriend...

"Should I *not* be?"

He closes the distance between us so quickly. It's only a split second before he's on me, pressing his wet body against mine. Taking my cheek in one palm, the other pressed against the door behind me, Pope tilts my face up to him. "You absolutely *should* be calling me that." He shakes his head. "Actually, it doesn't seem like *enough* for what you are to me. You are so much more than my girlfriend, Al."

And there he goes, saying things that melt me into a puddle of goo again.

Pope always knows exactly what I need to hear, and he never lets me question what we are together without setting me straight.

I hate the insecurity that sometimes creeps in.

But it has nothing to do with Pope and everything to do with what a mess I've made of my life.

Sometimes, it's hard to believe where I am—here, with this man, on our way to a future I didn't think could exist. It's what I dreamed about for so long and always thought was out of reach and could never be real.

Now, my palms pressed flat against his hard, slick chest, he's *very* real.

I score my nails down his chest, and he leans into me, his now fully hard cock pressed between us, making my core ache.

Squirming against him, I feather my lips against his. "You have twenty minutes, right?"

He issues a low growl and crushes his lips to mine. A hungry, fervent kiss his only response. But it's the only one I need. I wrap my arms around his neck and cling to him the best I can, the water making his skin slick.

That clean scent I always associate with him permeates the warm air, and I inhale it and him, wishing I could keep it there, in my lungs, and breathe nothing but this forever. Wishing I could put into words all the things my heart wants to say.

How much I love him.

How much I need him.

How much everything he's done for Benjamin and me has truly meant.

But even if I tried to say them, they'd get lost in our frantic kisses, our shared breaths, the groping hands and racing hearts.

He reaches between us and unhooks the towel from around his waist. His fingers dig into my hips, and he lifts me to wrap my legs around him so he can pin me to the door. He lightly teases his lips over mine. "You want it hard and fast?"

I nod, grasping his face between my hands and tugging his mouth back to mine fully, desperate to get another taste of him before he walks out of here and leaves me for the night.

It isn't often we're going to find time alone like this, but with Isaac and Jack busy with Viviana in the kitchen making dinner and the babies asleep in the nursery, this is the only chance I'm going to get—potentially for a few more days—and Pope seems to understand that, too.

After what happened the other night, we both need this, the carnal reaffirmation that we're alive and together, that as long as we stay that way, we can fight anything.

He reaches down and tugs at my thong, pulling it to the side. Thick fingertips drag through my arousal, spreading it up over my clit, making me twitch against him.

A low hum of appreciation vibrates in his chest. "Jesus, you're already wet for me."

More than ready.

I have been since the moment I saw him in nothing but his gym shorts standing in the kitchen and realized I won't see him again until he returns tomorrow after his shift.

It's impossible not to want more of Pope now that I have him again.

Impossible not to crave *this*.

"Yes..." I nod and keep kissing him, twirling my tongue along his as I thrust my hips forward against his hand. "Please..."

He chuckles, his chest rumbling. "Greedy, aren't we?"

I don't bother verbally answering him this time, just dig my nails into the back of his neck, probably hard enough to leave marks, urging him to stop toying with me.

We don't have time for games, and neither one of us really enjoys playing them anyway.

Not when we don't need to.

Honesty and openness will be the things that will gets us through the uncertainty, the tough times, the trials and tribulations we're sure to face—not trying to one-up each other.

Pope grins against my lips, and his hand between my legs vanishes, quickly replaced with the warm, wide head of his cock. He drags it through my wet folds and up across my clit, and I buck against him, gasping and pulling back slightly. My head bangs against the door, rattling it slightly, and we both laugh as he pushes into me slowly, allowing me to adjust to his size.

I squeeze around him, relishing the stretch and burn of taking him.

He grits his teeth. "You know that only makes it harder, Teeny."

Allowing my gaze to meet his again, I swim in the headiness

of seeing the pure fire scorching across his cognac eyes and knowing it burns only for me. "I know."

He presses his forehead to mine and plunges all the way to the hilt. "Christ, Allie, I fucking love you."

My mouth falls open on a silent gasp, my body aching and straining to accommodate him while his words cement us together even more than we physically are.

It isn't the first time he said that to me, but it's the first time I really *feel* the words deep down in my soul, a hundred percent confident that nothing and no one will ever break us apart again.

This connection with him has been the only thing that has kept me going through the days and nights I felt like I would completely fall apart, when it seemed like the world was crumbling and I couldn't do anything to stop it.

In this moment, I can almost pretend that isn't the case.

With his kiss, his touch, his love, I can almost believe we're truly safe.

He shattered my heart once, and for all those years, I tried to mend it any other way, when all I needed to do to put it back together was return it to the man who always owned it.

Keeping it from him, trying to ignore this pull, has only hurt both of us in ways we may never truly heal from, but the longer we're together, the easier it becomes to forget the pain of the past and concentrate on the here and now.

Which is *very, very* good.

Pope drags his hips back and plunges into me again, the door behind me rattling, but neither of us care. He squeezes my thigh with one hand and grips my chin with the other, angling my head to take my mouth as brutally as he is my pussy.

He pumps into me hard and determined to get both of us there quickly.

Pope has made love to me before, and it was delicious and decadent and beautiful, but this isn't that.

This is pure and primal.

This is both of us needing the connection and wanting it *now*.

His hips drive him into me deeper with each thrust, and my body starts trembling—the power and passion he possesses bringing me to another plane of existence.

He kisses my lips, my cheek, over my eyes, his mouth never stopping its movement as our bodies roll and meet. I squeeze around him on each withdrawal, allowing the head of his cock to drag against that perfect spot deep inside me that already has the slow, warm buzz forming at my core.

Pope moves his attention up my neck, and his lips find my ear. He grazes his teeth along it, sending a shiver through me and a spark straight to my clit. This position already gives me the most delicious friction, the perfect angle to get me there quickly, but that sends me completely over the edge.

Oh, God...

He tips my head back and catches my moan with a blistering kiss as my orgasm blindsides me.

A violent cataclysm of darkness and light, joy and pain, love and lust.

He clenches his jaw and comes right behind me, emptying himself deep inside me in hot spurts and baring teeth against my collarbone, like he wants to mark me there.

But he doesn't need to because I'm already his.

I always have been.

Even when I denied it to myself.

A mistake I won't make again.

Head still spinning in the post-orgasmic haze, I lift it and he does the same. Our hooded gazes meet, and a slow grin spreads across his lips.

His fingers twine in my hair and tilt my head slightly so he can kiss along my jaw. "Well, now my shift is going to feel even longer."

"What? Why?"

He presses his lips across my cheek. "Because I want to come home and do it again..."

"Mmmm." I tilt my neck to give him better access and clench around his still-hard cock buried inside me. "I wouldn't say no to that."

A strangled groan falls from his mouth. "But not now..." He pulls back and drags his hips away, his cock sliding out of me. "I have to go."

Not yet.

I drop to my knees and wrap my hand around him, leaning forward to flick my tongue across the head of his cock—the flavor of our combined releases dancing across it. "Not before I do what I intended to when I came in here."

"Christ, Al..."—he buries his hands in my hair, tangling the locks around his fingers—"you're going to make me late for work."

Grinning, I nod. "Maybe, but I know your boss, and you can come up with a better excuse than my girlfriend wanted to blow me."

17

POPE

The Hawkeye Club sign stands tall and proud—back where it should be. The repair Landon's guys did on it are so good that I can't even tell it ever came down during the storm, but I will never forget that sound when it slammed into the ground, seeing it laid across the road when the firefighters brought us out...or anything else that happened here.

That would be impossible.

Every moment is seared into my brain.

Every word Allie said to me.

Every confession she made.

All that anguish caught up in such a tiny woman.

It still blows my mind that she held in the truth as long as she did.

And this sign will be a constant reminder of what we went through together that night.

I pull into the club parking lot and glance across the street to where the giant oak once stood. Had that not fallen in Allie's way, things could have ended up so different.

She might've made it to Nana's safely and done what she always did back then by avoiding everyone's questions, locking herself away in a bedroom, and living in her own fear.

Or it could have been even worse than that.

That fucker, Roselli, might've managed to track her down and intercept her before she got there, and then, who the hell knows what would've happened?

A chill rolls along my spine, imagining the possibilities as I climb from my car and lock it. The two cars filled with the security personnel who have become my shadows to and from every work shift park on either side of me.

They're just doing their jobs, which right now means babysitting me when I'm not somewhere safe—like the club.

So, as soon as I walk in there, they'll have a few minutes off.

But I'm not in any rush to get in.

The warm summer air heats my skin, the sun threatening to set on the horizon. It would be a great night to sit outside with a bottle of wine. Maybe after I meet with Savage and the guys, I can take Allie onto Isaac's balcony and do that.

She deserves to really relax.

To go on a damn date.

Something I haven't been able to do for her.

Fuck.

I run a hand over my head as I tug open the door and step into the club. The deep, rhythmic bass vibrates through the floors and up through my feet, making my whole body buzz. Spinning lights illuminate the main room and bar, with a single beam directed at the girl on stage wrapped around the pole.

The place is alive again, so different from the last time I was here when the hurricane seemed intent on trying to tear it down, brick by brick.

Christ, has it really been two months already?

My mind still doesn't want to accept the fact that so much has happened in such a short period of time. Yet, it also feels like nothing has...

Allie and Benjamin have been in limbo.

Not able to move forward, but definitely not wanting to go back.

But if everything goes as planned, that's all going to change. *Soon.*

Byron waves at me from behind the bar, and I raise a brow at him and make my way over.

Leaning across it so he can hear me over the music and voices, I offer him a grin. "What are you doing here? You don't work the bar anymore."

He snorts and rests his elbow against it. "No, I don't. But since Luca needed to be here for your meeting, I figured I would help out because we're pretty busy tonight."

I scan the club—all the tables full, people standing and leaning against the bar without any free space, waitresses hustling around with full trays.

"Is everyone here?"

He inclines his head toward the second floor. "Yep, just waiting on you."

I glance at my watch. "Shit, I didn't realize I was so late. I got stuck at the hospital a bit longer than intended."

"Don't worry about it." He waves me off. "They know what your schedule's like."

"See you later."

He nods and watches me jog over to the elevator and punch the up button. It dings, the doors slide open for me right away, and I step in and hit the "2" to take me up. Leaning back against the inside of the cab, a vision immediately hits me of what Allie looked like doing the same thing that day I saw her at the hospital, the day all this kind of started.

She was so small, so scared, so shut down, so different from the woman who dropped to her knees and blew me before my shift last night.

The corner of my mouth twitches thinking about it.

I am finally starting to see the Allie I've always known and loved coming back. That broken, terrified, haunted woman isn't her—*shouldn't* be her.

Since the day she was born, Allie has always been a ray of sunshine, light and happy, seeking the things that ignite her joy and ways to bring it to others. It's what made her so good at her job at The Grind and why the customers love her so much.

It's why I fell in love with her in the first place.

She was always so bright, so inquisitive, so full of life and love—and I saw a glimpse of that old Allie who isn't bogged down in pain and fear. Knowing I was part of the reason she ended up that way only makes me want to bring her back to that more. Once all this resolves, I know I'll see *her* again.

The elevator dings, and I step out onto the second floor and stalk down to Savage's office. Voices carry out what sounds like a tense, serious conversation that straightens my spine.

I step in and find Savage, Gabe, Luca, Stone, and Dad seated or standing in various spots around the office. My eyes immediately zero in on the empty couch—the first time I'm seeing it since I helped the firefighters get an unconscious Allie off it.

Savage huffs and points at it. "No one will sit there even though I've had it professionally cleaned."

Everyone shares a chuckle, but the lightened mood doesn't last very long, not with what we're here to discuss. There's only one reason they would call me here—Roselli.

Gabe motions to the bar near Savage's desk. "Grab a drink before you sit. You're going to need it."

Fucking hell...

And I thought we were getting together to confirm that the first part of our plan is ready to initiate.

This seems far more ominous.

I release a heavy sigh and walk over, pour myself a bourbon, and take a seat on the couch, not afraid like everyone else. Dad chuckles at me from where he sits in one of the leather armchairs, and Luca offers me a hard smile from where he leans against a wall next to Savage's desk.

In a full suit, he looks every bit the mafia don he used to be, which isn't the norm for him these days. Since his retirement, he's enjoyed a much more casual vibe—but not tonight. And after this recent absence, it raises the hair on the back of my neck.

Inclining my head his way. "Where have you been?"

It's unusual for him to miss a family meeting, especially when we're discussing taking down someone in his former line of work, but no one mentioned the fact that he was missing the other day at my place when we first met to lay out the plan. Or that he hasn't been part of any of our discussions about the Roselli situation *at all*, really.

Luca takes a sip of his drink, crossing his feet at the ankles. "I have been *around*, talking with contacts, seeing what information I could dig up on Roselli and Satriano that might help us out of this mess."

Which *sort of* explains where he's been.

"Did you find anything?"

His lips twitch. "You wouldn't be here if I didn't."

I take a sip of my drink, enjoying the slow burn down my throat, then lean forward, resting my elbows on my knees. "Somebody want to fill me in on what's going on? Because I can tell you right now, Allie is not going to last much longer doing this. She can't live in seclusion her entire life. It isn't fair to her and Benjamin, and after what happened at my place, I don't think we can wait to take Roselli out. He got to us there..."

Gabe sighs and runs a hand through his hair. "Believe me, we know that, and we're sorry it's taking so long. I think everyone in this room will agree that we all feel like we have failed Alessandra by not being able to remove him sooner and free her from all this."

All this pain.

All this fear.

All this uncertainty.

It *will* completely destroy the old Allie if we don't do something—quickly.

I won't lose her now that I just got her back. That brief glimmer of hope that she's going to come out of this okay has to be stoked, not snuffed out.

"So, are we ready?" I look from Luca to Dad, Gabe, Stone, and Savage, who all wear far harder masks of concern than they should, even given how dangerous all this is. Something is wrong. "Has the plan changed?"

Luca bobs his head. "It has."

I sit up straighter and turn to Dad. "What the hell happened? I thought we had decided on the best course of action when we all met..."

Stone nods, his hand tightening on the top of the cane he now uses. "We did. But what we discussed with the entire family was never the real plan. Luca has been pursuing a different course behind the scenes."

Scanning the faces of all the men in the room, the sense of utter determination to accomplish the same task I want to stares back at me, but my blood still heats, knowing they all lied to us. We all sat in my living room and discussed how to get to Roselli and end things before he could follow through on his threat. "So, you all knew and lied to us?"

Savage's lips press into a thin line, and he nods. "Yes, we did."

I gape at Dad.

"I'm sorry, son, but we thought it was best to keep this information close to the chest. I promise you that we're sure this plan is the way to handle the situation. There's only one drawback."

Shit.

Nothing is ever easy.

I should have known there was a reason they brought me here to discuss this and didn't come to Allie and me at Isaac and Jack's place.

"What's that?"

Dad shifts uncomfortably in his seat, his broad shoulders tensing. "We need bait."

My back stiffens, my hand tightening on my glass. "You can't mean Allie and the baby?"

Dad scowls at me. "Of course not, son..."

He trails off and looks at Luca.

Luca stares into his drink. "I think I can get Roselli to come to a meeting with *me*, if I go alone. Ever since we learned he was Benjamin's father, I've been distancing myself from the family and making contact with old business acquaintances to drop hints, suggesting that I'm not happy with my role in the Hawke Enterprises empire, that I might consider backing Roselli in his bid for his father's throne. Even though I'm not in the world anymore, I still know people, and the Abello name still means something. My support would give him a sort of legitimacy he doesn't have otherwise in his battle against both Francis Gilardi and Satriano."

Holy shit.

What he's really saying is that *he* would be the bait.

"But you'd have to go alone..."

He nods slowly. "I think Roselli is smarter than we give him credit for. He's managed to stay safe for two months, with both Satriano and all of us looking for him. He won't just walk into a trap." Shaking his head, he pushes off the wall and walks over to the chair Stone sits in, resting one hand on the back of it. "I need to go alone. I need to determine what I can about his plans, make him think I'll not only back him but also help him get to Allie and the baby."

My stomach clenches, the bourbon I just drank threatening to come up.

Dad leans forward, catching my gaze. "We would be watching with hidden cameras, of course, and have audio, and the plan will be to follow Roselli after the meeting to his current base of operations so we can take him and his entire crew out *there*. It would be a controlled strike. Safer than setting a trap and hoping he doesn't catch on to it."

It makes sense, but it also means risking everything on Luca being able to convince Roselli of his hatred of the Hawkes.

"Shit, and you really think that's going to work?"

Luca nods slowly, swirling his drink before he takes a sip. "I do. Roselli is young and determined, but he needs someone like me behind him if he has *any* hope of consolidating the power now split between him and Gilardi or of defending his territory when Satriano finally strikes. He's desperate—and that desperation will work in our favor."

"And if it doesn't?" I look up at Luca—seeing both the ruthless don and the kind man who has always been an integral member of this family. "If Dan suspects you're playing him?"

A tiny grin plays on Luca's lips. "Then I guess I'm fucked."

ALESSANDRA

KENNEDY and Astrid lean over Benjamin on the play mat, tickling him and trying to get him to giggle.

I don't have the heart to tell them that most babies won't do it until they're closer to three or four months old—plus, I've been enjoying watching them try.

Benjamin seems entranced by them, and it's been so long

since I've been able to actually just *sit* with them and hang out. With Astrid covering my shifts at The Grind and Kennedy busy with the hotel, especially after the emergency repairs needed post-hurricane, I've barely seen either of them since Pope and I came back from our "cabin" in the woods.

Fighting back tears, I smile at them. "I'm glad you both came over...I needed some girl time."

Atlas throws up a hand from where he sits on the couch. "What am I, chopped liver?"

Astrid gives her brother the stink eye. "You are *not* part of this conversation!"

He snorts and returns to watching the MMA fights on Isaac's big screen. "Good. Didn't want to be, anyway."

Even though I know he's joking, his comment does needle me a little. Since we moved in here with Isaac and Jack, Atlas has had to step up and take on the babysitter role, moving into the rotation when Bishop, Gabe, or Saint are either downstairs manning the lobby or unavailable, having to handle other Hawke Enterprises concerns outside of keeping us safe.

It can't be enjoyable for him.

Sitting around, doing nothing sure hasn't been for me.

Kennedy glances up from Benjamin. "What time does Pope get off?"

I glance at my watch. "Oh, actually, he did a couple of hours ago. He worked a twelve-hour shift, so he should have been done around five. I wonder why he's not back yet. He may have had a patient who kept him late."

She scans the condo, blowing her blond hair out of her face. "And this is what you've been doing for the last two months, just sitting around, waiting?"

Astrid elbows her, her eyes wide. "*Kennedy!*"

The eldest of the Hawke cousins raises her hands. "Shit, I'm sorry. Was I not supposed to ask? I've been a little busy working on the hotel shit with Cass. And it's not like we've been having

Sunday family dinners since that asshole threatened all of us." She offers a shrug. "We haven't had a lot of time to catch up. I'm glad I was able to come over tonight."

"You didn't need to." I smile at her. "Just because Isaac and Jack took Vivi and Giovanni to his parents' house to see Aunt Nora doesn't mean I'm not perfectly capable of hanging out here alone."

Atlas turns on the couch and glares at me. "Seriously? Chopped liver over here!"

I roll my eyes at him. "I'm *not* going to sit with you on the couch and watch MMA, Atlas."

Astrid raises a hand. "Neither would I, for what it's worth."

He gapes at her. "And I shared a *womb* with you." Scowling, he turns back to the TV with an exaggerated huff. "Real nice."

Kennedy scoops up Benjamin and inclines her head toward the kitchen. "Why don't we go figure out dinner and let Atlas do whatever it is he's doing by himself?"

"I'm studying this guy." He motions to one of the two fighters pummeling each other. "He's a great boxer. Moved into MMA, but there's talk he might come back."

Astrid raises a brow, suddenly interested. "Is he in your weight class?"

He nods. "Yeah. Light heavyweight."

She narrows her eyes on the screen. "The dude looks *huge* for a light heavyweight."

Kennedy and I move closer to get a better look at the guy in the blue trunks.

Atlas motions to him. "He cuts a lot for a fight to make weight. He probably walks at closer to 195-200 and then gets down during pre-fight camps and final cut."

"Uhh..." Astrid snorts. "So do you."

He smirks. "Yeah, mostly because of Nana's Sunday dinners. Mine is lasagna weight. This guy is just naturally *huge* and a maniac. If he comes back and fights light heavyweight, I might end up having to face him."

Astrid stands behind the couch, crossing her arms as she watches the TV. "But can this really tell you much? Fighting style in the boxing ring is totally different than an MMA ring."

Atlas nods. "True, but I still want to watch him, try to figure out how he thinks in case I ever face him."

She leans down and squeezes her brother's shoulders. "You always were the smart one."

He rolls his eyes at her. "Ha, fucking ha."

Astrid elbows me playfully as we laugh and head for the kitchen. I turn toward her to ask what she's in the mood to eat tonight when the balcony sliding glass doors shatter to our right. Something whizzes past her head and strikes the wall at the far side of the condo.

Two sharp cracks sound so fast we don't even have time to react, more holes appearing in the drywall next to the first.

We all jerk away from the noise, whirling toward the now-empty door frame to see what caused it, too shocked to really process what's happening.

Benjamin lets out a sharp wail from Kennedy's arms.

Atlas jumps from the couch. "Get the fuck down."

What?

It takes me a second to register his command, but I recognize that sound.

Gunshots.

Kennedy and Astrid drop to the floor, eyes wide and scanning for where it came from. I do the same, crawling toward them to pull a frantic Benjamin from Kennedy's arms.

Atlas moves toward the window, keeping close to the wall, away from the open living room. Another shot cuts through the air and slams into the lamp on the end table only half a foot from us, sending the remnants scattering over us on the floor.

Glass and porcelain crunch under my legs as I shift and try to see out toward the balcony.

Kennedy glances the same way, the alarm evident in her gaze when she returns it to me. Given what happened to her the last time bullets flew around the Hawkes, her fear is warranted. "Someone's fucking shooting at us."

Not *someone*.

Daniele Roselli...

I fucking know it.

He may not be the one pulling the trigger, but this is *all* him.

My heart thunders against my ribcage, each breath getting harder to take, and Kennedy scrambles to get her phone from her pocket.

She finally manages to get it out. "I'm calling Bishop downstairs."

"You girls stay down." Atlas takes cover around the corner in the kitchen island and tries to peek through that window, but as soon as he sticks out his head, another shot collides with the marble, sending chips flying through the air. "Fuck." He drops down, his wide eyes meeting ours. "I'm trying to see where the shooter is."

Astrid glares at him. "Does it matter?"

"It does if we're going to get the hell out of here." He peeks around the corner again, and another volley of rounds tear into the island. Once they stop, he motions toward the door. "We'll go for the SUV in the underground parking..."

Kennedy releases a little relieved sigh into the phone when Bishop answers. "Somebody's shooting at us...I don't fucking know...Atlas can't figure out where they are...He's taking us to the car....Right...Okay." She ends the call and slips the phone back into her pocket. "She said she's going out after the shooter."

I jerk my head in her direction, cradling Benjamin to me,

his wails filling the eerily silent air now that the shots have, at least momentarily, stopped. "What?"

"She's going to see if she can figure out where the shots are coming from. So"—she looks to Atlas—"she needs him to take a few more."

You have got to be fucking kidding me.

Atlas squeezes his eyes closed, flexing his hands like he's preparing for a match. "Okay. Here's what we're going to do." He opens his eyes and meets mine with determination. "I'm going to step out long enough for him to take a shot while you three move for the door. I'll keep him distracted. I don't know where he is or what vantage point he has, so stay as flat to the floor as much as you can and move quickly. You got it?"

We all nod, and tears streak down mine and Astrid's faces. Kennedy just looks fucking pissed. Benjamin flails, inconsolable in my arms.

Dear God, let us get out of this...

"On the count of three." Atlas holds up his fingers. "One, two, three, *go*."

Heart in my throat, I crawl, cradling Benjamin with my hands and trying to stay low, using my elbows to advance with the girls on either side of me.

Two more shots ring out, and Atlas releases a pained grunt. I whip my head back to see him with his hand pressed against his shoulder, blood already seeping between his tattooed fingers.

"Oh, God. You're—"

"Go!" His scream tears through the air, and more shots ping off the metal balcony railing and slam into the couch, the coffee table, and the tile only inches from us. "Just *go*!"

Scrambling forward, Kennedy reaches the door and tries to unlock it, but a bullet slams into it, only a few millimeters from her reach. She jerks her hand back and hits the floor again. "What the hell do we do?"

Atlas crawls toward us, grimacing with each bit of progress he makes, leaving a bloody trail across the tile. "Get my gun out of my holster. Shoot out the lock and the handle, then we can pull it open faster."

Shifting my position slightly, I manage to get my palms over Benjamin's ears and turn him away from Kennedy, trying to protect him from the noise as much as possible.

Astrid grabs Atlas' gun, her hand trembling as she points it.

Kennedy takes it from her. "I'll do it."

She aims and pulls the trigger, the bullet biting into the wood just under the lock. The sharp sound only further agitates Benjamin, and he squirms against my hold as she fires off three more rounds.

Atlas reaches over with his good arm and grabs the ruined handle, tugging the door open. A barrage of shots whizz above our heads as he ushers us out into the hallway, still crawling and staying low. The moment we make it to the side, he motions ahead. "Run!"

We have to get out of here.

Away.

Somewhere safe.

Because even if *that* shooter fails, Daniele will send others. For all we know, they may already be on their way up...

Oh, God.

My chest tightens, and that familiar darkness starts to creep around the edges of my visions, but Kennedy grabs my arm and helps me to my feet.

We all scramble toward the elevator, but Atlas shakes his head. "No. Stairwell. They could cut the power."

Shit.

Even though the emergency generator should keep the elevator running, he's right—we don't want to be sitting ducks like we were in the condo if they somehow manage to kill the backup power, too.

He takes his gun back from Kennedy and leads us to the emergency stairwell, kicking it open with a booted foot.

Flashbacks of the smoke invading the one in Pope's building only a few days ago fill my head. My throat burns at the memory of that escape, rushing down the steps with Bishop and Benjamin, not knowing who or what might be waiting at the bottom.

There's no question now.

This has *all* been Roselli.

He knows how to draw us out of the places that are the safest, and this time, we might not be so lucky as to get away.

Benjamin's screams echo off the metal as we descend.

Turn after turn, our heavy footsteps slam against each tread and landing.

Kennedy pulls out her phone again and keeps dialing on our way down. "I can't get a signal in here."

Astrid looks back at her from two steps ahead. "Bishop will call Saint. He'll call everybody..."

For a split second, Kennedy's steps falter and her lip quivers. "She's not going to call Cass and Charlotte."

The real terror in her voice makes my heart ache for her.

She loves that little girl as if she were her own, the same way Pope loves Benjamin. And I can see the panic in her eyes, the worry that she's never going to see them again.

Where the hell are you, Pope?

The thought that his delayed return might be connected to the attack makes me stumble, and Astrid grabs my arm, holding me steady.

"We have to keep moving."

I nod, trying to tamp down the rising panic as Atlas leads the charge until we reach the basement parking garage.

"Shh. It's okay, buddy." I rock Benjamin, trying to soothe him, but he knows something's wrong, very wrong. The loud noises. The yelling. The sudden shift in the "chill" energy that surrounded him only moments ago. "Shh, I've got you. We're going to be okay."

The lie slips it out easily to a baby.

But everyone else knows we might be seriously fucked.

Atlas grabs the door handle with his bad hand, blood dripping from his arm to the concrete below. His gun raised and ready, he glances at all of us. "All right, I'm going out first. We have to cross half of the parking structure to get to the SUV. Keep your heads down in case there are any other shooters inside. Keep him covered and move as fast as you can."

We all nod our agreement, and Atlas tugs open the door.

Run.

Just run!

I pump my legs as fast as I can, with Kennedy and Astrid at my sides, helping me keep moving when my feet keep catching and making me stumble.

Atlas skids to a stop next to the SUV and reaches under the wheel well, pulling out a set of keys and unlocking it. We scramble in—Kennedy in the front seat with him and Astrid and me in the back.

The engine roars to life, and Atlas glances behind us. "Everyone, get down."

We all duck, lying against the black leather as Benjamin's cries go on and on, even louder in the close space.

Maybe he knows what I do.

As soon as we pull out on the street, we're exposed. At least, until we can put some buildings between us and wherever the sniper is. We're far from safe at this point. The bullets may not have killed us, but—

A sob slips from my throat. Picturing Pope. Ang. Jude. Mom and Dad. Everyone. "If anything happens to me..."

Astrid jerks her head up, her teary eyes meeting mine. She reaches over and wraps her hand around my wrist, squeezing it tightly. "No, don't."

Atlas peeks at us over his seat as he backs the SUV out of the spot. "If anything happens to *me*, you need to either get to the club or the hospital. They're both closer than any of the police stations and have armed security."

He throws it into drive and peels away toward the rolling garage door, which starts to rise as we approach.

I hold my breath, waiting for what I can feel coming, and press my lips against Benjamin's cheek. "I love you so much. It's going to be okay—"

We pull out onto the street, and a shot instantly hits the windshield, shattering it and tearing through the armrest between Kennedy and Atlas.

Jerking away from it, I press myself down into the floorboards with Benjamin pinned against my chest.

Another shot shatters the back passenger window, sending glass falling over Astrid as Atlas turns and races off down the street.

A block passes.

Another.

We're getting away...

Hope starts to bloom in my chest, but the final bullet enters through the back windshield...

And Astrid releases a sharp cry.

18

POPE

The red and blue lights from all the squad cars outside the building still flash in my vision as I stumble into the lobby filled with officers and our security personnel.

Dad's call only moments ago still rings in my ears, the words impossible to comprehend or accept.

A sniper shot up the condo. Bishop went after the shooter. Atlas left with the girls and Benjamin...

I hold out hope for a few brief moments that he was wrong, that the frantic call from Bishop was a mistake, a misunderstanding...

Until I see the looks on the faces of the people we hired to help protect us and prevent exactly this from happening.

No. No. No.

I stagger to the elevator to take it up. The only reason I'm even getting through is the Hawkes' connections in the force and the fact that the lead detective personally knows Dad and Gabe.

But I would fight my way to the penthouse if I had to.

The moment the cab reaches the top floor and lets me out, I storm down the hallway and through the open door to Isaac and Jack's place.

Cops swarm the living room and kitchen, broken glass and bullets littering the floor.

My heart lodges in my throat, making it nearly impossible to breathe.

I was prepared to spill blood to get here; I just wasn't prepared for *this* level of destruction or the confirmation that every word I was told was true.

Good God...

It looks more like a war zone than the opulent condo Isaac calls home, which had become our refuge for the last few days.

Isaac stands with Jack and Giovanni near a cluster of officers. He sees me and rushes over, his face grim, shoulders and jaw tense.

My body trembling, I take in the devastation. Bullet holes in the walls, furniture, and tile. Broken lamps and shattered windows. Benjamin's play mat spread on the floor with chunks of drywall scattered across it.

I fight the urge to vomit the bourbon I drank at Savage's office, struggling to swallow it down. "Where the fuck are they?"

Isaac shakes his head, his blue eyes filled with the same distress I feel. "We don't know."

Those words hit me as hard as these bullets would have.

"What the fuck do you mean that you don't know?"

Jack comes over, Giovanni sound asleep on her shoulder. "We were almost home from Stone and Nora's when he called to tell us what happened. Nora came and picked up Viviana before she saw any of this. They let us come up, but all we know is that it's been twenty minutes and no one's heard from them."

Twenty minutes might as well be a lifetime...

Scrubbing my hands over my face, I wrack my brain for any way to locate them. "Are their phones working? Can you track them?"

Isaac shakes his head. "We've been trying. Atlas, Astrid, and Allie all left their phones here. Kennedy is the only one who has hers, and either it's not on or it's dead."

"Fuck!" I pace away from him, glass crunching under my feet. "Where were they heading?"

Jack exchanges a nervous look with Isaac. "Atlas knows to get to the hospital or the club, but they haven't shown up either place."

"Fuck, fuck, fuck." I press my hands to my temples and stumble back a few steps, my eyes taking in the rest of the disaster in front of me from this new position. "Jesus...is that blood?"

My stomach turns for the first time in my life at the sight of it. A patient can come into the ER with a severed limb and it doesn't affect me, but the crimson drops and streaks across the tile are like a punch directly to the stomach.

"Is that, oh, God, who got hit? Who got—"

Isaac wraps his arm around my shoulders. "We don't know, Pope. Just take a breath."

"Take a breath?" I jerk out of his hold, the sheer panic threatening to overwhelm me. "We don't know where the fuck they are or who was hurt. How can you fucking say that?"

He grabs my arms and squeezes tightly, forcing me to still. "Because I've been there. I watched that asshole take Jack, and I didn't know if I was ever going to get her back. I've literally been where you're standing, okay? You having a meltdown isn't going to help anything."

His words snap me out of the fear spiral and help me focus. "We have to find them."

Giving me a firm nod, Isaac's confidence reflects in his steady gaze. "We *will*."

"There's a tracker in the car, right? Why weren't they using it?"

Isaac clenches his jaw. "We pulled it out when you took it up to Shreveport, just in case anybody figured out a way to tap into the tracking program and went looking for you."

"Shit."

The very thing we did to keep ourselves hidden then is making it impossible to locate them now.

A vision of Allie, terrified, hysterical, trying to protect Benjamin during all this, makes my vision darken until the room vanishes and all I see is *them*.

I shake my head, trying to clear away the worst-case-scenario images and come up with a plan. "Something must have happened. They would've been to the club by now, and I was coming from that way and didn't see them. If they reached the hospital, either Nora or I would have gotten a call from one of the staff, or one of *them* would have gotten in touch from there."

Isaac confirms my analysis with a grim nod, and I stumble over and drop onto one of the chairs, sucking in a shaky breath.

One of the police officers milling about approaches, giving me a concerned look. "Are you all right?"

"I..."

No. I'm not fucking all right.

"You were residing here, correct?" He raises a brow. "We're going to need to interview you."

"Yeah..."—I nod absently, still scanning the damage—"of course."

Though, it's the last thing on my priority list.

They don't need to do an investigation—we know who did this and why.

And everyone would have preferred to keep New Orleans'

finest out of this, but something as public and devastating as this wasn't going to be kept quiet. There wasn't any way we could have contained it. Which means the police are now going to be involved. It may help us find them faster, but it also complicates everything with our plan to take out the fucker responsible.

I look up at Isaac and Jack, who stand, watching me like they're waiting for me to break completely. "Do you think he has them?"

Isaac's jaw clenches again, and a muscle there tics. "I don't know who else would be shooting at us..."

Shaking my head, I stare out at the balcony, now wide open with shards of glass sticking up in places around the frame. "I don't get it, though. He wants Benjamin. Why would he risk..."

The words won't even come out—I can't say them.

I won't let myself believe that the blood belongs to any of them, even though the evidence says it must.

Jack hands Giovanni off to Isaac and squats in front of me, clasping my hands in her smaller ones. "Because when people get desperate, they do stupid shit. Maybe whoever he had shooting didn't follow orders. Maybe he was supposed to watch and ensure the baby wasn't in danger. I don't know."

Tears prick my eyes, and I pull my hands from hers and rub them away, determination taking over my panic. "I have to go look for them."

The police officer turns back to me. "Sir, I need to interview you before you leave."

I glance up at him. "I wasn't even here. I don't know anything."

"Sir—"

"Am I under arrest?"

The cop narrows his eyes on me. "No."

I push out of the chair. "Then I'm leaving. You can get my statement later."

Isaac smirks his approval, and Jack backs away, giving me room to move toward the door. Isaac follows me out into the hallway to the elevator.

He stops next to me, his brows raised. "Where are you going?"

I look at him and the baby, not that much older than Benjamin, sleeping so soundly despite the turmoil swirling around him. "I'm going to find them, and then, I'm going to kill that motherfucker."

Isaac punches in the elevator code, and the doors slide open immediately. I step in, turning to face him. He wants to come with me. I can see it in his gaze, but with his son in his arms, he has to stay.

And I completely understand.

His hard smile almost breaks me before the doors start to close. "Good luck."

Those parting words echo in the cab as the elevator zooms down, my stomach dropping with it. Each passing floor seems to take hours instead of seconds—every single one giving Roselli more time to find them if he hasn't already. Or if he already has them—

God...is this the kind of fear they all felt?

I squeeze my eyes closed, trying to fight through the cloud of panic that will impede my ability to think clearly.

The ding indicating I hit the main floor sets me in motion immediately, and I step out into the lobby that's crawling with police and our security personnel. Dad and Gabe stand, speaking with the detective who allowed me upstairs, but they break away from him when they see me.

I approach them, scanning the lobby. "Have you found out anything?"

They both give me bleak looks, and before either can even say anything, I brush past them toward the front doors.

"I'm going out to look for them."

Dad hustles after me, grabbing my arm to stop me from advancing. "Where? Where are you going to look?"

I shake off his hold. "I don't fucking know, but I can't just sit here, waiting, hoping that somebody finds them and that they're okay. There's blood up there."

They both cringe, and two of the strongest men I know are on the verge of tears.

Gabe nods and swallows thickly. "We know—"

The glass lobby doors open, and Bishop stumbles in, out of breath, her braids loose from her bun.

Holy shit...

Dad rushes to meet her, helping her to the wall so she can lean against it. "Bishop, where the fuck have you been? Did you find the shooter?"

She shakes her head, pressing her hand over her chest, then slides down to the tile. "I saw him three buildings over, corner window, but by the time I got over there and up, he was gone. The only evidence he was ever there was the open fucking window."

Gabe shoves a hand through his hair. "Shit. The apartment?"

"Unoccupied."

I slam my fist into the wall next to her. "Fuck."

She glances up at me. "Have you found them?"

We all shake our heads...unable to even say the words because we all know what it means.

Nothing good.

Bishop drops her head low between her knees. "This is my fault. I should have been upstairs with them instead of down here."

Dad squats in front of her, resting a hand on her knee. "This isn't your fault. What could you have done from up there?"

She shakes her head as tears slide out of the corners of her eyes. "I don't know, but I should have been with them. I should have been the one driving them out of here, then maybe—"

Gabe crosses his arms over his chest. "No, you did the right thing going after the shooter. He could have led us straight to Roselli. And maybe he still can." He motions to one of the officers milling around in the lobby and brings him over. "We need a rush on the testing of the bullets."

The man in uniform, whom I recognize as a "friend" of the Hawkes, flips open his notepad. "What do you need to know?"

"Manufacturer, caliber, anything that could help me track down the sales. If they're specialty rounds, they should be easier to find, and we can figure out who bought them. That might lead us somewhere."

Slowly, far too slowly.

Time isn't on our side.

The longer they're out there, unprotected, the easier it is for Roselli to finally get what he wants—Benjamin. And once he has him, Allie, Atlas, and Astrid won't stand a chance.

Bishop climbs to her feet, her gaze locked on mine. "Are you going to look for them?"

I nod.

She twists her hair back up and secures it, determination set on her face. "I'm going with you."

The officer holds up a hand. "Ma'am, we need to interview you. We'll need to have you take us over to where you think the shooter was set up."

Bishop gives him a look that tells him that absolutely isn't happening and follows me out the front doors and to my car.

ALESSANDRA

KENNEDY'S HANDS tighten on my arms, physically restraining me from launching myself at Daniele as he walks around the dingy warehouse, holding a screaming, hysterical Benjamin. She brushes her lips against my ear, trying not to let him or any of his men see she's talking to me. "*Don't.* You don't know what he'll do."

Considering he was willing to have someone fire shots into the place where his son was living...

She's right.

I don't know what he would do if I tried to take Benjamin from him. Though I suspect he would have no problem ordering one of his many goons milling about to kill all of us if I make the grab.

He threatened as much the moment he snatched Benjamin from my arms in the first place, and he doesn't seem to give a shit about the fact that Atlas and Astrid are deteriorating by the minute.

I drag my gaze from Benjamin and assess Atlas and Astrid beside us, bile rising up my throat at their condition.

Blood trickles from under Atlas' tattooed hand clamped over his left shoulder, and the red spreading across Astrid's shirt drips from her side to the filthy, cracked cement floor we're all sitting on.

If they don't get help soon...

Don't think that.

You can't *think that way.*

I try to control my mounting panic, inhaling long and slow before I risk opening my mouth to broach the subject with Dan again. Because this can't go on. I might have survived that shooting, but I *won't* survive hearing Benjamin in so much distress.

Tugging out of Kennedy's hold, I hold up my hands, trying to appear as unthreatening as possible. "He's terrified, Dan. And probably hungry. Let me take him."

His hard eyes cut to me—filled with animosity, hatred, and distrust.

They used to be so different, once held what I thought was affection when he looked at me. So much has changed about him that I barely recognize the man anymore.

Where is the affable, talented musician I tumbled into bed with?

It seems like he's completely gone now—not even a hint of the person I spent time with remains—replaced by this angry, violent man willing to hurt us to get what he wants.

He approaches me slowly, sneering, completely ignoring the cries of his son. "You think I'm ever giving him back to you again?" His humorless laugh echoes through the vast space, and he shakes his head. "Not. Fucking. Happening."

Turning away, he bounces Benjamin and talks to him low enough that I can't hear, which only seems to upset the baby more.

The more frantic his cries get, the more they eat away at my soul.

Benjamin has never known anything but gentle touches and pure love from me, Pope, or anyone else who has ever handled him. And even so tiny, he can sense something is wrong—that the man holding him is *wrong*.

It should be Pope.

Pope is his father in every way that matters, and Daniele is nothing more than a monster who will never offer him anything but fear and pain.

"Please, Dan..." I repeat his name softly, hoping to reach any small part of the person I knew who might be buried under all this hostility—"just let me calm him down and see if he's hungry. I'll give him back."

It's a fucking lie.

I'll hand my baby back to him over my dead body.

I try to keep my expression neutral even though I can feel

Kennedy tense beside me, preparing herself to intervene if she needs to on my or Benjamin's behalf.

Dan considers it for a moment, watching Benjamin wailing and thrashing in his arms, then narrows his eyes on me and shakes his head. "I don't trust you."

"Then why don't you just kill me and the rest of us?" The words come out before I can bite them back, the question slicing through the tense air around us.

Astrid gasps from my other side, and Kennedy's jaw drops as she looks at me like I've lost my mind.

She tugs me against her. "What the *fuck* are you doing? Why the hell would you ask him that?"

I push her off and climb to my feet. Dan watches me, and so do his men, trying to suss out what I'm doing as I approach.

As if I have a fucking clue.

But playing nice wasn't working, and I can't sit back and watch my baby suffer anymore. Not when Dan doesn't seem to give a shit about what's best for him.

I hold out my hands. "Give him to me."

Benjamin turns his head toward my voice, desperate for someone he knows, someone he trusts.

Dan hesitates for a moment, then looks at his screaming son, considering his options. "Five minutes, then you give him right back. And I'm watching you the entire time."

Thank God...

"Fine." I snatch Benjamin away quickly, before Dan can change his mind, and cradle him to my chest, whispering words of encouragement as I pace in front of the wall where Dan had us dumped when he led us in here at gunpoint. "It's all right, buddy. I have you. You're okay..."

Benjamin starts to calm slightly, but he turns his head toward my chest like he wants to eat. The poor kid has probably been hungry this entire time, and his douchebag sperm donor didn't give a shit about it.

That buys me more time with him in my arms and away from Dan. And right now, I'll take any win we can get, no matter how small.

I settle back on the floor beside Kennedy, casting a worried glance at Atlas and Astrid, who both look weaker and weaker by the minute.

Dan watches me with untrusting, narrowed eyes, and I turn away slightly to expose my breast and let Benjamin latch. That seems to appease him almost instantly, and he nuzzles against me, pressing one small hand to my neck and clutching my shirt in the other.

The man keeping us hostage doesn't look away for a second, and he still holds all the cards.

Now that I have Benjamin, I take a moment to examine Dan closely. Unlike the easy, laid-back man who used to play the most beautiful songs at The Grind, this version of Dan is jittery, on edge.

And why wouldn't he be?

His father was murdered basically in front of him, and he decided he wanted to run a criminal empire, knowing others would stand against him.

He started a war by claiming the Roselli territory.

If he had just let it go, Francis Gilardi would have stepped up, and he would have been the one to face Satriano. Instead, Dan has created a three-way conflict...one he's unlikely to win. Add to that his desperation to find Benjamin for the last two months and he's on the precipice of unraveling completely.

We can't do anything to push him in the wrong direction, or we'll suffer the consequences, especially Benjamin.

Maybe don't encourage him to kill us again, Al.

Now that I have my baby in my arms, it seems like a fucking stupid thing to have said to him.

Reckless.

But it got Benjamin away from that monster, so I can't regret it.

Not when I've been wondering it since we fled the condo and got intercepted by his goons...

Why didn't they shoot all four of us and take Benjamin?

Dan runs his hands through his hair, pacing and watching us with an unhinged gaze. He focuses on me, pressing his lips together, muttering something under his breath.

Kennedy levels him with her icy glare. "Did you say something?"

I cast a glance at her, begging her to be quiet with a look I hope she catches.

But it's too late.

He sneers at her, his agitation growing. "You want to know why I haven't killed all four of you yet? The only reason I'm keeping you alive is because I need you."

Kennedy shifts forward from against the wall, her curiosity piqued. "For what?"

Dan glances around the warehouse at his men, who all seem to be milling about, waiting for something. "I have a meeting with Luca Abello soon."

Luca?

My heart skips a beat, and I peek at Atlas and Astrid, who aren't in any condition to offer me their reactions. Kennedy's jaw drops, and she casts a quick glance at me.

Swallowing thickly, I adjust my hold on Benjamin, hoping Dan doesn't pick up on my reaction. "Why?"

He gives me a little satisfied grin. "It turns out he isn't very happy with the Hawkes and is interested in backing me."

No fucking way.

Luca would *never* help Roselli.

Not in a billion years.

It must be some kind of act, a ploy to draw Dan out when we couldn't find him for so long.

Trying to school my features, I meet his gaze. "If you have *him*. Why do you need *us*?"

He gives me a half grin. "Because if he shows up and it's any sort of trap, if he or anyone else in your family tries anything, then I have all of you as hostages. They know I would never hurt my son. I need people I *can* hurt."

Never hurt his son?

Rage fires through my blood, and I snap. "You fired *shots* into the fucking condo." I bite back the *worse* things I want to say. "You could've hit him."

Dan's jaw hardens, gaze drifting down to where Benjamin still feeds. "That was a mistake. I told him not to shoot unless he was confident the baby was in another room." He fists his hands at his side. "And that misstep has been rectified."

Icy confirmation that he killed the shooter. And while normally that idea would be revolting, he was the man who shot at Benjamin and us, so I hope he burns in Hell, along with anyone else who ever backed this psychopath.

Atlas releases a little groan, shifting himself up more and glaring at Dan. "Do you think that scares us? Telling us you killed him and want to kill us?" He sucks in a sharp gasp, his pain evident in his shaky words. "You know the Hawkes don't respond well to threats."

Apparently, there is some more fight in him than might appear evident...

Dan walks over to him and squats. "Ah, Atlas Hawke..."—his hard eyes trace over Atlas' tattoos—"the black sheep of the family. I heard you have quite a boxing career." His gaze drops to Atlas' injured arm. "If you survive this, that might be in jeopardy."

Atlas sneers and tries to push up to go after him, but one of Roselli's men steps forward and points a gun at him.

A cold grin spreads across Dan's lips. "I wouldn't do that if I were you. We're all going to sit tight until I have things squared away with Luca."

Kennedy scowls at the man. "And then what?" She raises a brow. "Have you thought this through at all? Let's say Luca agrees to help you, and you use us to prevent the Hawkes from trying to take you out. What then?"

I reach out and grab Kennedy's arm. This time, it's *me* trying to stop *her* from saying something to antagonize him. But she appears undeterred.

It seems we've all reached our boiling points.

Yet, watching Dan consider her question, a glimmer of hope flashes in the darkness of our current predicament.

For a split second, I thought we were going to get away from the condo earlier today. Even after Astrid was hit, I prayed we had a chance to make it to the club. But then four large SUVs cut us off, two in front and two behind, and I knew it was over.

Now, I'm not so sure.

Dan doesn't seem to have a plan beyond getting Luca to help him, which means there's still a chance we could get out of here alive if we don't set him off.

He glances down at Benjamin and me, his gaze softening for a split second before it hardens again. "The most important thing was getting my *son*. And now that I have him, I can set everything else into motion."

I bite back the argument that he "has his son" to see where he's going with this. "What are you going to set in motion?"

His brows rise. "You really want to know my plan?"

Kennedy and I nod.

"Once I have Luca's backing, the rest of you won't be necessary." He practically spits the words at us, then glares at me. "Especially you." Squatting in front of me, he releases a sigh. "Things could've been so different, Alessandra, if you had just told me about the baby. We could've raised him together. We could've had a life together, filled with power and money..."

He reaches out and twirls a strand of my hair around his finger. I jerk my head away from him.

"But you had to go and fuck all that up, didn't you?" Tsking, he pushes back to his feet and shakes his head. "Well, now you'll pay the price for it. You and the rest of the Hawkes."

19

ALESSANDRA

Daniele's men start getting antsy, their eyes darting around the warehouse, looking out through the partially boarded-up windows.

Luca will be here soon. For some reason, knowing that makes the situation a tiny bit more bearable. Gives me a flicker of hope.

Kennedy wraps her arms around me and leans in to ensure no one can hear what she's saying. "Do you think Luca has a plan to get us out of here?"

I snuggle a sleeping Benjamin against me closer and turn my head slightly so she can hear me. "My guess is this was part of Luca's plan the whole time. There's no way this was set up between when we were taken and when Dan told us about it."

"So, they must have had a plan before the shooting went down."

I give a little nod, praying I'm right. "If anyone can get us out of here, if anyone can convince someone as unhinged as

Daniele to let us go, it'll be Luca. And if all else fails, the cavalry will come in guns blazing."

Kennedy glances over at Atlas and Astrid. "It can't come soon enough..."

But they will come.

Pope will.

I know it deep in my soul.

He may not be as lethal as his father or sister or Gabe...but he will get to us. Any way he can. No matter what stands in his way. Including the men in this warehouse.

Dan moves between them, giving them orders but looking over here every few minutes to ensure we haven't moved an inch.

I've done my best to remain still so I don't draw any more attention to me or the fact that I still have Benjamin when Dan said he would take him back right away. But the utter stillness of the twins beside me screams just how bad a shape they're in.

I peek over at them, trying to keep Dan in my peripheral vision. "Astrid, Atlas, how are you guys doing?"

Atlas glances up at me from where he sprawls on the concrete, no longer even able to sit up. Eyes clouded and unfocused. His skin, at least what's visible of it that isn't tattooed, pale.

Astrid doesn't look much better, lying with her head on his thigh.

He groans. "Alive." He chuckles, and it turns into a wince. "But shit, we're not going to last like this much longer."

There wasn't any need to state the obvious. We all knew it. But for someone like him, who literally fights for a living and would never concede defeat, to admit that, it's bad, really fucking bad.

The makeshift tourniquets Kennedy rigged by ripping up her T-shirt and tying it around his wound and Astrid's don't seem to have helped staunch the flow of blood very much.

Pools have started to form under them.

And while I may not be a doctor, I know that kind of blood loss can be life-threatening very quickly. The longer we sit here, our freedom controlled by a rookie mobster with too much on his plate and too high aspirations, the worse it's going to get.

Dan sees me talking to them and narrows his eyes, coming over. "What are you doing?"

Squaring my shoulders, refusing to cower before him, I stand my ground. "I'm just checking on them."

"Stop."

"If they die here, what are you going to do?"

A contemptuous snort slips from him. "If Luca walks in and sees them, he won't care. From what I hear, he's pretty pissed off at your uncle right now." He looks at Kennedy. "Your father's greed is getting the best of him. He's going to pay for it now." He reaches forward to take Benjamin from me, and I jerk back, holding him tighter.

Dan glares at me, fury flashing across his gaze. "Give him to me."

I shake my head. "Do you want to be holding him during your meeting with Luca?" I raise a brow. "What harm does it do to let me keep him?"

Logic.

It's the one thing we haven't tried yet, but he seems unconvinced, reaching again and sliding his hands under him.

I don't know why I try to reason with him when the man clearly can't see any, but headlights flash through the warehouse windows, drawing his attention away before he can act.

One of his men jogs over. "Boss, they're here."

Dan stands and walks away without looking back, apparently not as concerned about Benjamin as he is the arrival of the man I've considered my uncle for my entire life.

I can see how the priorities go—business *then* son.

Which may actually play in our favor.

Kennedy shifts her position, sliding onto her knees.

"What are you doing?"

She glances my way briefly. "I want to be able to get up fast if I need to."

"Be careful. If they catch you—"

Leaning in, she scans the warehouse. "Look at his men. They're so terrified of Luca; they're not even watching us anymore."

I follow her gaze, examining each of the half-dozen armed guards scattered around who now move toward Dan, leaving a single armed goon at one of the doors.

The one Luca steps through.

My breath catches at the sight of him, hope bursting forward through the abyss surrounding us.

His hard, dark eyes scan the warehouse and pause on us momentarily. Somehow, he manages to fight his reaction to seeing Astrid and Atlas' conditions, advancing toward Dan.

Dan opens his arms. "Mr. Abello, thank you so much for coming to meet with me."

Luca steps forward, his shiny Italian loafers glinting under the overhead fluorescent lights. He offers Dan a half smile. "I am sorry about your father. I haven't had a chance to offer my condolences before now."

He sounds so sincere that *I* almost believe him, but all the Hawkes know how he felt about Cristiano Roselli.

Luca might have backed him to take over when he stepped down, but that didn't mean there were any sort of friendly feelings between the two. They tolerated each other—which kept the relative peace over the last thirty years.

That's all changed now.

Dan gives him a nod. "I appreciate it. It's been difficult."

Luca raises a brow. "Had I known he had a son interested in the business, I might've been able to assist you sooner."

"I wasn't always interested in my father's business, but times change, as I've heard they have for you and your relationship with the Hawkes." He glances over his shoulder at us. "Which brings us to where we are tonight."

Luca's penetrating gaze follows Dan's, landing on the baby and me.

God, he's a good actor.

If I didn't know him as well as I do, I would believe he didn't give a shit about any of us.

Giving nothing away in his gaze, he lowers it to Benjamin. "I see you got your son back."

A smile curls Dan's lips. "Yes, finally. I don't intend to give him up."

Luca shakes his head. "Nor would I. I understand the love a parent has for their child and what they're willing to do for them."

His words make the tears I've been holding back finally fall because I know what he did for Jude, and I know what Pope would do for Benjamin. The same thing I would—literally anything.

Dragging his focus away from us, Luca crosses his hands behind his back, surveying the warehouse with a slow turn. "I hope this isn't your base of operations. If so, it leaves a bit to be desired."

Dan offers a laugh. "Of course not, temporary digs. Until I can get rid of Francis and consolidate my father's power, I need to stay on the move."

Luca pauses, giving Dan a smug grin. "You don't need to worry about Francis anymore."

Kennedy grabs my arm, her fingers digging into it. "Is he saying what I think he's saying?"

I nod.

Holy shit.

Luca's taking this much further than I thought he ever would. After he went through so much to get out of the business, to move away from this life, in order to save us, he's had to go right back to it. By taking out Roselli's rival, he's making enemies out of others, those who supported Gilardi and who choose not to fall under the Roselli umbrella anymore.

That's the last thing any of us need—another potential enemy—but it may be the lesser of two evils in this situation.

Deal with the current threat, then look to any future ones later.

Daniele raises a brow at him. "He's gone?"

Luca offers him a hard smile. "Consider it an act of good faith so that you know I'm serious when I tell you that I'd like to back you and help you take your seat. Your father fought hard for it when I stepped down, and he controlled this area well for a long time. You deserve it. Not Francis, and definitely not Satriano."

At the mention of the name, Dan's entire demeanor shifts, his shoulders stiffening, eyes turning almost black. "He's been after me at the order of the Hawkes."

Nodding, Luca starts to wander closer to us—intentionally, I'm sure. "I'm aware." He stops a few feet from us and stares down at Kennedy, Atlas, Astrid, and me, his eyes bouncing between the four of us and to Benjamin. "It appears you've already taken care of at least two of them."

Dan joins him over near us and grins. "Those two won't last long."

"And what about the others? Allowing Atlas and Astrid to die will activate Gabe Anderson's full potential as a killer, and Kennedy is Savage's daughter. So, she holds a lot of weight. Alessandra, well..."

He doesn't have to tell Daniele anything about me. I stupidly told him everything when we were together, believing he cared.

Fucking idiot, Al.

Dan crosses his arms over his chest and watches us. "I

haven't decided yet. But unless you think they'd be of some use, I plan to get rid of them."

Luca looks over at Dan, his face dead serious. "That's probably wise. The Hawkes will come for them otherwise, and you don't want that. They're well-armed and well-prepared, undoubtedly searching for them already. They'll get *down* to business as soon as they find you."

Yes.

He's telling us there *is* a plan, and it's already underway. No way Luca would come to meet with Daniele Roselli and *not* bring the cavalry. And he just gave us the warning that when bullets start flying, we need to get down.

Kennedy shifts her position, making it easier to drop low if she needs to, and I do the same, ensuring Dan's focus isn't on me as I move.

They're coming soon.

I can feel the tension building in the warm, humid air.

Dan must sense it, too, because his spine stiffens and he narrows his eyes on Luca. "I imagine they are. But you wouldn't have been stupid enough to lead them to me, would you?"

Luca holds up his hands. "Of course not. As I said"—he inclines his head toward us—"I'm done with the Hawkes and Savage lording his power over me. I ran this city after my father's death, the same way you should. I still have more power than Savage ever will, yet he acts like he's my boss. I won't put up with it any longer."

"But you'll let me be your boss?"

A sinister grin curves Luca's lips. "I'd see you take the throne, but I don't have any intention of getting my hands dirty in the future. I'll support you. I'll back you. I'll make introductions and connections with people you may not know. Smooth things over with those who may have supported Gilardi or do support Satriano. Then I'll be a silent partner."

"For what sort of cut?"

"Forty percent."

Dan's eyes fly open wide. "Fuck no."

Luca's broad shoulders rise and fall in his tailored suit. "Then I guess we have nothing further to discuss."

He turns and walks back toward the door he entered through, but Daniele calls out to him.

"Wait."

POPE

ROSELLI CALLS OUT TO LUCA, and he freezes halfway to the door. From my vantage point, peeking in through one of the cracked, dirty windows on the far side of the warehouse, I can only hear bits and pieces of their conversation, but I can see enough to know that things are dire.

Astrid and Atlas lie barely moving on the floor beside Kennedy and Allie, their clothes bearing the evidence of their wounds. They've clearly been losing blood for a while, possibly since the shooting at the condo, which was hours ago.

If Luca doesn't wrap this up quickly so we can move in on them, it may be too late.

My gut twists at that thought, and I push it back out of my head, trying to force myself to think as a doctor and not family.

I can save them if I can just get in there.

But we're in standby mode right now, waiting for Luca to get clear so we can eliminate Roselli and his crew once and for all.

I glance over to where Gabe, Saint, and Bishop stand ready in tactical gear, tucked against the building, watching everything unfold and praying this all goes smoothly.

It could be deadly if it doesn't.

Rage floods my veins, growing stronger every moment we have to hold off on rescuing them. Watching Allie and

Benjamin cower against the wall, terrified and helpless, has only enforced the fact that there is no way to resolve this without Roselli dying. But it doesn't mean we can risk people we love getting caught in the crossfire.

I tighten my hand around my Glock, ready to do whatever I have to.

He won't hurt you again.

Never.

I silently make the promise to her, hoping she can feel it and knows I'm here, coming for them as soon as Luca is clear.

And Roselli just stopped him from leaving.

Shit. Shit. Shit.

Luca turns to face him, but headlights roll over us, and I have to duck into the shadows, unable to hear the rest of their conversation as I hide from the new arrival.

A dark SUV pulls up to the warehouse, and Satriano climbs from the back, buttoning his suit coat as he closes his door. His eyes bounce over to my hiding place immediately, then he scans the darkness, looking for what he must know is the rest of us.

"Dr. Clarke, why don't you join me inside?"

Shit.

This wasn't part of the plan.

If I show up, it could set Dan off.

But I can't exactly pretend Satriano didn't see me or that he's not standing here, waiting for some sort of response.

I rise from my crouched position, tucking my gun into the holster at my hip, and pull my shirt over it as I approach him. "What are you doing here?"

He grins. "The same thing you are."

"I highly doubt that."

A low chuckle slips from his lips, and he motions toward the warehouse door. "I heard there was a meeting happening tonight that I might be interested in. Didn't want to miss it."

"Why do you need me?"

Another slow grin splits his face. "You'll see. Shall we?"

He spreads his arm wide, indicating I should walk in front of him, and four of his men line up around us, leading our group toward the entrance.

I make eye contact with Bishop as I pass her hiding spot, and she warns me with hard bourbon eyes not to fuck this up.

Like I need another reminder of who is in there and what's at stake...

I step through the door, Satriano at my side, and Roselli's men are immediately on us. Luca's eyes widen, but he schools his features quickly.

Dan jerks his head toward Luca, already reaching for his own weapon. "What the *fuck* is this?"

Luca steps back, holding up his hands. "This has nothing to do with me. I don't know why they're here."

And for the first time tonight, he's telling the truth.

None of this was part of the plan.

Now, we're all flying by the seat of our pants, and if we don't make this work, it will be a fucking bloodbath.

My eyes dart to Allie, and her wide ones meet mine. Tears streak down her cheeks, and her lip trembles. She's terrified, but at least she appears unhurt and has Benjamin in her arms.

The same can't be said for Atlas or Astrid...

Roselli fumes, spittle flying from his mouth as he points his weapon at Luca. "Like hell you didn't. This was a fucking setup."

Luca shakes his head. "It was not."

Which isn't a complete lie.

Satriano was never supposed to be here, but it *was* a setup.

One that has now gone to shit because of the man standing beside me showing up uninvited. Satriano steps forward, holding up his hands. "Now, now. Let's not rush to conclusions. Mr. Abello didn't know I was going to be here this evening or that I was going to swing by and pick up Dr. Clarke on my way."

I release a heavy breath.

At least he didn't out me or the rest of the Hawkes for already being outside. Which means there may still be a chance to make this plan work.

Satriano approaches them, keeping enough distance that his men can provide cover against Roselli's. "I just didn't want to miss out on what appears to be such an important discussion regarding the future of New Orleans." He looks at Luca. "And from what I hear, the third interested party is no longer an issue, thanks to Mr. Abello."

Luca inclines his head but doesn't say anything else about taking out Francis Gilardi.

When he said he had been busy the last few months, he meant it. Using old contacts. Making new ones. Maneuvering himself into a position that allowed him to walk right into Gilardi's penthouse and end him with a single shot before his men even knew what hit him. And they were too scared of Luca Abello to retaliate for the death of their don. They let him walk out scot-free, something I don't know if we'll be lucky enough to accomplish again.

Satriano moves around Luca and Dan's standoff, urging me with him, until he can better see Allie, Astrid, Atlas, and Kennedy against the wall. "It appears we have a few injuries. Perhaps Dr. Clarke could go take care of them while we finish our conversation."

Allie's eyes stay locked on mine, pleading with me. And fuck, if it isn't the hardest thing in the world to have to stay rooted here until Roselli gives me the okay.

He looks between Satriano and Luca and me, confusion furrowing his brow.

The asshole doesn't know what to fucking do.

If his men start shooting, so will Satriano's. And if that

happens, the chances of him getting out of here alive are slim. The fucker doesn't realize he's leaving in a body bag, no matter what he does now.

Any attempt to exit the warehouse and either Gabe, Bishop, or Dad will end him with one fucking shot.

Satriano raises his shoulders and lets them fall, his gaze sliding over Astrid and Atlas again. "What could it hurt to let Dr. Clarke take a look?"

Not that I can do much without any medical supplies on me —but at least I can assess them and see how much time we have.

Dan shakes his head, locking his jaw as his hand tightens around his weapon still pointed at Luca. "He doesn't need to check them. They're irrelevant."

That draws a slow grin across Satriano's face. "They're far from irrelevant. I have plans for the Hawkes, and you're interfering with them."

The cold hand of dread squeezes my spine as I look at the man.

Plans.

It's the same warning he issued all those months ago at the hotel groundbreaking—the threat we've all been waiting for him to act on.

Roselli swallows thickly, debating whether he wants to further piss off a man like Satriano over such a seemingly innocent action, like letting me examine the injured. "Fine. He can go."

Thank fuck.

I rush across the cracked concrete and drop to my knees, pulling Allie and Benjamin to me and pressing a kiss to her lips. Pulling back, I take her face in my palms. "Thank God!" I run a hand over Benjamin's head, sound asleep through the standoff going on behind me. "Are you two all right?"

She nods as tears stream down her face. "Yes..."

Physically maybe.

But I can see how traumatized she really is by all that happened and continues to around us.

I look at Kennedy, scanning her quickly. "Kennedy?"

She nods. "I'm good. Astrid and Atlas have lost a lot of blood."

"I can see that."

Releasing Allie, I move over to them, checking Astrid first.

Though she's unconscious, her pulse and breathing are steady, and the tourniquet around her side seems to have staunched the flow of blood enough to keep her stable —for now.

I move on to Atlas, who is in a much more dire situation.

Weak, thready pulse.

Cold and clammy skin.

The wound on his shoulder still leaking like a damn sieve despite someone's attempt to stop the bleeding.

Fuck.

"Hey, Atlas." I tap the side of his cheek, and his eyes flutter open partially. Grabbing the hem of my shirt, I rip off a section and make a new bandage, tightening it around his arm as hard as I can. "Try to stay awake."

He winces and struggles to focus on me, instinctually attempting to move, but I keep him prone, hand on his chest. Finally, his eyes meet mine. "Pope?"

I nod. "Yeah."

Atlas' brow furrows as he attempts to look at the warehouse behind me. "What's going—"

I press my hand over his mouth, dipping my head closer. "We're all getting out of here. Just stay down and—"

"Hey!" Roselli's voice cuts through my conversation with Atlas, making me still. "What the fuck are you doing over there?" He comes closer, pointing his gun aimlessly back toward where Satriano and Luca stand. "That's enough. Back away."

I raise my hands and retreat, turning to face him. "They need to get to a hospital soon, or they're both going to die."

The words feel like acid burning across my tongue as I speak them, and the sob Allie releases behind me makes me wince. But the truth is, they don't have much time.

Especially Atlas.

Satriano *tsks* his tongue, moving off to one side and putting more distance between himself and Roselli as Luca does the same in the other direction. "I'm sorry, Daniele. As I said, I have plans for the Hawkes, and your interference over the last few months has made things difficult for me."

The singer-turned-mob boss snarls at him, his eyes wild and unhinged. He staggers away from us toward the center of the warehouse. "Are you threatening me?"

Satriano shakes his head, completely calm in the face of the younger man's rage. "I don't have to threaten you."

The shot comes so fast that Roselli's men don't know what's happening.

A single, clean headshot from the window in the far corner of the warehouse.

Roselli's goons take a stunned second to react, but it's all the time Satriano's men, Gabe, Bishop, and Dad need to take them all out—the sharp crack of gunfire explodes in the air, ringing in my ears along with Benjamin's frantic cries.

One by one, Roselli's entire crew drops to the concrete in bloody heaps.

It's over.

Finally.

My legs tremble, and I turn and drop to the floor to start working on Atlas and Astrid, doing what I can until the ambulances get here. I *know* someone outside is already calling.

Allie watches intently with tear-soaked eyes, whispering

something to Benjamin, who has been stunned by the sudden, catastrophically loud noises around him.

Kennedy moves over next to me. "Can I help you with anything?"

"Apply pressure to her wound and check if there's an exit."

I adjust Atlas so that he's in a better position for his airway and press my hand over where the bullet tore into him—really, the only thing I can do to help slow the bleeding now.

My gaze meets Allie's, and she completely loses it.

A sob wrenches from her throat, and she clutches Benjamin to her as Luca rushes over to us and pulls her into his arms.

Tears blur my vision, and I struggle to speak through the lump in my throat. "Shit. Teeny, I'm so sorry..."

For ever breaking up with her.

For all the years we lost.

For the pain she's had to endure.

For *everything*.

All I want to do is pull her into my arms and hold her now that we know she's finally safe, but with Satriano literally looking over our shoulders, we might not be.

20

POPE

I stand against the wall behind Stone's chair in his office, under his law school diploma and bar awards, staring at Satriano. He sits opposite us, casually reclined, one ankle propped up on the other knee, waiting for us to start as if this meeting isn't going to end up with someone getting fucked —likely us.

The longer this stare-down goes on, the thicker the tension in the room becomes, and given the number of angry people crammed in here, no one wants anyone to detonate.

There would be far too much shrapnel for anyone to survive it.

And after what we just went through, none of us wants any new trouble.

Especially me.

All I've wanted since the moment I left Allie's side this morning was to get back to her—and sitting here, letting the minutes tick by, only makes that prospect seem less and less likely.

Savage scowls from beside his brother, his frustration growing, and Isaac leans against the wall near the window, jaw locked, his hatred for the man responsible for Kennedy's, his father's, and his own injuries rolling off him in waves strong enough to knock someone over and drown them.

No one can blame him for his ire.

Damiano Satriano is no friend of the Hawkes—the man is a menace, just like his brother was before him.

Only he lurks in the shadows, showing himself when it pleases and benefits him. Usually when it hurts us, too.

Last night was no different.

It may have looked like he helped and came to the rescue, but that couldn't be further from the truth.

Which is why Gabe, Dad, and Luca all mill about the room, keeping a close eye on Satriano, fully strapped, while everyone else is rotating spending time at the hospital with Astrid and Atlas.

Which is where I should be, since Allie and Benjamin are there right now.

Fuck.

I thought getting rid of Daniele would make this ache go away, this longing need to always be with them, to ensure they're okay with my own two eyes, but if anything, it's only grown.

But today's meeting wasn't optional after what happened last night.

After a stony silence that goes on for far too long, neither side wanting to cross the battle line first, Satriano finally raises a brow as a sign of his impatience.

Stone scowls at him. "You are the one who wanted this meeting, so why don't you get down to it and tell us why?"

The silver-haired don grins. "I just thought after all the hustle and bustle of last evening and my having to rush out before the paramedics and police arrived that there were some loose ends and items we need to discuss."

Shit.

Everyone knew it was coming, that there were going to be consequences to Satriano's involvement, but none of us wanted to deal with it last night.

Not with Atlas and Astrid's lives hanging in the balance.

Now that they're stable, though, it's impossible to ignore the man sitting in front of us or the fact that he is now the head of the largest crime organization on the Gulf Coast.

He *isn't* just going to go away, no matter how much we might wish he would.

Savage stares down Satriano—the head of the Hawke family and the don of the Satriano family—each refusing to break. "Damiano, you already told us you would want a favor if you helped us find Roselli, but *we* found him without you."

Luca nods, crossing his arms over his chest. "*I* did."

Satriano chuckles. "I knew you'd try to weasel your way out of the agreement, claiming semantics, but you didn't stand a chance of getting all of them out alive last night, including your pretty little girlfriend and her baby." He looks at me pointedly. "If I hadn't shown up, Roselli's men outnumbered you three to one, and they would've taken out your family members before you ever got all of them."

Given Gabe's snarl, I don't think he agrees with Satriano's assessment of the situation, but I don't know that we're really in a position to argue with him.

We hold a lot of power in this city, but Satriano's family goes back generations in Italy, a powerhouse member of the founding group that still controls much of the organized crime there and in the United States.

Now that he's resurfaced and claimed both his brother's network there and Roselli's here, his influence has spread far wider than our wings.

And if we're not careful, they'll be clipped.

Satriano drops his foot to the floor and leans forward slightly. "Now that Luca has so graciously removed Roselli's competition, and I took out Roselli himself—"

Gabe snorts. "You mean *I* took him out."

The man we once knew as Damon smirks at him. "I guess I owe the Hawkes a debt of gratitude. You've made my position here much easier to claim."

Savage raises a dark brow. "Does that mean we're even?"

Like it would ever be that easy.

Satriano's low chuckle fills the space. "We will never be *even*, Mr. Hawke. Lest you forget how your family member murdered my brother in cold blood."

He looks at Isaac, who remains motionless against the window.

Isaac's icy blue gaze locks with Satriano's. "It wasn't in cold blood; it was for a very good reason."

No one in this room would disagree with his description of the situation—except Damiano himself. When a mafia don threatens your child and kidnaps your girlfriend to force her into marriage, the only way to end things is permanently.

All Isaac did was what any of us would do to protect our family.

If Gabe hadn't pulled that trigger and taken out Dan last night, I would have done it myself gladly.

Satriano snickers at Isaac's assessment. "Ah, yes. Love makes us all fools, doesn't it?" He pushes to his feet. "I'll make this quick so you can get back to your injured family members. I've decided what my first favor is going to be."

First favor?

Of how many?

We all exchange looks, and then his hard gaze lands on me. "Dr. Clarke. I've been studying you for a while now. You're quite impressive. Almost as impressive as Dr. Hawke." He glances at

Stone, who appears about ready to launch himself across the desk and strangle the man for mentioning his wife. "But I doubt Nora would be very agreeable to helping me, whereas you"—he gives me a sinister grin—"you have that girlfriend and baby to protect, which makes me think you'll be a lot more compliant."

Jesus Christ.

He isn't above threatening the very people he just swore to help us protect only six weeks ago—including an innocent child.

That means he's truly capable of anything.

Swallowing through my dry throat, I try not to let my voice waver. "With what?"

"From time to time, I've run into situations where one of my men is injured and, for various legal reasons, can't be taken to a hospital."

Shit.

I should have seen this coming after he called me out last night at the warehouse and emphasized my ability to care for Atlas and Astrid.

It was a fucking test.

One I apparently passed with flying colors.

A slow smile spreads across his face. "And lucky me, I hear the Hawke Enterprises clinic is very well-equipped. Plus, I'm more than willing to provide additional funding for more equipment. Whatever you might need that isn't already there in order to assist my men, should they need it."

The man wants me to treat his men off the books...

He's insane.

Shaking my head, I find the strength to stand up to him and voice my concern. "I could lose my license."

His unnerving eyes darken to an almost black. "That isn't my problem."

"I'm not a surgeon."

The corners of his lips twitch. "No, you're not, but Dr. Hawke is. She may be spending her time in the ER now, but I looked into her background. She did work as a trauma surgeon for a number of years before going back to emergency medicine. I'm sure if you get in over your head, she can step in and help, even if reluctantly."

Stone clenches his jaw, a muscle there ticcing. "So, you want them to be your on-call doctors? Is that it?"

A grin spreads across Damiano's mouth, and he nods. "I'm glad you're following along." He moves around the chair, makes his way to the door, and then turns back. "Make sure you leave your phones on in case I need you in the future." His gaze drifts to me. "And I look forward to our working relationship."

He opens the door, but before he can step out, Isaac pushes off the wall.

Oh, shit.

I want to scream at him to shut up and let Satriano go, to not poke the bear, but it wouldn't do any good if I did.

"And what about the truce? What about the promise you made to get back at us for what I did to your brother?"

Satriano turns around slowly and faces Isaac. "Consider the truce..."—he raises a hand and rocks it back and forth —"hanging on by a thread. I've discovered you Hawkes can actually be quite useful at times." His gaze cuts to me, again. "Like Dr. Clarke..."

Goosebumps break out across my skin, and I shiver as he walks from the room, leaving all of us stunned and silent.

After a minute, Gabe closes the door and turns back to face everybody. "Well, fuck."

Stone mutters a litany of curses under his breath and looks at Isaac. "Are you all right?"

Isaac gives a sharp nod and cuts his gaze to me. "I'm more worried about Pope."

I scrub a hand over my face as I pace the small portion of

the office not occupied by one of the Hawke men. "Jesus. He wants me to be his mob doctor." I scan the faces of the men in the room, the ones who lead this family. "Do I have a fucking choice?"

Dad exchanges a look with Savage, then approaches me, grabbing my shoulders and stopping my frantic movement. "You always have a choice, son, but if you say no, it could mean we'll stay at war with Satriano for God knows how long."

"And if I say yes, I risk my whole fucking career."

A sad smile pulls at his lips. "Is it worth it to protect Allie and Benjamin?"

Fucking hell.

Their faces flash before my eyes, and it's all it takes to know the answer will always be *yes.*

Anything is worth it to protect them.

I give him a sharp nod, and he pulls me into a hug and claps me on the back.

"I'm proud of you, kid. This has been a rough couple of months, but you have done everything asked of you and gone above and beyond for Allie and Benjamin. I can see how much you love them."

Pulling back, I nod and lock eyes with him. "I do."

More than I ever knew possible.

I thought what Allie and I shared all those years ago was *it*, but it was truly only the tip of an iceberg when it comes to my feelings for that woman...and now, her son, too.

Dad raises a brow, smacking me lightly on the shoulder. "So, why don't you go and tell them that?"

ALESSANDRA

I ADJUST the blanket around Astrid for the hundredth time, making sure it's just right and she won't be cold in this hospital room with the air blowing right on her like I was when I spent time here.

She smacks my hand away. "Will you stop hovering?"

Crap.

I was hovering, wasn't I?

Dropping back into the chair beside her bed, I hold up my hands and sigh. "Sorry. Habit."

A smile plays on her lips. "The whole mothering instinct thing is hard to turn off, isn't it?"

I laugh and turn to check on Benjamin, where he sleeps in his car seat on the floor beside me. "You have no idea."

Even knowing he's safe now, that Dan is dead and isn't coming for him, I can't shake these nerves.

The uneasiness.

The desire to keep my eye on him constantly, even when he's right by my side.

Atlas turns from his bed on the other half of the room. "Will you two stop arguing? I'm trying to watch this."

I crane my neck to see what's on his TV, and it appears to be some shoot-'em-up action movie. "Really? *That's* what you want to watch when you and your sister just had major surgery after being *shot*?"

He shrugs and immediately winces, placing his hand over his bandaged shoulder. "Shit. I have to stop doing that." Gritting his teeth, he inhales a few times before he opens his eyes and glares at me. "And for the record, *yes, this* is what I want to watch. It's mindless action and enjoyable. So, can you two keep it down?"

Astrid scowls at him and tosses an empty cup off the table beside her at him.

Atlas dodges it easily, grinning. "I guess my reflexes are still good."

A low growl slips from her lips. "We'll see about that when we get out of these beds."

The playful yet tense banter between the twins isn't anything new, but I chew on my lip, not wanting to bring up the elephant in the room—we don't know if Atlas is ever going to be back to a hundred percent.

His fighting career might be over all because he took a bullet for me to draw the shooter away so we could get to the door and Bishop could try to locate him.

I swipe under my eyes and try to turn away before Astrid can see me crying, but she narrows her gaze on me.

"Oh, here come the tears again." She grabs a tissue from the box on the other side of her bed and hands it to me. "You need to stop crying."

"I know." I dab at my eyes, trying to get my breathing and the tightening in my chest under control. "Believe me, I've been trying, but"—I shrug—"you know."

She nods. "I do know, but everything's okay now."

I raise an eyebrow. "Is it? Do we really know that? The guys are all meeting with Satriano, and who knows what the hell he's demanding of them?"

Likely nothing good.

When Pope told me where they were off to this morning, it felt like another blow I wasn't prepared to take. Only a few hours of feeling like things were settled, and we're right back where we started months ago—with Satriano thinking he owns us.

All because we had to make a deal with him to save Benjamin.

The door opens, and Nora and Caroline enter, carrying huge gift baskets with Ang and Jude trailing behind them.

"Oh, my God." I push up out of my chair and race over, throwing my arms around Jude. "You came."

He wraps me up and hugs me tightly, burying his face

against my neck. His familiar, comforting scent wraps around me. "I did."

Those damn tears return, flowing freely down my cheeks and onto his shirt. "I didn't think you would make it."

Leaving his place to come to a busy hospital is torture for Jude, and Ang and I weren't sure he was going to be able to handle it. I had planned to head over to their place to see him since all we've been able to do is chat on the phone since everything went down.

But he's *here*.

He pulls back and takes my face between his palms. "I told you I would try." A little shudder rolls through him. "Though I don't know how long I'm going to stay."

Angie reaches over and squeezes his arm, offering him support. "We'll get out of here quickly. I just wanted to check in on everybody."

Caroline smiles brightly, setting one of the baskets overflowing with fresh fruit onto the table along the wall while Nora sets the other at the foot of Astrid's bed. "Hello, everyone!"

Atlas barely acknowledges her arrival, waving his good hand at her half-heartedly without even looking at her.

Astrid rolls her eyes at him and grins at Pope's mom, examining the goodies. "Hi, Aunt Care, that looks amazing!"

Nora moves to stand beside Astrid. "How are you feeling?"

She bobs her head. "Decent. At least they're giving me the good stuff." She motions toward her IV drip. "But I would love some of that fruit tower thing."

Caroline grins and starts unraveling the cellophane from around it. "You got it, kid."

Nora smirks and pats Astrid on the leg. "Yeah. Well, thankfully, you only had some minor damage to repair, so I imagine you'll be feeling better quickly—even without the *good* stuff." She glances over at Atlas. "Your brother, on the other hand..."

Atlas tosses her a dirty look. "Do we need to talk about me like I'm not here?"

She moves over to his bed and leans in to speak with him privately, trying to maneuver around the landmine his prognosis seems to be.

No matter how many times anyone tries to speak with him about it or how he's feeling, he shuts down completely—much like I did when people were trying to get me to talk about Benjamin's father and I wasn't ready to face the truth.

So, I don't blame him for needing time to process what's happening.

I've been there.

Ang greets Astrid and sits on the edge of the bed while Caroline wrangles with the fruit display and manages to get several strawberries off and onto a plate for Astrid.

Jude squats down by the car seat, pulling back the blanket tucked around Benjamin to see him better. "There's my favorite guy." He looks up at me. "How is he doing?"

I shrug. "As well as can be expected, I guess. He seems fine today. You know, Pope and Nora kept me overnight to make sure that my heart was good, and they checked him out, too, said he's completely healthy. The shock of what we went through yesterday doesn't appear to be affecting him very much."

And I wish it were that easy for me.

No matter how many times I tell myself it's *over*, it never really *feels* over.

Too many things are left up in the air.

So much is still uncertain.

Jude climbs to his feet and wraps his arm around my shoulder. "And how is it affecting you?"

That's a tougher question to answer, and he knows it.

He reads me far too well.

And so does my sister.

Ang gives me a tight smile, knowing full well that I'm on the edge of losing all control of my emotions again. "I'm just so glad everybody's okay. This could have been a lot worse."

I nod, remembering that terror of the bullets flying past us in the condo, of Roselli's men pointing their guns at us and ordering us out of the SUV, of the shots at the warehouse echoing around us while we cowered against the wall. "It could have." And there's still a chance it could get worse. "Have you guys heard from anyone at the meeting?"

Jude presses his lips together, and he shakes his head. "Not yet. Though I imagine Luca will call me when they're done. I told him he needs to come over, and we need to talk."

No doubt they do.

When Jude learned what Luca has been up to the last few months and what he did to facilitate the meeting with Roselli, he was livid.

And I can't blame him.

I look up at him, searching his face for an answer I don't think even he knows. "Are you still pissed at him?"

Jude runs his free hand back through his blond hair, and it flops right back over his forehead. "Of course I'm pissed. First, he disappeared, barely around for two months, and then, he was willing to sacrifice himself without even giving me or Byron any warning. So, yeah, I'm mad, and so is Byron."

Their feelings are completely valid.

If Pope did the same, I would be furious at him for keeping me in the dark. Still, Luca did what he thought was right to protect us, and I don't see how else it could have gone. "Would it have made a difference if he had told you? What would you have done? Try to talk him out of it?"

He gives me a sympathetic look. "No, of course not. Not if it was the best way to get rid of Roselli and make sure you and Benjamin were safe. I just..." He releases a heavy sigh. "Wish he would've told me. That's all. So I could have been prepared for it instead of getting a fucking call from him letting me know what happened, all *after* the fact."

Ang gives him a tight smile. "I don't like that they kept it from us, either, but they had their reasons."

Caroline finally chimes in, resting her hip against the edge of Astrid's bed on the opposite side of Ang. "You know, when it comes to this family, there are always going to be secrets, even though we strive to always be honest with each other."

A knot forms in my throat at her words, and I think about the look Pope gave me in that warehouse last night.

There were things there in his cognac eyes.

Things that weren't said.

Things that need to be.

But we haven't really had a chance to talk after we rushed everyone here last night. Then he headed off to the meeting this morning.

Jude rubs my arm. "Are you good, Allie Cat?"

I nod. "Yeah, I'm just eager to get—" I stop myself. "I was going to say home, but shit." I release a sardonic laugh. "I guess I don't really have one. My apartment will never feel safe again, Pope's condo was destroyed, and now, Isaac and Jack's place is, too."

Caroline takes a bite of one of Astrid's strawberries and chews. "You could always come to our place. Saint and I would love to have you. I imagine Pope will be coming home…"

She trails off, likely as unsure as I am about what's really going on now that this ordeal is supposedly over.

We've spent so much time trying to make it through today and tomorrow that we haven't been able to think or plan for the extended future.

I imagine one in my head, with Pope, Benjamin, and me…

But it's hazy.

Unclear.

So, Caroline isn't the only one slightly unsure what to say about her son's situation with me.

I smile at her. "Thank you for the offer, Care. I'll just go to my parents' house. They went over this morning and got all our stuff from Isaac and Jack's, anyway, and I'm too tired to think about trying to move anywhere else." Turning to Astrid, I raise a brow. "I'm going to head out, if you're good."

She nods. "Don't worry. I have this guy"—she tosses a thumb toward Atlas—"and his pleasantness to keep me company."

He growls and turns back to his movie, ignoring Nora and whatever she said to him, not interested in conversation with anyone.

His life, his career could be over because of what happened.

Everything he has worked so hard for could disappear in an instant.

And that guilt sits squarely on my chest, weighing me down when I should feel like it's been lifted by finally being free of Dan.

Jude grabs Benjamin's car seat from the floor. "We'll walk out with you. We just wanted to say hi."

He leans down and gives Astrid a kiss on the cheek, and Ang hugs her gently before we pile out of the room. Nora and Caroline trail behind and close the door, leaving the twins to themselves for the first time since they came out of surgery.

Nora and Care step to the side, deeply engaged in a conversation clearly not meant for our ears, and we wave and head down to the elevator slowly, in absolutely no rush.

For the first time in what feels like forever, we're not running from something, not being chased or shot at.

We're just...living.

And, hopefully, the meeting with Satriano isn't going to change any of that.

Jude punches the button, and the doors slide open right

away. We step in, and I immediately lean back against the metal wall, dropping my head to it, letting the exhaustion I've been fighting finally overtake me.

The memory of seeing Pope that morning of my last doctor's appointment here flashes through my head, and I can almost see him.

Those doors parting.

His dark eyes meeting mine.

All that tension.

All that animosity I still had for him.

God, it was so stupid.

Given everything that's happened since that day, it all seems so futile.

All those things that kept us apart dissolved away so quickly when the world outside forced us together.

I just hope nothing will ever be able to pull us apart again.

21

POPE

I let myself into Storm and Landon's house and beeline straight for the bar in the living room, where I pour myself a bourbon—a double.

After what just happened, I need it.

My hand trembles, bringing the cut crystal to my lips, but the warm burn of the alcohol going down my throat helps, at least temporarily, calm some of my frayed nerves.

A mob doctor.

I run my hand over the stubble on my cheek, brace the other against the marble countertop, and squeeze my eyes closed, letting my head hang. Stretching the tense muscles. Trying to help the fog of anger clear from my brain before I see Allie.

The entire drive over here from Stone's office, I wanted nothing more than to get to Allie, to see her and Benjamin, but the closer I got to this house, the worse my body tensed, the more anxious I became. And by the time I walked in that door, I knew I was a fucking mess.

Not in any shape to see her and offer her support.

Not the man she needs me to be right now.

"*Fuck!*"

"Pour me one?"

I whirl toward Jack's voice and find her leaning against the fireplace to my left, watching me carefully, with much too observant amber eyes. "What are you doing here?"

She motions upstairs. "I came to help Allie set up all Benjamin's stuff from our place in one of the guest rooms upstairs."

"Ah..." I nod and take another sip before I set my drink down to pour one for Jack. "Is she okay?"

Pouring with my back to her, I can't see her, but I sense her movement as she comes closer.

Her hand slips past me to grab the tumbler, and her gaze meets mine. "She's okay. What about you? You want to tell me what's wrong?"

I raise a brow, moving away from the bar and her to pace the living room. "What makes you think anything's wrong?"

She snorts and rests her hip against the bar top, watching me carefully. "I may not have been around this family as long as everyone else, but one thing I've always been very good at is reading people. I read Isaac from the moment I saw him at that bar in Chicago. I knew who and what he was, that I could trust him, and I was right."

Sipping my drink, I wander to the couch and slowly lower myself down onto the leather. "And what is it you think you're reading with me?"

"That you're pretty fucking pissed off about something, and I'm assuming it has to do with the meeting with Satriano."

Hell.

Giacomina wasn't even there, and she can already sense how fucked up I am over what went down. If she can read me so easily, so will Alessandra. And the last thing I want to do right now is stress her out more about something that's beyond her control but that can be very dangerous for me—and for her and Benjamin because of their connection to me.

She pushes off the bar and settles in the armchair to my right, tucking her legs up under her, like she's getting settled in for what is going to be a painful talk.

Groaning, I drop my head back to stare at the ceiling. "Yep."

"You're upset about what Satriano is asking you to do for him..."

I lift my head and peek at her. "How the hell did you know about that?"

She smirks. "Isaac called as soon as everyone started leaving the office. He and I don't keep secrets from each other."

"That's good."

Their relationship seems very healthy, which is a miracle considering their history.

A two-night stand as strangers.

A daughter Isaac didn't know about.

Five years of time.

And a mob boss obsessed with Jack enough to actually take her and force her into marriage.

Those are the types of things that create immense trauma and PTSD.

But they're thriving and seemingly enjoying their lives.

Moving on.

How can Allie and I ever do that when I am at Satriano's beck and call?

Jack leans forward until she catches my gaze. "I suggest you don't keep any from her, either."

"What do you mean?"

She sighs. "You know how I grew up. Locked away. My parents were always so worried I was going to have another seizure that they didn't let me really live any life, have any friends. So, I spent my time watching and listening to my mom's business, to my dad's."

I snort and take another drink. "I bet that was interesting for a kid."

"You have no idea." She grins. "I learned a lot and grew up very fast. And one of the key things that I caught onto when it comes to *their* relationship and why it works is that they don't keep secrets from each other. Even if it might hurt, they tell each other everything. When they're pissed off, they tell each other why. When they're happy, they tell each other why. When they're ready to kill somebody, and I don't mean that metaphorically, they tell each other why."

"I get your point."

"This..." She waves her hand around aimlessly. "All of this, what's been happening since I arrived in New Orleans? It isn't your world. It's mine."

"You were trying to get away from it."

She nods. "I was. And believe me, if I hadn't found Isaac, if I hadn't come here, I'd probably be in Paris right now at art school. But I did and could *never* leave him. And she feels the same way about you."

Jack smiles.

"Which is why I don't want to see anything come between you, like keeping this from her. She needs to know what Satriano asked you to do. She needs to know why you're so upset so you two can talk it out."

Releasing a long sigh, I down the rest of my drink and twirl the empty glass in my hands. "Do you really think this will ever end?"

Jack takes far too long to respond.

Giving me exactly the answer I didn't want.

Finally, she takes a sip of her drink and shrugs. "Maybe. But if my mom and dad found a great doctor who could do what *you* do for their men, I can't see them ever letting him go."

Fucking fuck.

"Yeah...that's kind of what I thought."

And why my chest feels like it's been ripped open.

But there's only one cure when I'm feeling like this—that little dark-haired woman I came here to see in the first place.

I push to my feet. "Is Allie upstairs?"

Jack nods. "Yeah. I was just on my way out. Storm and Landon took Benjamin to Stone and Nora's house for some playtime with Giovanni. I think they could see Allie needed a little break."

"I'm surprised she let them take him."

She grins. "Me, too. But I can be very persuasive." She climbs from the chair. "I thought you two might need a little time to talk when you got here."

"Thanks, Jack."

Tilting her now-empty glass, she winks. "Anytime."

Who would have thought Jack would turn into the psychologist in the family?

She may not have the degree, but her insights were spot-on.

What I'm going to have to do is eating me alive.

And it will only continue to if I don't come clean with Allie and give her the opportunity to make an informed decision about whether she wants to stay tangled up with me—when I'm potentially going to be working for Satriano *forever* to keep this truce between him and the Hawkes.

Jack grabs her purse from beside the door and gives me a little wave goodbye as I set our empty glasses on the bar and look up to the ceiling.

Allie is up there somewhere.

Waiting for me.

Preparing a place for Benjamin to sleep and feel safe when everywhere he's been since his birth has been temporary and not really *his*. But I don't want her staying here with Storm and Landon.

I want her and Benjamin with *me.*

But it has to be her choice.

And she has to know what she's risking to do it.

I climb the stairs and wander down the hallway toward the open door of one of the guestrooms. Allie stands inside, holding up picture frames with different jungle animals in them up to various places around the walls, her bottom lip pulled under her teeth in concentration.

"The lion should go above the crib."

Allie jerks and whirls toward me, clutching the two frames in her hands to her chest. "Oh, Jesus Christ, you scared the crap out of me."

Way to go, asshole.

I rub the back of my neck and step in, scanning the work they already completed—the bassinet he's slept in since birth in one corner, a brand new white crib centered on the wall, a gray plush rocking chair, a dresser likely filled with his clothes brought over from the condo, and a stack of artwork for the walls.

"Sorry, I didn't mean to scare you."

She releases a shaky breath. "I didn't even know you were here."

I nod, moving toward her slowly. "Just got here. Talked to Jack for a minute, but she left."

"Ah..." Allie nods, watching me carefully. "Is everything okay? What happened at the meeting?"

So fucking much.

I'd love to pretend none of it happened and tug Allie against me, crush my lips to hers, and make love to her on this damn blue rug, but Jack's words won't stop repeating in my head.

She needs to know why you're so upset.

Her brow furrows, almost as if she's reading my mind. "What is it? Why do you look so..."

"Lost? Pissed? Confused?"

Allie nods. "Yeah, all of that."

I shrug. "Because I am all of that at the moment."

Worry clouds her blue gaze. "Pope, what's going on? You're scaring me."

Shit.

I step forward, pull the frames from her hands, set them on the floor, and scoop her up into my arms. She releases a little yelp, looping hers around my neck as I carry her over to the rocking chair and sit with her draped across my lap.

There's no simple way to tell her this.

No way to ease into the discussion of me working for the man who threatened all of us only a handful of months ago and was responsible for the shooting at The Grind that not only destroyed her sister's business but injured Stone, Isaac, and Kennedy.

I brush her dark hair back from her face, dragging my fingertips over her cheek. "I love you, Al. You know that, right?"

Her brow furrows. "Of course I do. I love you, too."

"Good, because you may not like me very much after I tell you what Satriano said."

Allie's entire body goes rigid in my arms, and her eyes narrow. "What did he say?"

I press my forehead to hers, inhaling her scent, hoping it's not the last time I get to hold her like this. 'He demanded his first favor for his assistance with Roselli."

She swallows slowly. "Which was?"

Pulling my head back, I meet her gaze. "That I act as an on-call doctor for his crew if they need any sort of medical treatment. Nora, too."

Her mouth falls open. "What? No...he can't ask you to do that."

"He wasn't asking, Teeny." I cup her cheek. "He made it very clear that if I didn't cooperate, it could put you and Benjamin in danger."

And this is where I lose the only woman I've ever loved in my entire life.

ALESSANDRA

It could put you and Benjamin in danger.

His warning should rattle me.

It should make me sob and completely lose my shit like I have so many times over the last few months.

It should make me rage and cry and want to throw something against the wall because we *just* managed to survive being saved from Roselli and now Satriano is laying down more threats.

It should make me hate Pope for putting me in this position again—having to choose between the man I love or protecting my son.

It should do *all* those things.

And Pope is clearly expecting it to, given how anxious he is and the fear in his gaze.

But with his gentle hand against my cheek, staring into his smoky-bourbon eyes, I don't do any of those things because the reality is so crystal clear to me.

So fucking clear that I'm not sure *why* I couldn't see it before this very moment.

"Pope, we're *always* going to be in danger."

His brows rise slowly as he processes my words. "What do you mean?"

My eyes start to mist, and I blink away the tears, needing to see him while I offer this explanation of the realization I feel like I should have had a long time ago that might have saved everyone some pain. "This whole course of events, everything that's happened, none of it could have been stopped, not completely. It was unknowingly set in motion, and the path of destruction was aimed squarely at the Hawkes.

"It was the same way over thirty years ago when Luca's father ran New Orleans. It's what brought all the people we love together. It's what created this family and helped us build Hawke Enterprises into the empire that it is. Because we were fighting against a common enemy then, one who pretended to be a friend, which is exactly what Satriano is doing now, and it means none of us are ever going to be truly safe." I suck in a sharp breath so I can get out the final two words. "Not *ever*."

It feels like a giant boulder has been lifted from my shoulders, the weight of carrying that guilt around with me removed by the truth I couldn't see until this very moment.

I close my eyes, leaning into his touch and the comfort he always brings me, wondering if my long rant just scared him off. But he caresses my cheek—his fingers brushing across my skin and over my lips.

Reverently.

Like a man wanting to memorize every piece of something he loves so he can close his eyes and still see it.

Maybe he wants to in case his warning ends things between us, but he needs to understand the truth I've laid out for him, the one we all need to accept.

Earlier today at the hospital, I didn't know why I couldn't shake that feeling, why I couldn't relax and stop worrying, stop feeling like there was a target on my back.

I thought it was merely the lingering effects of everything we just went through, not really processing that Dan was gone yet. But the truth is, I knew, deep down, that nothing was ever really ever going to be over.

It can't be.

Not with the people we are.

"We will always be in danger, Pope. You working for Satriano isn't going to change that." I finally let my eyes open to meet his, laying down the final painful truth. "I'm in danger just by being a Hawke."

A moment of silence lingers between us, filling that space between our breaths, and he contemplates my words, my warning, and my assurance that nothing he does will change anything.

"Shit..." He releases a heavy breath and lowers his forehead against mine. "You're right. About everything. We never will be safe. No matter how hard everyone tries to protect each member of this Hawke family, each of us will always be a target. I'm so sorry that all this is happening, that you and Benjamin can't just—"

I press my lips to his to silence him, to stop him from apologizing for something that isn't his fault.

Pope has been there for me more in the last two months than any other person has ever been there for me in my entire life, which is saying a lot, considering the closeness of this family and the connection I share with Jude.

Through all the panic and the pain.

The crying and the hysteria.

The dirty diapers and sleepless nights...

Pope has been there. Holding me. Cradling Benjamin. Taking care of any and every thing we could ever need.

He's what kept me from spiraling into a black abyss of despair I never would have found my way out of.

He is my rock.

And I can't bear to see it cracking.

I can't let him blame himself, like he wouldn't let me blame myself for the Daniele situation.

Maybe kissing him is playing dirty, trying to take his mind off where it was going to make it concentrate on something else. But he returns my kiss, his lips gliding over mine smoothly, the warm, spicy taste of bourbon he must have drunk before he came up here coating his tongue and mine.

He groans into my mouth, tugging me even tighter against him and sinking into the kiss. The push and the pull. The sweet ecstasy of loving Pope.

When he finally pulls away, his eyes roam over the room we've only just begun putting together for Benjamin. "I don't want you to waste your time in here."

I jerk back slightly. "What? What do you mean?"

"Shit"—he winces—"that came out wrong again. I have to stop doing that. I mean, this is beautiful, and you should leave it up for times when you might want to leave Benjamin here to spend time with your parents, but this isn't going to be his room permanently."

"It's not?"

He shakes his head and brings my lips to his again. "I meant everything I've said to you over the last two months about regretting what happened ten years ago, regretting losing you. But at the same time, if none of that had happened, we wouldn't have Benjamin, right?"

As much as I hate to admit it, he's right about that.

All the mistakes I've made since our breakup, all the stupid choices, all the reckless behavior, all of it led me to Daniele, and Daniele gave me Benjamin. So even though I hate that man, and I'm glad he's gone and hope he rots in Hell, I don't know that I could ever regret being with him.

Not when it brought me my precious angel.

A tear trickles down my cheek, and Pope swipes it away with his thumb. "Are those happy tears or sad tears?"

My lip quivers, and I bite it to try to stop it and shake my head. "I'm not sure. Confused tears, I guess."

Pope tugs me down against him, and I rest my head on his shoulder. He tucks me under his chin and rubs my arm, slowly rocking the chair intended for the baby. "What are you confused about?"

I shrug slightly. "Everything. What we're supposed to do now."

He presses a kiss to my hair. "We're supposed to find our own place, and we're supposed to go on living our lives the best we can, protecting Benjamin the best we can, while also navigating these things that are beyond our control, I guess."

It sounds so simple when he says it.

But we both know that's far from the truth.

Nothing will *ever* be easy when you're a Hawke.

We have too much power, too many things. We've created too many enemies over the years through our actions to ever be safe from looking over our shoulders.

Every day, I'll feel that hair rise on the back of my neck, always wondering if it's some old foe or new one watching and lying in wait.

It's something all our parents dealt with and lived through, and the Hawkes suffered the consequences then. The loss of Ben, of Angelina's father, shattered their lives. And the thought that something like that could happen to us feels all too real after almost losing Stone, Isaac and Kennedy, and now Atlas and Astrid.

Nothing can be taken for granted.

And I will never do it again—with any of the people I love.

Especially not Pope.

The man who owns my heart, who I want to build my future with, the one who will always protect me and defend me, no matter the cost.

"You're going to have to work for Satriano..."

I hate saying the words, but I know they're true and so does he.

He isn't the kind of man you say no to if you want to keep breathing, and Pope is far too intelligent to pick a fight with him about this and potentially endanger the rest of us even more than we already are.

"I know."

The sad resignation in his voice splits my chest open. "Do you think you're going to be able to do it?"

These aren't patients being brought into his ER.

These are deadly men, and if they're calling Pope, it means they've probably done stupid and illegal things to get them in that condition.

Working on them is dangerous in that regard alone, but it could also mean risking his career at the hospital, which is likely why he's struggling so much with it at the moment.

He doesn't know what to do with the conflicting feelings, with the guilt he already feels before he's even acted at Satriano's command.

Skimming my fingers across his arm, I watch the skin pebble. "I know a thing or two about guilt, Pope. I let it eat me alive from the inside out for my entire pregnancy. I blamed myself for being so stupid as to get involved with Dan without really knowing who he was and to get pregnant on top of that. I blamed myself for everything that happened after that. Even this morning, I was sitting in Atlas and Astrid's room, seeing how broken he is, feeling guilt for him being in that position because of me." Another tear falls from my eye, splashing against his dark skin. "It's okay, Pope, to do it. But don't let your guilt over it destroy you the way I almost did."

God, I hope that made sense.

It felt like one big, long, incoherent ramble that likely only confused the man when I was really trying to help him.

He tilts my face up and kisses me softly. "I'll do anything to keep you and Benjamin safe, Al, even if it costs me my soul."

I search his eyes, looking for the truth in his declaration. "Is that what you think this is going to do?"

Pope shakes his head. "I don't know. It feels like it, but then

I'll get to come home to you and Benjamin, and"—his shoulders rise and fall—"I feel like that's going to make everything okay, make it better. In a way only the two of you can."

Well, damn.

I grin at him. "You really do have a way with words, Dr. Clarke."

He feathers his lips over mine. "I hope I never say anything as stupid as 'it was a mistake' again."

"Me, either."

His lips twitch playfully. "Nothing with you could *ever* be a mistake."

EPILOGUE
TWO WEEKS LATER

ALESSANDRA

Watching the city fly by out the car window, I shift in my seat, getting antsy even though we've only been driving for a few minutes since we left Benjamin at Jude and Angelina's. "You are really not going to tell me where we're going?"

Pope glances over at me from the driver's seat with a smug grin. He shakes his head. "Nope. It's a surprise."

There was a time when I used to love surprises and being spontaneous, but now my nerves get the better of me, making my knee bounce. I huff and cross my arms over my chest in the beautiful, flowy, purple dress Pope bought me and insisted I wear today. "The last time you drove me somewhere without telling me where we were going ..."

I let my thought trail off, and he tosses me a dirty look.

"This is totally different, and you know it."

Neither of us want to relive that drive or the two weeks we spent trapped together in that house in the woods. Though, ultimately, that time is what brought us back to each other;

there's too much bad wrapped up with the good. Too much pain with the hope.

We'd both rather look to the future, and I would *really* like to know where he's taking me.

"Why couldn't Benjamin come with us?"

The corner of his lips twitches again. "Your sister and Jude just wanted some quality time with him."

I roll my eyes since they see Benjamin all the time and Jude has started watching him when I pick up shifts at The Grind and ease back into working. "Yeah. Ooookay. Rather convenient to have volunteer babysitters on the day when you're taking me somewhere mysterious."

He chuckles and winks at me. "You'll see in a minute."

That's what he said five minutes ago.

My knee continues to bounce as I scan the street he turns down.

I recognize the Algiers Point neighborhood—beautiful, old houses similar to the one Nora and Stone own line each side of the road, and stunning, massive trees stand near each curb.

It's the perfect, picturesque area.

"Whose house are we going to?"

"You'll see." He reaches over and squeezes my leg. "Don't be so nervous."

It's hard not to be.

I feel like it's a constant state these days, ever since he signed on to be Satriano's doctor. He hasn't received that call in the middle of the night yet, but we're always waiting, wondering when it's going to come and what he will be asked to do.

But it's a minor kink in an otherwise pretty normal return to our lives before the whole world went to shit, that I didn't think was possible even a few short weeks ago.

Of course, having Benjamin has changed my daily routines, and I'm still trying to figure out how to do all the mom things without failing miserably, but the Hawke women—and men—have all stepped up to help and offer advice when needed.

I never thought I'd *want* unsolicited advice from anyone, but being a mom has changed a lot of things.

Including me now imagining how incredible a house like the ones we're driving past would be to raise Benjamin in. Just as I admire another approaching one, we pull up to the curb in front of it—a huge white and pale pink Italianate with a massive front porch on both floors.

Pope shuts off the car and climbs out, then makes his way around to open my door for me. He holds out a hand, and I slide my palm across his and let him pull me up.

He drags me against him to steal a mind-bending kiss, then turns me to face the house. "What do you think?"

Anyone would be spellbound by the old home.

The stunning craftsmanship of the woodwork and beams, the history it must hold within its walls. It's the kind of house all the tourists come to New Orleans to see.

"I love it. It's...spectacular."

Pope leans in and brushes his lips against my ear, wrapping his arms around my waist and pulling me back to him. "It's yours."

It doesn't quite register, my mind too busy taking in all the ornate details.

"Wait...what?" I jerk in his hold and look up at him over my shoulder. "What do you mean it's *mine*?"

He waits for a moment to respond, searching my face to ensure he catches my reaction. "I bought it."

"No. You. *Didn't*."

His head bobs, and a slow grin spreads across his lips as he tightens his hold on me. "I did. And please, please tell me you're not pissed at me about buying a house without letting you make the final decision on this because I—"

I whirl to fully face him and throw my arms around his

neck, kissing him so he'll stop rambling before he ruins the moment with his completely unnecessary worry.

He groans into my mouth, squeezing me to him, returning the kiss with fervor before he finally drags himself away, breathless. "So...you're not mad?"

I shake my head. "God, no, I'm not mad. I just..." Peeking over my shoulder at it, I try to wrap my head around the fact that Pope now *owns* this magnificent home. Any free time Pope has away from his duties at the hospital, he's spent with Benjamin and me, which makes the fact that he was able to do this *without* me knowing about it even more surprising. "When did you have time to do all this and...I don't understand how this happened."

Clasping my hand in his, he drags me up the front walkway and through a small, bricked front garden area. "Let me show you, and I'll explain everything."

He pulls the key out of his jeans pocket and unlocks the front door, ushering me inside to an exquisite foyer.

Hand-inlaid marble floors sparkle, leading to a sitting room on the left and a formal dining room on the right.

A spectacular staircase takes up the center, leading upstairs, with red runners down the middle of each tread.

It's the kind of house you can *feel* the history in, and I spin, trying to take it all in.

"How old is this place?"

"It was built in 1850, but meticulously maintained. The kitchen's been upgraded. The bathrooms are state-of-the-art."

I gape at the interior as he leads me in deeper, through the living room, currently empty of furniture, past a massive fireplace that runs all the way up to the fourteen-foot ceilings and back through a kitchen with spotless, stainless-steel appliances and a stove that would make Nana faint.

God, it's so beautiful.

I press my hand over my heart, and Pope immediately narrows his eyes.

"Are you feeling all right? Is it your—"

"No, it isn't that."

Thank God.

I haven't had many symptoms from my heart condition in a long time, and Dr. Boggs continues to believe that I might make a full recovery, given time to heal and less continued stress. "It kind of takes my breath away. That's all."

"Wait 'til you see the upstairs."

Pope takes me to a second staircase that leads from the kitchen upstairs and shows me five bedrooms until we reach the one at the front of the house—the master, connected to the covered balcony that overlooks the street below.

He pushes open the glass doors, and we step out on it, staring down at the people riding their bikes, the beautiful flowers in the neighbors' yards, and other stunning, historical houses lining the street.

"You really bought this?" I look over at him. "You're not joking?"

That little grin plays at his lips. "I'm not joking. We can move in whenever you're ready."

I was ready three weeks ago, but we didn't have anywhere to go.

Nowhere that was ours.

Splitting time between Mom and Dad's house and his parents' place hasn't been ideal, but I never thought we would find a home like this.

Pope grasps my shoulders, turning me to face him, dipping his head slightly to meet my gaze without me having to stare up at him. "What are you thinking, Al?"

I chew on my lip, considering how to put the whirlwind of emotions and thoughts into words. "I'm thinking you did really well, but it's a lot..."

His brow furrows, true concern replacing the good vibes he's been emanating since we arrived. "If it's too much, we don't have to go see the other surprise I have for you."

"No!" I shake my head. "Of course I want to see whatever it is."

He drops a quick kiss on my forehead, then tugs me off the balcony and back through the house, down the front stairs this time, but then out through the kitchen to a back patio.

A wrought iron tea table sits in the center of it with two chairs and a spread of all my favorite things laid out to eat for lunch.

Damn.

"You really thought of everything, huh?"

He grins.

"You didn't have to do all this, Pope. You know I'm a sure thing."

Laughing, he pulls my chair out for me. "I know. I wanted to."

He helps me push it in, then goes around to the other side to take his seat. His hand disappears under the table, and he comes back up with a bottle of champagne. He pops the top, pours us two glasses, and holds his up. "To new beginnings."

I clink my glass against his. "To new beginnings."

It's honestly the best toast I could have picked for today's vibe.

Things are finally starting to feel like they're coming together, evening out, the past moving further away in the rearview and the future closer on the horizon.

Pope reaches back under the table and comes up with an envelope. "There's something else."

"Another surprise?"

His humor fades slightly, and the bubbles in my stomach turn.

"Pope, what is it? You look worried."

He clears his throat. "I guess I am a little." His hand shakes as he reaches in, pulls out some papers, and slides them across the table to me. "I need you to sign these."

"What are they?"

"It's so we can modify Benjamin's birth certificate."

My breath catches in my throat, and I look down at the papers in front of me, all filled out in Pope's meticulous handwriting—an acknowledgment of paternity required to amend the birth certificate to list him as the father.

POPE

ALLIE STARES AT THE PAPERS, tears streaming down her face.

I squat in front of her, pulling her hands into mine, hating the wet streaking down her cheeks because I can't tell what they mean. She hasn't said a word. "I'm sorry to just spring this on you, Al. I should have talked to you about it before."

"No." She squeezes my hands, inhaling sharply, trying to regain control of herself. "Pope, I'm crying because I'm happy. I'm just overwhelmed. This is a lot."

"It is, and I'm sorry. Maybe I should have waited."

It's only been two weeks since she and Benjamin were freed from Roselli. Two weeks since we were finally able to start going out, enjoying life, and being together without worrying— at least about him coming after the baby.

I should have given her some time to decompress, instead of springing the house *and* these papers on her all in one day.

She shakes her head. "No, you shouldn't have. This is perfect. But"—her brow furrows—"are you sure you want to do this?

Christ, after all this time, she still doesn't get it.

I tug her up from her seat so she can feel my heart beating

against her chest and know the truth of what I'm saying. "Allie, since when has this family ever been about blood? The Hawkes have always been about finding the people you care about and protecting them, creating your own family, no matter how it looks or how the people get there. That's what we're doing."

For some idiotic reason, I hadn't anticipated the amount of emotion this was going to bring—for her or for me.

My throat tightens, and I swallow past it to say the words she needs to hear, the ones I've been dying to say.

"Benjamin is my son. I'm the first person he saw when he was born. I'm the one who witnessed his first breath, who held him while he slept that first night. You and he are my heart, and you always will be."

She releases another sob. "I don't deserve you, Pope."

Tilting her chin up to force her to meet my gaze, I nod. "You deserve the world, Al. What happened in the past is just that. This house is our future. The place we'll watch Benjamin grow up and maybe give him some brothers or sisters to play with, out here in this grassy yard. We have all the time in the world and nothing stopping us now."

Even the fact that my phone might ring at any moment with the call I've been dreading can't spoil the moment or my plans for our new lives together.

Allie has never been able to think beyond tomorrow.

Since that day I broke her heart, she's spent each day looking for the feeling we only bring each other. And now that we have it, I know she will hang onto it as tightly as I do.

She leans forward and kisses me again, wrapping her arms around my neck and pressing her hips to mine. "I love you so much, Pope."

"I love you, too, Al."

Anything else either of us want to say gets carried away on the wind blowing through our yard, and our kiss grows almost frantic, with Allie clinging to me, desperate to get closer.

We definitely can't do this out here.

Snooping neighbors witnessing us having a nooner in the backyard on the first day in the house would certainly send the wrong impression.

I lift her to wrap her legs around my waist, then walk us back in through the open kitchen door, my cock growing against her as I move. By the time we reach the island and I set her on it, she's practically trying to rip the zipper off my jeans.

Chuckling against her lips, I nudge her hand away to do it myself. "I guess we're christening the house today."

She pulls back and smiles, and this time, I don't mind seeing the tears because I know why they're there. "I guess we are. How long will Jude and Angie watch Benjamin? Because there are a lot of rooms in this house."

I lean in and press my lips to hers again as she finally frees my cock and takes it in her warm hand, making me twitch. "We could always save some of them for when we formally move in..."

Brushing her thumb over the head of my cock, she spreads the precum, making me jerk in her hold.

A playful grin pulls at her lips. "That could be a fun way to celebrate each new day here."

Nodding my agreement, I slide my hand up under her dress and find her pussy bare and already slick. "No panties today, huh?"

She offers a slight shrug. "You didn't include them with the dress when you told me you bought me something new to wear for the surprise." Her brows rise playfully. "Did you have this in mind when you picked it out? Giving yourself easy access?"

I shake my head. "Actually, no, but it's a nice perk."

Feeling her response to me.

How a simple touch or kiss can ignite her for me.

It *always* undoes me completely.

This woman has given me her everything when she had

every reason not to trust anyone again, and I will never let her regret that decision.

I hike up her dress around her hips and drag her to the edge of the counter, putting her at the perfect height for me to line up my cock between her legs and drag it through her slick arousal.

Sweet mother of God...

The tease meant for her sends a bolt of pleasure straight through my body, and she bucks in my grip and wraps her fingers around the edge of the countertop.

A vision of spreading her across this marble and eating her for lunch flashes through my head, but we're both too far gone for that. Both needy and desperate for *this*.

I angle her hips slightly, then push into her slowly, watching myself disappear, her pussy swallowing me inch by inch.

The tight heat makes me grit my teeth, and she squeezes around me, making herself even tighter, torturing me even more with her cunt. I drag my hips back and plunge into her all the way, and her mouth falls open on a silent gasp as her knuckles whiten due to her death grip on the counter.

Taking her mouth with mine, I pull my hips back and drive into her again, pushing myself deeper inside her. She groans against my lips and rolls her pelvis to meet mine, setting a slow rhythm that will build us both up to that heavenly place where any troubles plaguing us are wiped away in a few sweet moments of utter bliss.

This is where we want to be.

This house.

Locked together like this in this place forever.

It's these moments that make it easy to forget everything else but each other and the things we can feel and touch and experience.

Right here.

Right now.

The drag of the head of my cock on that spot inside her. The way my fingers dig into her fleshy hips. The gasps and moans that tumble from her lips. The slap of skin on skin.

I reach up and grasp her chin, crushing my lips to hers in a bruising, searing kiss designed to seal the moment and convince her that she doesn't have anything else to worry about anymore.

Now we have each other.

We have Benjamin.

And we have a home.

We have a great life, an incredible family who supports us, and we'll never go back to those people we were only months ago, avoiding each other, volatile, so much pent-up animosity and unspoken words.

With every plunge of my cock and drive of my hips, I convince her that this is forever because there's nowhere else I would rather be.

She releases the counter to wrap her hands around my neck, scoring her nails down it, that little bite of pain, enough to make my cock twitch inside her and my balls pull up tight and start to tingle.

My orgasm hangs right there, on the edge, threatening to break. She clenches around me with each retreat, and her hips meet mine with every thrust until sweat trickles down my spine and also dampens her temples.

I reach behind her and grab her hair in my fist, tugging her head to the side, exposing her neck and giving me access to that spot behind her ear that I know she likes so much.

Licking, kissing, and sucking there, I keep pounding into her, until her body starts trembling, her legs and grip around me tightening. And finally, she explodes.

Her body convulses, her hips bucking frantically as I pump my hips, chasing my own orgasm. The walls of her pussy ripple along and clench around my cock, finally drawing it out, and I come deep inside her.

A release of those final vestiges of the horrors of the past.

I catch her as she comes down and sags back, then kiss her softly against her cheek and over to her mouth. "Welcome home, Allie."

Her eyes flutter open to meet mine. "Welcome home, Dr. Clarke."

ATLAS

THE DOCTOR STANDING in front of me blurs into an indistinguishable shape as my vision darkens around the edges at his words.

"Excuse me...can you...can you repeat that?"

He shifts nervously from foot to foot, the same way a rookie fighter does when they're nervous about stepping in the ring. "Of course. I'm sorry, Atlas, but there appears to me more extensive nerve and muscle damage in your shoulder than we originally anticipated. You're still recovering from the surgery, and there's always a chance that with physical therapy, you can regain somewhat regular control of the limb—"

"*Control* of the limb?" I gasp, my lungs seizing in my chest. "But...I'm a boxer..."

"I'm afraid that might no longer be an option for you, given the damage to..."

The rest of his words don't matter.

Nothing does anymore.

I HOPE you enjoyed *Reckless Hawke*. Delve further into the Hawke Family world with Atlas' redemption story in *Rebel Hawke*!

Get your copy: books2read.com/RebelHawke1

To stay up to date on news, sales, and releases from Gwyn, join her newsletter here: www.gwynmcnamee.com/newsletter

ACKNOWLEDGMENTS

I've been waiting years to tell Pope and Allie's story. I knew it would be unlike anything I've ever written, with their ten years of animosity and hidden feelings. And combined with the secret Al has kept for so long, it was as explosive as I thought it would be. This story couldn't have happened without my team who always bend over backward to assist me with my stories. I am truly blessed to have all of you in my life! Renee, Patricia, Stephie, and Caoimhe, you are all true rockstars who deserve a standing ovation. And a special shout-out to Renita for helping me do justice to Pope's character. Love all of you!

ABOUT THE AUTHOR

Gwyn McNamee is an attorney, writer, wife, and mother (to one human baby and two fur babies). Originally from the Midwest, Gwyn relocated to her husband's home town of Las Vegas in 2015 and is enjoying her respite from the cold and snow. Gwyn has been writing down her crazy stories and ideas for years and finally decided to share them with the world. She loves to write stories with a bit of suspense and action mingled with romance and heat.

When she isn't either writing or voraciously devouring any books she can get her hands on, Gwyn is busy adding to her tattoo collection, golfing, and stirring up trouble with her perfect mix of sweetness and sarcasm (usually while wearing heels).

Gwyn loves to hear from her readers. Here is where you can find her:

Website: http://www.gwynmcnamee.com/

Shop: http://www.gwynmcnameeshop.com/

Facebook:https://www.facebook.com/AuthorGwynMcNamee/

FB Reader Group: https://www.facebook.com/groups/1667380963540655/

Newsletter: www.gwynmcnamee.com/newsletter

Instagram: https://www.instagram.com/gwynmcnamee

Bookbub: https://www.bookbub.com/authors/gwynmcnamee

Tiktok: https://www.tiktok.com/@authorgwynmcnamee

OTHER WORKS BY GWYN MCNAMEE

Billionaires of New Orleans:

The Hawke Family Series

Savage Collision (The Hawke Family - Book One)

He's everything she didn't know she wanted. She's everything he thought he could never have.

The last thing I expect when I walk into The Hawkeye Club is to fall head over heels in lust. It's supposed to be a rescue mission. I have to get my baby sister off the pole, into some clothes, and out of the grasp of the pussy peddler who somehow manipulated her into stripping. But the moment I see Savage Hawke and verbally spar with him, my ability to remain rational flies out the window and my libido takes center stage. I've never wanted a relationship—my time is better spent focusing on taking down the scum running this city—but what I want and what I need are apparently two different things.

Danika Eriksson storms into my office in her high heels and on her high horse. Her holier-than-thou attitude and accusations should offend me, but instead, I can't get her out of my head or my heart. Her incomparable drive, take-no prisoners attitude, and blatant honesty captivate me and hold me prisoner. I should steer clear, but my self-preservation instinct is apparently dead—which is exactly what our relationship will be once she knows everything. It's only a matter of time.

The truth doesn't always set you free. Sometimes, it just royally screws you.

AVAILABLE AT ALL RETAILERS:

books2read.com/SavageCollision

Tortured Skye (The Hawke Family - Book Two)

She's always been off-limits. He's always just out of reach.

Falling in love with Gabe Anderson was as easy as breathing. Fighting my feelings for my brother's best friend was agonizingly hard. I never imagined giving in to my desire for him would cause such a destructive ripple effect. That kiss was my grasp at a lifeline—something, anything to hold me steady in my crumbling life. Now, I have to suffer with the fallout while trying to convince him it's all worth the consequences.

Guilt overwhelms me—over what I've done, the lives I've taken, and more than anything, over my feelings for Skye Hawke. Craving my best friend's little sister is insanely self-destructive. It never should have happened, but since the moment she kissed me, I haven't been able to get her out of my mind. If I take what I want, I risk losing everything. If I don't, I'll lose her and a piece of myself. The raging storm threatening to rain down on the city is nothing compared to the one that will come from my decision.

Love can be torture, but sometimes, love is the only thing that can save you.

AVAILABLE AT ALL RETAILERS:

Books2read.com/Tortured-Skye

Stone Sober (The Hawke Family - Book Three)

She's innocent and sweet. He's dark and depraved.

Stone Hawke is precisely the kind of man women are warned about—handsome, intelligent, arrogant, and intricately entangled with some dangerous people. I should stay away, but he manages to strip my soul bare with just a look and dominates my thoughts. Bad decisions are in my past. My life is (mostly) on track. even if it is no longer the one to medical school. I can't allow myself to cave to the fierce pull and ardent attraction I feel toward the youngest Hawke.

Nora Eriksson is off-limits, and not just because she's my brother's employee and sister-in-law. Despite the fact she's stripping at The Hawkeye Club, she has an innocent and pure heart. Normally, the only thing that appeals to me about innocence is the opportunity to taint it. But not when it comes to Nora. I can't expose her to the filth permeating my life. There are too many things I can't control, things completely out of my hands. She doesn't deserve any of it, but the power she holds over me is stronger than any addiction.

The hardest battles we fight are often with ourselves, but only through defeating our own demons can we find true peace.

AVAILABLE AT ALL RETAILERS:

books2read.com/StoneSober

Building Storm (The Hawke Family - Book Four)

She hasn't been living. He's looking for a way to forget it all.

My life went up in flames. All I'm left with is my daughter and ashes. The simple act of breathing is so excruciating, there are days I wish I could stop altogether. So I have no business being at the party, and I definitely shouldn't be in the arms of the handsome stranger. When his lips meet mine, he breathes life into me for the first time since the day the inferno disintegrated my world. But loving again isn't in the cards, and there are even greater dangers to face than trying to keep Landon McCabe out of my heart.

Running is my only option. I have to get away from Chicago and the betrayal that shattered my world. I need a new life-one without attachments. The vibrancy of New Orleans convinces me it's possible to start over. Yet in all the excitement of a new city, it's Storm Hawke's dark, sad beauty that draws me in. She isn't looking for love, and we both need a hot, sweaty release without feelings getting involved. But even the best laid plans fail, and life can leave you burned.

Love can build, and love can destroy. But in the end, love is what raises you from the ashes.

AVAILABLE AT ALL RETAILERS:

books2read.com/BuildingStorm

Tainted Saint (The Hawke Family - Book Five)

He's searching for absolution. She wants her happily ever after.

Solomon Clarke goes by Saint, though he's anything but. After lusting for him from afar, the masquerade party affords me the anonymity to pursue that attraction without worrying about the fall-out of hooking-up with the bouncer from the Hawkeye Club. From the second he lays his eyes and hands on me, I'm helpless to resist him. Even burying myself in a dangerous investigation can't erase the memory of our combustible connection and one night together. The only problem... he has no idea who I am.

Caroline Brooks thinks I don't see her watching me, the way her eyes rake over me with appreciation. But I've noticed, and the party is the perfect opportunity to unleash the desire I've kept reined in for so damn long. It also sets off a series of events no one sees coming. Events that leave those I love hurting because of my failures. While the guilt eats away at my soul, Caroline continues to weigh on my heart. That woman may be the death of me, but oh, what a way to go.

Life isn't always clean, and sometimes, it takes a saint to do the dirty work.

AVAILABLE AT ALL RETAILERS:

books2read.com/TaintedSaint

Steele Resolve (The Hawke Family - Book Six)

For one man, power is king. For the other, loyalty reigns.

Mob boss Luca "Steele" Abello isn't just dangerous—he's lethal. A master manipulator, liar, and user, no one should trust a word that comes out of his mouth. Yet, I can't get him out of my head. The time we spent together before I knew his true identity is seared into my brain. His touch. His voice. They haunt my every waking hour and occupy my dreams. So does my guilt. I'm literally sleeping with the enemy and betraying the only family I've ever had. When I come clean, it will be the end of me.

Byron Harris is a distraction I can't afford. I never should have let it go beyond that first night, but I couldn't stay away. Even when I learned who he was, when the *only* option was to end things, I kept going back, risking his life and mine to continue our indiscretion. The truth of what I am could get us both killed, but being with the man who's such an integral part of the Hawke family is even more terrifying. The only people I've ever cared about are on opposing sides, and I'm the rift that could end their friendship forever.

Love is a battlefield isn't just a saying. For some, it's a reality.

AVAILABLE AT ALL RETAILERS:

books2read.com/SteeleResolve

You can find information on the rest of Gwyn's books on her website:

www.gwynmcnamee.com